Amuletto Kiss

Magic & Mixology Mystery Series, Volume 5

Gina LaManna

Published by LaManna Books, 2018.

AMULETTO KISS

First edition. May 4, 2018.

Written by Gina LaManna.

To my husband: I love you!

Acknowledgments

SPECIAL THANKS:

To Alex—Here's to one year in Minnesota, six months married, and 95 pounds of chocolate consumed. я тебя люблю!

To my family—May the Fourth be with you.

To Stacia—For being the best BFF a gal could ask for! (And for not flinching when I email you this beast and say goodluckandsorry!) :-)

To everyone in LaManna's Ladies—For making every book feel so special. If I could blow you all an amuletto kiss, I would.

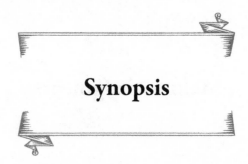

Synopsis

Hold your loved ones close, islanders...
Life for Lily Locke has not been normal ever since she learned of her witchy heritage, but now more than ever, her world is spiraling out of control. When a series of strange events begins to tear her beloved island apart, it's up to the famed Mixologist to seek out the most powerful wizard in the world and spare him from death. However, as Lily begins the hunt for the Master of Magic, she encounters a prophecy that could destroy everyone she's come to know and love.
...there is darkness on the horizon.

Prologue

THE FACTION HAS RETURNED...
This is Peter Knope, reporter for the *Wicked Weekly*, writing from
behind enemy lines. To all those back home on The Isle, consider
this message a warning:
Be wary, protect yourselves, stay alert.
This is war.
And above all,
Hold your loved ones close, islanders...
There is darkness on the horizon.
—Peter Knope

Chapter 1

I SET THE PAPER DOWN, my gut churning.

Sunday morning, front page. *How could Peter's story have ended up there?* I rubbed my forehead with my thumb and forefinger, easing away the stress.

When Peter and I had been held captive in Wishery, he'd entrusted me with this *exact* article. He'd requested I submit it for publication to his editors when I returned to The Isle, and I'd fully intended to do so...*soon*.

Someone had beaten me to it.

"I *thought* we decided to wait on this?" Ranger X burst through the front door of the bungalow, forgoing his typical morning greeting. "I asked for one more week before you had this printed."

"You did, but—"

"Why, Lily?" Ranger X looked at me with such heartbreaking hurt that I fell speechless. "I asked you specifically to give me more time before this news broke. We need to get the Ranger trainees formally initiated into the program—Zin included—before Peter's fearmongering letter wreaks havoc on the island. Though I suppose it's too late for that now."

I opened my mouth to respond and found I couldn't. My stomach flipped, torn between curiosity and frustration. I hadn't betrayed X's wishes—I wouldn't. A part of me sizzled with annoyance that he'd doubt me. After all we'd been through, hadn't I earned his trust?

"I have to go deal with this," he said, his eyes flicking toward my feet when the silence stretched long and weary. "I'm sorry, but I'll have to cancel our lunch plans."

I barely managed a nod before he was gone. I couldn't say how many minutes I waited, still as a gargoyle, before I exhaled a shaky breath. Gus found me sitting in the same position some time later.

"Well?" My assistant let himself through the front door and ground to a halt. "Why the long face?"

Startled, I shifted my gaze back to the newspaper. Without speaking, I pushed it forward.

Gus read through it quickly, his cheeks turning red. "Peter's an idiot."

"I promised him I'd publish this article, Gus."

"I thought you decided to wait another week before you made that call. Has X seen this? He won't be happy."

I raised my eyebrows.

"*Ah*. Now I understand the long face." Gus seemed unperturbed by my argument with X and shuffled toward the shelves along the back wall. He began tinkering with vials of rainbow colored liquids and jars of dried herbs. "Why'd you do it?"

I kept my silence until Gus turned to face me. My expression told him everything.

"You *didn't* do it," he said slowly, understanding. "But Ranger X jumped to conclusions."

"Correct."

"Shame on him, and shame on me," Gus said thoughtfully. "But that doesn't answer the burning question."

"I don't know *who* beat me to it." I shook my head. "I've kept the article in my nightstand since we returned home. Nobody outside of a few key people even knew about it. In order for someone to have a copy with this exact wording, they would have either had to find

Peter's original in my room, or they'd have had to go straight to the source."

"Well, I'll be..." Gus *tsked*, looking furious. "They can't have found Peter; he's still hiding with the enemy, so that eliminates him. Which means someone snuck into your bedroom and took that note."

"It must be someone I know. I haven't told anyone about Liam's visit, Peter's note, or the threat against the Master of Magic except for The Core and Ranger X. As far as everyone else on The Isle is concerned, it's business as usual here at the bungalow."

"Is the note gone?" Gus frowned. "I can tell you it wasn't me, and it wasn't X. Could that old bat have done this?"

"Which bat?"

Gus allowed himself the smallest smile, then shook his head. "Never mind. Hettie might get a kick out of stealing your things, but she wouldn't hurt you. Harpin *would* hurt you, but he's too lazy for this, and there's not enough glory for him in it. It wouldn't be Poppy or Ainsley or Zin—I know they're not Core members, but they hang around. They hear things."

"But nobody else knew—"

"*Someone* else knew," Gus corrected. "And we need to find out who."

"I'm going to see if the note is gone. Peter wrote the note specifically for me, in longhand, while we were being held captive. There's really no way another copy could be in existence."

"Did anyone else see the note between then and now?"

"Not that I know of."

"Then it can't be a copy," Gus mused, "which brings us back to square one. Don't you worry, Miss Locke—whoever stepped foot in your room will regret it. I'll make sure of it."

THE NOTE WAS THERE.

Set gently in my bedside drawer, completely untouched. Just as I'd left it.

I tucked the letter deeper into the drawer and threw a few pairs of socks over it, masking the crumpled surface completely. The paper, the drawer, my bedroom—as far as I could tell, nobody had tampered with a thing.

I breathed easier. In retrospect, it seemed highly unlikely that someone had crept into my bedroom without anyone noticing. There were spells protecting this bungalow, and more obviously, there were always people around. Someone would have noticed something.

I returned downstairs and relayed the news to Gus, who grunted in confusion. When he didn't have more to say on the subject, I distracted myself with work. I needed the physical movement, the sweeping and organizing and shuffling around. Otherwise, my frustration would get the better of me.

As I moved through the storeroom gathering up supplies for the day, I pondered who could have discovered the note—and how. *Who had gotten the article published before me?*

Even as I shuffled vials of champagne dust to reach the dried eel on the top shelf, my mind worked in overdrive. Ranger X was the only person who'd known about the article and where I'd kept it.

In theory, it would've been easy enough for him to grab the paper from my nightstand and return it looking relatively untouched. Nobody would have noticed since he came and went from the bungalow whenever he wished without question.

I knocked over a vase of apple cores in my haste to push the thought out of my head, ignoring Gus's quiet curse at the sound of shattering glass. Grabbing a broom, I began sweeping up the mess, my brain flicking through several unlikely scenarios.

"It wasn't him," Gus said. "You can stop breaking things. Ranger X didn't leak that story."

"I know." My voice came out quiet, broken. "But he should have trusted me enough not to barge in here thinking I'd done it."

"So should I," Gus said gruffly. "Men, we're idiots. Most people are, especially in tense times. Emotions are running high right now, and that article ain't gonna do us any favors. I still don't see why you intended to publish it in the first place."

"Peter asked me to, Gus."

"And you're loyal to a fault, Lily Locke, but I still think you should've waited. Peter would have understood. The last thing we need is a wave of terror sweeping across The Isle."

"Yet without his help, I'm not sure we would've escaped Wishery. I owed it to him after he sacrificed himself to stay behind."

"Well, it wasn't X. I think you should give him a break on this one and let his accusations roll off you. And that's saying something: You know I *never* side with that oaf."

"He's not an oaf."

Gus's stare found mine, pleading. An unlikely expression. "We don't need the two most powerful people on this island arguing. Not at a time like this."

My mind briefly flicked back to our mysterious encounter with Liam, and his request for help as well as the mention of a prophecy. Gus had a point; it certainly wasn't the best time to be struggling through personal issues, on top of everything else.

"I thought the sign said you opened at nine?" The question came from Magic & Mixology, from a faceless voice no doubt standing at the counter of the outdoor bar attached to the bungalow. "It's *nine-oh-two*. You're two minutes late."

Gus rolled his eyes. "Want me to get that?"

I shook my head. "But this conversation isn't finished."

I left the colorful, musty storeroom reluctantly. This room was a cozy little space that housed private conversations, deep research, and the familiar feeling of home—that feeling similar to loading up a car with all one's possessions in the world and sitting there, comforted by the sheer closeness of it all.

Breezing through the doorway between the storeroom and the bar, feeling the cluttered warmth slip away, I eased into the bright and open salty air of the beachfront bar.

The atmosphere shifted, and I sighed. The lake that surrounded us spread endlessly in all directions—superior to all others, as suggested by the name. Blue waters lapped onto the sugar-sand shore, the skies cloudless and pure.

"Sorry for the rush," a harried-looking woman said, brushing long brown locks behind her ear. "But I'm in a bit of a hurry."

I didn't know the woman, so I smiled and introduced myself. "How can I help you?"

"I live over near the library on the East Isle, and I'm looking for a protective spell."

I immediately understood she came from wealth. She lived in an area of The Isle flanked by the most exquisite housing and pristine grounds. I wondered if she worked for MAGIC, Inc. since most of the agency employees who retired to The Isle lived in luxury.

I frowned. "What sort of protection?"

"What do you have?" Her mouth pouted and her freckles gleamed. "I want the kind that keeps bad people away."

"Are you afraid of robbery, looking for a general alarm system, or just wanting a painless jinx that'll shock trespassers?"

She didn't look convinced at any of my suggestions, so I continued, waving to the general menu behind me as it flickered to life and populated with a list of available options.

"We have a wide variety of simple hexes and protections for purchase. The Seashell System is one of my particular favorites. Made from crushed shells and enchanted salts, the user just sprinkles the mixture around the perimeter of their home, and—"

"No, no, I need something stronger," she said. "Not your basic stuff. I need something that'll..."

"That will what?"

"That will hurt," she whispered. "That will hurt anyone who comes after my family."

A light bulb dinged over my head. "You read the article."

The woman shifted uncomfortably. "It was on the front page. How could I have missed it?"

"I don't sell harmful spells," I said flatly, gesturing to a sign on the wall where it proclaimed the famous *Do Good* motto of my predecessors. "I'm the Mixologist."

"Isn't it *good* to help citizens protect themselves?"

"Let me be clear," I said, leveling my voice. "I don't sell anything that is purposely intended to harm another person. Period."

The woman looked slightly annoyed. She leaned forward and rested her elbow on the counter, her chin in her hand, surveying the menu. "What's this Yard Yelper I see up there?"

"You can set a spell where unfamiliar footsteps on your lawn set off an alarm," I said a little stiffly. "It sounds the alarm, but it doesn't hurt anyone."

"Ah," she said, looking disappointed.

"There's a logical reason for it. These spells are too easy to fool," I continued, for some reason feeling the need to back up my moral code. "The newspaper delivery person or a surprise guest arriving earlier than expected—you wouldn't want to hurt someone you *love*, would you?"

"No, but what if it *is* a person intending my family ill will?"

"The article..." I hesitated.

I wanted to tell her the article had been an overreaction, but I couldn't bring myself to negate Peter's words. He'd saved our tails in Wishery, and though he'd had the opportunity to leave, he'd chosen to stay in Faction territory to get the first-hand story. I owed him.

"Yes?" she prompted. "You were *there*, weren't you? You saw The Faction alive and healthy with your own eyes?"

"I was with Peter for a bit, yes," I hedged. "But I still think the letter—"

"Were things really as bad as Peter said? Is war on the horizon?"

I turned her question over for a long moment, my gaze drifting downward as I shuffled through a stack of ingredients. I averted my face so it didn't give me away as I stalled, thinking.

Finally, I selected a small array of Security Spell Sets for beginners. "The world is complicated at the moment," I explained. "Do I think anybody will appear at your door to hurt you and your family? No. Do I think The Faction is a problem? Yes, probably. Do I believe the Rangers and the appropriate law enforcement agencies will take care of it? Absolutely."

Instead of comforting her, my words seemed to have the opposite effect. The woman's eyes flicked to the supplies on the counter. "I'll take all of them."

"I didn't mean you needed—"

She grasped at three Security Spell Sets and hoarded them to her chest like the last pieces of food on a desert island. "All of them."

"It's completely unnecessary," I explained. "These three sets all do the same thing."

But the woman had already tossed payment on the counter and whirled around, heading for the door. At the last moment, she stopped and peered over her shoulder at me.

"Miss Locke," she began uneasily. "Do you know where I could buy something stronger?"

"No. And looking for something to harm another person will only lead you to trouble."

She left, looking chastised, as two more people entered the bar area and approached the counter one after the other. I offered my help to both.

"Do you have, uh..." The first man was smaller, ruddy in complexion and thick in size. He cleared his throat. "Can I purchase security spells from you?"

I reached behind me, feeling an expression of stone settle into place as I retrieved a few more Security Spell Sets for beginners and set them on the counter. "Is this what you're looking for?"

The second man, as tall and lanky as the first was short and stocky, crept toward the counter and pulled a box possessively into his arms.

"This says it's for beginners," the lanky one said, offering a smile that showed he was in dire need of a dentist. "We ain't beginners."

The other man bobbed his head in agreement.

"I have a few more things," I said, already feeling the exhausted monotone that came with the same explanation over and over again. "Yard Yelpers, Sidewalk Sweeps, Bug Blasters. I can make custom potions for anything you find on the menu."

I handed over a folded and laminated piece of stock paper that pre-populated a menu for an individual customer's tastes. As I ran my finger along the outside of it, neat little scrolls listed a variety of rather harmless security spells on the page before me.

"I can get half of these at the supply store," the first man said, referencing my aunt's shop not far from the bungalow. "These are no more than glorified pranks."

"They're very effective alarm systems," I said. "I'm not sure what more you're looking for."

The first man shifted uneasily, but the second bore no hesitation as he pressed against the counter and leveled his gaze on mine. "We read that article. Joey and me, we're neighbors. We have families and friends and things to protect."

"Listen, that article—"

"Weren't you there?" the smaller man asked. "Did you see The Faction?"

"I saw Peter for a short while," I said, sounding cross, "but I think there's a slight over exaggeration about how much danger the islanders are in. At least, in your own homes."

"But you don't deny The Faction is preparing for some sort of war?"

How could I deny such a thing after all I'd seen? My slight pause, the firm set of my jaw, was the only answer the men needed.

"If you won't help us," the tall, lanky man warned, "we will go elsewhere."

"Fine," I said. "Good luck to you."

"That's it?" The shorter of the two rose to his toes and leaned further over the bar, his face now inches from mine. "You're the Mixologist, Miss Locke," he said on a hiss. "I thought you were supposed to protect this island. Or, maybe you don't care since you just showed up here out of the blue. Some of us—we love this place. Our families are here. We can't just leave—"

"It's not like that—"

"Gentlemen." Gus's gravelly voice rolled over the beachfront as he appeared in the door, his cane pounding extra loudly against the floor. "What seems to be the problem?"

It wasn't that Gus looked intimidating: He was an old man, gruff and rumpled with pale eyes that surveyed the room with startling clarity. In terms of loyalty to the island, however, there wasn't a soul who could question Gus's. He'd served willingly as the assistant to the Mixologist for more years than many islanders could remember.

"Nothing," the shorter man grumbled, leaning back on his toes. He stabbed a finger randomly at the menu. "I'll take that one."

I raised an eyebrow. "Are you sure?"

"Of course I'm sure, it's—" His face reddened as he read the selected name. "Fine, I'll take this one. And this one."

He jabbed at a few more intimidating looking spells. While I surveyed them, calculating the necessary ingredients on the spot, the taller, lankier man settled against the counter and leveled his gaze at Gus.

"*I've* got a problem," he said, his voice low. "What's this newbie doing telling us we can't protect our family?"

"She ain't a newbie any longer," Gus growled. "She's done more for this island in her short time here than most people have in a lifetime."

"She's not a lifer," he argued. "I want to protect my family. I need a spell stronger than..." he paused, glancing at the menu and selecting one of the gentler ones. "Rabbit Repeller."

My face flushed red. "That's just listed as a gardening aid!"

"If you want a stronger spell, here's how you get it." Gus clacked his cane on the steps as he climbed down. When he reached the bottom, the sand swallowed the familiar thumps. "You can head to the mainland and inquire at MAGIC, Inc. like the rest of us. Or, if you fancy a quicker fix, I'm sure The Faction leaders will have no problem trading you a few spells for your loyalty."

"That's not what I'm after. You're twisting my words."

"I'm not twisting anything." Gus inched closer. "I'm giving you some options. Lily says she don't sell spells that hurt others; you want to hurt others, you go to The Faction. What's so hard to understand?"

"I want—"

"You protect yourself and start injuring innocents, and you're no better than them. Get out of the Mixologist's bar."

"Gus, you know me; you know my father," the taller man argued. "We're loyal. You saw the article. We need to be ready."

"We *are* ready. The Rangers are initiating new recruits at a faster rate than ever. We're surrounding this island with more complex spells than you can comprehend. We have guards on high alert and more—so much more than you or I could ever understand. The best are on it, Jimmy."

Jimmy flushed at the nickname. "I hope you're not wrong."

Gus merely crossed his arms. "There are other avenues for you to pursue if you're looking for curses. We know that's why you're here."

Though I felt like a bug on the wall, I couldn't help my mind flashing to Liam. If anyone could acquire complex, potentially dangerous supplies and spells, or even curses, it was him.

In retrospect, Liam's morally ambiguous connections now made sense. He had connections high up in The Faction—as high as one could get. It was no wonder he could move next-to-illegal supplies easily on and off the island undetected. The Faction had probably been feeding his business this entire time.

I felt stupid for not seeing it earlier. For not looking deeper into the man behind the mystery, for not asking the right questions when I put in orders for difficult-to-find supplies. Everyone had seemed so certain, so sure, Liam had The Isle's best intentions at heart. Finding out it wasn't so, being made a fool in front of my father, had been a difficult blow to move past.

Even now at the thought of it, a surge of anger coursed through me. A crackle of blue electricity snapped between my fingers, and I quickly moved them below the bar before anyone could notice. Gus, forever observant, barely blinked, but I could tell he hadn't missed it.

"I recommend you make your choice and get out of here," Gus said, probably before I could explode at our customer. "What'll it be, Jimmy?"

"I'll take what he got," Jimmy said, nodding at his shorter neighbor, his voice turning to a grumble. "And I'll take the Rabbit Repeller, too. Nasty bunch of critters this season——they're eating my wife's lettuce."

"Now, *that* we can do for you," Gus said, sounding mildly appeased. "Lily—you got the order?"

"Yes," I said tersely. "I'll have to Mix a few things. Does tomorrow morning work for pickup?"

The men nodded and took their leave, the taller one somewhat begrudgingly. As they left, I collected the menus and slid them back into place, flexing my fingers to make sure the sizzle of magic had calmed.

"Shouldn't be too bad," Gus said nonchalantly. "I think we have most of the supplies on hand. I'll head inside and start preparing the ingredients for you."

"Gus?"

He stopped, his cane resting on the first step going into the storeroom. "Yes, Lily?"

I narrowed my eyes at him. "What was that all about?"

For a moment, he feigned innocence. "Which part?"

"Don't," I said, more snappish than I'd intended. "Please don't patronize me. You didn't need to come out here; I could have handled them myself."

"Jimmy was being a clown. I've known him since he was..." Gus paused to gesture around his waist. "He needed to see reason—seems he forgot the point of the Mixologist's duty."

"*I'm* the Mixologist. I can remind him. I'll handle my customers."

"I'm your assistant." Gus didn't back down. "I serve the Mixologist in *any* necessary capacity, and I won't sit around when someone like Jimmy's being hard-headed. He needed some sense knocked into him."

"Let me knock it next time."

This was my home, my bar, my career—my life. My entire existence had somehow shifted since I'd learned from my aunts that I had witch blood in my veins, that I'd been born into the role of Mixologist.

I no longer thought of myself as *a* Mixologist—I simply *was* the Mixologist. It would forever be linked with my identity.

"Try to understand, Gus. I can't have people thinking I'm weak. Not in a time like this."

"Anyone who thinks you're weak is a fool."

"You saw the article; they're scared." I glanced down at my hands, unable to ignore the blue glow on the tips of my fingers. "Tensions are high all around, and we need to be the ones keeping up appearances. Those of us facing The Faction need to be strong, and we need to appear strong for everyone else. Please, Gus, for the island."

He looked ready to argue again, but before he could open his mouth, another set of feet wandered toward the bar—a set attached to very long legs, a wispy body, and the face of a supermodel.

"Hello," the woman purred. "I'm here to order—"

"Here you are," I said, handing over the menu of security spells. "I assume you're looking for this?"

"Actually, I'm throwing a party, and I need to purchase ten vials of Long Isle Iced Tea."

I blinked in surprise. "Ten vials? That's a hefty amount."

She laughed deep and hoarse, a strangely exotic sound. "It's a big party. You know, rumors still circle the island about the success of yours."

"Sure," I said. "Let me see what I have in stock. It's been flying off the shelves lately."

Gus silently disappeared into the storeroom. Faint clanks of vials led me to believe he'd begun preparing the orders of security spells, and I was grateful for his unspoken display of support.

"Let's see, I have nine right here..." I shuffled a few vials. "It'll be somewhat expensive—the ingredients are difficult to find, especially with a silver this pure."

The woman pulled out a pouch and set it down, clinking it against the counter. "Cost is no issue."

"Wow. That's some party."

"Don't tell anyone." She inched toward me with a conspiratorial wink. "But it's for one of the largest magical institutions in the world."

"MAGIC. Inc.?" I blurted. Then waved a hand. "Forget I said that."

She winked. "Call me Rhonda. You must be Lily."

I extended my hand and shook hers. "Are you a party planner?"

"Something like that."

I silently tallied the vials once more, but we were still at nine. "Let me check the storeroom," I said, and ducked inside for a moment.

Gus was there, ready with a vial. "This is the last prepared one. Are you sure you want to sell it?"

I shrugged. "Why not? Let's get another batch started."

He confirmed with a grunt and returned to the table. I could practically see his To Do list growing, and I made a mental note to make sure he got out of here on time this evening. If Gus started working late again on a regular basis, Mimsey would have my head. The two had been seeing each other for months now, and their honeymoon phase didn't seem to budge with the passing of time.

As I returned to the bar, my thoughts of Gus brought about a pang of longing for my own relationship. A relationship that now felt strained, despite my best efforts. I'd worried things between X and I wouldn't go back to normal after his near proposal at the end of my time spent in Wishery, and it appeared my concerns were coming to fruition.

I clutched the vial tight in my hand, so tightly I nearly cracked the glass as I replayed Ranger X's promise. He had said he'd wait until the end of time for me to be ready. *Could that possibly be true?*

"Everything okay?" Rhonda's eyes scrunched as she watched my stiff movements. "Not a huge deal if you don't have that last vial."

"Oh, I have it." I forced a smile. "Let me grab your change, here."

"Keep it." She waved a hand and winked. "It comes out of the party fund."

I nodded my thanks and packaged up Rhonda's purchases. Money didn't mean much to us on the island—we took care of our own around here. If someone needed a Mix and couldn't afford to pay, it'd never stop me from providing them with the necessary one. However, Gus and I did need to make purchases from afar at times, and money happened to be a universal language understood in all corners of the earth.

"Have a nice party!" I offered her the parcel, relieved to have an order that wasn't a security spell. "Let me know how it goes."

Rhonda flashed me a winning smile and agreed, then picked up her package and sashayed out of the bar. While she left, I counted up the coins, forcing myself not to wonder where Gus would get the pure silver and stardust needed to replenish my supply of Long Isle Iced Tea now that our relationship with Liam was, in a word, *complicated*.

I delayed my return to the storeroom by puttering behind the bar for a few moments. I put on the ingredients for a Caffeine Cup and polished the counter while I waited for the beverage to brew.

My mind crowded with thoughts of Ranger X, wondering what damage control would look like. The article had surprised and affected both of us. I took a few deep breaths, knowing I should explain myself to him—that it'd be easy enough to clarify I'd had nothing to do with the article being published early.

He'd believe me. He was my love. He was a good, honest man—as well as an incredibly powerful force to reckon with, and his reaction to seeing the headline in the paper had been nothing but a knee jerk emotional one. I knew all that.

However, I'd had my own emotional reaction to *his* outburst that left me wondering. Unease percolated in my gut, and there was a deep sense of unrest in realizing that X's immediate conclusion had been to assume I'd leaked the article in spite of his wishes.

As I scrubbed, harder and harder, I couldn't help the flash of hurt that racked my body. I would never betray him, yet somehow, he'd believed it possible. Somewhere deep down, he'd suspected me of going behind his back for something as stupid as Peter's article—and *that* worried me. Against everything else, we needed to trust one another. *Isn't that what love is all about?*

Ranger X's doubt hurt worse than Liam's betrayal, even though the latter had become a man I'd viewed as a friend, a confidant, a well-intentioned—though dangerous—fixture of the island. He'd fooled Ranger X, Gus, and a slew of islanders into believing his loyalties had been firmly on our side.

I'd spent the last few weeks tracing back over every one of our interactions, struggling to unearth signs I should have seen.

The thoughts brought me nowhere fast and always led to the same place: betrayal, darkness, and anger.

Despite Liam's murky loyalties, Ranger X and I had agreed to work with him on a mission that was larger than all of us. We needed to save the Master of Magic. He was the man—the entity—who controlled our magical world.

According to the stories, without the Master of Magic, our world would crumble. Life as we knew it would cease to exist if the balance of magic was destroyed. Liam had claimed the Master of Magic was The Faction's next target. He hadn't shared the when, the how, or the why, only that we needed to be ready at a moment's notice.

I took a few deep breaths, rotated my shoulders, and cracked my knuckles as the Caffeine Cup setup gurgled to completion and left me two piping hot cups of magical coffee. I gathered them, forcing the swirling thoughts to the back of my brain as I re-entered the storeroom.

"We'll need more silver and stardust," I began as I climbed the stairs. "We're wiped out of Long Isle Iced Tea as you've noticed. I'll also need the basics for the Security Samplers: rosemary, a hint of acid—I don't think we keep that on hand—ginger, lemon—"

"Don't you dare ruin this, Lily Locke!" The front door burst open, and in typical fashion, Zin stormed in, her short black bob cutting sharply around her face. "I swear, if you ruin my chance to become a Ranger, I will..."

She trailed off at the sight of Gus holding a very sharp knife over a vanilla bean. Meanwhile, I gently set the Caffeine Cups on the table in the center of the room and faced my petite, dark-clothed cousin.

"What's that, Zin?" I asked, my hand raising to land on my hip. "Did you need something?"

Her eyes clouded, but she was outnumbered. Not that she'd do anything rash, but she'd clearly come for an argument, and frankly, I was glad. I needed someone to be honest with me, to hash things out so we could move on with our lives.

"Never mind," she grumbled. "I was just—"

"Tell me what you came to say," I said, an edge to my voice. Raising one hand from my hip, I gave a warning sign to my assistant. "Stay out of this, Gus."

"Ranger X is on a tear," Zin said, some of the fire coming back into her voice. "That stupid article. Did you have something to do with it? Because the only time Ranger X ever curses at his employees is when you've done something that upsets him. And let me tell you, my mother would've washed his mouth out with soap after our meeting at HQ this morning."

A terse smile at the thought of Trinket swirling soap around Ranger X's mouth broke off a corner of the tension. "I'm not dragging you into my relationship with the details, but yes. He's angry with me."

Zin's eyes crinkled. "What'd you do?"

"Nothing," I said curtly. I refused to have an argument with Zin that really needed to be had with Ranger X. "How am I ruining your chances of becoming a Ranger? I thought you were a shoe-in. The ceremony is in just a few days."

"It is." Zin pursed her lips. "I have one last assignment that needs completing before my paperwork is official."

"What's the assignment?"

"It's confidential," she said, thoughtfully. "Ranger X hasn't told you?"

"Not if it's confidential Ranger business. We're in a relationship; we're not colleagues."

Zin shrugged as if the two were interchangeable, but she seemed mildly appeased. "Well, with this stupid article, all of the Ranger and trainee schedules are being eaten up by bogus calls and paranoid people. Our free time is *zilch* for personal cases."

Chills went down my spine. "Things are that bad?"

Zin raised a hand to her forehead. "You really didn't do anything, huh?"

I shook my head. "I *did* know about the article—I have it here, in fact. I planned to publish it according to Peter's wishes."

"What do you think about its contents?"

I sat at the table, my hands encircling the Caffeine Cup as I passed the other to Gus. Zin stepped further into the room and plunked herself down opposite me.

"I think," I began slowly, "that there are valid points to it, but—"

"It's a fear-mongering piece of fiction that's meant to terrify the islanders," Zin said, poison in her voice. "We need people to stay calm. Not rise up in a panic."

"It's not fiction," I corrected. "Not all of it. There's danger in our world, and The Faction..." I trailed off. She was nearly a full-fledged Ranger. She knew the dangers. "I agree the timing was unfortunate, and the panic is certainly distracting."

"I have one assignment left." Zin's voice turned into a thin, pained line. "My time is planned out for the next three days following up on calls about Peeping Toms and evil spells that don't exist. I'll spend all my time assuaging concerns about *nothing,* and my assignment will fall behind."

"Ranger X will understand—this is part of your job, too. Surely he knows that and won't hold back your initiation because you've been swamped."

"I'm bound to complete this assignment. Magically," Zin explained, shifting uneasily in her seat. "Not to mention, it's important."

The slight waver in her voice drew my attention. "What is it, Zin?"

"I can't say, but I need to take care of it. I need to, Lily, for us."

She seemed to be trying to tell me something with her gaze, but I couldn't read her mind. Gus cleared his throat, warning us of his presence. Anything Zin said, he could hear too, and his meaning was clear: She shouldn't get herself in trouble by spilling confidential information.

"I should be going." Zin stood and gave me the slightest smile. "Sorry I barged in here, Lily, Gus."

"Zin, wait. Can I ask a favor of you?"

"What is it?"

"I am the only person who had a copy of Peter's article," I said, my voice low and layered with meaning. "I didn't publish it."

The light flickered on behind Zin's eyes. "Where'd you keep it stored?"

"My bedroom. I swear to you, I didn't show anyone else."

"I'll look into it," Zin assured me, battling back the uncertainty in her eyes. "I'm sure there's an explanation for it. I'll ask a few questions at the *Wicked Weekly*—someone will know."

"Of course," I agreed. "There has to be a logical explanation."

"In the meantime," Zin moved toward the door but stopped with a hand on the knob. "Stay alert, Lily."

After Zin left, I turned to Gus. "That last part, the bit about staying alert—that wasn't about the article. Do you think it had something to do with her assignment?"

Gus frowned. "She's worried about something."

"You think?" My sarcasm came on strong. "What did Ranger X assign to her?"

"If you want my opinion, you've got enough to worry about on your own. These Mixes ain't gonna make themselves, and you've got a line of customers waiting already."

I hadn't heard the gathering at the bar outside, but sure enough, no less than seven folks were waiting for my attention.

"Those orders?" I pointed to the paper where Gus was listing out the ingredients we'd need to stock the shop. "Triple it."

Chapter 2

I SPENT WHAT WAS LEFT of the morning, as well as the afternoon and early evening, slinging what Security Spells I had available over the counter. I took backorders for the rest, including a week's worth of Long Isle Iced Tea. It'd take me forever to get ahead with how fast the vials were flying from the shelves.

I finally had to put up a sign that declared a handful of spells out of stock and unorderable until further notice. That didn't do me any favors with the already antsy crowd.

I hadn't seen X all day, nor had Zin returned. I figured they were busy, as we all were. Gus barely moved from the storeroom, hawking orders to suppliers and shuffling around the room with the vigor of someone half his age.

By the time the moon inched onto the horizon and the waters around the island grew dark, my feet ached and my head pounded. Formulas for potions flitted randomly through my head, as if my brain had short circuited and all I could process were bits of ingredients here and there.

A pinch of thyme, a teaspoon of salt. Brew until bubbling. Cool until calm. Add Dust of the Devil—*strain out the bits of pineapple pulp.*

Finally, the closed sign appeared out front, and with a sigh of relief, I eased onto a chair behind the bar and let my shoulders slump forward. The six—*seven?*—Caffeine Cups had helped me through the rush, and now I was feeling the crash. Hard.

My eyes drooped, and I was just on the verge of either sleep or tears—hard to tell which—when footsteps sounded behind me.

"Sorry, we're closed," I called. "We open at ten tomorrow."

"It's me," a soft, clipped voice said. "Sorry to bother you, Lily, but I thought..."

As the voice faded away, I looked up to find my aunt Trinket, Zin's mother, inching toward me. She wore her usual smart clothes—a long, neat skirt with a white shirt and a sensible cardigan over her shoulders—but the look on her face was different. Softer around the edges, save for her eyes. Her gaze burned with intensity that would lead us to yet another argument.

"We're out of it," I told Trinket. "I'm sorry, but we've already discussed your wishes. My answer is still no—it's simply too dangerous to continue."

"Please, Lily, just once more." Her bony fingers gripped my arm. "You must have faith. She's trying to tell us something."

I let her squeeze me, the slight pain in her grip a welcome jolt back to reality from my exhausting day at the counter. "I've already made my decision; I will not help you with this any longer."

"*She* needs you!" Trinket's voice grew shrill as she pleaded, until Gus peeked through the door to see who we had for company. "She needs you to help her."

I shook my head at Gus, who thankfully eased back into the storeroom before Trinket could see him.

"Even if I wanted to take Long Isle Iced Tea again, I don't have any, and I won't for a few days at the very least. It's been selling off the shelves," I said, gesturing to the sign that declared Long Isle Iced Tea out of stock and unorderable. "I've never had so many backorders for one potion."

"Surely you have some in your reserves."

I turned, finally easing myself out of Trinket's vice-like grip, and shook my head. "Nothing I will use for your purposes."

Her eyes went dark, something like bloodlust appearing there. "Lily, you don't understand—"

"I do understand," I corrected her. "I'm simply telling you no."

When Trinket and Mimsey had first presented me with the matching half to the necklace I'd worn since my birth, they'd explained the charm was a form of protection. It had come straight from the Order of the Heart, as started by the goddess Hecate herself. The inscription inside read *Follow the Heart*, though I'd never known its meaning until my aunts snapped the matching half in place. The heart had warmed and glowed, proving I belonged in the supernatural world.

I hadn't thought much about the necklace during my time on The Isle—not until I'd returned from Wishery. However, on the night of Poppy's birthday party, the necklace had glowed in an entirely new way—bright blue, scathing hot to the touch. Since then, it hadn't been the same. It'd flickered here and there, warmed for unknown reasons, as if something had upset it.

That had also been the night I'd taken Long Isle Iced Tea and turned into my mother for the first time. I couldn't believe that was a coincidence. The potion had transformed me into a mere illusion of her, yet one that had disturbed Trinket. The potion had been created as a simple party trick, not a way to interact with the deceased, yet Trinket seemed to think otherwise.

Once Trinket had caught a glimpse of her dead sister, she'd craved more. Her eyes grew darker, wilder every time she asked for my assistance in seeing *her* again. At first, I'd agreed. I'd taken the potion once or twice more at her insistence, but eventually, I'd had to stop—for Trinket's sake. The wait times in between incidents had grown shorter, and the thought of seeing her sister again had begun to drive Trinket mad.

"Trinket—go home to your children," I told her. "Is Zin with them?"

She nodded. "I *know* you have a way to bring her back to me."

"She's gone, and we cannot bring her back. This is becoming unhealthy. Not to mention, it doesn't work," I explained, straining for patience. We'd had this conversation nearly a hundred times over the past few weeks. "Overuse of the potion is dangerous. I won't risk it for either of us."

Trinket eased back, her hands retreating to her sides. "You don't want to see her? You don't want to know what happened to her?"

"She's my mother!" I stood, the stress, the anger, getting the better of me. "Of course I want to know what happened to her, but that doesn't mean we can bring her back. She's gone—we can't let our lives go to waste looking for a figment of our imagination. It was me underneath that potion, not her, and I'm sorry I can't change that."

Trinket seemed startled back to reality, which made her next whispery phrase all the more potent. "Your necklace glowing on the beach—that wasn't an illusion. We both saw it. We both watched it turn to light. I'm sure you felt it."

"She's not coming back," I murmured. "I'm sorry."

Trinket turned on her heel, having the sense of mind to look ashamed, and stumbled toward the exit. Pausing on the edge of light and dark, her face half shadowed as she looked to me, she appeared ready to say something.

However, the words never made it out. Her eyes grew in size as she stared at my neck with such intensity it gave me a start. I was so distracted by Trinket that I didn't feel the warmth until I glanced down and saw the heart around my neck gleaming a bright, crystalline shade of blue.

"I knew it," Trinket whispered. "You must listen, Lily."

"It's nothing." I clasped the locket, warm to the touch, and tucked it inside my shirt. "It does that on occasion. It doesn't mean anything."

"How long has it been doing this? Did it happen before that night, before you changed into her?"

I didn't answer. There wasn't an answer that would banish Trinket's theory back to where it belonged—out of sight and out of mind.

Trinket stumbled toward me, her feet clumsy and her hands clammy as they found mine. She'd crossed the room in seconds. Still holding me, she collapsed to her knees, her voice raspy. "You must, Lily, please!"

"No! She's *gone*, Trinket!"

Trinket clasped tighter. Her chest heaved with rasps and her eyes sparked with desperation. "My sister—it's my fault, I should have told someone about Lucian..."

"It's not your fault." I struggled to pull my aunt's hands from my body, but her sheer will was enough to overpower me. "Trinket, you're hurting me."

At this, she retracted her hands as if licked by flames. She stood, her gaze unseeing as she stared, alarmed and distracted. Her lip trembled, but no tears fell.

"Why?" I managed. "Why is this so important to you? Nothing is going to bring her back."

"She was murdered." Trinket's whole body trembled this time, on the verge of convulsing. "You know as well as I do that it wasn't a *mugging* gone wrong. Your mother was a powerful witch—her death was no accident."

"Trinket, if you know what's good for you, you'll back away." Gus appeared livid at the door. "That's your niece you're bruising. Get off her."

I hadn't realized it, but Trinket had reached for me, her nails like talons digging into my arm and leaving red indentions on my skin. I could see them as I ran a hand over the locket, which had since returned to its normal shade and temperature. There'd be bruises tomorrow, almost certainly.

"You know I'm right," Trinket whispered on the verge of a hiss. "You feel it, too."

Before I could respond, Trinket turned, hobbled toward the darkness, then fled into it.

When I recovered from my surprise, I could hear my breath rasping double time.

"Don't say a word about this," I told Gus. "To *anyone*."

"She's not well. Mimsey or Hettie need to know."

"This is not their business," I said, still rattled from the encounter. "Not yet."

"She all but attacked you."

"This is between Trinket and me," I said with finality. "I'm exhausted. I'm going to bed. Goodnight, Gus."

As I trudged upstairs, I grudgingly acknowledged my appreciation for the soft clattering of vials and beakers downstairs. Chairs scraped against the floor and thunks of the cane signaled Gus's continued labors into the night. Mimsey might be upset at his long hours, but I couldn't bear to send him home; I needed the company. Even distant company.

I showered, soaping gently over the fingernail marks from Trinket which stung just a bit where she'd broken skin. I left the locket on, even as the water burned over my shoulders. Something pulled me to leave it across my collar, to never undo the clasp my aunts had fastened behind my neck on that first day so long ago—back in the bar where I'd learned of my destiny as a witch and had begun the rest of my life.

History quickly played out in the back of my mind as I washed my hair, then quicker still as the timeline in my memories grew nearer the present. Eventually, I flicked the water off and stepped into the steamy room, wrapping the towel around my body.

As I selected a soft nightgown from my self-populating closet and curled into bed, I couldn't seem to disconnect the memory reel. Trinket's bottomless gaze haunted me and each thought of X sent my stomach winding in knots. I'd give anything for him to be here next to me, but I knew that was impossible. Judging by his silence today and Zin's concern, the Rangers were swamped. He'd probably work through the night.

Which reminded me of the article. Rolling over, I pulled open my drawer and scanned the dirty scrap of paper I'd tucked underneath my socks. How could someone possibly have gotten at this note without my knowing? I'd kept it a secret from very nearly everyone. I hadn't felt the need to lock the article in the safe because nobody knew of it in the first place.

Correction: I'd *thought* nobody had known about it. I'd also thought nobody had cared enough to steal it. I'd been wrong on both counts, and not only had it hurt the island as a whole, it'd hurt me on a personal level. Very personal. My relationship with X was already in new territory, what with the balancing act between marriage and love and life together. We didn't need the additional tension, not *now*.

With a rush of frustration, I slammed the drawer shut and flopped back into bed. No use protecting the article now that it was out there for all to read. My thoughts on the matter flipped back to Zin, and I wondered if she'd have any luck uncovering the identity of the thief with her inquiry into *Wicked Weekly* headquarters.

That's if she had time to follow up on my worries while dealing with the article's fallout and her latest assignment—one I was dying to be let in on, though I wouldn't hold my breath. Like everyone else, she had her own crosses to bear.

Which left me with the biggest outstanding question of all: *When* would Liam return with news?

As I fell asleep, I felt as if the storm was closing in on me. I might be in the eye of it now, the deceptive calm, the swirling mess of hot and cold fronts that left me frustrated and anxious, but it wouldn't last forever. I ached with the anticipation of it all, knowing the pressure was building, squeezing, tightening the noose.

Sooner or later, the storm would break.

When it did, I would be ready.

Chapter 3

WOMAN'S KNICKERS IN A TWIST
...over stolen laundry.
Late yesterday evening/early this morning, Betty Baumgarten's bot-
toms were swiped right off the clothesline in a surprising twist of events.
Betty, who's been living on this island for sixty-four years, has never
*seen anything like it. All of her clothes—*poof!*—gone.*
"It's unfortunate, really," she says in an exclusive quote to Wicked Week-
ly reporter Dawn Dingum. "I stitched that dress out of my husband's
old shirts. I'd really like it back. The undies—those, they can keep. I was
buying new ones for my birthday anyway."
There are no leads to the theft of Betty's bottoms at the time of printing.

*ALL TOMATOES STOLEN FROM SUPERMARKET IN ROT-
TEN DEVELOPMENT...*
*In another random event early this morning, all of the toma-
toes—every last cherry tomato—was taken from Magic Market. The
store's produce section was wiped clean, and as of publication, there are
no leads as to who needs a supermarket's worth of the vegetable.
With any leads, please get in touch with Wicked Weekly reporter Lulu
Beluga.*

BUBBLE, BUBBLE, TOIL AND TROUBLE...

Someone has dumped gallons of dish soap onto the Lower Bridge. As of publication, efforts to remove the coating of soap across the bridge have been unsuccessful, as each washing only irritates the sudsing and brings more bubbles to the surface. Please avoid using the Lower Bridge until mid-morning when it will be cleared by Magical Maintenance.

For any news or sightings of the culprit, please reach out to Cindy Sherbert at the Wicked Weekly tip line.

I TROOPED BACK UP THE stairs holding the newspaper in one hand and a cup of regular coffee in the other. I hadn't had the energy to make a Caffeine Cup this morning and had merely flicked on the old coffee machine stashed in the kitchen cabinet.

The headlines this morning exhausted me for some reason. On behalf of X and his exponentially increasing workload, my eye twitched in agitation. The last thing everyone on this island needed was an influx of petty crime. Not only petty, but nonsensical. *Tomatoes*? Who in their right mind could possibly need a wheelbarrow full of tomatoes? Not to mention Betty Baumgarten's bottoms—an even bigger head scratcher.

Glancing at the third story, I briefly wondered with unabashed selfishness whether the bridge's closing would lighten the influx of customers this morning. Since the West Isle Witches were the only ones gutsy—or foolish—enough to live on the same side of the island as The Forest, all customers had to cross either the Upper or Lower bridge in order to reach the bungalow. Since the Upper Bridge led straight into The Forest, there was only one normally viable option. One that was now down for cleaning.

I tossed the paper on the bed, then shortly after, I followed its trajectory and crawled back under the covers. Just for a minute, I told myself as my eyes closed. Just one little minute.

One little minute...

Many minutes later, I opened my eyes to find the early morning darkness had lightened to a shimmering sunlight and the sound of Gus clattering below filled the previously silent house.

I stretched, noting the loud clamor to Gus's movements. He had the habit of pounding around louder and louder as the morning grew later in hopes of waking me at a reasonable hour. To him, reasonable was before eight a.m. We had different definitions of reasonable, though it had been months since I'd slept in past seven. The customers of yesterday must have kicked a new bout of exhaustion through my bones.

Unable to procrastinate longer, I slid out from my cozy covers and muttered a prayer of gratefulness to my self-populating closet as it suggested an array of choices for my mood this morning. Mostly black dresses. Apparently, my moodiness was obvious even to an inanimate object.

On second thought, I pushed past the dresses and pulled a more unlikely ensemble off the racks—a sweater, thick and chunky and knitted with gusto. Despite the always-summer conditions of the island, I tossed the sweater on with a pair of jean shorts and bright blue flip flops to match.

The material was airy enough to prevent me from dying of heat, but more importantly, there was enough material to hide an unwanted glow. Tucking the charm inside the neckline, I waited, watched, and sure enough, there was the now-traditional morning flash of light from the heart.

The sweater didn't hide it entirely, but it would work for now. By the time I finished my morning routine, Gus's clattering downstairs had reached epic proportions. If I didn't join him in the storeroom soon, he'd send a hex upstairs to drag me down by the ears.

"Morning, Gus," I said, stepping lightly into the storeroom, determined to put on a positive face. "How's it going?"

He grunted his typical greeting without looking up.

"Great," I said. "I'm feeling well, thanks for asking."

His eyes flickered to me, then did a double take at my attire. "You are?"

"Oh, this? Just switching it up," I told him. "I miss the seasons from the mainland, especially sweater weather."

Gus didn't look convinced, but he could care less about fashion—especially when there were more pressing matters on his mind.

"I picked up the supplies on my way over this morning. You were still sleeping."

"Thanks."

"The silver and stardust are on backorder, what with..." Gus trailed off and cleared his throat. "Let's say my usual line of supply has been interrupted."

Liam. Liam had been Gus's line of supply, and therefore mine as well, and he was no longer a welcome man in these parts. Though Ranger X and I had begrudgingly agreed to work with him to save the Master of Magic from attack, we couldn't instantly forget Liam's recent wrongs.

"Fine," I said. "I'll leave the sign out that Long Isle Iced Tea is unorderable. Hopefully it'll be a slower day today, what with the bridge being sudsed."

"About that..." Gus moved creakily toward the door to Magic & Mixology and pressed it open a crack. "Take a look."

The door creaked as I stuck my head through which, in retrospect, was a huge mistake. A sea of people swiveled their expectant expressions toward me as they waited impatiently for the bar to open.

I slammed the door shut and stared in open-mouthed surprise at Gus. "What's that?"

"High demand."

"I thought the bridge was closed."

"Someone set up a damn ferry. A ferry to shuttle people across."

"Why?"

"Isn't it clear? They want to see you."

I inhaled a breath, struggling for calm. "I am already behind on the Mixes I was supposed to create for today. The backorder list is going to become astronomical, and who knows when..."

I was about to say *when Liam will return*, but I stopped myself short.

"When what?"

"My relationship with X is already bumpy thanks to the stupid article," I said, changing the subject to love. Gus hated to discuss love, especially with me. "I was hoping to talk to X today, but I won't get away from the bar at this rate."

Gus frowned, probably not convinced, but distracted enough. "I'll clear them out. Keep the shop empty. Not much we can do if we've run out of supplies, anyway."

"We can't do that. I'm here to serve the islanders. To help keep people safe and, more equally it seems these days, to help them *feel* safe."

"We aren't a store. They want to buy ingredients, or spells, they can head to the supply store or talk to MAGIC, Inc. You're the Mixologist, Lily."

"And being the Mixologist takes on different forms depending on what people need," I said. "You know that. It's not a simple nine-to-five."

"Nine'a'what?"

"I'm just saying, this isn't a job I can take off for a day whenever I want."

"You might be superhuman, but you aren't invincible," Gus argued. "You can only do so much in a day."

I exhaled a breath that felt stale, as if it'd been stuck in my lungs for ages. Sucking in fresh air, I shook my head again. "I'm going to open the bar for a bit. I'll take a long lunch hour to talk to X and get started on the outstanding orders."

"Your choice," Gus said. "What would you like me to do?"

"Prepare the ingredients. If they're separated, chopped, diced, soaked, washed, etc., Mixing will go a lot faster."

Gus nodded, pleased with my assessment. He was likely also pleased that I'd given him the job that required silence and concentration in the background. He had never been one who played nicely with crowds, preferring to study magic in quiet solitude.

As I stepped toward the door, a burst of warmth around my neck gave me pause. A quick glance down gave me the news I'd expected: My mother's charm glowed pale blue. I hesitated, holding a hand to it as I waited for the glow to fade.

Turning to Gus, I tried for nonchalance when I spoke. "Do you know any spells that deal with items?"

"What do you mean?"

"You know," I began, then paused. For some reason, my mother's necklace and its newfound quirks felt private to me. Only Trinket had seemed to notice, and she hadn't exactly handled it well.

Gus waited, still, thoughtful. His eyes flicked once to the hand I'd clasped at my throat.

I dropped my hand. "*Things*. A spell where you can take an item and read what the user is thinking or hear the last words they've spoken. Or something similar. I don't think I've ever read about one."

"Why?"

I had the feeling Gus knew I wouldn't answer the question, so I dodged it easily. "No reason. Just wondering."

"I haven't ever used one," he said, "but that doesn't mean one can't exist."

"I suppose."

"I'll take a deeper look this afternoon," he offered. "But you do remember, Lily, that you're the Mixologist. If a potion doesn't exist...you make one."

Gus's response startled me. "Yes, but it would be incredibly complicated, and—"

"And what?"

I fell silent.

"Don't tell me you're not ready for it," Gus said, ambling toward the vials, his eyes already alight with the hint of a challenge. "You've been through years, decades of magic since you've arrived. You've improved by leaps and bounds— more than I could've ever dreamed."

Gus pulled a book off a shelf, cradled it to his chest, and turned to face me. "It's a pleasure to serve as your assistant."

"Gus—"

"You might be the strongest Mixologist yet." Gus stepped across the room, his eyes fixed on the chain around my neck. At the last moment, he lifted his gaze toward mine. "Don't shy away from your powers. Don't busy yourself as a clerk. You have the ability to help people on a scale grander than anyone on this island can comprehend. You cannot lose sight of that."

Gus's comments felt like a chaste reminder, a warning, and a compliment all in one. It took me several long seconds to comprehend all of it. In that time, Gus shuffled back to the table and cracked the book open, easing himself onto the bench before it.

"Go on," he said, flicking a pair of reading glasses onto his nose. "I've got work to do. Also, I ordered more To-Go vials. This ain't a store, as I mentioned, and we didn't have enough. Mimsey will bring them by later."

In a bit of a haze, I stumbled back toward the door of Magic & Mixology, taking a moment to gather myself. I took a calming breath, then pasted on the peppiest expression I could muster and stepped through the entryway, greeting the customers with a wide grin.

"Hop in line," I instructed. "As you'll notice by the sign, we're out of several ingredients due to the high demand, and..."

I trailed off as a series of squeaks and giggles sounded from the back of the crowd. A pleasant voice preceded the wake of destruction, muttering apologies as she pushed herself to the front.

"Sorry about the toe," Poppy said, her blond hair bobbing merrily in the sea of other heads. "Out of my way, sorry—important Mixologist business."

As my cousin burst through the crowd, I caught myself stunned into inaction as I watched her carry a dusty old box forward. Leaping to attention, I took the package from Poppy's arms and poured her a glass of water.

"Poppy! What's going on?" I asked. "You look dusty."

"I was helping my mom and Trinket at the supply store this morning—you know, day off dispatch at Ranger HQ." She grinned happily at me. "I heard Gus talking about the crazy business you guys have been drumming up and thought I'd help."

"You don't have to do that, Poppy. We're okay, really."

She glanced skeptically at the sign, the list of out-of-stock options that seemed to grow with each passing breath. "Right. Well, here are some back-up vials and bottles. They should last you through lunch at least, and my mom is having more delivered tonight. You might want to give them a quick rinse, though—they're sort of dusty. Found them in the attic."

"Thank you, Poppy, that's—"

"Alrighty, folks," Poppy shouted, clapping her hands. "Get in a single file line. I'm the store clerk for today, so if you want something, you'll have to talk to me. Lily's going to be focusing on her Mixes."

"Let's go," someone moaned from the back. "Pick up the pace. I've been waiting for forty-five minutes."

"That's your own darn fault for getting here an hour before the bungalow opened," Poppy snapped back. "Stop complaining, Chad, or I might just ignore your order."

The patron named Chad grumbled some, but it seemed to do the trick. An awkward line formation trickled into place, and before I knew it, Poppy was passing out menus and taking orders like her life depended on it.

"Well?" she said, a minute later with a bright smile. "Whatcha waiting for? These orders aren't going to Mix themselves."

I returned Poppy's smile with a grateful one of my own and hurried into the storeroom. Gus, ever efficient, already had the supplies for the Security Sampler Spells laid out and ready. He offered me one wry glance which I returned, and that was the extent of our communication. It was my way of thanking him and his way of acknowledging me, and nothing more was needed.

By lunchtime, we'd made huge progress on the backorders and had moved on to the recent purchases made that morning. At this rate, we'd be all caught up if we worked well into the evening.

Rolling my sleeves up, I wiped a thin layer of sweat from my brow. The sweater was still too warm for this weather, and it'd been made warmer still by the intermittent glowing and heat bursts from the charm around my neck. I ignored the discomfort and pushed another set of potions ready for packing toward Gus.

He packaged them automatically, reading quick snippets from an ancient spellbook between stopping up the vials and setting them snugly into boxes. He'd tried to be discreet about his reading, but eventually gave up and read openly.

"I'm going to give Poppy a break. Take one, too. Say hello to Mimsey for me," I said pointedly. "Get out of here, Gus. We'll be late tonight."

He looked up as I spoke, as if surprised he wasn't alone. "Right, right, I'll just finish up with this and head out," he said, in another surprising move. Gus always argued, and he hated taking breaks.

I watched him, wondering what he'd found in his research and if he was, in fact, looking up ancient spells having to do with items or possessions like I'd asked. I shrugged it off, heading out to Magic & Mixology where I gave the rest of the waiting line tickets to hold their place, then propped up a closed sign.

"Thank you," I told Poppy sincerely once everyone had cleared. "Seriously. We are almost ahead on orders, and I would never have been able to do that alone. Gus and I were drowning over here."

"I know," she chirped, as she led the way back into the storeroom. "I'm happy to help. What are your plans for lunch?"

I cringed. "I'm sorry, I was going to try and find Ranger X. We have a few things to discuss. But if you want to catch a bite first or something, we can do that on the way."

"No, no," she said, waving a hand. Her bright expression didn't diminish for a beat. "I'm going to head home and shower. I'm so dusty you could vacuum me right up."

On an impulse, I reached out and hugged Poppy. She stood still for a moment in surprise, then reacted, her arms squeezing me tightly back. I savored the moment, the feeling of camaraderie and family. Unlike everything else these days, Poppy stood alone as a happy bright spot, dressed in a flowery skirt and pink tank top and glitter encrusted flip flops.

As we parted, a tickle of the dust coating her clothing drifted toward me, and as my eyes watered, I gestured for her to head home.

"I'll go shower," Poppy said, unable to suppress a giggle. "Want me back this afternoon?"

I gave a shake of my head. "You've done plenty—thank you. I do have one more question, though."

"Ranger X is at HQ," Poppy said slyly. "Elle can help you find him."

I tried not to look sheepish. "Thanks."

"Zin's there, too," Poppy said, this time with a frown. "She's been hard to pin down lately."

"I'm sure she's busy. She said something about having one more big assignment to finish before her induction ceremony."

"She did?"

Poppy's surprise startled me. Not only did Poppy work at Ranger HQ, but she and Zin were close—probably closer than Zin and myself.

"Er, maybe not," I said. "She was in a mood about the article. I probably misunderstood."

"Right. Sure. Well, I'll catch you later, Lily." Poppy pulled the door open but stopped short. "Um, you have company."

It was my turn to frown as I approached the door. I hadn't heard anyone knock, and I couldn't see anyone outside. Stepping closer, I spotted the reason for my confusion. A disgruntled gnome with a squashed-tomato nose stood there with a hand on his hip.

"What'd I tell you about getting a step stool out here?" Chuck snapped. "I know you're busy, what with doing Mixology things, but seriously."

"Maybe you should consider coming back when the shop is open," Poppy said, sidestepping my guest. "The sign says closed, Chuck. Get in line with the rest of the island."

Before he could respond, Poppy raised her eyebrows at me, mouthed *Sorry*, and scurried down the path. I waved goodbye weakly in her direction.

"What can I help you with?" I asked, aware of Gus's disapproving gaze on the back of my skull. "We are closed for lunch hour if you're looking to get something from Magic & Mixology."

"Lily, you've got to help us."

"Us?"

"The gnomes," he said, twisting stubby little fingers together and pulling his squat lips into a pout. "We ain't as magical as the rest of the folks. Spells are hard for us to understand."

"Why would you need spells all of a sudden?"

"Because..." Chuck peered around me, surveying the bungalow as if someone were listening.

Someone was listening. *Gus*. And Gus didn't look very happy.

"What's he doing here?" Chuck pressed. "This is a private matter."

"Whatever can be said to me can be said to Gus," I said firmly. "What's happening out there, Chuck?"

He stepped through the door, scanned the beachfront behind him, and once he'd determined it clear, he spoke in a harsh whisper. "We need to keep ourselves protected. You will help us, won't you, Lily? The Grove of Gnomes is vulnerable."

I'd never known gnomes had a name for their town. I had been to their home for the first time recently to deal with a mislabeled haunted house. Chuck apparently figured we were old pals after that.

"Why now?" I suspected I knew the answer, but I wanted to hear it from the mouth of an islander. "What's making everyone so nervous, Chuck?"

"The article," he said simply. "Surely you saw it. You were there with The Faction, weren't you?"

"For a bit. The article—"

"There's more," Chuck said, heaving a sigh. "You haven't heard the latest?"

"No."

Though he feigned disappointment, underneath was a tremor of excitement at his being the first to deliver the news. "There's a rumor floating around that it's a Ranger pulling all the local hijinks."

"That's insane. What sort of Ranger would do that? I assume you're talking about the tomatoes, and the—er, Betty's things missing, and the soap."

Chuck nodded, no longer bothering to hide his glee at being the bearer of bad news. "Betty Baumgarten said she saw him."

"Him?" My heart sank like a rock. "Who's him?"

The gnome had the presence of mind to look ashamed. "I-I'm sure it's not true, but..."

"Spit it out."

"Your, uh...beloved."

"Ranger X?" I gave a short laugh of disbelief. "Yeah, right. He wishes he had enough spare time to steal all the tomatoes from a grocery store. That sounds like a high school prank."

"A high—what?"

I'd forgotten the gnome had likely never been to the mainland, let alone integrated into modern human society. "Forget it. I promise you it's not him."

"The clerk at the grocery store..." Chuck hesitated, surveying my face. "Er—never mind. I should shut up now."

"I'm sorry for snapping," I said quickly. "Please tell me the truth. If I'm to help protect this island, I need to know the truth."

"The clerk at the grocery store described seeing a figure as he came to open the store. The man was wearing all black."

"Okay, I'm sure plenty of men wear all black," I said, telling myself the first flutterings in my stomach meant nothing. "Let's think about the big picture. What would ever be gained by Ranger X—or any Ranger, for that matter—pulling these stunts?"

Chuck had an answer. It came lightning quick, so quickly it told me he hadn't come up with it on his own. "Maybe he's trying to drum up business for the Rangers. You know, make sure he keeps his hero status."

Another bark of laughter. "I'm sorry, but he's Superman enough without drumming up his own business."

"Super—who?"

"Forget it." I shook my head. "What do *you* think, Chuck?"

"Er—I don't know."

"Obviously, you think something, or else you wouldn't be knocking on my door."

"*Attempting* to knock on your door," he corrected with a gleam in his eye. "You really need to install a second knocker for us shorter folks."

"Can we put that on the to do list?" I called over my shoulder. "Thanks, Gus."

I could feel Gus's unhappiness at the task, but he didn't question me. Not in front of guests, though I'd most certainly hear about it later.

"Well?" I prompted. "What do you think is going on?"

"I think..." Chuck's eyes flicked toward the ground. He toed at the wooden boards there for a long moment, likely weighing the pros and cons of lying. "We don't know who to trust."

I swallowed back a retort. "I understand."

"You do?"

"I don't know if I agree with you," I said. "But if you're feeling unsafe, that's a problem. I'm going to do my best to help rectify the situation."

"Rectal-what?"

"To help you. I want to help, Chuck. You're worried about your safety, and I want to put your minds at ease."

"Right." He nodded, sinking into a rhythm. "The Grove of Gnomes has always been close enough to The Forest where we don't get random wanderers strolling through. We normally don't need protection from outsiders, but times are changing."

I pictured the little valley of homes built into the side of hills, of the stream trickling through it, a little palm tree filled oasis just north of Hettie's house. "What has changed?"

"Well, normally we call the Rangers to handle anything that requires magical protection," Chuck said. "But if we can't trust them, who do we have?"

"You're here because you want to set up your own shields."

"What good is a lock on the door if the thief has his own key?" Chuck lamented, raising his shoulders. "We have to look after our own, Lily. Please, I don't mean any ill will toward your beloved—"

"You can say his name," I said. "He's called Ranger X."

"Ranger...er, X." He tested the words out, looking as if he didn't like them much. "I don't personally have any reason to doubt him, but if the other islanders are convinced he's not doing his job, who am I to disagree?"

"Would you jump off the Lower Bridge if everyone else did it?" Gus mumbled. At my sharp glance, he shrugged. "Just saying."

"It's different," Chuck argued, giving a dirty look past my shoulder to Gus. "We're trying to be proactive."

"Thanks, Chuck," I said, assuring him again that I'd help. "I'll be over to set up a few shields for you this week."

"This *week*?" He leaned forward, ready to argue, but must have seen my expression. "Right. Thanks. I'll, uh, be going, then. We'll be expecting you."

With that, Chuck turned and hopped down the stairs, waddling in his uneven gait down the path. I watched until he vanished from sight.

By the time I turned around, I realized Gus hadn't moved a centimeter; it was so quiet in the storeroom, I wondered if he'd even exhaled.

"It wasn't X," Gus said softly. "You know it. I know it."

"You'd heard the rumors already." It wasn't an accusation; I merely stated a fact. "You heard about the culprit being a Ranger—*allegedly*—before Chuck got here, and you didn't say a word."

"I had heard things."

I clenched my fingers at my sides. "You didn't think it was imperative to pass along the news?"

"You don't need more on your plate."

"I think I should decide what's on my plate and what's garbage for myself."

"You've been busy all morning."

"Not busy enough to ignore news like that," I snapped, feeling tears pool in my eyes. "I'm sorry, I just..." I took a deep, settling breath. "It's not him, is it?"

"Of course it's not. We all know that."

I nodded, hardly hearing him. "X has been acting off lately. I don't know if it's me or something else."

"He's juggling an entire island's safety. We're in the fog, Lily, the morning mist just before daybreak. Everyone is confused."

"What does daybreak bring?"

His silence was enough.

"War," I whispered. "It's really happening."

"We're trying to avoid it. We don't want to confront The Faction, but if they need dealing with, who will stand up for The Isle if not us?"

I could only offer a succinct nod. "I'll be back after lunch sometime. Can you hold down the fort until then? I know I told you to take a break, but there's something I need to take care of."

"If Magic & Mixology doesn't open this afternoon, it's not the end of the world," Gus said in a rare showing of sympathy. "Do what you need to do."

I straightened my sweater, tucked the charm underneath the thick fabric, and headed outside. As I closed the door behind me, I surveyed the list of things that needed care.

The most pressing was also the most intimidating.

My feet pulled me away from the bungalow, past The Twist, toward the entrance to The Forest. As I entered the shadowy piece of island home to the stuff of nightmares, my footsteps fell softly against the pine needle laden floor. After another few steps, I found two trees with a muted lightning burst between them—the entrance to Ranger HQ. Interesting, seeing as I hadn't alerted anyone to my plans aside from Gus and Poppy.

Someone on the inside was expecting me.

Chapter 4

"LILY!" ELLE, A BEAUTIFUL, centuries-old woman of Elfin blood, trilled her greeting in a pleasant voice. "Welcome."

"Did you let me in?" I asked, sidling over to the front desk. "I was going to Comm Zin, but the portal was open already when I got to The Forest."

Elle winked. "I had a feeling you'd be needing an entrance. That, and Gus gave me the heads up."

"Of course, he did," I said with a sigh. None of my movements stayed a mystery for long on the island. "I assume you know why I'm here?"

"Ranger X?" she chirped. Then, she hesitated. "Or maybe you'd like to talk to Zin, first?"

"Why?" I stepped closer, narrowing my eyes. "Is X busy?"

She raised a thin shoulder, then tapped long, meticulously manicured golden fingernails against the counter. "Er—he's indisposed at the moment. Meetings," she added hurriedly. "But I can call him down here if it's urgent."

I struggled to hold onto my composure. "Of course, I understand. Is Zin around? I was actually looking for her, too."

Elle glanced down at a ledger on her desk. A blush crept onto her pale cheeks, making her look much younger than her several hundred years of age. "My mistake, Lily, apologies. It appears Zin is out on a mission."

"You wouldn't know where—"

"It's confidential," she offered, and reading the disappointed look on my face, she continued. "I don't even know where she is. I'm sorry. It looks like she's on The Isle, but...tracking our Rangers gets a bit wonky when they're checked out on a confidential task."

"No, I understand," I said, my shoulders feeling suddenly weary. I needed to talk to Zin, to find out if she'd gotten news from the *Wicked Weekly* on the leak for the article. "The bungalow has been busy, anyway. I should get back. The Rangers are probably keeping busy, too?"

Elle's look of sympathy was almost too much. My futile grab for information wasn't lost on her.

"It's a difficult time for all of us," Elle said. "Are you sure there's not something wrong? If it's urgent, I can call him for you."

"Is something wrong?" A deep, thundering voice echoed the question behind me. "Lily, what are you doing here?"

I turned to find my broad-shouldered, tall and gorgeous boyfriend standing before me looking positively ragged. Despite the dark circles under his eyes and the unusually messy mop of hair on his head, he was a breath of fresh air. If Gus had predicted correctly that we were all in the dawn before war, Ranger X was the dew that sparkled in the new morning light.

I moved to him, rested a hand on his shoulder. To my surprise, he flinched. Elle looked away, and I didn't blame her.

"I'll, uh—" I tried to excuse myself, but the words felt like swallowing peanut butter.

"Let's talk in private." Ranger X recovered, linking his arm through mine and marching us away from the desk. "Elle, cancel my next meeting."

The click of her nails against the ledger was the only confirmation Elle dared to give him.

I kept silent until we reached a small room different than any I'd been in before at HQ. While the rest of the building had been outfitted in sharp black lines, shiny silver casings, and glistening marble slabs, this room looked like the misfit breakroom. A nook meant for relaxation, for meetings unrelated to official Ranger business, for a brush with a book over lunch.

With unusual caution, I took a seat in one of the squashy, yellow-flower patterned armchairs while Ranger X sat across from me on a lumpy brown couch. He gestured toward the small fridge, silently offering me a beverage. I shook my head.

"Lily..." he started. "I'm sorry."

"For what?"

He shied away from the question, looking pained at my response. "Everything, I suppose. I'm on edge. I'm not myself, I'm...well, look at me."

Sure enough, when I looked closer, I noticed an unusual phenomenon: Ranger X glowed. A small halo outlined his entire body, latent magic sizzling to escape.

"But, we just camped last weekend." I struggled to understand. "I thought you wouldn't have to worry about Lumiette if you released your magic once a month. How is this possible?"

He shrugged. "I don't exactly have a doctor's note on the subject."

We shared a small smile.

"I imagine it's a natural defense mechanism." His face lost its smile and grew somber. "Now that I've cracked open the magical reserves, my powers are itching to protect me. I can't seem to get rid of it—it's a natural body response, like my heart beating or my lungs breathing."

"That's good!" I hoped to sound calm and collected instead of revealing the bumbling mess of nerves jumbled inside my stomach. "I'm glad you have it as a tool to use if you need it."

"Did you need something?"

Ranger X's abrupt change of subject had me reeling for a moment. "Yes, actually, I came to talk to you about a few things."

"If it's about the article..."

"It is. X, I didn't—"

"I'm over it, Lily," he said shortly. "I love you. We're dealing with the fallout from it, and that's all. It's in the past."

His words felt like a slap to the face. I took a sharp breath. Piecing the sweet, sensitive man who shared my heart with this edgy professional had my head spinning.

"No, X. I didn't *mean* it like that. I meant—"

"I *know* you didn't mean it," he said, softer, more soothing. "It's done and over with. There's nothing more to discuss."

A wave of horror washed through me. He didn't *understand*. Somehow, he still believed I'd gone behind his back and purposely released the article before we were ready. We'd *known* publication would send a rustle of panic across The Isle—that part wasn't the surprise. The surprise was that he actually believed I'd done it.

It took me a moment to process. My chest constricted, and I felt drowned. My lungs were strained, wheezing to take in enough oxygen. Spots danced before my eyes, and I finally raised myself to stand on shaky legs.

"I'm glad that's settled, then," I said, knowing in the back of my brain that I should fight harder to correct him. But I couldn't. The hurt was too strong, too sharp. He should *know* I'd never do that. "There's one more thing. I heard a piece of news today that I wanted to pass along."

X raised his eyebrows, waiting.

"There's a rumor—I heard it from the gnomes—that the person responsible for the random events around the island is a Ranger."

Judging by his unsurprised expression, I realized that he, too, had already heard the news. My shoulders inched lower still, the weariness turning to a dull numbness.

"I see I'm late on that uptake, too," I said, resigned. "I'm going to get going. This is clearly a bad time."

"I didn't do any of those things," Ranger X said evenly, ignoring my attempt to leave. "You have to know that I would never turn my back on The Isle for *any* reason."

I swallowed, and it felt like a knife slid down my throat. The words burned as I whispered them. "I know that. I trust you."

He nodded once, oblivious to my double meaning. The childlike part of me wanted to scream, to throw a tantrum and demand he listen, demand he trust me as much as I trusted him, but the more adult side of me refrained. It would help nothing.

I couldn't *make* him trust me, just like I hadn't *forced* him fall in love with me. Just like he couldn't *make* me accept his marriage proposal. These things, these feelings, emotions, choices—they had to come freely. There was just no other way.

He'd fallen in love with me all on his own. I thought we'd had the trust, too. Though I couldn't put my finger on where it'd gone, I could feel the hollow emptiness in my chest.

"I need to ask a favor of you," he said, rising to join me. His posture was unnaturally tight, bringing his already tall figure to impressive heights. He appeared positively giant in the small room—broad and strong and unrelenting.

Normally, I'd swoon being this close to him. I'd melt into his steel arms, rest my face against his rock-hard chest, and know the softness I'd find in his gaze.

This time, I couldn't find the softness.

Ranger X took my silence as a path to continue. "I have a press conference scheduled for this week, and I'd like you to be there with me."

"Why?"

For the first time all day, Ranger X looked surprised. "As a show of solidarity. The Rangers, the Mixologist—together we can inspire confidence in the community. We have to fight the backlash from..."

He hesitated, leaving the article's name unspoken. "We have to show we're capable of defending ourselves."

"Are you saying people don't trust us to protect this island any longer?"

Ranger X leveled his gaze on me. "Yes."

The word sliced out, killing him inside. I could read it across his face, and despite my own selfish frustrations, my personal hurts, a crush of sympathy for Ranger X melted my resolves. I still loved him more than anything in this world, and I had no doubt he reciprocated it. I reached for him and rested a hand on his wrist.

It was the lightest touch, but I could feel him trembling, and suddenly, I understood. Ranger X had given his life, his very *existence*, to the Ranger program, and the community was letting him down. The trust he'd worked to gain over the years, that of the islanders, of his fellow Rangers, of himself, was crumbling before his eyes.

"I'll be at the conference." Easing onto my tip toes, I planted the softest of kisses against Ranger X's cheek, the action more difficult than I would've liked. He didn't recoil, but he didn't respond either, and that tore me to pieces.

Feeling the sting of tears on the backs of my eyes, I reached past him and opened the door. I barreled through, down the hallway, toward the front desk, choking out a request to Elle to *get me out of here* before I collapsed into a weepy mess right on the spiffy marble floors.

"Lily, are you—"

"I'm fine," I told Elle, gasping for a breath. "I just need some fresh air. Please."

Over the years, Elle had learned when to demand more during high pressure situations and when to back off. She correctly read the situation at hand and retreated, giving me access to the outside world with nothing more than a sympathetic murmur.

Once outside, I found myself wandering along the edge of The Forest, ducking into the shadows as my mood turned gloomy, reappearing into the sunlight as my reserves to stay strong grew.

By the time I reached the bright little oasis that signaled the start of the Grove of Gnomes, I'd managed to dry my tears, swipe the salt from my cheeks, and retrieve some semblance of a stable voice.

Feeling around in my pockets, I uncovered a few vials I'd stuck in my travel belt this morning at the bungalow. The potions inside were Security Sampler Spells—simple, effective alarms that I could set up for Chuck and his family.

Like I'd told the other customers, these spells wouldn't rid their property completely of intruders, but they would certainly make the status quo more difficult to upset. More importantly, these spells would provide a layer of security to bolster the gnomes' trust in the island's sworn protectors. If nothing else, it'd give them a sense of independence and proactivity.

I found Chuck sunbathing. I'd never seen a gnome in a small bathing suit before, and I wished I still hadn't.

"Lily!" He scrambled for clothes the second he saw me. "You should have told me you were coming."

"I thought I did. Next time, I'll be more specific." I peered closer at him and tapped my nose. "I have Aloe Ale if you need. You're looking a little burnt."

Chuck waddled over and peeped into the river. He gave a most-pleased smile at the sight of his shockingly red nose. "Oh, red noses around here are a thing of beauty," he said, preening under the compliment. "All the ladies are gonna love it."

"Is that right?" I murmured. "Well, I don't want to keep you from your beauty ritual. Maybe I can get started implementing the Security Spells?"

"Sure, but I want to know everything you're doing."

I sighed. Apparently, the trust wasn't back yet. In good faith, I allowed Chuck to tail me around the Grove like an untrained puppy as I sprinkled the Yard Yelpers and Sidewalk Sweepers in a circle around the gnome settlement. He stepped in everything. Asked inane questions that took ages to answer. He never let up, even as my answers grew shorter and shorter.

Still, it was a good way to spend the afternoon. Being outdoors was pleasant work and exhausting enough to distract me from the situation at Ranger HQ. For good measure, and because I wasn't yet ready to be alone again, I included an extra salt treatment on the outskirts of the oasis.

I explained several times to Chuck—and to the small audience of gnomes he'd proudly gathered to watch—this particular potion stemmed from the same salt crystals we used to anchor the island's protective shield. The spell would make it difficult for an intruder to accidentally stumble into the Grove.

Somewhat satisfied, Chuck gave a grudging nod when I finally declared myself finished.

"We'll see if it works," he said, putting on a brave show for his friends. "I'll keep you posted, Miss Locke."

"Thanks," I said, subduing an eyeroll. Then, I dropped my voice and stepped closer to Chuck. "In return, can I ask for a favor? I need someone to keep me posted on the rumors going around The Isle. I need to know how to help, and I can't do that if I'm not aware of what's happening."

Puffing his chest out for the other gnomes to see, he accepted the challenge with a nod. "I'll let you know what I hear."

I thanked him once more, waved goodbye to the rest of the gnomes, and carefully picked my way across the stream and headed in the direction of home. As I reached the edge of the Grove, I heard a particularly giggly female gnome complimenting Chuck on his bulbous, Rudolph-red nose.

Gnomes. I'd never understand them.

Somewhere along the route home, my feet changed paths almost before I could compute the updated trajectory. Before I knew it, I found myself outside Mimsey's home—a cozy little cottage not far from the supply store that my aunt Mimsey ran with her sister, Trinket.

I was in the mood for company, and frankly, the only person I could think of that might bring about a smile was Poppy. I hoped she'd be home. I wasn't ready to return to the bungalow and face a deluge of islanders reminding me that our home wasn't as safe as we thought.

I took a few steps up the path to the door, stopping when a rustle sounded from the bushes. Then a rustle came from the other side of the house. My head swiveled between the two. Something was amiss. *Two* somethings, technically, because there was no way one creature could move that fast.

Immediately, I dropped to a crouch and felt in my pockets, but my travel belt and all my vials were empty, thanks to my work at the Grove. Raising my hands, I muttered the incantation for a spell that'd render any attacker temporarily frozen at the first touch of my skin. It might not stop them from striking me once, but it'd stop them from getting a second chance.

A sharp, familiar female voice cursed from one side. "I almost had him."

"Zin?" I dropped my hands and the blanket of electric current shimmering across my skin faded to nothing. "What are you doing in Poppy's bushes?"

Zin had clearly been in her jaguar form, judging by her exceptionally sleek black hair and eerily gleaming golden irises. I watched as her hair lengthened and her eyes darkened to mere glints of metal. Her claws visibly retracted to perfectly shaped black-painted fingernails.

"Had who?"

Zin looked startled to see me, though I knew I hadn't surprised her. "Nothing," she muttered. "You spooked him."

"Who?!"

"Forget it," Zin snarled. "It's confidential."

"I'm in no mood, Zin. Why were you lurking outside Poppy's window?"

Zin's gaze flashed behind her at the glass pane in question.

"I *heard* the other visitor. Who was he?"

"Lily, I can't..." Zin trailed off, struggling for an argument. "My assignment."

My brow furrowed. "What does your assignment have to do with Poppy? Is she in danger?"

Zin bit back her response.

"Poppy is my cousin, too. I care about her. When she was kidnapped, I told you everything."

"Everything you *could*," Zin said. "You've never mentioned the actual location."

Even now, the thought of Wishery sent shivers down my spine. A part of that stemmed from the binding MAGIC, Inc. document I'd signed, promising to keep quiet about its existence. "I physically *can't*. You know that. Please, Zin, give me something. I won't tell a soul."

After an extended glance around, Zin's breath caught in her throat as she struggled to speak. "I can't tell you everything."

"I'm not asking for everything," I said quickly. "Just something."

"There's an unwanted *guest* on the island," Zin said, leading me on with a knowing gaze. She nodded for me to venture guesses on my own. "And..."

I followed her prompt. "And this *guest* has an interest in Poppy. He's probably not wanting to ask her out for a friendly coffee."

Zin didn't nod; she didn't need to say anything. There was someone on The Isle lurking outside of Poppy's home. I felt useless.

"*Why*? What can I do to help?"

"It's *my* assignment." Zin curled possessively inward, her arms stiffening at her sides. "You asked for information. I'm asking you not to interfere. It's a hunch at this point, nothing more."

"If this is about Poppy—"

"I can handle it," Zin said. Then, softer, she continued. "I will let you know if, or when, I'm in over my head. If you hadn't spooked him today, I'd have this guy in custody already."

"Sorry."

Zin shook her head. "I hesitated on the jump—it's my own fault. I'm just glad X wasn't here to see it."

"Yeah," I agreed, sullen. "Me too."

"Is everything—"

"Who forgot to invite me to the party?" Poppy appeared in the doorway. "What are you guys up to?"

Zin and I were bad actors, and we did a terrible job of keeping straight faces and coming up with a plausible story.

"I was hungry," Zin started. "So, I came by."

"Seeing if you were free—" I continued. "For a snack."

Zin smiled weakly. "Hey, Poppy."

Poppy was no fool. As she climbed down the stairs, she surveyed us with a hurt expression. "This is about me being a weakling, isn't it?"

"What?" Zin and I exclaimed together. I finished for both of us. "Not at all!"

"Ever since I got kidnapped and my memory wiped in that *place*, you—along with my mother and Gus—have treated me like I'm some little dolly in need of protection." She stuck her finger out, wagging it at both of us. "Drop the act. That's why you're here, isn't it?"

"Yes, and we're sorry," Zin said, deliberately ignoring my look of confusion. "I've been checking in periodically to make sure you're okay. It's my fault."

"See, I was *actually* coming over to hang out," I told Poppy, "but I ran into Zin."

Poppy's eyes narrowed. "I want this to stop. No more checking in on me, no more babying me, no more keeping secrets you don't think I can handle."

Zin nodded, pained. "Sorry."

"Sorry," I added, though I wasn't sure why I felt the need to apologize.

"Fine," Poppy said. "Let me fight my own battles, or at least let me fight them alongside you. You're my family first, not my guardians."

I reached for Poppy's hand and gave it a squeeze, then changed to safer topics. "Zin, did you get a chance to talk to the reporters at the *Wicked Weekly*?"

Zin quickly explained the article mishap to Poppy, who frowned at the Ranger X developments.

"I'm sorry, Lily," Zin said in conclusion. "It was an anonymous tip. Someone left a sealed envelope with no defining characteristics on the desk of the gossip columnist."

"Did you interview—"

"I talked to *everyone*," Zin said emphatically. "I flashed my badge up and down the hallways. Nobody's talking. I really think they got lucky on this one. Someone dropped it in their laps, Lily. Someone wanted it out there, but they didn't want to be associated with it."

"But how did they get the text?" I pressed my fingers to my lips. "It was in my bedside drawer this whole time."

Poppy looked horrified at the idea, but Zin looked more intrigued than anything else. We chatted for a few more minutes, struggling to come up with a list of suspects. Nothing popped out at us. Eventually, I grudgingly declared that I should be returning to the bungalow.

Zin also took her leave back to HQ, and Poppy had agreed to dinner with her mother. We parted ways, promising to keep each other in the loop on any developments. Except, I thought wryly, for Zin's mysterious assignment, which she'd successfully managed to keep under wraps from Poppy.

Who in the world could be after *Poppy*? And why? I grumbled about it all the way home, wondering if Ranger X would give me some insights. He'd likely been the mastermind behind the confidentiality flag on Zin's assignment in the first place. Then I dismissed the idea at once, annoyed that I'd let my relationship cloud my professional judgement once again.

Blowing through the front door of the bungalow, I bypassed Gus with a grunt. I'd worked myself into a right tizzy on my walk home, and I needed to do something about all the questions, or I'd burst from anxiety.

Stomping upstairs to my bedroom, I marched straight over to the bedside table and threw open the drawer. I wanted another look at that note—to examine it more thoroughly. To ensure it was truly the original copy, and that it hadn't been touched.

However, a surprise met me instead. A second note rested gently on top of the first.

I whirled around, half expecting to find someone—the author of said note, for example—hovering in the dusty corners of my bedroom. My heart raced, my palms dampened with sweat, but there was no one. Of course, there was nobody. Gus had been here the entire time.

Yet, whoever had placed the paper in my room had wanted it found.

With caution, I raised the slightly crumpled sheet of paper from the drawer and examined it from all sides. Like the reporters had claimed of the envelope they'd received, this paper contained no distinguishing marks or hints as to the writer behind it.

When I'd exhausted all my skills, including a quick tracking spell that petered out into nothing, I flipped the note over and focused on the words written there instead. Loopy cursive spelled out a message that I couldn't make heads or tails of even after I'd read it through fifteen times.

Use what you have.

The writing was almost child-like, which made its meaning even more diluted. I squinted, waiting for inspiration to hit, but no brilliance descended on me, and instead, I found myself growing more and more exasperated. Eventually I gave up and placed the note back in the drawer. Then I ran through a list of protective spells I should really implement in my own bedroom. I had to catch my anonymous visitor.

A visitor who simultaneously wanted to hurt *and* help me. While the publishing of the article had torn apart The Isle, this note seemed intended as assistance. The pair of actions were contradictory.

My pondering came to an abrupt stop as one end of my room began to tremble like an earthquake. A low rumbling sounded as the floorboards shook beneath my feet. I lurched forward, holding onto the bed for balance, the sounds growing louder, growling from the closet.

I struggled for an incantation, but the words were ripped from my mouth as I crumbled to the ground, landing on my knees. When I looked up, the tremors had stopped and the rumbling had silenced.

The door to the closet slid open and there stood the last person I wanted to see.

"Liam," I gasped, and scrambled away from him. "What are you doing here?"

He looked a mess. A disaster actually—terrifying in his disheveled appearance. As he stepped from the closet, his gray hair lay straggly against gaunt cheeks, and his face was worn. He raised both hands in surrender, though his fingernails were grimy with dirt and mud and blood.

I found my voice somehow as I cowered against the bed. "What *happened* to you?"

He merely opened his arms wider and looked up, past the ceiling, past the skies. His eyes rolled back into his head as he stumbled forward, his voice a low intonation as he spoke. "The time has come."

Then he collapsed motionless to the floor.

Chapter 5

MY FIGHT OR FLIGHT responses abandoned me.

Instead of calling for Gus or hightailing it down the stairs, I went to Liam. Despite his recent betrayal, he looked utterly destroyed, a fragment of himself lying crumpled on the floor. My hands were gentle as I tilted his head toward me.

Liam's face was clammy and distressed, even in unconsciousness. I found myself patting his cheeks gently, murmuring his name, begging for him to wake. Friend or foe, he'd promised to help us dismantle a threat against our entire existence. A threat bigger than The Faction versus The Isle.

"Liam," I whispered, unsure why I kept my voice lowered. Surely Gus had heard the bungalow's very skeleton quiver with our guest's arrival. "Liam, wake up. What did you mean *the time has come*? For what? Who hurt you?"

It took another minute or two of prodding and a lifetime of nervous anticipation before Liam sucked in a raspy breath, turned on a grin, and opened his eyes.

"I thought you were dead," I said, feeling my eyes widen as I backed away. "What happened to you?"

"I've been traveling," he said, easing into a sitting position on my drafty wooden floorboards. "Nice space you have here."

His offhand nature caught me by surprise, and I paused to glance around at the lofty attic-like bedroom I'd made my own. Airy curtains billowed over the window and a plump mattress sat fatly on its bedsprings. Frilly, feminine pillows lined the bed and window seat along the far wall, and over the last few weeks I'd stuck up a few family photos on the walls.

"Don't change the subject." I turned my attention back to Liam just in time to catch him wincing with pain as he forced himself to his feet. His hand clutched at his ribs, and I fought back the urge to assist him using my Mixology training. I could whip up pain elixirs with the flick of a wrist, but I didn't trust him enough to turn my back. "How'd you get into my house? My *room*?"

"Your closet." He thumbed over his shoulder, each word breathier than the last. "You really should get that looked at. I know a guy who's a great security consultant if you want a referral."

"Yeah, we know. You know a *lot* of people."

Liam's eyes cut sharply to me. "Self-populating closets are great, but spells can be hacked. You really should place it away from your bedroom and get some security sensors around it."

"Everyone's looking into security these days," I grunted to myself. "You haven't explained your injuries or your presence. I've given you more time here than you deserve. Another minute longer, and I'll holler for Gus. He probably already knows you're here."

Liam gave a tight shake of his head. "The sounds and shakes—those are isolated to the room. Gus is oblivious."

"Why didn't you come through the front door?"

"Lily..." He *tsked* and gave a small smile. "Most people on this island aren't very happy with me at the moment."

"Myself included." I crossed my arms over my chest. "Start talking."

"I've been looking for the Master of Magic. My latest..." he hesitated. "Let's call it a quest—makes me sound more noble—brought me a little closer to ancient history than I'd like."

I blinked. "You're not making sense."

"The Master of Magic can only be found via the Keeper—the person responsible for hiding the Master's whereabouts." Liam eyed me knowingly. "Find the Keeper, and you find the Master."

"That would help if I knew where to find the Keeper."

That fleeting smile was back, and for a moment, I wondered what Liam had to be happy about. Broken and bruised, an outcast from his home, he was pursuing a journey that could lead to his death—or any of ours. I couldn't return his smile.

"I've been looking myself to no real avail. What I *did* learn is that the Master is protected by the ancients."

"What do you mean, the ancients?"

"I mean that the Master of Magic is a position in our society that goes back *centuries*. Thousands of years or more. As long as there has been magic, there's been a Master of it." Liam raised an eyebrow at me. "Doesn't it make sense the most powerful, the most ancient of figures, would be his guards?"

"So why would The Faction go after him now?" I asked. "And why are you here if you haven't found any new information to share?"

"Because I've run out of time," he said simply. "Your father is ready to move."

"Does *he* know where the Master of Magic is located?"

"Not yet." Liam's gaze tightened. "I am almost certain he wouldn't keep that secret from me. I've been searching for the Keeper under his direction and so far have only reported losses. Sometimes devastating ones." He examined his hands, as if they were proof. "If he knows, it's on his own time."

"How kind of you to share *nothing*," I said dryly. "How do I know this isn't a trap?"

Liam raised both arms in surrender and extended them to me. "I suppose you don't."

"Then what do you *suppose* I do about it?"

"Find the Keeper. The Keeper and the Master cannot be manipulated."

"Anyone can be manipulated."

Liam shook his head. "The Keeper is carefully chosen and will never—can never—be found unless he reveals himself."

"Which makes him impossible to find."

"He has a way of knowing when someone is wanting his attention." Liam chanced a smile in my direction. "In fact, I'd venture a guess that he's already here on this island."

My mind briefly flashed to Zin's last task. Could her assignment be a misunderstanding? Did Ranger X have Zin tracking the only person who could lead us to the Master of Magic?

"I see you don't disagree with me." Liam capitalized on my silence and moved a step closer. "Perhaps you've noticed...*things* happening around you."

"Nope," I said fiercely, popping the *p* in frustration. "And if I did, I wouldn't tell you. How does my father plan to reach the Master if not through the Keeper?"

"Lucian has connections beyond your wildest dreams," Liam said with a frown. "He seems ready to move forward with his plan. If he knows a way to the Master, he hasn't shared it with me, but I can sense we're hovering, waiting for something to happen. And when it does..."

"Lily, I found something!" Gus's voice interrupted the tense conversation. "Get down here. I need to show you now."

"That's my cue to head out." Liam stepped into the closet and raised his hand in a wave. "Send my greetings to X."

"X?" I didn't mean to sound startled, but it came out that way.

Liam sensed my uneasiness. His face crinkled with confusion. "Is everything okay?"

"Lily!" Gus hollered again. His footsteps sounded closer to the staircase. "You have to see this!"

By the time I turned back to the closet, Liam had gone.

I stared after him a moment, peering through the layers upon layers of fabric that I'd grown to love and appreciate in this nifty little closet. A closet I'd now have to destroy. Or at least install some protective measures to prevent people from arriving next to my underwear drawer.

"I'm coming," I yelled down to Gus. "I'm just getting dressed."

I figured that would buy me a few minutes. I needed to think. Wandering around to the other side of my bed, I inched the drawer open once more. *Use what you have.* Could that be Liam's note? If so, why hadn't he told me the information firsthand? And if not, then who in the world had slipped in and out of my bedroom without my knowledge? Had they, too, hacked my closet?

Gus's frenetic pacing eventually drew me downstairs. The second I appeared on the bottom stair, he whistled and waved me over.

"Take a look at this." Gus dove right in, first showing me the cover of the book he was reading. "*Masters, Myths, and Magicks,*" he read off the title page. "I couldn't find a spell to do exactly what you wanted, but this might interest you."

I scanned an almost encyclopedia-style entry in the book. The words were old, written in thin, looping script, some of the letters smudged and worn.

Kissing Curses

A sort of magic that's intimate. Often times requiring an item of the subject's to be held, used, burned, or tasted. When a Kissing Curse is properly concocted and managed, it can reveal the subject's thoughts, desires, or wishes.

"Don't you see?" Gus nearly shook with excitement. "There is a magic that will let you uncover the last words, wishes, or thoughts of a subject."

"Kissing Curse," I murmured. "Why is it a curse? Is it harmful?"

Gus scanned the rest of the entry as well as the potential side effects for this type of magic. His face paled. "I—er, well, it could be dangerous."

"Is it harmful?"

Another long pause as Gus scanned. "Doesn't seem so, unless the user is planning to steal the subject's thoughts for nefarious action. The actual doing of the spell doesn't appear to cause anyone harm. So long as the item you take from the subject isn't...well, important or valuable. Then that's just *theft*—magic or not."

My hand clutched desperately at my mother's chain. "Then why do they call it a curse?"

"Because it's invasive, Lily. It's an intimate thing to be inside someone else's head. I don't encourage it." Gus's fluffy eyebrows drew together in a more serious gaze. "I don't know why you're asking about it, but I trust you have a good reason. If it were anyone else, I'd bury this article."

"I try to avoid curses."

"Curses aren't *always* harmful by definition, though many can be dangerous. Most magic is."

"Thank you for finding this, but I can't use it. *Do good*," I murmured. "I can't break my code. Can we just forget I asked?"

Gus looked hard at the necklace dangling beneath my sweater. "Here are the necessary ingredients." He sat down and scribbled out a quick list. "In case you're wondering, I wouldn't judge you for taking a glimpse, Lily. It could bring you closure."

I swallowed, accepting the list of supplies. "A curse, Gus—"

"Every spell has its place in this world." He folded his hands on top of the table. "The word *curse* has only taken on a bad meaning because of the wizards who misuse it as a form of magic." Tapping his fingers against the wooden slab, his eyes returned to the book. "Curse magic is a category of magic, no different than hexes, spells, or jinxes. It's possible to use a curse in the very way it's intended—to help."

I folded the ingredients list and slipped it into my pocket. "I'll be careful."

"That, there," Gus said, gesturing to my pocket. "Isn't a complete list. Those are the base starting points from the ancient spell. You'll have to tweak and adjust and revise it to fit your specifications. As for the ferns mentioned, you'll want to be getting them quickly. It's high season now, but once the supply is gone, they're done for the year. There's a farm to the northeast. Annabelle will know how to serve you."

I nodded, quickly committing the items to memory.

"I think we'll keep Magic & Mixology closed the rest of the day," Gus said, reading my thoughts. "You can get a start on those ferns. I'll leave an order sign up outside so people can put in their requests. It doesn't make much sense to keep the store open if we're fresh out of supplies."

I considered arguing, but in the end, I gave up before I started. My heart wasn't in it today. I needed those ferns, needed to get to the bottom of this glowing necklace. Needed to find out who had been in my room without permission, aside from Liam.

With a murmured thanks, I gathered up my travel belt and a few miscellaneous potions, stuck them into pockets, grabbed a tote for my errands, and hollered goodbye to Gus.

My feet set off toward the Lower Bridge out of habit. There were only two bridges on the island—one in the north and one in the south—and the latter was significantly less dangerous than the first. Hopefully the crew had cleaned up the sudsing soap by now so I could skip the ferry.

Halfway there, footsteps sounded behind me, and I turned to find Poppy breathing hard as she jogged to keep up.

"Power..." she gasped. "*Walker.*"

"Poppy!" I issued a genuine smile, then paused until she caught up. "I thought you had dinner with your mom?"

"We had a quick bite to eat. She had to get back to the supply store. Trinket called in sick today."

I frowned. "Trinket's sick? I can whip up a Fever Fighter or a Stomach Spelunker if that's the issue."

"I don't think it's serious." Poppy wrinkled her nose. "It's odd, isn't it? Trinket never calls in sick. But I suppose she deserves a day off, so my mom's covering, and I'm here because I wanted the company."

Together we finished the trek to the Lower Bridge in near silence. Poppy was still struggling to catch her breath when we arrived, while my mind was busy worrying about Trinket's supposed illness.

"That's what I call squeaky clean," Poppy exclaimed with a laugh. "Look, the bridge is back open."

Sure enough, the Lower Bridge had never glistened brighter. It shone as though the wooden panels were brand new instead of decades old, and for the first time, I noticed some intricate carvings along the sides. Goldfish and dolphins swimming in circles below the bridge continued to leap and dance, though I glimpsed a few lingering bubbles shimmering against the surface of the water.

"Odd, isn't it?" Poppy suggested as we crossed. "These pranks. Who could be behind it?"

"I wish I knew."

Poppy chattered the rest of the way, in much higher spirits than a few hours ago when she'd caught Zin and me lurking outside her home. I couldn't tell if she'd pushed the incident out of her mind, or if she was doing her best to ignore it, but I was glad either way. I had enough worries for the both of us, and her pleasant conversation helped ease some of the tension.

"Have you heard of Annabelle's farm?" I asked. "Gus pointed me in her direction for some ferns."

"Oh, of course! Pointe Farm," Poppy explained. "It's on this weird little peninsula that looks like a finger pointing out to distant lands."

She demonstrated, crooking her pointer finger like a candy cane. "Supposedly, she has the best soil on the island to grow a few really exotic plants. I'm sure Gus uses her supply often; my mother even has a few of her dried herbs in the supply store."

"I hope she has the Forgotten Ferns."

"Oh, it's high season for them," Poppy said with a wide grin. "They'll be giving them away, she'll have so many. What're you using them for anyway?"

"I'm trying to add another signature potion to my Mixology Menu, but I haven't ironed out the details yet. I'll let you know more as soon as I do."

"Do you have a name yet?"

I considered it. "Not yet. I guess we'll see how the potion turns out. I don't even know what it'll do yet."

Another few minutes and we came to Main Street, the core shopping and meeting center for islanders. Storefronts sat open, shopkeepers leaning against doorways and calling greetings under the sunny skies as we padded through. Poppy called back first name greetings to everyone.

"Here we are," Poppy said, raising a hand and crooking her finger again against the horizon. "Do you see it?"

If I squinted and positioned myself *just so*, the outcropping of land sure did look like a pointed finger.

"You made it faster than I thought! Whew-*wee*!" A woman with shocking red hair and a spattering of freckles across her nose stomped toward us, a hoe in one hand and a watering can in the other. She wore a plaid red shirt under overalls and looked like Pippi Longstocking come to life. "Thought it'd take you a few minutes to get here, at least."

"A few minutes for what?" Poppy asked. "Annabelle, this is Lily."

"Lily *Locke*? The Mixologist?" A startled look overtook Annabelle's face as she glanced at me. "Wait a minute. Why are you both here? I was waiting for the Rangers. Don't you work for them?"

"Why would the Rangers be here?" Poppy's pleasant chatter turned more severe as she stepped closer. "I checked the HQ logs earlier, and I didn't see any visits planned for the farm inspections."

"Well, it wasn't planned!" Annabelle's voice leaned toward huffy. "I didn't *plan* on someone stealing half my gardens."

"Someone stole your gardens?" A pit sunk in my stomach as I moved to Poppy's flank. "What did they steal?"

"I'm not saying." Annabelle's lip flipped down in a pout. "I want to talk to the Rangers."

"I work for Ranger HQ," Poppy interrupted. "What happened, Annabelle?"

I rested a hand on Poppy's arm. "It's your Forgotten Ferns crop, isn't it?"

"How could you *possibly* know that?" Annabelle rounded on me sharply. She straightened at Poppy's stern look, and then sighed. "*Yes.* It's my Forgotten Ferns—my babies. My little loves. They're completely wiped out."

"When did this happen?" I asked. "Was there any warning?"

"If there was warning, I would have protected my livelihood," she snapped. "Of course there wasn't warning. I just noticed it a few minutes ago. Whoever did it must have been here within the last twenty minutes because half an hour ago, I was out here watering my babies."

"But how could someone..." I dumbly began to ask how one person could have wiped out an entire field within so short a time, but Annabelle read my expression and answered.

"Magic," she said. "They took armloads of it, from what I can tell. A few patches of the fields were burned, but not much. Most of it was taken."

"They've probably already left the island," I said grimly. "I suppose we could check, but there are ways on and off The Isle that are too hard to detect."

"Why are my ferns so important to the Mixologist?" Annabelle looked between us. "I've always supplied Gus with materials for your work, but never has a Mixologist come banging on my door in person."

"It's very important," I said, sighing as both women stared and waited expectantly for more information. "Gus uncovered the makings of an ancient spell I needed in a book just today. Actually, it wasn't more than an hour ago that he told me about it."

Poppy's expression tightened. "Do you think someone was listening? That someone was deliberately trying to sabotage you?"

"Unless there's another reason to steal the ferns." I looked to Annabelle for an answer.

"They're valuable, of course—the land here is perfect for raising them into healthy plants, but I grow them every year; I have since I was a child and they towered over me." She smiled at the memory. "Nobody's ever stolen one before. My plants are safe and protected. Speaking of, why didn't my alarm spells go off?"

"That's a question for the Rangers," Poppy said. "If you sent word for them, they'll be arriving at any moment. They're busy right now, or else they'd have beaten us here. The island has been a little crazy lately. Maybe it's the same person who stole all the tomatoes."

"That sounds like a prank. Wiping me out of a year's supply of my most famous product?" Annabelle shook her head. "That takes premeditation. Or, at least, a cold heart. That's my livelihood."

"Someone was listening." I backed away from the pair. "I'm so sorry, Annabelle."

"What are you sorry about?"

"Gus was telling me about your plants for the first time this afternoon. Someone must have been listening," I explained. "They wanted to prevent me from getting my ferns for some reason."

"You think all this is because someone is sabotaging you?" Annabelle gave a short laugh and shook her head. "Sorry, Mixologist, I know you're important and all, but I can't believe that's the case."

"Why not?" Poppy pressed.

"I have *fields* of the stuff! Someone would either need very impressive magic to wipe them out without burning it all, *or,* it was a premeditated action. If you didn't even know about the ferns until this afternoon, I doubt this is your doing."

I shook my head, but Poppy raised a hand. "Do you have any left, Annabelle? *Anything* that Lily could use?"

"Not a spec of it. It'll be months before anything even starts to regrow. What's the spell you're trying to make, anyway?" she asked. "Why's it so important?"

"It's—"

"Lily? What are you doing here?" Ranger X appeared in a patch of trees nearby. He strode toward us with a smaller man, one I didn't recognize, at his side. "Poppy, did you receive the call? I thought you were off today."

"I was," Poppy said. "Er—I am. I was hanging out with Lily."

"Thank goodness someone is here to help." Annabelle swung her hand around. "Ranger X and..."

"Ranger J," the shorter, stockier man filled in.

Annabelle nodded a greeting. "My Forgotten Ferns are completely gone."

Ranger X's gaze lingered on me for a little too long before turning to Annabelle. "Destroyed or gone?"

"Hard to say," she hesitated. "I think *gone*, though. I'm fairly sure of it. There are a few small patches that look burned, and the rest...it's like someone magicked off entire fields of it, and I can't figure out how or why."

"Has anything like this ever happened before?"

"I think we'll get going," I piped up before Annabelle could answer. "I have some things to take care of."

"Not so fast," Ranger J snapped, turning stony faced to Poppy and myself. "You're at the scene of a crime. You made it here before we did. We'll have questions for you."

"You can't think we're suspects?" My response was directed at Ranger X. "If anything, we think someone's trying to sabotage *us*!"

"Why do you think that?" Ranger J asked curiously.

Ranger X must have seen my hesitant expression because he chose that moment to step in. "You surely recognize the Mixologist," he said to Ranger J. "Let them go. I know where to find them; I'll handle their questioning myself."

Ranger J looked dissatisfied, but he didn't argue with the direct order from his boss.

I turned to X. "Are we free to go?"

"I'll find you later," he said with a stare most curious. "But before you leave, what *did* bring you here?"

"Lily thinks someone's watching—er, listening to her." Poppy barged in before I had the chance to answer. "Gus *just* told her about a spell that required Forgotten Ferns. And now they're gone. Coincidence?"

"Coincidence," Annabelle said assuredly. "There's no way someone could move all those ferns in twenty minutes without pre-planning."

"Maybe not by themselves," Ranger X said grimly. "They could have had a team."

"It'd take an incredible amount of magic to be so thorough." Annabelle frowned. "I haven't a scrap of it left."

"Incredible magic," Ranger X said quietly. "Yes, I expect so. Annabelle, can you give me the details of your day? Start from the top. Any detail you can remember is important, no matter how small..."

Poppy took that as our cue to leave, though I wanted to stay longer and listen. "Come on," she urged, tugging me along. "This is not our place. You can grill X later. I'm sure he won't forget to stop by for a chat."

"Lovely."

"Is something off between the two of you still?"

"It's nothing. We both have a lot on our plates."

"If you say so," Poppy said with a wince. "But that didn't feel like sexual tension to me back there. It just felt like regular old tension."

I kept silent on the walk back.

"Hey, Lily, this isn't about the ring I saw X wearing on my birthday, is it?" Poppy asked as the bungalow came into sight. "I know I should mind my own business, but I want you to know it's okay if you're not ready. Or if you want to talk about it, I'm here for you."

"Thanks," I said, then added truthfully, "I suppose that's been on my mind. Along with other things."

Poppy took my hand and squeezed. "You'll know when the time's right. If I were you, though, I wouldn't go wandering off this evening, at least until X swings by. He's probably not happy about the theft, and he'll be even less happy that you might be the target."

I remembered Poppy's blurted information—her theory that someone had listened in at the bungalow. I realized she'd deliberately shared her thoughts with X so he'd come around to examine the bungalow for holes in security.

"I'm sorry I told him," she said, reading my face. "But he had to know. I'm sure it's nothing, but it's better safe than sorry."

"Sure," I said, coming to a stop outside the bungalow. "Thanks for the company. I mean it—I needed someone to talk to today."

"Of course. By the way, what *is* this spell that's so important?"

I forced a smile before climbing the porch steps. At the top, I turned to face Poppy. "Doesn't matter now, does it? I can't make it anyway."

I SPENT THE REST OF the day zipping around the storeroom keeping as busy as possible. Mostly, I wanted to forget the fact that I was essentially imprisoned, held here by an unspoken agreement with Ranger X to wait until he could ask his questions.

Gus sensed my mood, and together we worked in silence. We worked hard, and by evening, most of the potions we needed to back-fill were either bottled and ready or well on their way to completion.

We'd decluttered the table in the center of the storeroom, and in place of the normal debris, we'd lit small fires that hovered mid-air. Above them, we had a series of little tables balancing cauldrons over the flames.

The Security Sampler cauldron was the largest—it'd be enough to supply half the island with spells. A variety of medium cauldrons carried all sorts of defensive spells, which were not meant to harm, of course, but to stun, to alarm, to warn.

The smallest cauldron bubbled with a potent mixture of Long Isle Iced Tea. It'd be another day or two before it was brewed to proper strength. I'd purposely made a small amount of it. Though the vials had been flying off the shelves, there was safety in having a limited supply. Safety, I didn't want to admit, from my own aunt.

"You mind if I check out for the evening?" Gus wiped his brow. "I have something I need to do."

His ask for permission caught me off guard. "Of course. Are you headed to Mimsey's?"

Gus's silence was enough of an answer.

"Oh, I see what's happening," I said as he glanced at the clock. "You're just leaving because you don't want to be here when X arrives."

A knock on the door sent a jolt of surprise down my back.

"That's my cue," Gus said, grabbing his cane and heading for the door. "Enjoy your evening."

"Coward."

Gus paused in the doorway. "No, I'm choosing my battles. This ain't mine to fight."

He pulled open the door, greeted Ranger X with a typical grunt, and slipped by. X smoothly took his place in the entryway to the storeroom, waiting uncomfortably for an invitation inside.

"Come in," I said, gesturing for him to cross the room. The gesture was an awkward one since he'd never previously needed an invitation. Usually, X came and left as he desired, and this new hesitation had me on edge. "How are you?"

"Let's not do this." X crossed the room in a few steps, his lips meeting mine with a touch of anger. He kissed me, his hands reaching for the sides of my face as he held me close, closer, until finally I relaxed. "There," he said, after a long moment. The smallest smile appeared on his face as my eyes drifted back open. "That's more like it."

My heart pumped from his touch, the desperate roughness of it joined by the wild familiarity of him all at once. To give myself time to think, I brushed past Ranger X's shoulder to close and lock the door. By the time I returned to the center table, my expression was again carefully passive.

"I know you didn't have anything to do with the ferns," X said at promptly. "What I don't understand..."

He trailed off, his gaze landing on the shelves as he paced around the room. His eyes traced every vial, beaker, even the flames that licked and danced around the boiling potions on the table.

"X, I wanted to tell you—"

He held up a finger, silencing me. Then, he closed his eyes and murmured an enchantment lasting long enough for me to tune out halfway through. I didn't recognize the language he used.

"What was that?" I asked, when his eyes reopened and his gaze defogged. "I've never heard anything like it."

"One of the oldest spells around that's still practical," Ranger X said. "It's a temporary shield—it'll block everything we say and contain it to this room. All the words we speak here tonight will be safe."

"Unlike earlier today."

Ranger X gave a succinct nod, but he didn't look convinced. "This bungalow has been protected by security spells throughout its existence. They were set a long time ago," he clarified at my questioning face. "I didn't find any holes in it when I checked this evening."

"What does that mean?"

"I don't think anyone *was* actually listening to you. Did you bring any articles inside the home recently? Something someone gave you?"

I shook my head. "We get a lot of customers at the bar and many visitors in the storeroom, but they never go into my private quarters."

X shook his head. "Those areas use separate security charms. The storeroom and your living quarters are most heavily protected. The bar has to be more open due to the nature of it."

I frowned, remembering the note in my drawer, as well as my earlier visit. "Didn't you say that Liam knows some big security specialists?"

"What's he got to do with this?"

"I'm just saying, if he knows how to set it up..." I hesitated. "He'll know how to break it down."

"But Liam—"

"He was here. Earlier today."

Any sign of camaraderie that'd lightened Ranger X's eyes vanished at once. "Here? On the island?"

My heart stuttered with nerves as I shook my head. "In my room."

X's hands clenched and unclenched. A slight halo of gold appeared around his head, the sheen dancing off his tanned skin, his sharp black suit shimmering with it. I had to calm him down before it grew out of control.

"I meant to tell you," I said. "But things happened, and I didn't get a chance. He didn't do anything to hurt me."

"How'd he get inside?"

"The closet."

"The..." Ranger X blinked. "That self-populating piece of—"

"He said *the time had come.*"

"Meaning The Faction is ready to make their move?"

I paused, realizing how shaky Liam's information had been. In retrospect, I should have asked more questions, demanded more from him. As I repeated the information to Ranger X, I felt almost ridiculous at its barrenness.

"Let me understand," Ranger X said. "We are supposed to find the Master of Magic, but we don't know where he is. We're supposed to find the keeper of his location, but again we don't know where he is, what he looks like, or when he'll appear...if he chooses to do so at all."

"That's about right."

"And Liam had no solid information to offer about the plans of Lucian. Except that he's on the move or looking to be on the move shortly."

"When you put it like that, yeah. We don't have much."

"At *best* we don't have much. At worst, we're being played," Ranger X growled. "If anything, I'll bet he wanted into the house for a different reason and merely used the information as a diversion. How long was this before you and Gus discussed the spell and ferns?"

My cheeks burned, and I felt annoyed with my naivete. It was embarrassing that I hadn't put the pieces together sooner. "Immediately before. We were interrupted by Gus calling up that he had found something, and then Liam left."

Ranger X closed his eyes, pinched his hands together over his temples. "What was the spell you and Gus were working on that was so important?"

"We weren't working on anything *yet*. I'd come up with a spell I wanted to create and add to the Mixology Menu. It doesn't even have a name yet. Gus thought he'd found something that might be helpful to get me started."

"It's purpose?"

My hesitation to share clearly showed through. "It's not even a spell, yet—"

"If Liam heard, if he's after it, then I need to know." Ranger X stepped toward me, one of his hands circling my wrist as he gripped it tightly. "I need to know as much as possible—everything *they* know—in order to have a chance to close in on them. We might never be a step ahead, but we have to try. We'll fail before we start if there are gaps in the knowledge that we *do* have."

"My spells have nothing to do with The Faction," I finally whispered. "X, you're hurting me—let go."

With a shocked look, X loosened his grip around my wrist and backed away as if my words had licked him with fire. "They have nothing to do with The Faction?"

"It was for my mother's locket, okay?" I grabbed for the chain around my neck and, feeling the prick of anger prodding at my eyes, held it out for him to see. "It's been glowing ever since the night of Poppy's party. The night I changed into *her*—and I need to find out why."

"How will the spell help?"

"I need to know what truly happened to her. Trinket doesn't believe it was a mugging gone wrong, and I tend to agree with her." I hesitated, the bubbling of potions setting a backdrop for the moment that was dryly fitting. "Gus uncovered some information in an ancient book of spells this morning—references to old magicks and the ingredients that could potentially lead me to my mother's last thoughts."

"Of course." Ranger X smiled, and to my surprise it was gentle, indulgent. "He found a legend about the *Empath* family of magic. Don't get your hopes up."

"All I have is hope! If you're familiar with these types of spells, can you help me understand how they work?"

"I'm familiar with the stories, but I'm afraid I can't help you."

"Why not? I need this, Cannon. You have to understand how important this is to me."

My use of his true name didn't go unnoticed. He knew I was begging, desperate, and I could tell he was trying to let me down easy as he continued.

"I can't help you because Empath magic doesn't exist."

"But—"

"You said Gus found the notations for a spell in an ancient book?"

I nodded.

"Was there an actual spell attached?"

"Not really, but—"

"That's because nobody has ever created one that works." Ranger X's proclamation dropped heavily into the room, bringing the earth around me to a standstill. "Those spells are made of myths. It's a hopeful thing that's never been proven real."

"I don't believe you." The fierceness of my whisper came as a shock even to me. "Why would it be written about in books if it didn't exist?"

"Why are stories written? To give us hope. Understanding. Entertainment."

"This wasn't some dreamer writing fiction," I said. "It was in an ancient textbook."

"Then if it exists, why has another Mixologist not uncovered it? Why are we not all using these spells? Because they have never worked."

My fingers shook, and I couldn't sort through all my frustrations. It hurt to realize the one spell I'd hinged all my hopes on was a notion stemming from fairytales. Waves of sadness followed, made harsher by the fact Ranger X delivered the news with such nonchalance.

"I don't believe it. Until recently, I thought ancient gods were the stuff of myths. Magic and witches and vampires. Hidden societies and tropical islands in the middle of a frigid Great Lake. None of that was *real* until I found it."

"People have tried, Lily," X said, sensing my spiral to the edge of sanity. "It's not a new idea—people have tested Empath magicks for years."

"*I* haven't," I said. "And until I test it and fail repeatedly, I'm going to believe there's a chance."

Ranger X raised his hands. "I never intended to doubt your skills. My only desire is to not see you get hurt."

I took a few deep breaths, my chest aching. I forced myself to bite back my snappish words. "I know. I'm sorry, too."

Ranger X stepped closer to me. "If anyone can create this spell, it's you." His hand came up, brushed my hair to the side. His lips pressed, like the petal of a rose, against my forehead. "I only want you to be happy. Safe and protected, of course, but also happy."

I sunk against his chest, letting my head rest there as his arms came to circle my back. "I know. I want the same for you. Why is it so *hard* to stay happy?"

Ranger X lifted me then, cradling me to his chest as my arms eased around his neck and pulled us closer. My fingers played through his dark hair, the curls intertwining due to their length. He needed a haircut, but something about the mess of curls there gave him a softer look, almost boyish. On an impulse, I pressed a kiss to his nose.

"The rest of this conversation can continue tomorrow," he said, climbing the stairs to my bedroom. "We're done with professional business tonight."

He laid me gently on the comforter, taking a moment to glance at the closet and mutter a spell that sent up a shimmering bubble of a shield against it. Once satisfied at the defenses, he returned to me, his eyes glinting with darkness.

"Now," he said slowly. "Where were we?"

Chapter 6

GUS MUST HAVE GOTTEN the memo. Somehow.

I assumed Ranger X had found a way to discreetly get in touch with my assistant because Gus was nowhere to be found the next morning. Ranger X had likely put the kibosh on Gus's early morning puttering around the store in order to let me rest.

It worked; I slept, undisturbed, until half past eight. Ranger X sat next to me as I stretched to consciousness, a cup of coffee in one hand and a paper in the other.

I couldn't help it. The sight of him made me burst into laughter.

Ranger X flinched at my reaction, so jerky in his movements that coffee splashed from his mug and landed on the white comforter in an ugly patch of brown. A few muttered words from him had the stain wiped clear in a second, but not before he'd managed to wipe the look of incredulity off his face.

"Lily?" he asked, cautiously. "Is everything okay?"

"Don't look at me like I've been jinxed." I snuggled closer to him. "It's just funny, in an ironic sort of way."

"What's so funny?"

He was so mystified it was cute. I reached a hand to his face, toying once again with those locks that were just a little too long. His face was blank, clear and bright in the morning light, his lips parted with confusion.

Resting a hand against his bare chest, I giggled again. "It's just so...*so* normal."

"What's normal?"

"You! Us. This moment." I let my fingers trail over the solid line of abs visible above the startlingly white comforter. "You let me sleep in, you're reading the paper in bed, sipping coffee...it's like any old Saturday morning."

It still hadn't clicked with him, and he shook his head. "And?"

"We could be normal humans," I said with a wry smile. "Just a pair of non-paranormals, with no more care in the world than a long commute."

Ranger X's face finally relaxed into a smile, his arm coming to pull me closer to him. "Then let's let this moment last for a while longer."

I reached over and stole a sip of his coffee. "How'd you get out of work this morning? And Gus—where did you send him?"

"Gus got a surprise shipment of materials," Ranger X said, a smile tugging at his lips. "As for Ranger HQ—I've clocked seventy out of the last seventy-eight hours on the job. I mentioned to Poppy I might be late this morning. She cleared me until noon."

"But Magic & Mixology..." I said, a frown pulling my smile back down. "It'll be filled with people waiting in line—angry customers who want to kill me for being late."

"The store opens today at noon," Ranger X said. "Hours are changed due to a new shipment of supplies."

I blinked, feeling like a child given a balloon and a stick of cotton candy. "You're telling me I don't have to *go* anywhere?"

"We have a few hours," he said with a crook of an eyebrow. "You're welcome."

That's all the information I needed to hear before Ranger X's coffee mug crashed to the floor, and he pulled me back under the covers with a delicious smirk.

By the time we got around to cleaning up the spilled coffee, I was positively buzzing from happiness. The bliss would surely come to an end in the next half hour once the store opened, but until then, I'd cherish the quiet comfort of our moments together.

As I magically mopped up the spell and pieced together the shattered mug, I heard X's movements in the shower. The spray of water turning on, the soft, almost indiscernible humming coming from behind the door that signaled a rare great mood from Ranger X.

I smiled, picking up the paper he'd been reading, and settled into bed to wait for him with a fresh cup of coffee from downstairs. I flipped past the first page to a gossip column near the back. Ranger X hadn't ventured this far along, judging by the unwrinkled sheets. Once there, I came face to face with a headline that nearly stopped my heart.

ARE RANGERS BEHIND THESE *CRIMES?!*

A list of recent crimes followed, from the tomato stealing to the bridge of bubbles to the newly minted disappearance of Forgotten Ferns. Beneath it all was a theory that the culprit was one of our very own.

If the Rangers can't protect us, then who can?
Lily Locke, island Mixologist, is quoted saying she's refusing to sell protective charms.

"I did not say that!" I shrieked. "I said nothing like that!"

Is she in on it, too? She has been rumored to be in talks of marriage with her current squeeze, the Head Ranger known to the world as X.

"Did you say something?" Ranger X called from the bathroom. "Lily, is everything okay?"

I stayed still for a moment, the coffee cup perched halfway to my lips as I reread the article a few more times. It went on and on, a dithering mess of theories based on anything but logic. Finally, after Ranger X called my name a few times, I was startled into action by the water shutting off.

Leaping from bed, fueled by adrenaline, I slammed my coffee cup onto the bedside table and tore into the bathroom.

I pushed the paper into X's face, past the shower curtain to where he stood sopping wet. It was a testament to my shock and outrage that I barely took a moment to appreciate the sight of him naked.

"Did you see this?" I demanded. "What is *wrong* with people?"

Ranger X's eyes darkened as he scanned the article. "I hadn't gotten past the first page this morning before you..." He coughed. "Before I was distracted."

"I did not say *anything* of the sort!" I exclaimed again, jabbing my finger against the newspaper. Angry black splotches appeared beneath my touch. "I *also* didn't comment to any reporter, so whoever wrote this was reaching out on a limb. Maybe they talked to my customers—people who came to me in confidence."

Ranger X pulled the shower curtain back and reached for a towel. It gave me half a second's pause before the shuddering anger returned and my fist balled again.

He wrapped the towel tight around his waist. Then, hands finally free, he took the paper from me and fully read the article. I watched him, watched his eyes fluctuate from intrigued to angry to curious. When he finished, I watched for his reaction.

"Squeeze?" he asked finally. "I'm your *squeeze*?"

"That's all you took from the article?"

He shook his head slowly. "The allegations that a Ranger is involved in these crimes are serious."

"Of course it's not true." When X didn't respond immediately, I looked at him in surprise. "It's *not* true, right?"

"I don't believe so."

"But—"

"But I never make any assumptions." He let a heavy sigh escape. "I'm looking into it. Internal Affairs is never a happy business."

"Do you need any help?"

He looked weary now, and sad. "No, it's my responsibility. The glory and the dirty work."

"You don't seem like you get a whole lot of glory." I reached out, forcing my own frustrations away. They were mild compared to what X had to face. "I'm sorry. I wish I could do something to make it go away."

"I'm sorry, too," he said, leaning forward to kiss my forehead. "We had twenty minutes left on the clock, but I'm going to have to cut our time short."

"Of course." I followed him to the bedroom; the scent of him fresh from the shower lifted my mood just a bit.

He dressed quickly and efficiently, pausing only for a wink when he caught me staring. "Lily," he said, once he'd slipped into a clean suit he'd previously stashed in my closet. "You asked what you could do to help."

"Yes?" I watched as X forfeited the top button of his shirt and worked to roll his sleeves. I went over to help, gently adjusting the stark white fabric so the folds rested nicely against his arms. "Whatever you need."

"In light of the article, I'm going to move the press conference up to tomorrow morning. Will you still be there?"

"Of course. Is there anything you need me to say?"

"We'll discuss it in the morning. Most importantly, I'd just like you by my side."

I fell against X's chest as he pulled me into a ferocious hug, one that stole my breath and nearly cracked a rib. When he finished, I stepped back and offered a smile. "You're some squeeze."

He cracked a smile, laughed. "I love you."

"I love you."

I walked him out the front door, grateful we'd fallen back into sync. Drifting along without him had tilted my life out of orbit. It was a lonely road to travel alone.

As the noon hour rolled around, footsteps inevitably approached. Gus came first through the door, his entrance followed shortly after by the low chatter of guests filtering into line outside at the bar.

Gus's way of greeting me was to drop a huge duffle bag full of supplies onto the table. Then he clomped over to the potions still hovering mid-air and sniffed around. "The Long Isle potion is just about ready," he announced. "You could've taken the Security Sampler off this morning if you'd wanted."

"I was busy."

Gus stiffened, narrowed his eyes at me. When I didn't offer more information, he turned back to the potions and began adjusting the flame levels.

"Do you want to start bottling and handle the pickups?" I asked, switching to business mode. "I'll get started on the new orders."

Gus reached into the duffle and withdrew a carton of beakers. "We've got to be running out of islanders to help, don't we? You've served just about everyone I've ever met."

Apparently, there was no shortage of folks looking for an additional layer of protection. Especially with the new article breaking this morning, the line today was longer than ever. However, instead of the chattering mess of people I'd grown used to, this group was silent.

I caught wind of hushed whispers, of people comparing their potions with one another as they retreated from line. It wasn't until I overheard my name whispered in conjunction with X's that I realized the truth: these people no longer trusted me—likely due to my affiliation with Ranger X. The accusations against him, against his program, had rocked the island to its core.

The next few hours flew by as I helped one customer after the next. It wasn't until the *Closed* sign miraculously appeared that the flow of customers began to slow.

"We kept up with all the orders," Gus said proudly as I retreated inside. "Not a single backorder for tomorrow."

"Nice work." I meant the compliment sincerely, but it was difficult to muster up excitement. "How's the Long Isle potion coming along?"

"Nearly there. Should be ready in an hour. I'll stick around to finish her up."

"You don't have to do that." I slumped at the table, pulling the plate of food Gus had prepared toward me. I offered a grateful moan of delight as I sunk into the sandwich. "Thanks for your help."

"What's got you down? You seemed all skippy this morning."

"What have I ever done to break the trust of our people?"

"Excuse me?"

"The guideline is posted right there on the wall. *Do Good*. Have I ever acted in a way that would make people think I'm *not*?"

"Why are you asking?"

"You saw the article this morning. Islanders are turning against one another. People *believe* that Rangers could commit these random crimes. Apparently even the fact that I'm dating one makes me part of the problem."

"Who said that?"

"They didn't need to say it directly to me. I could hear it and see it on their faces. People were comparing their potions as they left as if, I don't know, I'd tricked them or something."

"They're fools, Lily. Pay them no mind." Gus rolled up his sleeves as he sat across from me. "I think we should close the shop for a few days. They don't get to have it both ways. They can't doubt you and expect you to care for them all at once."

"No. That won't help anything. We can't give them a reason to lose faith in us. That's the *opposite* of what I'm trying to do."

"These people need their eyes opened. They don't know *half* the things you or the Rangers do to ensure safe daily life on this island. They take it for granted."

"No." I stood, my voice firm. "We can't react out of fear or anger. I was just venting. It seems lately like every little thing on this island is tearing us all apart."

"Wouldn't *they* like that," Gus growled. "We're doing their jobs for them."

"Who?"

"The Faction," he spit out. "They'd just love it if we took ourselves down from the inside."

I paused, the sandwich halfway to my mouth. "Do you think this is all part of their plan?"

"How do you figure?"

I set the sandwich down and stood, pacing as I thought. "What if somehow, The Faction has planted someone here who's doing all these things, wreaking havoc on the island. It's working, isn't it?"

Gus raised a hand to his chin and scratched it, pondering. "We haven't had many visitors to the island lately. If it's someone from The Faction, it's a local."

"Any ideas?"

"I'm not convinced this is The Faction's work. It's too odd, too illogical. If The Faction had a presence here, they'd be after you, or the Rangers, or something bigger."

"Something bigger..." I looked up, hesitant. "Gus, why didn't you tell me that Empath magic doesn't exist?"

"Who says it doesn't exist?"

"Ranger X." I watched his reaction, but there wasn't an ounce of surprise there. "You knew I'd figure it out."

"It's well known that Empath magic is a myth."

"Then why'd you get my hopes up with all that talk about the Kissing Curses?"

Gus straightened. "Because I know differently."

"How? Have you seen it performed before?"

"Well, of course not. Then Empath magic would've graduated from myth to *fact*. No, Lily, I know different because I know you." Gus stopped talking and followed my pacing with his eyes before he continued. "Myths are only that until they're proven."

"If none of the Mixologists have proven Empath magic, what makes you think I can do it?"

"That's it!" Gus's eyes shone. "Because *you're* the part that's different, Lily. You're stronger than the rest of your predecessors in many ways. I don't know how, I don't know why exactly, although I do have a suspicion."

"What's that suspicion?"

To my surprise, Gus raised his hands in surrender. "If I tell you, then you have to promise not to kill me."

"That's an odd request."

"You'll understand in a second." Gus lowered his hands, then steepled his fingers together and looked uneasy as he continued. "I *think* it's because you're a woman."

"Er..." I hesitated. Gus's statement had shocked a retort right out of me. "Sorry, but *what*?"

"Empath magic is rumored to have been discovered, created, however you want to say it, by the female gods of ancient times. This type of magic delves deep into thoughts, feelings, intuitions..." Gus paused. "Something men don't always excel at understanding."

"Now you're making sense. *Do* go on."

"We've never had a female Mixologist before." Gus rose, stretched, and took a stance in his proud old body. "I'm pleased to serve as your assistant, Lily. It's my belief that you possess skills stronger—different—than anyone I've assisted or studied. What was impossible for others, may not be so impossible for *you*."

His little speech made me uncomfortable, so I gestured for him to get on with it.

"You must study the text." Gus shoved the ancient manuscript into my hands. "Read it. Soak in the knowledge and the hints. Then, throw the damn thing away."

I looked up in alarm. "Throw it away?"

"Not literally," he growled. "I want it back. It's a figure of speech. All I mean is you have to learn and understand, and then throw that knowledge away to the far recesses of your mind. Let your intuition take over. Break the rules. You won't uncover a new form of magic by following instructions. There *are* no instructions to be found."

"I don't understand."

"Lily, this is truly the first opportunity you've had to create your own magic."

"But Long Isle Iced Tea, Jinx and Tonic, Witchy Sour and Hex..."

"Those are all brilliant little Mixes," Gus admitted. "But it's nothing like rousting magic that's been buried for centuries—possibly untapped forever."

I stepped back, still reeling from the news. My heart pounded at the sudden pressure of what Gus was asking of me, and my head swung back and forth in denial. "No, you're wrong."

"I can't help you much on this, aside from the slicing and dicing. Give me instructions that I can follow, and I'll be there for you. But that is where my skills end."

Because I needed something to do, I plunked back onto my seat and polished off the last of my sandwich. As I chewed, I thought. "I don't know what to say."

"Think about it." Gus glanced at the Long Isle Iced Tea brewing on the counter. "I'm going to get back to work and finish—"

"I'll handle it. Take the night off and spend some time with Mimsey. I'll see you in the morning. Actually—" I held up a finger. "I won't be here in the morning. I'll be with Ranger X at the press conference."

"Why does he need you there?"

"To show a united front."

Gus's eyebrow crept upward. "*Really?*"

I tried not to look miffed. "Why's that so hard to believe?"

"I'm just not sure the two of you seem united on this front at all."

"What's that supposed to mean?" I stepped closer to him, blocking his path to the door. "Why don't we seem united?"

"Forget I said anything," Gus said. "I'm not getting mixed up in your personal life. Goodnight, Lily."

Gus moved past me, ducking into the darkness as I watched him leave. I stood in the doorway long after he'd disappeared, wondering what he could've meant. *Had something happened?* Just this morning X and I had seemed back on the same page. My fears over a crumbling relationship had been quelled, and I'd found a bounce back in my step.

I hoped it was nothing. I prayed it was Gus's paranoia and nothing more, but somehow, I knew I'd have my answers soon enough. In the meantime, I couldn't focus on the *what-if's* or the hypotheticals. I had potions to finish and new magic to uncover.

My night was just beginning.

Chapter 7

TWO HOURS LATER, THE Long Isle Iced Tea glittered a pretty pink in its final beaker. I capped it, but not before inhaling the sweet smell with a smile. In a way, this drink had been created for Poppy, and it had a bit of her personality in its very essence: bright, bubbly, and sweet. Long Isle Iced Tea might stand for many things now, but it would never have existed without Poppy's influence.

As I capped the beaker and moved to set it down, something tugged against me. I frowned, feeling uneasy as I lifted the beaker back to eye level. As I did so, I realized my mother's necklace had begun to glow. The closer the potion came to my body, the brighter the necklace shone. By the time I pulled the beaker to my chest, the charm was so hot it burned against my skin.

I gasped in surprise. I yanked the cap from the beaker and threw my arm out, fully extended, pushing the potion away from me. The second I caught the scent of the potion once more, the burn against my skin faded to nothing. The light from the charm burned down from its fierce anger into a warm and comforting glow.

Confused, I peered into the potion, inhaled again, and was rewarded by a flickering of the heart on my necklace, as if it approved. "That's impossible," I muttered to myself. "Impossible."

I glanced behind me, checking to confirm I'd locked the front door. I had closed up while I'd cleaned the storeroom in preparation for the next morning; I hadn't gotten much restful sleep the night before, and I had an early morning tomorrow, so while all was calm in the bungalow, I intended to get to bed early.

Except for the niggling feeling of unfinished business. For some reason, I couldn't help but wonder if my mother's charm had other plans for me.

Maybe one sip of potion won't be so dangerous, I thought to myself. After all, Long Isle had been created as a party trick. A fun little way to escape into costume.

After a few minutes, I'd convinced myself that this was the best solution. Ladling a small portion of the pink liquid into a clear glass chalice, I brought the mixture to my lips and paused. The charm on my necklace seemed to come alive, practically humming with the proximity of the Mix. Encouraged, I took the first sip.

Before my eyes, I morphed gently, slowly, into *her*. I downed the rest of the potion I'd poured as my mother's features slid into place. Once the transformation was complete, I grabbed a mirror and took a seat on the fireplace hearth. Finally, I studied my face in it. *Her* face.

My somewhat sharp cheekbones rounded into softer curves, and the stress lines on my forehead disappeared. My lips filled out, my hair changed to soft waves, my eyes brightened at the sight of it all.

"Where are you?" I raised my fingers, pressed them to the glass, and realized the question was a silly one. *Dead*, that was the answer. My mother had been dead since the year I'd been born. "What do you want from me?"

My mother's eyes softened, and the face in the mirror shook her head at me. With a start, I wondered if I'd shaken my own head. I couldn't remember; I couldn't tell where I ended and she began.

"Why does your necklace want me to see you so badly? It feels like...it feels like it's trying to tell me something. But *what*?"

There was no response this time, but curiously, the face in the mirror looked so deeply into my eyes I lost track of our differences. The similarities between mother and daughter were uncanny, but it was more than that. As if the reflection in the mirror had a personality of her own.

"Mom?" I whispered, feeling the tears prick in my eyes. "Are you still here somewhere?"

No response this time, but the eyes in the mirror glistened back. I forced myself to remember it was me in the room alone. *Me.*

"What happened to you?" I shook my head at the futility of questioning my own reflection. Instead, I changed tactics. "Your family doesn't believe you were killed in a human mugging gone wrong. I swear I will find out who took you away from me—from everyone who loved you." At this, the illusion flickered. "No, stay! *Please* don't leave me!"

My voice infused with desperation as the image began to fade. I had taken a small portion of Long Isle Iced Tea, and I'd lost track of time, burning through the potion before I was ready to revert.

"Mom! *Wait*!" My fingers clawed at the mirror, trying to drag her back.

It was too late. My cheekbones had returned to sharper points, and the bags under my eyes and lines across my forehead were back, deep and threatening. My eyes dimmed from the light of hers, turning to glassy red-rimmed gems.

"No!" I leapt to my feet, lunged for the table in the center of the room. I grabbed the ladle with such force some of the contents splashed onto the table and left a trail of faint pink sheen.

I'd just poured myself another goblet—a much larger dose—when a knock on the door sent my spine stiffening. I stood still, hoping my visitor would vanish if I remained silent.

As the knock sounded again, a sense of horror set in. *What if it was X outside?* Did I so badly want to spend time with the dead that I'd forget the living?

Battling curiosity and shame, I quickly capped the potion and slid the beaker onto the shelves. As for my goblet...I looked wistfully at it, then emptied the contents into a fresh vial and corked that, too.

By the time I opened the front door, I'd mildly put myself back together, though I didn't trust the look in my eyes. I felt frenzied, and the annoyance at my visitor bubbled near the surface.

"Trinket?" I gaped in surprise. "What are you doing here?"

Her face was pointed down, her hands clasped before her. "I wanted to apologize."

As she turned her gaze up, her eyes came to rest on my face. She studied my expression with excruciating detail. I shrunk back under her gaze, realizing at once that I hadn't tucked my mother's necklace back into my shirt.

I scrambled to hide the charm, but it was too late. She'd seen the glowing necklace, as well as my haste to hide it from her. *She knew.*

I wasn't prepared for her to lunge. She reached for my necklace with fervor. My breath vanished as we landed in a lump on the floor—our bodies tangled around one another. I might be younger, nimbler than she, but my willpower and strength to overpower a member of my family was no match for hers.

Her bony hands gripped my shoulders as she yanked me toward her, bringing our faces close enough to touch with the slightest movement. "Where is she?"

"Trinket!" I struggled to back away, but her grip was too strong. "What are you talking about?"

"*Delilah*. You changed into her—you've been swearing you'd never do it again, and I came to apologize tonight for pressuring you into it. But *you*. You've gone and done it anyway." She narrowed her eyes at me, her voice rising to the screechy octaves. "Behind my back."

"I haven't! I just needed to see—"

"What did she tell you?"

"Nothing! It's not *her*, Trinket—it's me. It's a reflection. It's why I'm getting rid of the whole thing. I'm not brewing more."

"You have the potion here, I can smell it." Trinket's grip tightened as her eyes raised over my shoulders and surveyed the storeroom behind me. "A fresh vial, over there on the shelves. You were going to take more, weren't you? Weren't you?"

I finally got up the courage to grip Trinket's hands in mine and extract them from my shirt. I scrambled backward, away from her. "You've got to take a breath. What I do as Mixologist is private business."

"This isn't Mixology business." Trinket stood, leaving me unattended on the floor as she glided across the room and retrieved the recently emptied goblet. Then, she found the newly corked vial, surveyed it with a smile, and then extended it toward me. "Drink."

"No, I don't want to take more—it's not safe."

"*Drink*. I want to see her. I need to know what happened."

"No. I refuse."

"You were going to before I interrupted—rewind just a few minutes, Lily."

"It's dangerous!" I exploded. "I don't know what happened tonight. It felt like—it felt like it wasn't me in that reflection. That's not supposed to happen! The potion is all sorts of wrong. It's a dangerous Mix, and if we don't watch out, we'll turn it into a curse. We will get lost staring into the mirror at a dead woman. Is that what you *want*?"

Trinket hissed as she stepped closer. "I'm here now. I'll pull you out of it. She's your mother—she died for you. Don't you want to find out why? Who murdered her? *Drink*, Lily."

"I won't—"

At my refusal, Trinket reached for me, clasping one hand behind my head, dropping the goblet with a clatter to the floor, as the other thumb flicked off the lid of the vial and brought it to my lips. "Let me *see* her!"

The taste of Long Isle hit my lips, and suddenly, it was the only thing I wanted. I desired so desperately to see *her* again, to touch her face in the mirror, to pretend she was real. I closed my eyes and licked a drop from my lips, hungry for more.

But something held me back from parting my lips and taking the rest of the potion. The wildness in Trinket's eyes terrified me. The feel of her fingers pinching against my neck pinned me to reality.

"Stop!" I shouted, but her steel grasp didn't budge. "Trinket, let me go."

"One sip, Lily," she said. "One *sip*, you stubborn child!"

"*Protectum Possibile*," I yelped, reeling away from her as the spell launched from my lips.

I bent in half, hugging my stomach as Trinket's body flew backward. The vial crashed to the floor and shattered, the pink liquid seeping into the floorboards. The din of it all sent jolts of nervous energy across the room, punctuated by the quiet *oomph* that came from Trinket as she hit the front door and slid to the floor.

At once, I was apologizing, my neck knotted in nerves as I sprinted to her side. "Trinket, are you okay? I didn't mean to hurt you—I'm so sorry."

Trinket's eyes remained closed, but her breaths were heavy.

"I *can't* drink more. I can't lose myself to her, do you understand me?" My breath came in gulps and my words were a garbled mess as I let my hands flutter over Trinket's body, feeling for any injuries, looking for signs of blood or hurt.

She seemed fine, save for a small lump on her forehead where the vial had cut her as it shattered. I reached to my travel belt and removed the Aloe Ale, peppering some onto the nick and murmuring a charm to slow the bleeding.

She swatted me away before I could finish. I watched her struggle to her feet, a droplet of blood sliding over her cheeks and down to her chin. It gave her an eerie look.

I sucked in a sharp breath as she leaned toward my chest. As she moved to her feet, I stepped away from her. When she took a step closer to me, I flinched.

At my retreat, Trinket took one look at herself, then at me. Panic set in, replacing the wildness, the desire, the demand. Her entire body trembled as if the protective spell had knocked sense into her. Though her hair stood messily on end and her face was streaked with blood, the gut-wrenching remorse in her eyes couldn't be clearer.

"Lily..." Her lip trembled. She reached toward me with thin fingers, but on second thought, pulled them back. "I'm so sorry."

"Trinket, please, forget it. It was the potion talking back there; it wasn't you."

I trailed off because Trinket clearly wasn't listening. She back stepped until her hand reached the doorknob, and she yanked it open. In a flash of swirling skirts and a now-loose bun of hair, she gave me one last glance, then turned and fled into the night.

I left the door open, staring into the darkness as I struggled to catch my breath. I'd barely begun to survey the mess of potion on the floor when a voice spoke from outside. Cautious at first, then concerned.

"Lily?" Footsteps turned into a pounding jog. Ranger X appeared in the doorway breathing heavily. "*Lily*?!"

"I'm right here. What's wrong?"

"What's *wrong*?" He stopped, surveying the room with a question on his lips. "Why was your door open in the middle of the night?"

"It's not the middle of the night," I said, glancing at the clock. "I'm just cleaning up before bed. The door—well, Trinket stopped over and she just left. I was airing the place out."

Ranger X's sharp eyes took in the scene, and I could sense the calculations ticking through his brain. "What did Trinket want?" His voice sounded casual, but his demeanor had tensed. "Seems like a nasty spill there on the ground. Don't step on the broken glass."

"Just dropped a potion as I was showing her something," I said, forcing a smile as I reached for the broom. "What brings you here, anyway?"

"Is that Long Isle Iced Tea?" Ranger X stepped toward the table where some of it had spilled. He swiped a finger over the liquid and took in the scent. "I wasn't aware you were brewing more."

"I brew things all the time for customers. I didn't know I needed to submit a log of them." I sounded snappish. Before I could apologize, I was distracted by the appearance of another figure in the doorway—the same Ranger who'd been shadowing X at Annabelle's farm. "Can I help *you*?"

Ranger X looked behind him. "Ranger J and I were following up on some leads when we saw your door open. I wanted to stop by anyway, and he was with me, so he came along. I hope you don't mind."

I stared at Ranger X curiously. "Of course I don't mind. But you still haven't told me the purpose of your visit."

"We're here with a *decree*," Ranger J spoke up, his chest puffing proudly in the background. "The Rangers are ordering you to—"

"Shut *up*," Ranger X snapped in a startling display of temper. "You don't speak to the Mixologist like that."

"The Mixologist?" I asked. "Or your *girlfriend*? What's this about, X—is this visit personal or business?"

Ranger X met my gaze without flinching, but I could see he was affected by my cool tone. Ranger J looked downright sheepish, hovering back into the shadows with his lips sealed.

X sighed. "It's official business. I'm sorry, Lily."

"Then let me have it; I'm in no mood for games." I propped the broom against the table. "What's this *decree*?"

"We have issued a ban on the creation and distribution of the potion known as Long Isle Iced Tea," Ranger X said, the entire statement heavy and solemn. "I'm sorry, Lily."

"Don't apologize." I picked the broom back up and gripped the handle so tightly it might've cracked in two. "It's just *business*."

"It's not just *business*. You're turning this into something it's not." Ranger X ran a hand through his hair as he glanced at his partner. "Wait outside, will you? And shut the damn door."

Ranger J was apparently more used to X's harsh tone than me. He leapt to attention and followed orders. Once he was far enough outside, Ranger X let down part of the shield, his eyes softening as they turned to me.

"I'm really sorry about that," he said. "Ranger J has been...*struggling*. That's why he's my partner. I've made it mandatory for Rangers to work in pairs so that..."

"All of you have consistent alibis," I said. "You need to be able to vouch for everyone's whereabouts at all times because of whatever's happening."

Ranger X gave a hesitant nod. "He spoke out of line about the decree, and I apologize. He shouldn't have said that."

"Oh, I have no beef with *him*." I let one hand off the broom and rested it on my hip. "He told me the truth. I have a problem with whatever's happening between us."

"I love you, Lily—"

"I love you, too. That has never been the question. The *question* is..." I paused in thought. The question was more difficult to formulate than I'd expected—I was still partially in shock. "What is going on, X? A *decree*? Since when have Rangers restricted Mixology magic?"

"I'm sorry, I had to do something. We have the press conference tomorrow, and there are rumors..." He closed his eyes. "There are rumors of people seeing Rangers at the scenes of these crimes. There are laws against impersonating Rangers, and it's extremely difficult to do."

"But?"

"But you saw Zin on the night of Poppy's birthday party," Ranger X continued. "She looked like me. Maybe not identical, but enough where...enough that she could have been mistaken for me from a distance."

"Are you trying to say I sold Long Isle Iced Tea to a member of The Faction?"

"This isn't about you, Lily! You did nothing wrong. But you did create a potion so powerful it can be used like a curse. The Isle is hurting, and I need to staunch the bleeding."

I swallowed, unable to argue with him. I'd seen the unrest on the island with my own eyes.

"I don't *know* the potion is responsible, but I am at a loss for what to do to stop this from happening again. We have no leads, nothing solid. Nobody's been seen at the scene of the crimes except for a few mentions of someone in Ranger clothing."

"It can't be the potion responsible—"

"We need to do *something*!" Ranger X roared. "I'm sorry. Sorry," he muttered at once, shrinking back. "I am running low on options."

I set the broom down gently against the table, my arms sliding into a hug around myself feeling weak, tired. "Why didn't you just ask? I would've stopped selling it if you had just come to me and *asked*."

"I made a rash decision," he said, the pain of it evident on his face. "There was another incident tonight—someone took all of Marty Yesterbag's unicorn horns. Those cost a fortune. I'll give you one guess who he thought he saw climbing out the window of his barn where he stored the stuff."

My silence was enough of an answer.

"A Ranger," X said, and the full weight of the day was visible on his face. He ached with the stress, and I ached for him. "The reporters were there already. I can't figure out how they were tipped off, and none of them are talking—they're just happy for the dirt."

"Right."

"I didn't mean to march in here demanding things. I was heated when I left Marty's, and I *should* have taken a minute to calm down." He crossed his arms over a broad chest. "I needed to give the reporters something. It's been too long without anything from Ranger HQ, so I told them we'd ban Long Isle Iced Tea from being served on the island until we sort things out. I *meant* to ask you, I promise."

"Well, thanks for letting me know." I bent down to retrieve the full dustpan, then on second thought, zapped it with a cleaning spell. It helped to burn off some of my frustrated energy. "I'm sure you have a long night ahead of you, so I'll let you get back to it. I'll see you in the morning."

"Lily, don't do this."

"Do what?" I tried to put myself in an understanding, forgiving mood. My tone wasn't quite there. "I will be at the press conference tomorrow, if that's what you're worried about."

"I'm sorry."

I rested against the broom. "Do you want to stay tonight?"

Ranger X glanced painfully over his shoulder at J. "We have to finish up—"

"It's fine," I said. "Understood. Goodnight, X."

He seemed prepared to offer another apology, an argument—something, but it never came. Instead, he leaned forward and pressed a kiss to my forehead. "Goodnight."

When he left, I locked the door and sent one more spell sweeping through the room to scrub the spilled Long Isle Iced Tea from the floor, the table, the shelves. Then, I grabbed the full beaker and stomped outside with it.

I tipped the glass container completely upside down, watching the potion drain to uselessness in the sand. In theory, it was stupid to waste such valuable ingredients. But I couldn't leave them in my house.

My necklace still glowed bright, brighter than ever before, and the memories of my mother's face flashed painfully into my head. I pushed those thoughts away. Long Isle Iced Tea had only brought me problems, and I had enough problems existing already without creating more.

I returned inside and washed the last dregs of potion from the beaker and my hands. The room smelled blissfully like lemon and clean pine, and thankfully, the taste of Long Isle had departed from my lips after some vigorous teeth brushing.

I climbed into bed and flicked open the drawer next to me. The press conference was on my mind, and the thought of appearing united with Ranger X while we were on rockier ground than ever before had me in fits of nerves.

Instead, I pulled the new note from between my socks and read it over.

Use what you have.

Use what you have, I mused. All at once, it felt like I had everything...and nothing.

Who'd left the note, and what could it possibly mean?

I drifted to sleep with the paper clenched between my fingers. My necklace continued to glow against my chest, and as dreams crept into my mind, I sunk deep into visions of my mother's eyes as they stared back at me through the mirror.

Chapter 8

"ARE YOU SURE YOU'RE ready to do this?" Ranger X asked one last time as we prepared to climb on stage. "If you want to back out, I'd understand."

"I gave you my word," I said, striving for calm. "Plus, I don't have to say anything. I think I can manage standing still and holding your hand."

"That's what the PR team is saying would be best."

As a vote of confidence, I reached out and grasped Ranger X's hand in mine. "I'm ready if you are."

My small gesture worked like a miracle. The tension snapped in X's shoulders, and he folded forward, dragging me into an embrace almost stifling in its thoroughness. His hands found my back, pressing me to his stone-hard chest, harder and harder until I relaxed into him.

My arms encircled his neck, and I pressed an olive branch of a kiss just below his ear. He shivered under the touch, shuddering as he stepped back, his gaze filled with a cornucopia of emotions.

"I don't want any of this mess to come between us," he said. "I meant my apology last night."

"I know. It was a rough night all around."

"Are we ready?" A woman holding an official looking clipboard scurried toward us. "Can we get moving? I like the look in his eyes right now. There's some vulnerability in there, and I want to capitalize on it. Let's *move*, people."

Shock replaced the vulnerability as Ranger X turned his gaze to me. "I look vulnerable? Since when do I look vulnerable?"

"Well, now you look paranoid. Forget what that lady's saying; just be yourself out there."

"Be myself," he repeated, but there seemed to be a question behind it. As if he'd forgotten exactly what it was like to be himself.

The thought made me sad. It had been impossible for him to avoid taking the islanders' lack of faith as a personal attack on him. I'd never expected to see Ranger X's confidence shaken, but lo and behold, the earth he walked on seemed to have shifted.

With a surge of my own protective instincts, I gave his hand another squeeze. A harder one. The PR lady rushed us forward, but I gave her a sizzling stare that bought us a few moments.

"Hey," I whispered to Ranger X, leaning on my tiptoes to reach his ear. "You are *Cannon*. You're the love of my life, and you're the best protector this island has ever had. You can be both, you know. You don't have to choose between the two."

Ranger X slid an arm around my back, holding me against him, his grip tight.

"I'm sorry I was upset about the stupid decree. I know you're just doing what's best for The Isle. So do the rest of the people here—they don't doubt you, not really. They're just scared."

"We seriously need to move it along," the PR lady barked. "Show's starting, folks."

"Ready?" He expelled a breath and seemed to visibly steady himself. "Here we go."

Together, Ranger X and I stepped from behind the curtain in the sizable amphitheater and faced a sea of curious faces. There was a long, extended moment of silence as the islanders, reporters, and guests, took in the united front before them.

Then the silence shattered, and chaos broke loose.

"*Where's Peter?*"

"Who brought that article back?"

"Has The Faction infiltrated the island?"

"Crime is out of control! Why aren't the Rangers doing anything about it?"

"Why aren't the Rangers protecting us?"

"Miss Locke, what actually happened while you were with The Faction?"

I turned to X, leveled my gaze, and squeezed his hand. He took a breath, and together, we faced the fire.

"The Rangers and the Mixologist have joined forces here today to answer your questions," X said boldly. "The first rules of the conference: no magic is allowed in the venue as a courtesy to everyone. We will not answer any personal questions. Ten minutes are on the clock, starting now."

More questions pelted toward him, quicker than X could keep up.

He waved a hand for a moment of quiet. "I'll start by addressing the article. It's true that it was penned by one of our own, Peter Knope, who is currently believed to be a prisoner of the enemy."

"Is it true Miss Locke left him behind when she escaped?" asked another. "Did Lily use him as bait?"

Ranger X handled each question with as much grace as possible, protecting me from having to field a single one myself, just as he'd promised. However, one shot after the next hurled his way, and it no longer began to matter what he said—his voice was barely audible over the growing roar of the crowd. The crowd's fury built to a deafening din, as if a balloon of fear was expanding too quickly and on the verge of eruption.

It wasn't long before the questions devolved into insults. The mob's unrest fed off itself, growing to a boiling mass of anger. My heart raced from fear of something happening, some spark setting this tinder alight.

That's when I saw it: the prick of a spell in the center of the mass of bodies. It grew larger, gleaming and swirling green as it hurtled toward us. I barely had time to open my mouth in surprise. I began to shout a warning, but X's reaction was faster than mine.

Before I could utter a word, Ranger X stepped between the spell and me, raising both hands and projecting a golden glow that swallowed the spell whole as it hurtled toward us. There was a *whoosh* as the two magicks collided, and then a sudden silence.

Ranger X whirled toward the side of the stage, a fury so deeply ingrained into his face I didn't argue as he took my arm roughly and swept me behind the curtain. As we left, the sounds returned outside, less furious, more curious in nature.

"Who let that happen?" X demanded at the PR team. "What the hell was it?"

The woman with the clipboard stood still, her mouth gaping open. "I'm sorry, I didn't know..."

"We're done." Ranger X pulled me away from her, from the rest of the backstage personnel, while barking orders to the Rangers standing by at attention.

The faces of the other Rangers, too, were grave. I couldn't find Zin, and I vaguely wondered if she was off working on her secret assignment and had been excused from security detail. I knew, however, that if she'd been here, she would also be wearing a scowl of disapproval. When one Ranger was attacked, it was aimed at the team. The *family*.

The first Rangers swarmed through the crowd, presumably looking for the person who'd dared light a spell at such a public event. They were under sharp orders from X to waste no time bringing in the culprit.

"When we find him," Ranger X said to me, then quickly amended, "or *her*, they'll pay."

"It's fine, I'm okay—nobody was hurt."

"We have rules for a reason. That spell was a Soul Suck—a curse, a poison. Have you ever seen someone affected by it?!"

I inhaled deeply and shook my head. "No."

"It's deadly," X said simply. "We're going home. I'm taking you to my place, and—"

"Don't I get a say in this?"

Ranger X slowed at the softness in my voice, the pleading there. "Of course, Lily. I'm just worried about your safety. Anyone who launches an attack against you launches one against me. And an attack against me is an attack against the Rangers."

"It's business. The spell could've been aimed at you."

"No," he said, hoarse. "It was aimed at you, and that's what made it personal for *me*."

A rough touch of his lips against mine sent the familiar singe of fire lighting down my spine as the kiss lingered. Disappointment followed the second we broke contact.

"I can't go home with you now," I murmured to him. "I have something I need to do."

He frowned. "It's not a good idea. Whatever it is. I'd like you to stay close to me." As an afterthought, he added, "*Please*."

"It'd take me away from The Isle," I said, surprising both of us with my newest plan. "I need to go to the mainland."

"Why?"

My confession confused me almost as much as it did him. It was an idea that'd popped into my head earlier this morning after I'd woken with thoughts of Liam's visit on my mind. It hadn't solidified until just now.

"The Master of Magic is in danger," I whispered, tugging X deeper away from the crowd. "The morale on The Isle is in shambles. Something is *wrong*. I found a note in a drawer in my bedroom yesterday morning that had advice on it. But how could someone have gotten into my bedroom?"

"What did it say?" he asked sharply. "Why didn't you tell me?"

"*Use what you have.*"

"Excuse me?"

"That's what it said, word for word," I said. "I don't know what it means. I meant to tell you, but things got busy."

I could see Ranger X's hands clench into fists.

"I know you want to lecture me about safety, but let me assure you, the note wasn't the most alarming thing of the morning, which is why I forgot to bring it up," I said. "Liam appearing in my closet was a *lot* bigger surprise, so please, don't lecture me now. Someone just tried to curse me, X. We have bigger fish to fry."

He digested my plea, though his fists didn't loosen in the slightest. "What's on the mainland?"

"I don't know, but it's somewhere different than here. My presence on the island is making things worse all around—plus, it's distracting you from your work. I'd like to visit Ainsley at MAGIC, Inc. and see if she has some information on the Master of Magic."

"She won't. Nobody does. He's not connected to MAGIC, Inc. He was around long before the association ever existed."

"I know, but they must have resources or thoughts on it."

He didn't disagree, and that gave me a bigger boost of hope than I'd expected.

Don't fight me on this, X. I'll be safe; I'll go straight to MAGIC, Inc. I need to investigate somehow, to do something."

"Use what you have," Ranger X pondered. "What could that mean?"

"Nothing," I said, shrugging my shoulders helplessly. "Or everything. It could refer to a potion in one of Gus's spellbooks, or it could mean my friendship with Ainsley. If I don't start looking somewhere, I'll never find anything."

"Don't do anything rash." Ranger X's hand came up, brushed a stray strand of hair off my forehead. "I love you, and I trust you, but I worry about you."

I nodded vigorously. "Thank you. Maybe it'll free up some time for you, too. You won't have to babysit me while you have other things going on."

"I never babysit you, Lily," he said sounding cross, his eyes flicking over my shoulder at an outburst from the crowd. "I just wish—"

He stopped short.

"What is it?" I asked. "What's wrong?"

"There were extra spells set up around here to prevent magic to-day," Ranger X said, crossing his arms as he stepped back to survey the hall. "How the hell could someone have conjured a Soul Suck when we had all spells blocked?"

"Why don't you solve your problem," I said, leaning up to kiss him on the cheek, "and I'll solve mine. I'm going to arrange transport with Kenny. I'll Comm you when I get to Ainsley's."

"Promise me," Ranger X said, gruffly, "that you'll wear your device at all times and let me know the second anything doesn't go according to plan."

I raised my wrist and showed off the magical Comm. "I promise. MAGIC, Inc. is one of the safest places to be."

"I'd like to go with you; I hope you know that."

"You need to be here."

Ranger X grudgingly agreed. We both knew his offer had been merely show, a token of his desire to keep me safe. He offered another chaste kiss to my forehead before walking me away from the crowd and back to the bungalow where Gus would surely be waiting. We had a ten-minute walk together, but it ended all too soon.

"Go," I told him, sensing an urgency in X's footsteps as our feet landed on the white sand outside of the bungalow. I knew he was itching to study the scene of the spell. "I'll let you know when I'm back."

"*Back*?" Gus interrupted from the top of the stairs. "Where are you going?"

While X took his leave, I climbed the stairs to the bungalow and began gathering supplies. As I tucked vials and potions into my travel belt, I explained my theory to Gus, along with the discovery of the note in my sock drawer.

"I'm sick of sitting around," I said, double-checking my supply belt. "I need to do something about that message. I have to look for information somewhere."

Gus nodded, but beneath his nonchalance was a shred of worry. I was grateful he had the good sense not to argue, and instead, he tapped his cane thoughtfully against the floor. "Say, if you find something on the Tortoise Wars, I'd love a copy."

"What are you talking about?"

Gus winked. "I'm sure Ainsley will take you to the only place in the world with more magical knowledge than me."

"Where is that?"

"Let's just say..." Gus mused, a smile quirking his lips upward. "You're in for a treat."

Chapter 9

"AINSLEY IS VERY BUSY," a tart little blonde explained as we strolled through the shiny hallways of MAGIC, Inc. "I'm not sure she'll have time to talk to you."

"Well, it doesn't hurt to check. I've traveled all the way here, so it'd be a waste not to stop by and ask."

The young woman who had introduced herself as *Nevada*—likely a new intern—peered at me through glasses magicked to sparkle along the edges. "Who'd you say you were again?"

I pointed to the nametag I'd been assigned after verifying my identity at the front desk. "Lily."

Her eyes roved over it, catching the last name there and turning it over in her head, muttering my name several times under her breath. "I swear I've heard the name before."

I made a noncommittal noise in my throat.

"Lily Locke," she said again, unsure. "What do you do for work?"

I hesitated, which spared me an answer.

"Ah, here's her office. She got a recent promotion, you know," Nevada said. "I'm her assistant now."

"That's great. Ainsley deserves the promotion."

Sounds came from inside the closed office. It sounded like quite a commotion in there, and I wondered if Ainsley might actually be too busy for a visitor—a fact I stupidly hadn't considered before setting off for the mainland.

"I can wait outside if she's dealing with something," I said. "I don't want to interrupt."

"I *told you* she was busy," Nevada said crossly. "She's always in demand around here, and—"

"She shoots, she *scores!*" A loud, booming male voice roared. "Ainsley for the win, ladies and gentlemen."

Nevada stopped short as the door to Ainsley's office swung open. Out came a flood of six or seven folks, all dressed in business attire wearing broad grins on their face. The grins disappeared into guilty expressions as they found Nevada and myself waiting patiently in the hallway.

Through the door, we could see Ainsley perched on her desk, fists pumped in the air as if she'd won the world series. "Y'all owe me lunch, folks! I'm expecting—*Lily*? Hey, boss! How's it going?!"

Nevada's mouth dropped open as Ainsley completely ignored her assistant and barged out of the room, sweeping me into a grand hug. I wasn't sure if Nevada was more surprised by the term *boss*, or by Ainsley's dramatic display of affection.

"What brings you to these parts?" Ainsley was clearly still riding high on whatever fumes were coming from her office: her cheeks were flushed, her voice higher pitched than usual, and a slight amount of sheepishness snuck into her gaze as Nevada caught sight of the monitor behind her.

"Is that..." Nevada inhaled a sharp breath. "Miss *Shaw*, is that the confiscated game?"

"Nope," Ainsley quipped just a little too quickly. "Fine. Maybe."

Nevada looked gobsmacked. "But that's supposed to go down to the Dismemberment Committee."

"It'll get down there. But they couldn't transport it until this afternoon, so..." She shrugged. "We sampled it. It's research, Nevada. We have to know what types of video games are hot on the market these days. Otherwise, how can we confiscate them?"

Nevada's eyebrows cinched together, as if debating the pros and cons of believing her boss. "I thought it was declared dangerous?"

"It's mostly dangerous to humans." Ainsley neatly evaded the question. "Anyway, we have more important business at hand. Nevada, next time Lily arrives, bring her straight to my office—do you understand?"

Nevada nodded dumbly.

"Great. Now, how about you call Dismemberment and tell them to come grab the computer? I need a little time with our Mixologist here. I'm so glad the two of you met."

"The Mix..." Nevada stuttered. "Lily *L-L-Locke.*"

"Who'd you think she was?" Ainsley's eyes landed on Nevada. "There's only one Mixologist in our universe."

"I didn't...I-I'm sorry, Miss Locke, you'll have to forgive me."

"Nothing to forgive," I said quickly. "It's been a pleasure to meet you. Can Ainsley and I have a minute?"

"I assume this is confidential." Ainsley took me by the arm and marched me down the hallway, leaving behind a speechless Nevada. "I know just the place to talk. By the way, sorry about my assistant."

"Why? She was fine."

Ainsley rolled her eyes. "She's new, and she thinks she runs the world. She probably gave you the excuse I was too busy to talk, or whatever. For some reason, she loves me—she imagines I fart glitter and rainbows. Not a clue what gave her that idea."

I laughed, pleased to be reunited with my friend. Ainsley knew how to lighten up a room, and that was exactly what I needed. We continued pleasant small talk for a few minutes as we wound through the magnificent building located in the middle of the Twin Cities. The lower half was disguised as a bank, while the upper floors were rendered invisible to human eyes by a series of complex magical spells and charms and hexes.

"You seem a little blue," Ainsley ventured once we reached a huge glass doorway that seemed to open into the center of the building. "What's eating you, boss?"

I sighed. "Are we okay to talk here?"

Ainsley grinned. "This is the best place in the entire building to talk. You could admit to murder and there's not a thing we could do about it."

I squinted around us as she pushed the door open and we stepped through it. I gasped as we did so, not having expected to step into a whole new world. Behind us, we'd left a mess of corporate hallways, sharp corners, clean to the point of dull fixtures with nary a comforting painting to spice up the walls.

Before us sat a roomful of life.

It was like we'd stepped into an exotic conservatory of the magical variety. A mix of rainforest and greenhouse.

Shaggy moss hung from limbs in every direction, and thick stalks of greenery protruded from the dirt beneath our feet. Glistening leaves as big as an elephant's ear waved in the light breeze, though I couldn't for the life of me find an exit to the outdoors.

"Magic," Ainsley said with a smile. "Don't forget, Lily, my dear—you're a witch."

I grinned back, soaking in the musty smell of dirt, the click of Ainsley's heels on the unevenly laid stones. The path wound through the jungle-like greenhouse, the air thick with humidity and heavy with quiet.

Save for the sounds—sounds I hadn't noticed until I truly listened. The slight rustle of leaves, a heavier clomp here or there. The crack of a stick and a buzz—an unending buzz that began to give me a headache if I concentrated on it too hard.

"You noticed," Ainsley said, pleased. "The jitterbirds."

"The what?"

"Jitterbirds. There, see? It's got a silver feather through the tail."

I found the bird, a crow-like thing except smaller, much smaller and thinner. Sure enough, there was one long silver feather protruding from its behind.

Ainsley waved a hand, and I moved my gaze to follow her gesture. Sure enough, once I truly looked, they were everywhere. Five of them sat on the branch just above my head, and a few hopped along the path next to my feet. Three more jitterbirds fluttered their wings on a nearby leaf the size of a small boat.

"They make this place work," Ainsley said, happily whistling a tune as we moved along. "This is the largest population of jitterbirds in the entire world."

"Why—er, do you have a jungle in the middle of your office building?"

"Fresh air," Ainsley said with a wink. "That, and these jitterbirds block out sound up to twenty yards away for anyone to whom it's not intended."

"But I can hear you."

"I haven't induced the confidentiality bit of it yet. Here, I'll invoke the charm and show you how it works. You're going to love it." Ainsley put a hand on my shoulder, spun me to face her, and looked into my eyes with a bright smile. "Lily Locke, listen to me."

I nodded, not understanding. Ainsley gestured for me to repeat her phrase.

"Lily Locke—" I began.

"No, it's like a repeat-after-me, but you say my name. I'll restart. *Lily Locke, listen to me. The sound of the jitterbirds sets us free.*"

"Okay," I said. "Er, *Ainsley Shaw, listen to me. The sound of jitterbirds sets us free.*"

At once, it was as if we were in a tunnel. Just the two of us, deep under water. Nothing about the outside world changed except for the ringing of intense silence now in my ears.

When Ainsley spoke, it was crystal clear. Dainty. As if I could hear nuances in her voice that I'd never heard before, never knew existed.

"Neat, huh?" she said, and it was as if she'd pounded a drum. "It takes a second to get used to."

I nodded, listening to the reverb of her question bounce around my skull for ages longer than normal. It was as if all other sounds had been vacuumed away. Even my own breath sounded like someone banging a gong.

"This is how sound *really* works. You know, when it's not diluted by everything else," she explained. "Nobody has a chance in Hades to hear what we're talking about now. So, if you have any gossip, now's the time to spill."

I smiled weakly. "I wish that were the case. I am actually here on a quest for information."

"A quest. Fancy. What can I do for you?"

"Have you heard of the Master of Magic?"

Ainsley burst out laughing. When she looked at my face, her laughter morphed into a cough of confusion. "Are you serious?"

"Yes. It's very important."

"Oh, well, yes of course. I just figured..." Ainsley held a hand over her mouth, exhaling slowly. "I'm so sorry. It's easy to forget that you spent so many years being human. I feel like we've been friends forever. Plus, you fit into the magical world like you were born to be there. I mean, you were, but you didn't *grow up* hearing the tales."

"So, everyone knows of him? Or her?"

"It's most definitely a *him*," Ainsley corrected. "Every master has been male since the beginning of time. Children born to magical parents, well, we hear the stories. I suppose some might call him a myth, like Santa Claus, but we all know Santa is real."

"We do?"

"How else do you think the presents get all across the world in one night?" Ainsley shot a me a look that said I was being incredibly thick before continuing. "The Master of Magic is real. We've got extensive evidence that points to this being true. I can go more deeply into it, but I'll wait since I'm guessing you have more to your question."

"How do I find him?"

Ainsley began another laugh but cut this one short too. "Lily. You can't be serious."

"Deadly serious."

"Thank goodness for the jitterbirds," she said, tugging a hand through her hair. "I'm not sure anyone else would believe this even if they did hear it. Lily, it's a death sentence to look for the Master of Magic. Many have tried, none have succeeded."

"None that you know of maybe, but surely someone has found him?"

"Like you said—none that I know of." Ainsley's brows knitted together. "You're really serious about this, aren't you?"

I nodded, then sighed. "I wish I weren't. I've been sworn to secrecy by my source, but I have information that suggests the Master of Magic is The Faction's next target."

Instead of laughing, Ainsley's face drained of blood, her dark hair framing cheeks where slight freckles visibly popped. "That can't be."

"I don't think they've found him yet, but—"

"Then they won't." A bit of confidence returned to her step. "It's impossible to locate him just because one *wants* to."

"What if it's not? Is it worth the danger of writing this off as an impossibility?"

Ainsley sighed. "No, I suppose not. Have you heard about the last time he was injured?"

I frowned and shook my head.

"Researchers have said," Ainsley said, her tones hushed despite the protection from the jitterbirds, "that the last time the Master of Magic was *hurt*, World War II broke out. Obviously, the consequences were devastating to recover from. The world still isn't fully recovered."

"But—"

"You *must* understand, Lily, that this is a huge theory you're suggesting. If the Master of Magic were attacked, it wouldn't only be the end of the magical world, it would be...it would be a global disaster."

"How was he hurt last time?"

She shook her head. "I don't know. I just know the story. He was unable to tend to the laws of magic, and the world just about fell off its axis. It was a disaster, Lily—millions of innocent people died."

"Most of them humans, I'm willing to bet," I said grimly. "No wonder The Faction has their sights set on the Master. It'd be one of the quickest ways to wipe out the non-paranormals. The Faction wouldn't even have to do anything; if the laws of the universe are off balance, it seems like the humans will take care of the destruction themselves."

My statement must have rung true to Ainsley because the paleness in her cheeks lightened further, leaving her chalky in color. "What are you planning to do to try and stop them?"

"I *have* to find him first. I'll offer my protection, my skills—if there's a way to help him, I'll do it." I could see Ainsley wasn't yet convinced, so I dove into my bigger plea. "Look, I know this sounds impossible, and maybe it is. But I am sick of waiting around for The Faction's next move—I'm ready to act first, to take the offense instead of the defense. If you can help me, please, consider it."

Ainsley gave a short nod of agreement. "I think you need to talk to Millie."

"Who's Millie?"

"Millie is…" As Ainsley debated this, she hooked her arm through mine and marched me toward a hidden doorway that loomed behind a splashy waterfall in which jitterbirds played. "Let's just say she's a bookworm."

"How will she be able to help me?"

Ainsley gave the first real smile since I'd told her of my plan. "According to the legends, the Master of Magic is protected by the ancient gods. You want to find the Master? You'll need to uncover the gods."

"And Millie…"

"Has read everything on the subject," she said, leading me to a familiar desk where we proceeded to check out a set of broomsticks. "Let me introduce you to the Library of Greats."

"You're coming with me?"

She squished up her face. "We'll see if they let me in. Last time, I nearly burned the place down. I highly suspect they revoked my library card."

"Huh."

"Long story," she said. "I'll explain another time."

And then we were off from the flight deck, sailing through the air toward the only hope we had left.

Chapter 10

MILLIE TURNED OUT TO be a young woman with the most soft-looking brown hair I'd ever seen. She wore round glasses that made her eyes look three times their normal size, and though her expression was mostly pleasant, she frowned at the sight of our broomsticks as she met us at the front door of a very normal looking library.

"Ainsley," she warned, "what have I told you about riding here on your broomstick?"

"Sorry, sorry." Ainsley quickly eyed the librarian situated behind the front desk with concern. Then, she leapt with lightning speed to lock up the broomstick in a closet that looked as if it were for coats. "See, it's actually a human library," Ainsley whispered to me as I followed suit with my own broom. "I forget we're not supposed to fly here."

"You didn't *forget*," Millie chastised. "You know the rules. And anyway, Ainsley, isn't it a little...*soon* to be back? The librarians haven't forgotten your last visit."

"I wouldn't be asking you for a favor if it wasn't important," Ainsley said, parroting the same logic I'd used on her earlier. "Hear Lily out—that's all I'm asking."

Millie turned to look expectantly at me, so I launched into a quiet conversation as we began to stroll through the library. Along the way, Millie waved a few badges at the front desk to check us in, and then she led us upstairs. The entire way, the librarian behind the desk watched us like a hawk.

"Mrs. Flutterbing is not a huge fan of me," Ainsley said, glancing sideways at Millie. "I'm not getting you in trouble, am I?"

Millie wrinkled her nose and shook her head. "She's just concerned for the books. You have a talent for...well, you know. Not keeping them in one piece. Ah. Here we are."

I looked up at the sign to which Millie pointed. It was labeled with the headline: *Intestinal Issues and Severe Stomach Struggles*.

"Er, *actually*," I said. "I was hoping to find books on the Master of Magic."

"Exactly." Oblivious to my discomfort, Millie led us down a dead-end aisle, and when I was just about ready to suggest we turn around and leave the intestinal issues far behind, she reached forward and ran her finger down the center of one of the books.

Before our eyes, the shelves split in two. Ainsley glanced behind us again to make sure we were alone to witness the spectacle while I watched with rapt attention. The jam-packed shelves folded in on themselves to reveal an entryway through which Millie stepped without hesitation.

"Come along," Millie said, her voice leaping with excitement. She glowed the second she stepped through, and it was easy to see she belonged. "Feel free to peruse as you wish."

I surveyed the most magical expanse of books as I stepped into the cavernous room, overwhelmed by the sight of the utterly secret library. The ceilings were lofted high above the floor with shelving units covering every inch of spare wall. Ladders extending as tall as houses slid along the edges, while various scholars dressed in the traditional Cretan robes sat behind old mahogany desks.

There was no electricity, cell service, or modernity of any sort within the magical library. Instead, lanterns cast flickering glows over the creaky floorboards, leaving long shadows reaching into the belly of the library. Piles upon piles of haphazardly arranged books wobbled in stacks on every surface, creating cozy little caves behind which writers and students studied and scrawled on parchment before them.

I inhaled a shuddering breath, awed and astounded and hopelessly lost. "Um, do you have any suggestions for where to find information to locate the Master of Magic?"

"Sorry, I can't help you find him," Millie said again, apologetically. "You've come to the wrong person."

"Why?" Ainsley demanded. "Millie, this is really important."

"You want to *find* the Master of Magic." Millie's eyes narrowed at us. "I don't have that information. It doesn't exist—nobody has it, and therefore, I cannot help you find him."

"Any information on him would be helpful," I said, trying not to sound desperate. "Do you know of any works that reference him, by chance?"

"Ah!" Millie perked up significantly. "Now, that I can do."

"She's one of those artsy types," Ainsley whispered to me as Millie flounced away, running her hand along a variety of manuscripts as she moved, pulling one out here, another there. Her choices appeared random. "I don't always understand how their brains work."

"I just hope there's something here. If not, I'm at a loss for what to do next," I admitted. "I hate to sit around and wait, but I can't think of another path forward."

"Let's see what Millie brings back." Ainsley sounded confident. "She's never let me down yet."

I had high hopes for the books Millie brought back, and sure enough, she didn't disappoint.

"Here's one that briefly references how his magic system is supposed to work." Millie flipped through a detailed reference book with complex illustrations and loads of colorful images. "It's a theoretical book since obviously nobody alive has seen his work."

"That's the problem," I murmured. "I don't know all of this *obvious* information everyone else seems to have. I didn't grow up on these stories; I grew up human. I'm learning everything from scratch."

Millie's eyes widened. "Fascinating. Tell me about being human. Did you ever come to this library? Who are your preferred non-paranormal authors? Did you read books on magic and wonder if it existed? What's your favorite form of non-magical travel?"

"Millie." Ainsley cleared her throat. "I think our friend Lily is on a time crunch."

"Right, right, of course," Millie said. "Well, in that case, let me introduce you to this one."

I accepted the slim, brightly illustrated paperback that nearly crumbled in my hand with age. "What is this one?"

"It's a children's story," Ainsley interrupted, leaning over my shoulder. "My mom read me this one. *Masters and Magic*. It's almost like a, oh, I don't know, a comic book for magic. It's got his origin story and all that. It's a story about the man who saved magic as we know it, and how he continues to this day to provide balance in the world. It hints at the destruction that will follow should the balance go awry."

I clutched the book closer to my chest, then surveyed the pile of massive manuscripts Millie had prepared, including a collection of books on Greek, Roman, and Norse mythology. There was even a book with Russian lettering on the cover. "Thank you. This is an incredible start; I think I'll need some time to look through all these."

"You can take them home," Millie suggested. "But I recommend spending an hour here flipping through them and finding which ones you need. If you tell me which ones you like, I can find others more in depth on specific subjects."

"Which would you suggest I start with? Anything that might *hint* to where the Master lives?"

Millie's eyes flashed again. "Let me be clear: You are not going to find information on how to locate the Master of Magic in these books. It's simply impossible."

"If I can't find him," I shot back, "then what in the world should I be looking for? I refuse to sit here and do nothing."

"You're not doing nothing," Millie said with a curious smile. "You're doing quite the opposite."

I crossed my arms, not in the mood for games. "What's that?"

"You're not looking *for* him," she said lightly. "You're preparing to be found."

Chapter 11

PREPARING TO BE FOUND was more difficult than expected.

I pulled Millie's quickly-scribbled list of suggestions toward me and reviewed it yet again as I closed the book on Norse mythology and scratched my head. *Nothing.* Not a thing in the book except information on Norse mythology and gods—information that Millie had said would be important when I was found. *If* I was found. *If* I were chosen to be led before the Master of Magic.

While I read, Ainsley had been studying, too. She'd been in charge of covering various biographies of people who claimed to have met the ancient gods. While reading, she'd jotted down a list of etiquette she'd gathered from the books.

I pulled the list toward me and read, in Ainsley's sloppy handwriting, her suggested etiquette:

<u>Etiquette around gods:</u>

1. Don't give any of the gods a reason to punish you.
2. Let them teach you their ways.
3. If you have the opportunity to meet a god, don't.
4. Repeat.

It didn't *exactly* inspire confidence, I thought.

"Millie," I called, flagging Ainsley's friend from where she shelved returns with a surprising gentleness. "Do you know what Ainsley meant about this punishment bit? I think she's off getting a snack."

"Oh, that? Well, gods are notoriously fickle entities. In their day and age, punishment meant eating babies and tearing apart limbs."

She sighed heavily. "They have *tried* to progress with the times but, you know, old habits die hard."

"Oh. Right." I returned my eyes to the page and pointed toward the next rule. "What about this teaching part?"

"Oh, that's easier." Millie grinned. "Gods *love* to talk. They *love* to impart their wisdom and stories on people—how do you think the myths began? For example, if you ran into Aphrodite, she'd want to redo your love life. If you meet Ares, he'll want to go on and on about strategy and war and *yada, yada*. If you meet Dionysus, he'll probably bring out the wine and talk with you for hours."

"And this third one," I said, deciding I was in a constant state of shock. Hearing about mythical gods as if they were real would do that to a girl. "If you have an opportunity to meet gods, don't?"

"Refer back to one," Millie said simply. "They're dangerous beings, there's no way around it. Not only have they been around the longest, but they're vastly more powerful than the average witch or wizard."

"Why have I not seen any? Or even heard they exist?"

"They keep to themselves, and most people are happy to leave them alone," Millie said. "See points one through three on the list earlier. There's a very good reason why they're said to have their own colony—that's why Olympus was formed a long time ago. In fact, it's impossible to find the colony of the gods. There's only one creature alive who has access to its location."

I raised my eyebrows.

"He—or she, I suppose—is called the Keeper." Millie answered my unasked question. "Only the Keeper can grant another creature the knowledge of the gods' location. It's magic as old as time. As long as the gods have lived in secret colonies, they've had a Keeper."

"How does one find this Keeper?"

"Again, one doesn't. He finds you." Millie shrugged at my look of disappointment. "I know it's not what you want to hear, but it's the truth. The Keeper has arguably the most important job in the universe in protecting the Master of Magic."

"And how do the gods play into it?"

"Wherever the gods choose to live is the safest place on earth," Millie said. "It's believed—though not confirmed—that the Master of Magic resides in the modern version of Olympus, wherever that may be."

"Let me get this straight. The ancient gods have their own colony that nobody can get to unless the Keeper invites them in," I said. "It's there that the Master is housed for safety."

"So we think."

"Yet there's no way to look for the Keeper. One must simply wait to be found."

Millie's eyes glittered. "Now you've got it. Do you see why I couldn't promise to help you find the Master of Magic? It's impossible!"

"Great," I muttered. "Everything is crystal clear."

"I figured you'd understand it," Millie said easily. "I mean, you're sort of *like* them after all."

"Like who?"

"The gods!" She gave a knowing laugh. "It's almost as if they're a separate breed of paranormals than us. Their magic is different than ours: it's more innate, less manufactured. It's simply *who* they are."

I shifted my weight from one foot to the next as Millie scratched her nose, then continued her explanation.

"Most of us, we learn spells and potions, and we practice magic, and hopefully over time, we get better at it." Millie raised a hand and sent a few books flying back to the shelves with a short incantation to prove her point. "But you, you're the Mixologist. That's different. According to legend, you're simply born with certain magical tendencies and powers that nobody else will ever possess."

"I had to spend a lot of time learning," I said. "It wasn't all natural."

"Sure. But no matter how much I want to be the Mixologist, I'll never be able to look at a potion and see it the way you do. Tell me if I'm wrong, but you are rumored to be able to sense what's needed next in a potion, to smell, taste, touch, and simply do—to create magic in a way that we can't. I can never fully understand what it is you do, or even who you *are*. Because it is a part of you, Lily, it's part of your very spirit."

I didn't have a good answer to this, so I took a moment to think. My mind wandered, flipping through the stages I'd gone through since learning of my true nature. The denial, the anger, the realization, the grudging acceptance, and then, finally, the wonderful sensation of true understanding.

Millie watched me with curiosity.

"Sorry, I was trying to think of a way to explain it to you, but..." I hesitated. "It's hard to put into words."

"I'd think it would be," she said cheerfully. "As a matter of fact, I've always wondered if the Mixology family tree contained mythical bloodlines. It really is uncanny the similarities between you and the other ancient deities."

To my relief, Ainsley reappeared then and clapped me on the shoulder. "Find anything yet in those books?"

"Mostly random bits of history." I turned to Millie on a sudden impulse. "Actually, that reminds me of something Ainsley said this morning."

"What'd I say?" Ainsley asked. "I hope it was smart."

"You said that historically, every time the Master of Magic is out of commission, odd things start to happen in the world."

Millie nodded. "Of course. If the balance is off, there's no saying what might happen."

"If nobody can find him, how can that happen? How can he be *hurt*?"

Millie and Ainsley exchanged a look. "I might have mentioned World War II," Ainsley admitted. "I told Lily I'd heard stories that the Master had been injured, and his duties were neglected while he was out of commission."

"Oh, that's not a story." Millie reached behind her ear for the pencil she'd stashed there, retrieved it, and tapped it against her palm. "I have a newspaper somewhere that explains it. I'll pull it for you, Lily."

When she vanished, I questioned Ainsley. "You know more than you're telling me, don't you?"

Ainsley hesitated. "It's a dangerous assumption. I think we should wait for Millie to explain. I've only heard theories."

Millie returned, oblivious to the uneasy silence and flashed the article before us. "Okay, ladies. Here you go. The text speculates that a demigod—a person born with both mortal and immortal blood-lines—can track down the location of the gods because they are part deity. Therefore, it's assumed that whoever attacked the Master of Magic around the time of the second world war was a demigod—specifically, a descendent of Ares."

"One who inherited his penchant for war," Ainsley said, wrinkling her nose. "He didn't manage to wipe out the Master, but he came close."

"I pulled another article from last month," Millie said, adding it to the stack. "There are rumors circling that the current Master of Magic's time is coming to an end."

"What's that supposed to mean?" I asked. "He's not immortal?"

"Oh, no," Millie said. "He's not a god—he's a wizard, much like yourself."

"There's been talk at MAGIC, Inc. that supports that theory," Ainsley agreed. "The Master of Magic ages like we do, Lily. Well, not exactly. They have long, long life spans, but we all age. Eventually, one

Master is replaced with a new one. It's very possible the new Master of Magic has been born already and is waiting for his calling to emerge. He's probably some normal little boy running around and playing Hex Marks the Spot—completely oblivious that his powers will be manifesting shortly."

"Well, that's a lot to digest." I shifted under Ainsley's piercing gaze. I added the articles to my stack and faced Millie. "How do I check these out?"

"Let me handle that," Millie said, shifting the books with a spell and carrying them alongside her toward the door. "Browse for a few minutes, and I'll call you when they're ready."

Ainsley dipped her nose back into the book she'd been reading while I let my feet pull me toward the shelves and wander. My mind wandered right along with my feet, churning through the pile of information I'd received this morning in a frenzied struggle to digest it all.

I can't find the gods, but I can prepare to be found. It frustrated me that the only solution was to wait around some more. The whole purpose of me coming here was to move forward with my investigation. If I could guarantee one thing, it was that The Faction wasn't sitting around waiting for things to happen.

A sudden thought sent my nerves into a tizzy. Maybe they *weren't* waiting for a lightning strike—maybe The Faction had found a workaround.

Maybe, they'd found a demigod.

"Millie!" I called out, only to be shushed by a nearby librarian with a tight bun in her light brown hair. "Sorry," I muttered, surprised to find myself lost in a stack of books. I'd wandered deeper into the library than I'd realized.

Before I found my friends, however, the most curious thing happened. My necklace awakened with a glow—bright blue and searing hot. Burning, boiling hot. So hot it nearly crippled me as I bent in half and struggled to breathe.

I tore at my neck, trying to remove the chain before it swallowed me whole, but I couldn't do it. I couldn't unclasp the lock. It was as if it'd melded together, seared into one by its molten temperature.

Through sheer survival instincts, I stumbled backward, trying to pull away from the metal. Just as suddenly as it'd begun, the heat retreated. Still breathing heavily, I forced myself to a standing position, holding the charm away from my skin. A lingering burn in the shape of a heart was still imprinted against my chest.

"What is *wrong* with you?" I muttered to the necklace. "I thought you were supposed to protect me."

Taking another step forward, I held the heart as far away from my chest as possible. The burn mark began to fade. However, only two steps later, the pain was worse than ever.

Searing, burning, boiling.

My mother's face flashed into my mind as delirium set in, a wildness that pulled on my survival instincts and threaded the strings into messy chaos. A hand—*my hand?*—reached out, stroked the mirror in my memories. I touched her face, my own face...

When I finally opened my eyes, I was surprised to discover that I was on the floor. A cold sweat had swept my body and left me chilled and weak. I must have collapsed, fainted maybe. The images flashing through my mind had to be that of a nightmare.

I rose to shaky feet, gripping onto the shelves for support as I gingerly touched the charm around my neck. It hummed with a pleasant glow, luxuriously warm, but no longer scorching.

I was too afraid to move. Though the burns hadn't left behind marks, the pain was unbearable. When I finally gathered the courage to take a step, it was with a cringe, a wince, and the crippling fear of not knowing when the pain would return.

For support, I held onto the shelves and inched my way along, nearly whimpering in anticipation of its next angry flare. To distract myself as I cautiously moved toward the front of the library, I focused on reading the titles of books around me.

Witches and Warlocks: a history of our kind.

Spells and Enchantments: Volume IV

Charmed by the Boss: A collection of paranormal office romances

Coincidence or Fate: the role of magic in our lives

"Coincidence?" I fingered my necklace once more. "Coincidence...or *fate*?"

The word triggered something in my memory. The last time my necklace had burned so harshly, I'd felt as if it had wanted to tell me something. As if it had *wanted* me to drink the Long Isle Iced Tea potion and see my mother again.

"Bogus," I muttered. The necklace hadn't *wanted* me to do anything. I'd simply wanted to drink the potion and had used the necklace as an excuse. I hadn't even thought twice about that event until now, until it had happened again.

It *must* be coincidence.

As a quick test, I retraced my steps backward. I moved slowly, cautious, wincing with every breath. Eventually, I noticed the sensation between my fingers. The charm grew to a comfortable temperature once again, projecting a pure, crystalline shade of blue that radiated to the end of the aisle in either direction. It'd never glowed so brilliantly.

"What do you want me to do?" I asked of it, feeling delusional talking to a piece of jewelry. "I don't understand."

I kept walking back, retracing the steps I'd taken until the temperature grew to a low boil once more and discomfort set in. I stopped before it could become worse, then moved forward again.

The temperature reverted to a comfortable one, lukewarm and pleasant, the glow almost blinding. I looked up, soaking in the sights around me to find nothing but books. *Lots* of books.

If, in fact, the necklace was charmed to somehow guide me in certain directions, I'd guess it was wanting me to locate a book in this section. The thought had me exhaling in exhaustion. It'd take me forever to get through just this section.

But, if I couldn't leave this section without the book or my necklace charring me to ash, I might as well get started. I read the titles one by one, but the necklace didn't seem happy with that choice either, judging by the growing heat. I reached out a hand to steady myself, and my finger brushed against the books.

At once, it calmed.

I ran my fingers over several more books on the shelf. Then moved to another shelf. This seemed to keep the charm satisfied, and as I worked, I couldn't help but wonder what sort of enchantment my mother had put in place. Some sort of Seeking Spell, maybe? Could it know what I needed to find? Or was it something broader, something bigger—something unexplainable?

As I pondered this, I lost track of the titles I'd been reading. With a sigh of frustration, I let my hand slip down the current shelf, realizing I'd have to start all over. However, as my hand slid to a rest on top of a thick volume, my necklace flashed once, blindingly bright, and then extinguished.

Startled, I glanced to where my fingers landed. They rested on the spine of a book with a title so dusty, so old, I had to squint to read it. When I deciphered the lettering, it was only a word: *Ceres*.

I snatched the book from the shelf, clutched it to my chest, and tentatively began my journey back toward Ainsley and Millie. Along the way, I grabbed a few more books that I expected Gus would like from the Tortoise Wars era and carried them with me.

When Millie saw my additional stack, she rolled her eyes but gave me a knowing smile. "Great place, isn't it? I could live in this library my entire life and never get bored."

Millie warned us that the doors would be closing soon, so she rushed the three of us through another round of checkout. Soon enough, Millie, Ainsley, and I stood outside the library under the watchful eye of the Head Librarian. Mrs. Flutterbing hadn't released our broomsticks yet, explaining we could only travel once it grew dark.

"I have some work to do," Ainsley said with a frown. "Lily, do you want to come hang out with me for a bit? I'll get you home after the prison guard releases our brooms."

"Mrs. Flutterbing is *not* a prison guard," Millie said, pulling us both into hugs as she murmured goodbye. "I have to get back to tidying up the library. Let me know if there's anything I can do for either of you. It was a pleasure to meet you, Mixologist."

"Lily," I corrected, hugging Millie back. "Thanks for everything. Oh, and Ainsley, there's something I need to take care of this afternoon. Do you mind if we meet up later?"

"Sure." Ainsley looked surprised. She waited until Millie returned to work and left us alone. "Is it something you'd like help with?"

Ainsley stared intently at the small little bag I'd received from the front desk. The librarians had brilliantly charmed the parcel to carry all manner of books and old tomes—while weighing less than a pound. I briefly wondered where such a charm had been during my college years.

"Actually, no. Just some personal errands," I said, waving her off. "It's been so long since I've been on the mainland, and—"

"I'll come with you. My work isn't that urgent."

"If you don't mind, I'd prefer to handle it alone. Go ahead and do whatever you need to do. We can meet back here later?"

"Better idea," she said with a wink. "Do you have to be returned home tonight? I know my parents would love to meet you. Will you come by and have dinner with us? We have a spare bedroom. I'll get you back before your day starts at the bungalow tomorrow. Gus will never even know you're gone."

"Actually," I said, quite pleased at the development. "That sounds wonderful. Thank you."

"Oh, wait until I ring my mom! She'll faint again with excitement. And my dad! I've told him I'm friends with the Mixologist, but I don't think he believes me. Thank you, Lily!" She pulled me into a tight squeeze. "Apologies in advance if my grandmother stops by. She's a character."

I was laughing by the time Ainsley pulled away. "I'm so ready for a normal night. That sounds perfect."

Ainsley winced. "I wouldn't call my family normal. But," she said, raising a finger, "if you're looking for a distraction, look no further. Plus, my dad might have some information on the Master of Magic."

"Really?"

"He worked as a Guardian for MAGIC, Inc. for years. One of the best in the business," she boasted proudly. "He had to retire because, ah...well, you'll see soon enough for yourself. Anyhow, good luck on your errands. Comm me if you need anything?"

I raised my wrist to indicate the device and nodded. "Thanks, Ainsley—for everything."

After she gave me her address and promised to take care of the broomsticks for me, we parted ways, and as I maneuvered to my next destination, I gave Ranger X a quick Comm, updating him on my itinerary. He seemed happy I had a safe place to stay for the night. To my additional surprise, he admitted he was familiar with Frank Shaw's work. Apparently, Ainsley's father was quite a legend in the business.

"He's a very talented wizard," Ranger X said. "It's so unfortunate about...well, never mind. I hope you have a nice time. Come back to me in one piece—please?"

"I love you, and I promise. Oh, one more thing," I said, before he could hang up. "How are you doing with your investigation? Did you find out anything about the Soul Suck from the conference—who generated it and how?"

Silence extended for a moment. It lasted for so long that I suspected our Comm had been severed somehow. And then he sighed.

"I don't know, Lily, it's so bizarre. The protective charms were all in place—absolutely solid. No patches, nothing. Our defenses were untouched. Whoever set off that Soul Suck was very, very skilled to evade detection. I'm just afraid..."

"What, X? What are you afraid of?"

"I'm afraid of *what* they are. There's no wizard registered on The Isle who could set off that Soul Suck without detection. Unless they had help from someone—or *something*—else."

We hung up minutes later, the Comm ending on a decidedly somber note.

I took a moment or two to gather myself, to sort through my upcoming task, to put Ranger X's concerned tone into the back of my mind. I was still shaky when I set off on my errand.

I dipped and dodged as I moved, circled back and overlapped across my own path to avoid detection. I even smashed a hat onto my head to ensure I wasn't easily recognized or followed. My next errand was decidedly private and somewhat risky. I was determined to go at it alone.

Once I could be sure I hadn't been followed, I wound my way to end at the police station. I took a deep breath, reached down, and unclasped my Comm. I slipped it into my bag, wincing as I did so. I *should* have told X about my plan, but he would've instructed me not to follow through with it, and I didn't feel like being told what to do.

Today, I needed to do something for me, for Trinket.
I needed closure.

Chapter 12

I MADE IT INTO THE building easily enough. Surprisingly *easy*.

When I'd been living the human portion of my life, I'd been so by-the-rules that I'd never seen the inside of a police station. Frankly, I had no clue if my little mission would be helpful in uncovering the information I needed, but I had to try something.

Slipping into the bathroom, I glanced behind me before I shut the door. I was alone in the room which was exactly what I needed for phase two.

Phase two of my plan began by summoning the clearest image to mind of the lady cop I'd *just* witnessed strolling through the corridors. I focused on the blues of her uniform, the flash of metal around her waist, the badge on her chest, and I held the image there, wishing with all my heart.

I focused so intently that, as I pulled out a small vial of the Long Isle Iced Tea potion I'd recently brewed—the portion that hadn't gotten dumped into the sand—I felt a bubble of excitement that this transformation would work.

I gulped it back and the potion began to work instantaneously. As I swallowed the pink liquid quickly, I relished the tingle that spread throughout my body. A part of me had expected to turn into my mother once again, but I'd *hoped* that my desire to find closure for her would outweigh my desire to see her. And in order to find closure, I needed to look like a human cop during this leg of my journey.

The spell worked just a little too well.

I gasped, glancing in the mirror, realizing I hadn't merely turned into a policewoman like I'd hoped, but I'd turned into the *very one* I'd seen strolling the halls minutes before. I could have been her twin.

While this was a sign the potion had worked perfectly, it was also potentially dangerous. I absolutely couldn't run into this woman while disguised as her, or there'd be one magical mess I had no hopes of cleaning up on my own. If that happened, MAGIC, Inc. would be called, and this wouldn't be the last time I saw the inside of a police station. Exposing magic to the human population was most certainly a crime that came with severe consequences.

I'd have to be careful on all fronts. It'd *also* not look good if I was caught and reported to be using Long Isle Iced Tea not one day after Ranger X issued the decree stating I shouldn't sell it. Technically, I hadn't sold anything, and I'd brewed this *prior* to the decree—so theoretically, I hadn't crossed the line.

However, the meaning had been clear: Until further notice, Long Isle Iced Tea was a banned substance on The Isle, and it wouldn't look like a very "united front" if the Head Ranger's significant other was caught breaking his rules.

I tossed the vial back in the magicked book bag and slung it over my shoulder. I hadn't brought much of the potion, and time was ticking, so I had to get a move on before it ran out. I had no time to re-think my plan now. Instead, I slipped out of the bathroom and prayed for the best.

I eased into the light flow of traffic in the corridor, turning down a less populated hallway in an effort to think. I needed to find files. Technically, since I looked like I belonged, I should know where they were, which meant I couldn't just ask someone for help without looking suspicious.

I jumped in line behind a pair of burly men, also in uniform, strolling easily down the hallway and having a rowdy conversation about the weekend. They each had a mug of coffee in one hand and looked to be going nowhere fast.

"—my kids had a soccer game, and..." The shorter of the two trailed off, turning to look at me. "Diane? Did you need something?"

I glanced down, taking a beat longer to respond than I should've. "Er, yeah, actually. I had someone asking a question about an old case. It'll have been nearly twenty-six years ago by now, I guess, and it was a mugging gone wrong. You know where I'd find it?"

The second officer looked mildly miffed. "Over in archives. He thumbed past his shoulder in the opposite direction from where they were headed. "You looking for the primary on the case, or...what case did you say it was?"

"Thanks," I gasped. "I, ah, I'm in a rush now. Gotta run."

As I looked up in the direction I needed to go, I was horrified to find myself staring at the very woman I'd impersonated. The *real* Diane had just turned the corner at the other end of the hallway and looked to be meandering straight toward me.

I ducked into the nearest office, waiting, listening, as the two men mumbled about inept new officers. They continued down the hallway moving none too quickly. I held my breath as the real Diane neared them, coming from the opposite direction.

"Er, Diane?" the skeptical one said. "Didn't we just talk to you?"

"Nope," she said, smiling. "Have a good night, guys."

"I could've sworn..." the shorter one put a finger on his lip as Diane continued down the hallway. "That's so weird. I could've sworn she was *just* here."

Diane kept moving, completely oblivious that she'd left the two officers staring behind her as if they'd seen a ghost. I suddenly liked Diane quite a lot.

Once the hallway was cleared from the close call, I slipped back out and made my way purposefully down the corridor. I surveyed each sign on the wall, trying to keep my ineptness discreet, studying for any sign I was headed in the right direction.

Finally, I found what I was looking for: *Archives*, a small sign tucked between a derelict coffee machine and the ladies' room. I popped in the women's restroom first, checked to make sure I was still solidly in Diane disguise, and then returned to the Archives doorway where I slipped through with a handy little Lock Lifter spell.

I'd vowed to use as little magic as possible while out in the human world. While it wasn't illegal to use magic on the mainland, it was frowned upon to bewitch, charm, or otherwise hex humans without their knowledge. But an unlocking charm hardly hurt anyone, I thought, scanning the rows upon rows of filing cabinets that reached to the ceilings as I stepped foot through the door.

A few desks sat pushed against the far wall, the weak outside light filtering through and giving the space an odd, bluish tinge. One desk was empty, the other was covered by a lanky man whose nameplate read Andy Dinker.

"Well, howdy, Diane," Andy said, leaning back in a creaky old chair. "How are *you* doing?"

I froze, ready to retreat and call it a day when a burst of determination planted my feet to the ground. I offered a bright smile that just barely hid the terror brimming behind it, reminding myself this might be the only chance I'd get to uncover my mother's files. What if I didn't look *exactly* like Diane? What if my voice came out sounding nothing like hers?

With a sigh of relief, I realized I had heard Diane speak. I focused on the brief words she'd exchanged with the duo of cops in the hallway and concentrated on returning Andy's greeting.

"Hey," I said cheerfully. "How's it going?"

"After last night," he said with a wink, "pretty spiffy, if I say so myself."

Oh, Diane, I thought to myself as I realized what was happening. *You can do so much better, honey.*

Nothing against Andy Dinker's personality, but he wasn't exactly a looker or a charmer. As he stood, he exposed pants hiked up to his belly button. Every inch of his uniform was positively *slathered* in animal hair. A slight odor hovered around his desk, and I prayed to every one of the mythical gods that Andy Dinker wouldn't try to kiss me. Er, *Diane*.

"Yeah," I said, channeling Diane's raspy, firm voice. "I know what you mean. Last night was...*great.*"

"Say, Duke's out to lunch." Andy gestured to the other desk. "I was thinking we could take *advantage.*" He raised and lowered his eyebrows a few times. "What do you say, sugarbun?"

"Oh, I *wasn't* thinking that, sorry." I must have sounded sharp because the poor guy looked crestfallen. I reminded myself that I was *Diane*. Not wanting to ruin a budding relationship that wasn't mine to ruin, I gave him what I hoped was a sweet smile. "I mean, the thought is...*er*, you know, *there*. But I have some urgent business I have to take care of, and we all know you're the best. I was hoping for a little help before...*ah*, playtime?"

I added a slight purr to the compliment, and that did the trick. Andy melted under my gaze, sinking back into his seat like Play-Doh, all gooey and malleable. He moved like a slinky, one arm and then the other, then his torso, then his legs.

"What can I help you with, darling?" He preened under my stare. "Anything for my sugarbottom."

I winced at the nickname. "There's some new information coming in about an old case—it's been nearly twenty-six years, though, and I'm not sure if you'll be able to find what I'm looking for."

"Sure thing," he said, in action mode. "What's the name of the primary?"

"I don't know," I admitted. "The victim was Millie Banks."

Two *Millies* in one day, I thought. One a fake and the other real.

"Looks like I've got a hit. You want whatever I can find?"

"That would be great," I gushed. Then, in a moment of goodwill toward Dinker, I added, "Sugarbottom."

He gave me a salacious wink that ruined any moment of bonding we might've had, and I backed far, far away, pretending to examine the names on the files at the opposite end of the room.

While there, I chanced a glance out the window and stopped, ramrod straight in my tracks. *Diane.* The real Diane was en route to this very location. *Crap*!

The way she was looking over her shoulder had me thinking she didn't want to be seen—or followed. Judging by the smug look on Andy's face, there was one thing Diane was looking for, and it was more of Andy Dinker. If she walked in here while I was standing dumbly behind the door...

"Andy, babydoll, sugar-fairy," I said, struggling. Ranger X wasn't huge on endearments, and I had little to no practice with them. "You have anything? I'm sorry, I've got to run—stomachache, er...you know, so much fun last night."

"Aw, I'm sorry, baby! Let me take care of you. Maybe if we both called in sick, we could—"

"No, I'm sorry, I'm really, *really* not feeling well. Could I just grab the file from you for now?"

"Dollface, you know I can't give these things out."

"Er, *dollboy*, this is really important. The boss is asking for up-dates, and..." I hesitated, wondering if policewomen had bosses. "I need to get a head start, but I'm also feeling terrible. I'll return it once I'm through."

"I don't think I can do that," he said, frowning. "Maybe I could make a quick copy for you, but you'd have to destroy it when you're done. Seriously, Diane, we could both get fired if you don't."

"I promise! I'll get rid of it just as soon as I scan through it. This is really important. Thank you, *er*, angel hair."

"Angel hair?" he frowned, and I hoped he hadn't realized I'd grabbed the name from a pasta box above his desk. "*Huh*, I like that one. My mother always did say I had beautiful hair."

I winced at the thinning strands over a rather large bald patch and tried to arrange my face into a positive expression. I couldn't be sure it worked, but luckily, Dinker finally received the picture and began making copies.

I peered out the window and saw Diane drawing nearer. I only had a few minutes left until disaster struck. I tapped my foot, waiting for Dinker, when another officer rounded the corner and stopped Diane. Judging by their stiff shoulders and official-looking stances, they were discussing business.

Good, I thought. Just a few more minutes, and I'd have everything I came for. I scooted nearer to Andy to supervise, but not too near that he'd grab me in some unwanted sort of kiss. I sincerely hoped Diane liked the guy. He seemed nice enough, and if he got me the pages I needed, I'd make him the love potion myself.

"Almost done," he said. "Just a few more. Can I just say, I love the look of you from behind?"

I'd been peering out the window into the hallway once more, tapping my finger against the doorknob in anticipation as the older officer dismissed Diane, then gave a parting wave in her direction. The two separated, Diane returning on her trek to find Andy Dinker.

When I turned to find Andy staring, I couldn't possibly mask the look of discomfort on my face, so I opted for impatience. "That's great. I need to be going now. Hope you understand. Thanks, baby-face. Er, whatever. Bye."

I snatched up the papers and returned to the door. I sent a tiny little firebolt streaking from my finger as I silently muttered an incantation too soft for Dinker to hear.

"But, that's not all of it!" Andy was busy looking down at the last few pages of the file, still being copied, so he didn't notice anyway. "I've got the last ten pages here for you. Actually, there's the last one now. Here you go, honey."

Diane had her eyes glued to her feet, so she, too, didn't notice the ball of flames hurtling through the air to land in a small trash can just behind her. With a Smoke Screen spell, I dragged a few streams of smoke up from the fire and danced it around underneath the fire alarm.

A few seconds later, a loud metallic shriek told me the job was done.

"I'll keep you safe!" Andy called valiantly as the fire alarm continued to blare. "Let me bring you to safety, my princess."

"Sure, just one second," I said, reaching toward him with an apologetic smile as I snatched the rest of the pages from his grasp. Then I turned away from Andy and yanked open the door, slipping into the hallway as other cops did the same. In seconds, the hallways were swarmed and minor chaos had gone into effect.

It was just the break I needed. I hightailed it in the opposite direction of the real Diane, pausing behind a water fountain to watch the pair's reunion. Andy went straight for a kiss that had me cringing, relieved I'd missed out on that attack. Diane looked surprised but not displeased, and it was then that I knew I hadn't ruined anything.

"Thank you, Andy Dinker," I muttered, tucking the files into my bookbag.

My work here was done. I left the hugging pair and concentrated on navigating my way from the building. I moved quickly. The slightest tingle of the Long Isle Iced Tea wearing off had hit, and I needed to get to the bathroom before I morphed mid-hallway and created a statewide disaster.

I wound through the hallways, some less populated than others. The first few times I felt a pair of eyes land on my back, I assumed it was because I was one of the few women around. But the third and fourth time it happened, I grew suspicious.

As I rounded one particularly sharp corner, I glanced back at the last possible second and caught sight of a man whose eyes were fixed intently on my figure. He looked shiny: shiny blond hair, shiny badge, shiny shoes—all of it *too* shiny.

I tucked my backpack tighter to me and barreled toward the bathroom. I took a few detours, mostly by accident, as I couldn't remember where each hallway led. Once, my pursuer swung particularly close to me on a turn, and his hand reached out, his lips pouted in thought.

The motion set off alarm bells clanging in my head. I murmured a quick protective spell that crackled around my body. The humans wouldn't be able to see or feel the protective spell, but it might help ward off an attack. If nothing else, it would make it more difficult for the man to follow me.

I moved quicker through the corridors, focused on getting to the door. I wracked my memory, wondering if there was a window in the bathroom. That wouldn't be a half-bad escape route, and I hoped it would be enough.

As I hurried along, the ends of my hair began to change color and the blues of my clothes faded at a rapid rate. Turning a corner, I broke into a jog. I glanced behind me, relieved my shadow hadn't kept pace. The restroom was close, mere yards away.

I could feel the features of my face twisting from Diane's back into my own. The chaos of the fire alarm helped to deter others' attention, and thankfully, nobody cried out in shock at the clear signs of magic happening right in the middle of the police station.

I flung the bathroom door open with an exhale of relief, skidding inside just as the transformation into my own body picked up speed. I made the mistake of glancing over my shoulder and caught the piercing blue eyes from my shadow landing on me. He registered my escape route and broke into a run.

I glanced around, horrified at the lack of window in the room. At least, not one large enough for escape. There was a tiny little thing that let in enough light to highlight the bland, paint-chipped walls and cracked faucets, but that was it. The walls were solid cement. There was no way out of here except back through the door and straight into the attacker's waiting arms.

The final bout of transformation back to Lily Locke hit me with a searing burst of energy. I lurched forward, holding onto the sink as the Long Isle Iced Tea left my system. It was getting harder and harder to change back each time I took the potion, I noticed. It wasn't supposed to be painful, but this time around, it felt as if needles pricked every inch of my skin while I morphed.

As I clung to the sink and waited for the discomfort to pass, I had one last idea. Possibly the only idea that'd get me out of here without using magic.

Glancing in the mirror, I scanned myself over. The transformation was complete. I was back in my normal clothes with my normal brown hair and my normal face. Save for my eyes—my eyes were wide with fear.

I allowed one second to wonder who the man was and why he was after me.

Originally, I had guessed him to be a cop—a logical choice, seeing as he wore an officer's uniform and hung out in a police station. *Unless,* he'd followed me here.

But how? How had he gotten a uniform? I'd watched myself for a tail, but there'd been nothing unusual about my trek here that I'd noticed. Not to mention, a human cop shouldn't have been able to follow me so closely once I'd launched the protective spell.

Did the files I'd taken from Dinker's office have some sort of tracking device on them? Some sort of alarm that'd sounded when

Dinker recalled the files? It was possible there was someone out there who *didn't* want these files re-opened. But who? And *why*?

The only logical explanation left was that the man was indeed a cop—a cop who'd worked on my mother's case. He might be a cop who had something to hide, a cop who'd received a payout to cover up certain information. I hugged my bag close to me, praying the files held the answers I needed.

The fire alarm's sudden silence jerked me back to reality. Hoisting my backpack onto my shoulders, I walked toward the restroom door and bit my lip. I had only one plan to get out of here, and it would require huge amounts of charisma and zero percent nerves. I had to fool my attacker face to face.

He was following *Diane*. I now looked like *Lily*.

It would have to be enough.

Sighing, I pulled the door open and offered a bright smile as I came face to face with the blond man who had followed me here. He straightened, surprised by my sudden appearance.

"This is the women's room," I said to him quickly. "You should probably head down the hall to the men's room. There's someone in here who asked for privacy."

It was by sheer willpower that my hands didn't shake. I'd plopped my hat back on my head and looked away from him. I folded my arms in front of me and gripped my waist so hard my nails dug into my skin.

Every nerve in my body screamed for me to move, to get out of there, to get my legs pumping and carry me away from him, but I fought back. I forced myself to play it cool and offered a smile before I set off.

He stared at my back as I left.

My breath hitched, but I didn't stop.

It took every ounce of self-control not to look back over my shoulder. I forced my feet to carry me forward. When I reached the safety of the outside world, I sprinted, my lungs screaming for air as I rounded the corner and ducked into the nearest coffee shop. A few cops hovered around the counter, each holding a piping hot mug of coffee and a donut as they discussed the faulty fire alarms and miserable city budgets.

I hopped in line, shielding myself behind a particularly rotund man in a suit, and waited. I didn't have to wait long. After a few seconds, my follower ran from the building and drew to an abrupt stop. He ran a hand through his hair as he hissed out a curse word I couldn't decipher.

My heart thumped in my chest. I was sure the man next to me could hear it pounding. When it was my turn at the counter, the barista asked me multiple times for my name, and even after I finally heard her question, I was too upset to respond.

My hands shook, and the last thing I needed was caffeine. With an apology, I slipped from line and took a side door out to the opposite street. My follower remained standing in front of the building, talking to something near his wrist. Some sort of Comm, no doubt.

I hesitated. *A Comm?*

Could the man be a paranormal? Could he... I hesitated, not wanting to think it. But after all the assassin talk from Millie and Ainsley this morning, combined with Liam's convictions that The Faction was ready to move forward with a plan, I had to wonder... could I have faced off with a demigod?

I shuddered and pulled my clothes tighter to my body as I made my way toward Ainsley's house. I muttered a quick Map Maker spell and input the name of Ainsley's house so that every time I glanced at my palm, a shadow of an arrow would point me in the right direction.

I had no clue who the man might be, but the more curious issue was *how* he'd found me. My plan *couldn't* have been leaked. It was impossible. Not a soul in the world had known of my stop at the police station today. Not Ranger X, not Poppy, not Ainsley, not Hettie.

I'd come here alone. Completely, and utterly by myself.

Except... I hadn't been alone.

Chapter 13

"I'M AT AINSLEY'S NOW," I told Ranger X, curling up in the spare bedroom on the comforter Ainsley had said was mine for the night. "Her mother's cooking dinner, and it smells delicious. We'll be eating soon, but I just wanted to check in."

"Have a nice time, okay?" he said. "You deserve to relax."

"Are you sure you're feeling alright? You sound tired."

"I'm tired, but nothing I can't handle. Don't worry about me—I'll see you tomorrow when you're back."

"Did you learn anything else about that Soul Suck?"

"Since we last talked?" He laughed. "No. However, there was another incident."

"Oh, no."

He grimly agreed. "Nobody was hurt, so that's the positive. Unfortunately, there was another report of a Ranger breaking into someone's house."

"To do what?"

"I have no idea." Ranger X hesitated, and when he spoke again, he sounded uncertain. "Reported missing was a sandwich and all the photographs from the wall frames."

"Why would someone take a sandwich and someone else's pictures?"

"You've got me."

"But, it *can't* be a Ranger, right? First, I can't imagine what any of the Rangers could possibly want with that stuff. And secondly, aren't all the Rangers working in pairs? That would mean everyone has an alibi."

"*Almost* every Ranger has been accounted for during each of the crimes."

"Almost everyone?"

Ranger X exhaled. "Two of my staff lack alibis for all of the events."

"Oh."

"Right. And I refuse to use truth serum on my own men—*er*, men and women," he corrected quickly. "We are a family, and I won't break their trust by doubting them."

"But?"

"But one of the reporters has caught on to the noticeable lack of alibis, and they're calling for a suspension of the two Rangers in question until the culprit is found."

"What happened to innocent until proven guilty?"

"I know, Lily, I'm not going to listen. That doesn't mean the islanders aren't hearing it."

"I'm sorry," I said. "I really am. Is there anything I can do to help?"

"No, in fact, I'm glad you have some time away. Get a good night's sleep."

"You too," I said, knowing that wasn't on his agenda. "At least promise you'll try."

"Sure."

I could almost feel him nodding halfheartedly. "I really miss you, and I'm excited to see you again."

"Me too. Goodnight, Lily."

We bid our goodbyes, and I took the remaining time before dinner to shower quickly and change into some of Ainsley's spare clothes. We were close enough in size that she had some yoga pants and a sweatshirt that fit me comfortably. Once I'd dressed, I curled back onto the bed and slipped the files from Andy Dinker out of my bookbag.

With shaking fingers, I began my study of the pages. The first few sheets contained monotonous red tape information. *Name, date, disclaimers*, etc., and I scanned through them, committing any important names and places to memory: officers who had worked the case, the reported name of the victim, and the location where she'd been found.

When I got to the names of the two suspects in her murder, I stared at the handwritten print: Adam Sherman and Samuel Palmer.

The names meant nothing to me.

Human or paranormal, innocent or guilty, alive or dead, I knew nothing about the two men who'd been convicted of my mother's murder. For some reason, I'd expected to feel something when I reached this section: a spark of recognition or a surge of hatred. The thrill of the chase or the sadness of seeing the story in black and white.

I *hadn't* expected to feel the blankness. But it hit, and it hit me hard, because along with it came the realization that after all this time and effort, holding the official file in my hands didn't change a thing. My mother was still dead, and she wasn't coming back.

With trembling fingers, I dropped the papers onto the guest bed and relaxed against the pillows. As I closed my eyes, processing it all, a pit lodged in my stomach. Weary, that's what I was. Weary of the mess, of this complicated existence, of a never-ending battle. Exhausted because I hadn't had time to recharge. To laugh with my friends. To snuggle my love. To eat a good meal.

I rested uneasily until the dinner bell rang. As I stood, I forced myself to ignore the pit in my stomach and focus on the evening ahead. I took the stairs down to the main living area, pleased to find the Shaw's home warm and intricately cluttered. Every shelf, every wall, every cupboard was filled with life and family and the very things that I longed to have.

For just one night, maybe I could forget the rest.

"I JUST CAN'T BELIEVE you're here!" Ainsley's mother tittered with excitement. "The *Mixologist* is over for dinner. Wait until mother hears she missed this, Frank."

Frank Shaw, Ainsley's father, gave a lopsided smile from underneath his mess of untidy hair. "Wait until she hears indeed. I'm sure she'll be terribly disappointed."

"Believe me," Ainsley said, leaning closer to me. "You're lucky it's just us. My grandmother can take some getting used to."

"We can *hear* you, Ainsley," her mother said, though she didn't seem all that upset. "Anyway, let's eat."

Dinnerware and plates of food floated in from the kitchen, and as everything settled in its place, I was struck by the oddities of having a magical family. It seemed surreal to me even now, the concept of growing up with levitating meals and table talk of hexes. To the Shaws, it was just another day in the neighborhood.

"Tell me about that handsome man of yours." Mrs. Shaw kicked off the conversation with pink cheeks. "You two make the most gorgeous couple."

"Mother! Will you stop already?" Turning to me, Ainsley gave an apologetic shake of her head. "My mom's been reading that rubbish newspaper. *Wicked Weekly* or whatever—I swear, they will print anything to make a quick buck."

I gave a snort of agreement.

"I'm just making conversation." Ainsley's mother helped herself to a dinner roll and loaded it up with butter. "How long have you two been together?"

"Awhile now. We started dating not long after I arrived on The Isle," I admitted. "Ranger X is doing well. He keeps plenty busy with his work, but that's normal."

"I'm sure." Frank raised his eyebrows. "Say, have you kept in touch with much from your human days, Lily? I read something in the *New York Times* that got the old brain ticking away. *Self-driving cars*. What do you know about them? How do they work? Seems to me a bit like magic."

"Don't quiz the poor girl, Frank," his wife said, just before she turned to me with a cheeky smile. "Tell me more about this boyfriend of yours. Do I hear wedding bells in the near future?"

My smile must have frozen on my face. A second of extended silence stretched across the table before Ainsley threw me a lifejacket. "Mom. Dad. If you can't stop being nosy, Lily and I are going out for dinner and not coming back until you're asleep."

Mr. and Mrs. Shaw glanced down at their plates, picking through the first bites of pasta. Angel hair, I noticed with a wry smile, and thought fondly of Dinker and Diane.

"Are we allowed to ask about your work?" Mr. Shaw directed the question at me, but he looked to Ainsley. "I'd love to hear about any potions you're working on, Lily."

Ainsley shot me a raised eyebrow, and I nodded, grateful to latch onto a topic that didn't involve rings and vows.

"Actually, I have a few things I've been working on," I said, diving into an explanation of my recent surge of Security Spells. "I'm working on a new one—er, I was, until a shortage of ingredients put the kibosh on that."

"Which ones?" Frank asked, his plate nearly empty after my long-winded explanation of Mixology. "Anything I can help you find?"

"No, I don't think so. I was looking for Forgotten Ferns," I said, forlorn. "I've heard they grow specifically on The Isle, on a particular farm."

"Ah, I see," he said thoughtfully. "Any news when they'll be ready?"

"Likely not till next year," I said on a heavy sigh. "Unfortunate, but what can you do?"

Frank sat, paused in thought. "So, what brings you to the mainland?"

"Just a visit to Ainsley and the library," I said. "I've never been before and figured I should pay a visit."

"What's the topic of your trip?"

"Frank," Mrs. Shaw interrupted. "Honey, leave our guest alone. Ainsley's already annoyed we're asking her so many questions."

"No, really, it's okay," I said, feeling the dawn of an idea. "Mr. Shaw—"

"Frank, please."

"Frank, then," I said. "Do you know anything about the Master of Magic?"

He analyzed me with a piercing gaze. I ducked my eyes for a moment, caught off guard by the intensity of his stare. Then at once, it ended and a mildly pleased, somewhat confused look took over.

"Oh, no," Ainsley murmured under her breath. "He was doing so well."

"What?" I asked softly. "What happened?"

Frank hummed, his eyes glimmering with brightness as he sat back in his chair, surveying the table. "Delicious dinner, darling. What were we talking about?"

I looked to Ainsley in confusion. She'd warned me something unfortunate had happened to her dad, but I'd gotten the impression it wasn't any of my business. I hesitated to press further without her permission, and judging by the steely set of her jaw, she wasn't thrilled to share.

Ainsley muttered something unintelligible under her breath as she stood, then tossed her napkin to her seat. She stalked to the kitchen without another word.

"Sorry," Mrs. Shaw apologized, gesturing to her daughter. "It still upsets Ainsley when her father...*forgets.* Don't worry dear, there's nothing wrong. It's nothing you did, it just...happens sometimes. He'll snap out of it."

Mr. Shaw leaned in toward his wife and threw an arm around her shoulder. Then he shot an unnerving glance in my direction. "And who are you, might I ask?"

"I'm, ah—Lily," I said, thrown by the complete blankness of his stare. "Lily Locke. I am a friend of Ainsley's visiting from The Isle."

"Give him a few minutes," Mrs. Shaw said under her breath. "He'll be back."

Frank stayed in *la-la-land* until halfway through dessert. Ainsley had returned to the table a few minutes after the incident, and though more subdued, she'd kept the conversation going with her mother.

"You're looking for the Master of Magic, aren't you?" Frank shot me a sharp look out of the blue. One with such clarity and vitality I could hardly believe it was the same person who'd forgotten my name minutes before. "That's not a good idea, Miss Locke. That sort of mission can get you killed."

"And, he's back," Ainsley muttered. "Sorry, I know it can feel strange to see him flip like that without warning."

I smiled at Ainsley, letting her know I wasn't bothered by it—just surprised. "Mission? I don't know that I'd call it a mission. I'm just looking for information on him."

Frank nodded knowingly. "I won't pry for details; I imagine whatever you're working on is quite confidential. But I'll urge you to proceed with caution."

"What do you know about him?" I leaned forward, greedy to hear Frank's knowledge before he fell into his blank abyss once more. "Have you ever encountered the Master in your work?"

"Of course not." Frank issued a light smile. "Nobody has."

"Except for the demigod," I said pointedly. "Ainsley explained how that works."

"The assassin." Frank nodded. "There are more demigods running around than you'd know out there. Don't get yourself involved with any of them, Lily."

"Assassin?"

"The demigod intending to take out the Master of Magic had trained as an assassin," Frank said. "You didn't read that far, I imagine?"

"I haven't gotten a chance to finish the article," I said apologetically. "It's a lot of information. How does one know if they're dealing with a demigod?"

"Well, they're supposed to be registered with MAGIC, Inc." Ainsley said. "It's the law to report a birth with mythical bloodlines."

"We mustn't forget that all laws exist for a reason. This particular one has been broken many times." Frank shot his daughter a serious look. "See, most demigods consider it discrimination that they have to register, so many don't. It's easy enough for them to fly under the radar."

I tried a new tactic. "How would one go about finding the gods?"

"One *doesn't*," Frank said firmly. "It's best we keep ourselves out of their business."

"What if it's *my* business to find the Master of Magic?"

Frank exhaled a large sigh and offered a glance at his wife. "More coffee, please?"

She nodded, patted his head, and then flicked her finger and the coffee pot floated in from the next room over.

When it arrived, Frank poured himself a cup in the delicate china. "If you're sincerely after the Master of Magic, the Keeper will already know you. The only way to the colony of the gods, and therefore the Master of Magic, is through him."

"He has been most impossible to find."

Frank laughed. "That's the point." He emptied creamer into his cup until it was milky white, and then he swirled it with a spell and a swish of his finger. "The Keeper will lead you to himself once he decides you're worthy. *If* he decides you're worthy."

"And how—"

"I don't know much more than that, I'm afraid," Frank said. "Just that my only experiences with the ancient gods have been dicey at best. I sincerely recommend being careful, Lily."

"I will be."

"I do suppose, however, that if anyone could find the Keeper, it'd be you."

"What makes you say that?"

Frank shrugged. "You have a peculiar set of powers. I'm not sure any of us truly understand what exactly you're capable of—least of all you."

I bowed my head and accepted the pot of coffee as Mrs. Shaw floated it by me. I truly hated when people referenced my powers; it left me feeling awkward and unsure of an appropriate response. Most people meant their words like a compliment, but to me, it felt like one I didn't deserve. I'd been *born* with this; I hadn't created it myself.

"Now, there's an interesting idea," Frank said, sounding fluffy and far away, as if he were drifting off again. "Interesting indeed."

"What's interesting, dad?" Ainsley prompted. "What idea?"

"Wouldn't it be something if Lily trained with the Master?" Frank's eyes sparkled at the thought. "Just think. One of the greatest minds in magic joined with one of the most powerful witches in the world. *Unstoppable*."

"Oh, I'm not powerful," I said. "I mostly Mix up little drinks. I'm not out there saving lives like the Rangers or protecting the world like your daughter."

"But you will be powerful," Frank said with startling confidence. "You have no idea, Miss Locke. If you ever do find him, promise me you'll learn all that you can."

I couldn't look away from his eyes. I merely nodded. Then just as quickly as before, Frank slipped into a happy state of confusion and dinner concluded. Ainsley excused us from the table with her voice pinched in pain. We stood, and she led me to the guest room once more.

"Sorry about that," she said as she let me in. "Nothing like my dad putting the weight of the world on your shoulders, huh?"

"Oh, your parents are great. I really appreciate them letting me spend the night here."

"You made their *year*." Ainsley gave a good-natured eye roll. "My mom was bursting at the seams with excitement, and my dad..." She took in a deeper breath. "Those were incredibly long lucid periods for him. It was really good for him to focus, so I owe you a thank you. I think you helped him, and I sincerely mean that."

"I didn't do a thing." Embarrassment nudged at me, blooming red onto my cheeks. "He's the one who helped *me*."

"I don't know if he helped anything at all, but he does enjoy discussing his work. He always does better when he has a problem to work on—that's why he tinkers so much with human crap."

"Speaking of human crap..." I glimpsed at the bed where I'd foolishly left the papers sitting out. "Your dad wouldn't happen to have a computer around here, would he?"

"Three of them." Ainsley shrugged her shoulders. "I don't understand it, but he loves 'em." She left the room and returned a few minutes later with an old model. "Will this work?"

"Perfect." I accepted the laptop and hugged it to my chest, then gave Ainsley a squeeze with one arm. "Thank you."

"Night, boss," she said. "See you in the morning. Better get you back on the island bright and early before Ranger X comes hunting me down."

After Ainsley left, I smuggled the computer under the covers with me and pulled the copied files closer. It'd been a while since I'd worked in a traditional human office, and I found my typing came back clunkier and slower than I'd anticipated.

It took me a few minutes to plug the names of both men who'd been arrested for my mother's murder into a few search engines. The first man—Adam Sherman—was easy to find. He'd been dead for over twenty years. He'd died in prison after being convicted for my mother's murder.

The other man, Samuel Palmer, was more difficult to pinpoint in my searches. Eventually, I landed on a small article in an independent news website that covered his release from prison just over a year earlier—he must have been released just after I'd been taken to The Isle. From what I could tell, he didn't have much in the way of family or friends, nor could I find any current address or phone number for him.

I gave in finally and muttered a version of my previous Map Maker spell over the computer, hoping that a little magic mixed with technology might work. I'd never bewitched electronics before and wasn't sure it was possible, but it *probably* couldn't hurt. Probably being the key word.

I held my breath until the results kicked back something positive. It wasn't much, but it was an address. An old address, but the only one available. It appeared Samuel Palmer hadn't ventured far most of his life; this record listed him in the same Minneapolis neighborhood where he'd grown up.

As I shut off the computer and pushed the files into a more secure location at the bottom of my magicked book bag, I was left to ponder Samuel's current whereabouts. I shut off the light and pulled the fluffy comforter tight to my chest, wondering where I'd go if I'd gotten out of a twenty-four-year stint in prison and had nothing to my name.

Would I go somewhere completely new?

Or would I try to pick up my life where it'd left off?

I drifted to sleep while my brain churned through the makings of a plan for the next morning. It would surely be a Hail Mary, a shot in the dark, a prayer for blind luck, but it was better than nothing. The files had given me a name—the name of the man who'd served a short lifetime for the murder of my mother.

Trinket and I needed closure. I needed to hear the confession from his lips.

And if, in fact, he was innocent...how had a human been locked up for the murder of a witch?

Chapter 14

"WE'RE SAD TO SEE YOU go," Ainsley's mother said as I stood on the front steps of the Shaw family home the next morning. "Are you sure you aren't due for a vacation? You're leaving so soon, and we'd love to have you stay for just a bit longer."

"Ma, she's in the middle of a huge mission," Ainsley said. "Leave her alone."

"Sorry, we just *love* to see Ainsley with a friend." Mrs. Shaw winked at me. "It's been so long since she had a real nice girlfriend. That Millie is wonderful, don't get me wrong, but she's always been so interested in books!"

"Mom, I'm right here, and there's nothing wrong with Millie," Ainsley said. "Also, I work a lot! *Hello*, that doesn't leave a ton of time for *people* friends. Also, you neglected to mention my boyfriend."

"Praise be, she found a man who'll put up with her crazy schedule," Mrs. Shaw said making praying hands toward the heavens. "I never thought I'd see the day. Anyway, I'd better let you get going. Frank, let's go inside and leave the girls to chat."

"Actually, do you have a second, Lily?" Frank asked, stepping forward. "I wanted to ask you about a few human things quickly. Ainsley, don't yell at me darling, it'll just take a second. I'll walk her to the bus stop."

Ainsley looked to me for permission, and I nodded. "Sure, Mr. Shaw, no problem."

"Be careful, dad," Ainsley said, and I could see the worry in her eyes. "I'm going after you if you're not back in twenty minutes. And if we have to trace you to Florida again because you took a wrong turn and got lost, I will be royally pissed."

Frank let out a big laugh, an action that put smiles on both his wife and daughter's faces. "I'll be back. I've got my tracker on." He raised his wrist to show off a small device that looked like a watch. "Shall we head out, Lily?"

"Great! I've never actually taken the magic bus," I admitted. "It'll be nice to have someone show me the ropes."

After one last round of hugs and a bag of cookies for the road, Frank and I set off at an easy pace down the street. We walked in silence for half a block before Frank wrinkled his nose.

"Can I help you with something?" I asked. "I'm guessing you don't want to talk about human things."

"I wasn't convincing with that excuse, huh?" Frank asked, though it seemed rhetorical. "Yes, actually, I do need to talk to you about something. *This,* actually." Frank pulled a small baggie from his pocket. Inside, there were beautiful little ferns, dainty and perfectly preserved. "They aren't as fresh as I would've liked, but they should do the trick."

I sucked in a breath as I took the bag from him. "Are these Forgotten Ferns? Where did you find them?"

"Better if you don't know."

"You didn't have to do this, Mr. Shaw—er, Frank. How much do I owe you for the trouble?"

"Nothing. It's my absolute pleasure. Maybe just, *ah*, keep this quiet from my wife. I don't think she'd much like knowing I have a little stash of herbs in the attic closet."

"Of course."

"There's one more thing, Lily." Frank reached into his pocket and pulled out a scrappy little piece of paper, dirtied and old. He handed it over. "This is yours. I didn't realize it until late last night."

"What is it?"

"Someone entrusted it to me a long time ago," he said. "They told me I'd know when I needed it."

"Are you sure it's meant for me?" I stared at the sheet of paper and saw what appeared to be an address. The letters and numbers meant nothing to me. "What is this for?"

"I'm not exactly sure." Frank said. "But the previous Keeper entrusted this to me before he retired."

"You *knew* the Keeper?"

"I met him once while I was working. I believe this is a place where you might find him. He instructed me to never make copies, never memorize this, and never give it away...until the right time."

"How do you know this is the right time?"

"Because there's not a doubt in this mind." Frank tapped his head. "And these days, my mind is full of fog and doubts. Believe me, Lily, he meant it for you."

I swallowed, tucking the Forgotten Ferns into my book bag and slipping the piece of paper into my pocket. "I don't know how I can ever repay you."

Frank frowned. "I don't know what you'll find at the end of this journey, but it's my duty to help you if I can. You know, us Guardians never truly retire." He gave me a wink in conclusion. "It really has been my pleasure, Lily. I wish you the best of luck."

A tremor of emotion shivered over my skin. I tried to thank him again, but none of the words on my lips were sufficient, so I merely nodded.

"Ah, here we are—don't worry, the humans can't see it." Frank pointed to a supernatural sign above my head that read: *THIS WAY TO THE ISLE*. "Goodbye, Lily."

ONCE AINSLEY'S FATHER left me at the bus stop, I waited an appropriate amount of time before stepping back from the curb and taking a closer look at the Forgotten Ferns. When a bus arrived flashing a matching sign that read **THIS WAY TO THE ISLE**, I quietly slunk away as a few witches climbed down the stairs and emptied onto the sidewalk.

I watched from behind a nearby building as one witch hurried away from the bus dragging a briefcase while another paused to light up a cigarette on the sidewalk. I waited until the bus drove away accompanied by a flash of light and a loud bang, wincing as it careened around a telephone pole.

Once the bus chugged out of sight, I kept hidden for what I considered a sufficient amount of time while the newly departed passengers scattered in their respective directions.

I continued to scan the area as I muttered a Map Maker spell onto my palm and input a new address. The address I'd found on the laptop last night; the address of the only living man who could tell me the truth about my mother's murder.

I knew from my previous Googling that the address wasn't far, so I opted for the brisk half hour walk instead of using public transportation. The sun was shining and the breeze was cool, but my fast pace kept me plenty warm. By the time I reached my destination, my heart was pumping and my nerves were at full tilt.

I studied the dingy building in a small little bubble of Minneapolis, not quite in the downtown hustle and bustle, but in a tiny little community that fed off the lights, the action, the city itself.

I suspected rightfully that the apartment complex in question would be quiet this time of day; it was the sort of place where people rolled into bed in the wee hours of the morning and emerged only after most of the workforce had put in a full day at the office.

A quick Lock Lifter got me through the front entrance, but it was there that I stopped short. A woman stood checking her mail, and I realized I'd dumbly forgotten to peep through the door and make sure the lobby was empty.

The woman turned, shooting me a curious expression. When she didn't appear to recognize me, she frowned. She held a set of keys in her hand much too big for any one person, and with a gasp of both horror and surprise, I realized she was likely the landlady.

"What are you doing? You don't live here." She hesitated, scanning me up and down. "You're awake far too early to live in this building, and it looks like you've got yourself a proper paying job, which also counts you out as a potential tenant. Are you a cop?"

"No, not at all," I said, relieved she hadn't questioned my Lock Lifter spell. "I'm actually looking for someone."

"I'm sorry." A protective shield seemed to settle over the landlady. "I don't know him."

"I didn't say—"

She locked the last mailbox with a resounding thud. "I don't know him, don't know her, don't know whatever or whoever it is you're looking for."

"Please, Miss—"

"Hubick," she filled in. "What don't you understand, lady? Unless you've got a warrant, I'm not talking. My name would be mud if word got out I ratted on my tenants."

"I'm trying to help," I said, struggling with an idea. "My cousin got out of prison, and I just heard the news recently. I figured he must be hurting for money, and I want to help him out."

Miss Hubick brushed a stray strand of black hair from her face then crossed her arms. "Well, ain't *you* a Mother Theresa."

"He was convicted of killing a woman. He didn't do it, Miss Hubick—I know he didn't. Life's thrown my cousin a few hardballs, so when I heard he'd been released, I had to see if I could help him out.

Maybe see that he gets whatever pieces of his life together that he has left."

Miss Hubick stared piercingly at me, and for a moment, I wondered if she had some sort of magical tendency. Her gaze went straight through, chilling me to the bone. Only when she shifted her weight did the spell break. She was *incredibly* perceptive for a human.

"Which one?"

"Which, er..." I hesitated. "Excuse me?"

"There's more than one man convicted of murder living here," she said, giving a nonchalant shrug of her shoulders. "Which one's yours?"

"Oh, um..." I couldn't help the slight sheen of perspiration at her casual mention of those unsightly statistics. "His name is Samuel Palmer."

To my surprise, her face brightened. "He was one of my favorites."

"Was?"

"Lady, he got out of prison almost two years ago. He's long gone. I liked the guy, but if someone doesn't pay rent, they're outta my house. I got a mouth to feed. *Mine*. And he wasn't working, so he couldn't pay. My hands were tied."

"Do you know where he went?"

She gave a wry smile. "This ain't a Christmas-card sending sort of place, lady. People don't leave forwarding addresses. What'd you say your name was, anyway?"

"Um, Zinifred," I said, blurting out a horrible nickname my grandmother used for Zin. "My name is Ainsley Zinifred."

"What was your mother smoking when she named you?"

I winced. If I wanted to play undercover, I'd better come up with a better cover, and quickly. "It's been a tough life with that name."

"Your mother was on Sam's side of the family?"

I gave a noncommittal shrug. "Any thoughts on where he might've gone?"

"Lady, Zinnyfreddy, whatever—do me a favor. *Next* time you go making up a name, will you make it something I can pronounce?"

Flushed with embarrassment, I could only nod. "Look, I know you might not know where he went, but do you have any guesses?"

With a long sigh, the woman considered. "I suppose the first place he would've gone is down around Filbert Street. There's a group of guys that hang around there. Mostly ex-cons that don't have anywhere else to go."

The thought of wandering into an area of men or women convicted of horrible crimes had my stomach churning and the blood draining from my face.

"Yeah," Miss Hubick warned. "I wouldn't go down there alone, pretty little thing like you."

The note had an element of crassness to it, almost a challenge. I convinced myself not to panic. After all, I had magical powers, and the ex-cons didn't. With any luck, I'd dance right in and dance right out, practically unseen.

"I see you sizing the idea up, and I'm warning you..." She shook her head. "I wouldn't go down there. You got money you want to give to Sammy?" With a cackle, she held out her hand. "I can watch it for you."

"No, no, I think that's fine," I said, backing away. "I'll get my boyfriend to go with me."

It had become more and more clear over the course of our conversation that Miss Hubick was well-suited for her job. The woman could handle herself. She was sharp as a tack and armed with wits and survival instincts: a combination to be admired on some other day.

"Smart idea to bring your man with you." The landlady's eyes fixed on me like a hawk as I backed away. "Hey, Fake Zinnyfreddy—one more thing before you go."

I hesitated. "Yes?"

"Why do you *really* want Sammy? He's a good guy. You hurt him, the others will get you. They protect each other on Filbert. I know you're not a cop, but there's something weird about you."

"I'm not a cop," I said, ignoring the weirdness bit. "And I do have money for Sammy. I want to help him. I have to talk to him."

"Oh, shit. You want to see if he did it."

I didn't bother to deny it. Pulling the door open, I stepped through and made to shut it, but Miss Hubick's foot blocked the doorway. She'd moved like lightning across the room.

"I can tell you this, sweetcheeks," she said in soft tones. "They said Sammy killed that woman. They're wrong. I don't know who did it, but Sammy lived here for ten years before that, and he wouldn't hurt a fly."

"Why are you telling me this?"

She hesitated, then shrugged. "I liked having him as a tenant. He didn't deserve what he got."

I pursed my lips and gave a nod in her direction.

"I think you're like me," she continued. "You don't think he did it. If you can set his life a little on the right track...well, I think that'd be the right thing to do."

"Thank you. I appreciate—"

Apparently, Miss Hubick had used up her last ounce of niceties for the day because clearly she was done talking. The door slammed shut in my face.

"Great," I said speaking to the wooden panel. "Nice to meet you, too."

It *had* been nice to meet Miss Hubick. She was an odd soul and an intriguing woman, but she just might have given me what I needed to find Samuel Palmer.

"Filbert Street," I muttered into my palm as I resumed the Map Maker spell.

Since I didn't have an exact address, this was the best I could do. Unfortunately, Filbert Street was quite long. It ran the length of the city, though I suspected the *down and dirty* part I was looking for wouldn't be too difficult to find. And so, I resumed my hike.

As I moved, I quickly popped onto the Comm to let Ranger X know I wouldn't be back until later this evening. He wasn't available, so I left a brief memo at HQ for him to retrieve on his next break.

I found myself thinking of him as I walked. I sincerely hoped he hadn't worked through the night again; the man would run himself ragged, something I'd worried about ever since he'd been taken down by a bout of Lumiette. It was harder to keep control of his powers on little to no sleep. The last thing he needed was a flare-up in public.

Thankfully, I'd gotten a good night's rest as a guest at the Shaw house. With an extra pep in my step from a full eight hours in which I'd slept like the dead, I continued toward Filbert.

My last chance to find Samuel Palmer.

Chapter 15

EIGHT HOURS OF SLEEP wasn't enough to sustain me for a full day of traipsing the city. The first few hours I'd spent wandering around Filbert Street had led me to a whole lot of nothing, and by the end of it, my feet were beginning to drag.

When the sun hit its peak and started its descent, I grabbed a sandwich from a sketchy deli on the nearest corner and inhaled it quickly. I wouldn't call it delicious, but it contained calories, and I needed energy if I was to continue.

I ducked back into the store to throw the trash away, a new idea brewing as the bell tinkled over my head. If Sammy did live in the area, he'd have to get food from somewhere.

"Can I help you?" The guy behind the counter was big, burly, and bored. "Cash only."

"I, uh, just bought a sandwich from here." I pointed to the garbage where my wrapper sat on top. "I have a question, actually."

"You need a soda?" he leered. "Bag of chips?"

Apparently, this was a neighborhood where information didn't come free. "Sure. Diet Coke," I said, reaching into my bookbag where I had precious little human money left. "Do you know a guy named Sammy?"

The clerk looked at the bottle of pop. "That's all you want?"

With a hefty sigh, I added a bag of Twizzlers to the mix. "How about that?"

"Yeah, I know Sammy."

I hesitated, then added some M&M's as well. "Does he live around here?"

"He does."

I added a postcard on top of that. Any more candy, and I'd have more cavities than I could count. "I'm sorry, I'm running low on cash. He's family, and I need to find him."

The cashier rang me up, looking somewhat appeased by my explanation. "He got out of prison, oh, I don't know—over a year ago at least. I saw him around here last Christmas, so I know it was at least that long ago."

"And now?"

"Now, he wanders. He's a Filberter for sure—lives and scrounges in this area. Makes his home with that pack down by the train station."

I frowned. "Do you know where he is now?"

"Didn't you hear me lady? He's a wanderer. Nobody knows exactly where he is. The closest information you're gonna get just came out of my mouth."

I swiped the candy into my bookbag and left a ten-dollar bill behind as a tip. It was my last bill greater than a one. I tore open the pack of Twizzlers and popped one into my mouth while I cracked the Diet Coke open in my other hand.

Down by the train station. I started in that direction. It wasn't a whole lot to go on, but it was a start. As I walked, another idea dawned on me. So far, I'd only ever input *addresses* into my Map Maker enchantment.

When I'd initially learned the spell, Gus had explained that most witches and wizards wore a small array of spells across their body—like a spritz of a perfume—called a Spell Splash. Basic protection that would foil a simple tracking spell. In fact, I owned a similar potion and wore it daily.

But humans wouldn't have a wink of protective spells around them due to the nature of their kind. I decided it'd be worth a try, and instead of giving an address to my spell, I spoke Sammy's name as discreetly as possible toward my palm.

Nothing happened. I watched as the Map Maker struggled to register the name, the worry building with each passing second. By the time I looked up, my heart thumped hard against my chest and blood pounded against my ears.

After *all this*, I might not find Samuel Palmer. The idea stung as it settled into place. While I'd gotten a few lucky breaks right off the bat from people who knew him, it was now obvious he didn't have any sort of stable home base. *A wanderer*, the clerk had said. If he'd wandered too far, and I couldn't find him...all of my efforts would be for naught.

I gasped with relief as Samuel Palmer's name registered with the spell. He popped up as a moving target just a few blocks away, and my blood pressure spiked with adrenaline in response.

I hiked up my bookbag and set after the blinking dot; I didn't chance a break in eye contact from my palm. I was determined not to lose him now that I'd come *this close* to getting answers.

I scrambled the last few blocks in what seemed like a flash. Finally, when the slow-moving dot came within speaking distance, I chanced a look up and saw a man in a heavy jacket, ratted old pants, and a surprisingly clean-shaven face.

"Hello," I ventured, holding up a hand in greeting. "Are you Sammy Palmer?"

"Who wants to know?" His eyes were of such a pale blue they appeared washed out. As if they'd once gleamed bright and now subsisted on something less.

"Me." I stopped, gasping for breath as I shook the spell from my palm. "I'm looking for you."

I stopped dead as his gaze landed on mine and we watched each other. It was Sammy, alright. His photo was plastered all over the borrowed files in my backpack. Those eyes gleamed back from the mugshot. *Those eyes* might have watched my mother die.

"You should know who I am," I said, my voice low. "My name is Lily."

His eyebrows pinched together. "You're too pretty to know who I am."

"What about my mother? Was she too pretty, too?"

Concern etched over his face. "Look, lady, I ain't your father, if that's what you're wondering. And even if I was, don't you think it's a little late to be looking for money? You're a full-grown adult."

"You went to prison for the murder of my mother, Millie Banks," I said, giving her human alias. I wasn't sure if that was the name she had used while alive, or if that was simply the name the police had slapped on her file in order to close her case. "*Now* do you recognize me?"

"Where were you during the trial?" he asked, then calculated my age. "You must've been just a babe."

I stepped toward him, surprisingly bold considering he'd been let out of prison a mere two years earlier. "You're pretty good at math for a murderer."

"I didn't do it."

"What are you talking about?"

"Lady, I didn't do it." He looked worn, spent, maybe, but completely unafraid. "I know the charges against me, and I know the truth."

"How can you say that? You served over half your life in prison for the crime, and you expect me to believe you're innocent?" I *had* to push him. Each passing second had me believing the police had caught and punished the wrong man, but I had to know for certain. I had to see if he'd break. "You made me an *orphan*."

"Why would I lie about it now?" He raised his arms on either side of his body. "I served my time. I'm a free man now, whole lot of good that's doing me. I could confess to you, and they can't touch me. Double jeopardy."

I bit my lip, studying him. "Then tell me the truth. We're talking about my mother's murder!"

"How *dare* you come here accusing me?" His eyes went flat. "Look, lady, I'm sorry about your mother. In fact, I'd wager a bet that nobody's sorrier than me—*yourself* included."

"That's impossible. She was my mother."

"You got to live your life, didn't you?" Sammy gestured to himself. "Look at me. I'm on the cusp of retirement age. I was in my prime the night I got arrested, did you think about that? I was considering settling down, marrying, having a family. I'd just gotten a job that paid me regular. I even had my eye on a gal," he said, cautiously.

I crossed my arms, waited.

"You somehow figured life out even without your mother. Look at you—you're well dressed, clean, you even got good skin—" He ran a hand over his face, looking more and more exhausted. "Hell, you probably ate three square meals yesterday. Me?" He gave a squeaky laugh that bordered on hysteria. "I don't know if I'll make it out alive from one day to the next. I haven't eaten a warm meal in over a week. The lady I had my eye on won't talk to me after I missed rent because guess what? I'm a washed up ex-con. *Nobody* wants to hire me."

I took a step back as he edged closer. Though my gut told me he was innocent, he looked every bit the murderer in his dirty old clothes and determined expression. The glassy look in his eyes accentuated the red lines there.

"I gave all of that up for *what*? A crime I didn't commit!" He roared the last words, his entire body shaking. It took him a long second to calm, and when he finally did, he spoke softly. "If I killed that woman, I'd tell you. I had never seen Millie Banks in my life—not until they showed me a picture of her dead body."

"Then why were you arrested?"

"Me and Sherman were both arrested."

"Adam Sherman."

"Yeah, we was hanging out that night. He was looking to score a bit of coin..." Sammy peered at me through his lashes. "Figure I can tell you since it's been so long now."

"I'm listening. I just want the truth—I'm not here for anything more than that."

"Adam was a little hopped up on something...er, *special* that night. He made a stupid choice to nab a lady's purse, but it wasn't your mother's. The woman whose things he swiped—well, she was a black lady. Really dark-skinned and pretty and curvy. It can't have been your mother. Millie Banks was white as a ghost and thin as a rail—I couldn't have been more surprised the day they showed us her picture. I never seen that woman before in my *life.*"

"Then how were you sentenced to over twenty years in prison?"

"They have security footage of Adam nabbing this woman's purse a block away from where the murder occurred. They figured we went on a bender looking for money, attempted a second mugging that night that went belly up, and then we killed your mother and ditched the scene."

"You're telling me that's not how it happened."

"Of course not. I've never murdered anyone. I was trying to stop Adam from doing anything else stupid. I didn't appreciate him breaking the law while I was in his company. Like I said, I had my eye on a gal, the landlady, and she's not a big fan of convicts."

"Miss Hubick."

"Ah, so that's how you found me." His eyes flicked in my direction. "She must have liked you if she talked to you."

"We understood each other."

He blinked, as if this cemented his own decision to share his take on the story. "Anita doesn't take crap from anyone, least of all me." He paused for a forlorn smile, probably picturing the stern Miss Hubick. "I wish...forget it. Doesn't matter what I wish."

"Mr. Palmer—"

"Sammy."

"Sammy," I started again, raised my hands in a relenting gesture, then let them fall to my sides. "I'm really sorry."

"You believe me?"

I nodded.

He seemed indifferent to learn this, as if the answer didn't really matter. I supposed it didn't since he'd already served the time. If he was innocent and knew it, there wasn't all that much more to be afraid of—the worst had already happened.

"It's a waste of a life, you know? Two lives." Sammy offered a blank smile. "Then again, I suppose better someone like me get thrown into prison than someone like you. I wasn't—how do they say it politely?—I wasn't *going anywhere*. I had fallen in with the *wrong crowd*. It was just such a *shame*. Heard lots of them buzzwords that made it easy for them to justify locking me up."

"Them?"

"The lawyers, the judges, all those people in their fancy suits and shiny briefcases. Nobody listened to me, least of all my own suit. The lawyer they assigned me was a moron. I considered firing him and defending myself, and the only law I know is from the movies."

I couldn't hold back a quiet laugh which surprised both of us—me most of all. I'd expected to come here and, at worst, find a horrible murderer roaming free on the streets. At best, I thought I'd get confirmation that the man hadn't done it. Never in a million years had I expected to feel sympathy for Sammy, and even the beginnings of an oddly forged bond.

"Look, I'm really sorry," I said. "I don't know why, exactly, but I'm sure you didn't do it. And it's awful that the law didn't find her true killer, and you were punished instead."

I didn't explain further because I couldn't. There was no good way to tell Samuel Palmer that I suspected witches or wizards had been behind my mother's murder, and when push came to shove, human cops were no match for magic.

"Yeah, I'm sorry too," he said, dryly. "I am sorry about your mother. It's just a little hard for me to sound sincere when two people lost their lives that day."

"Your life isn't over." I swung my bookbag down and withdrew all the candy I'd purchased, along with any remaining cash I had left. "Here. I wish I had more for you, but this is all I have."

Sammy frowned as he took the items from me. "This is all you have?"

"I know, it's not even real food, but..."

He looked up, a kinship behind his bloodshot eyes. "Thank you. I wish I could help more with your mom's case, but I have no clue who offed her or why. I *wish* I did, believe me—it would've saved me a lot of time and heartache."

"For whatever it's worth," I said, backing away with a touch of a smile. "I don't think Miss Hubick's as *over you* as you might think."

He glanced down at himself. "Look at me. I can't go back to her now."

"It's not about what's on the outside."

He gave a dark chuckle. "It's not like I have all that much to offer on the inside, either. I'm washed out, Miss...what was your name?"

"Lily."

"Miss Lily." He extended a hand and shook mine. "Best of luck. I'm sorry I can't help you more."

"Best of luck to you, Sammy."

He covered my hand with his much, much larger one, and the warmth and sentiment behind his grasp made me forget the reason I'd come here in the first place. It wasn't until he'd let go and disappeared around a bend in the alley that I looked up and truly saw around me, realizing hints of stars pecked through the early evening glow. Evening had snuck up on me, and I needed to get off Filbert Street.

The sun set early around this time of year, and my lunch had been a late one. The entire day had passed in a blur, and though I hadn't learned much new information about my mother's murder, I was confident on one front: *Trinket's theory was correct*. And, since the suspects who'd been convicted hadn't committed the crime, the real murderer was still out there.

On that somber note, a sudden itchiness slithered over my skin; I recognized the feeling of watchful eyes following my every move. As I hesitated, I noticed a movement behind a dingy curtain, and the clatter of a trash can tipping over nearby. While I hadn't felt frightened on Filbert Street during the day, the night brought with it far more terrors, and all of Miss Hubick's warnings came back in a rush.

I backed out of the alleyway and continued on the street. I made it a few blocks before I realized I was headed in the wrong direction. Glancing at my palm, I muttered the words to the bus station where Frank had dropped me earlier. Another bus to The Isle left within the hour, and I could make it if I hurried.

Seeing a U-turn blinking on my palm, I flipped around to head in the direction from which I'd come. A few steps later, the itchiness returned. I hadn't looked up from my palm, partly in fear, partly in concentration. That turned out to be my biggest mistake.

By the time I looked up, there were at least five of them. Four big, burly men and one skinny little woman with mangy hair creeping toward me. I thought I spied a sixth figure in the shadows, but I was too busy with the first five to pay much attention to anything else.

"Hey, pretty, pretty girl," the woman cackled. "What were you talking to Sammy about? We saw you handing out some goodies, darling, and we want to play, too."

"I don't have any more goodies." I cinched my bookbag tighter subconsciously. I didn't have any money, but I did have a slew of valuable library books as well as my Forgotten Ferns. "I'm sorry. I wish I could help you, but—"

"Don't lie, precious dolly," the woman said. "We're your friends. You and I, we women have to stick together, don't we?"

I glanced behind me, but the sixth shadow had solidified into another figure, bigger than the rest, and he inched closer from the rear.

"I just got lost around here, er, looking for my boyfriend," I said. "He's a cop. He's supposed to meet me around here soon."

"Whaddya think, Binky?" The woman looked to the large man behind me. "Is she lying?"

The man referred to as *Binky*—the largest man of all—gave a positive grunt, and the woman slunk toward me like a rabid fox. She reached for my hair, swirling the ponytail around her finger while I stayed stock still, trying not to show my fear. I sensed an animalistic instinct in her, and there was no doubt she'd latch onto the first display of weakness.

"What a pretty little doll," she said again, surveying me. She jerked her head toward the huge man looming behind me. "Know why I call him Binky?"

"I have no idea," I said, struggling not to quiver in his shadow. "It doesn't seem to fit."

"Because that was the name of my dolly," she said with a fierce laugh. "And big Binky here is just an old teddy bear. He protects me, just like my little dolly did. Do you know what else?"

I shook my head. My palms grew sweaty, and my chest felt on the verge of cracking with the rate my heart was pounding.

"I like to collect dolls," she said, curling a finger under my chin. "And you're a pretty little thing."

The woman was nuts. Absolutely crazy, but she also seemed to be the leader of the gang. I *had* to go for her first. I had a decision to make. My first option was to forget about privacy laws and bust out magic in public—and suffer the ensuing consequences. My second choice was to die.

Pretty easy decision, in retrospect.

I immediately launched into an incantation with gusto. I didn't care who heard, who understood. MAGIC, Inc. certainly couldn't find fault with self-defense, and even if they did, I couldn't care less. Without a spell, I might not have a life to defend.

The spell grew in my palm, a blinding light I tried to hide for as long as possible. I shielded it from the woman as she circled me, studied me like a designer might study her muse.

Binky noticed it first. "Car," he grunted. "Her hand."

At first, I thought he was mentioning a vehicle, and I chanced a look behind me.

But the woman responded to him, as if it were a nickname. "What is *that*?!"

Her screech brought me back to attention, and I swung a hand toward her, muttering the final words that'd launch the spell. However, mere milliseconds before I could release the magic from my body, concentration was ripped from me again, this time by brute force.

And...*fur*.

A snarling, beautiful, terrifying jungle cat knocked me from my feet and sent me skidding to the curb. As I hurried to stand, I watched as Zin went straight for the woman's throat. She pulled back from the kill shot at the last second, letting her claw gently graze the woman's face.

Even so, a gentle graze from a jaguar is a dangerous thing. A line of red bloomed from the woman's cheek, across her forehead. The pack of men watched as Zin circled their leader, sniffing the scent of her blood.

Crazy or not, the woman clearly wasn't an idiot. She knew when to run.

"Binky!" the woman screamed. "Get me out of here!"

The monstrous man looked between Zin and the woman and shook his head, just once. Zin's golden eyes dared him to step forward.

The woman struggled to get out from under Zin, but the fight was too easy for the latter. Zin kept the woman pinned to the ground, her posture just *begging* the men to step forward in a rescue attempt. To end things, she let out a terrifying growl that sent even Binky scattering to the dark recesses of the city.

Only once the men were completely gone did Zin back away and allow the woman to wobble up and stumble toward the alley. She disappeared into blackness while Zin licked her paws and watched, her posture proud.

A few minutes passed in which I caught my breath on the sidewalk, trembling with relief, fighting back frustration and all-around confusion. I'd just begun to see straight when I looked up to find the jaguar sauntering deeper into the alley.

"Zin! Leave her alone—she's not worth it," I called, scrambling to my feet and launching after the sleek figure. I couldn't keep up with Zin in her current form, but I had to try. I worried she'd take things too far with the human, and I couldn't let that happen.

"Chill, Lily—I wasn't going to *eat* her." Zin's voice tinkled from the depths of the alley. She gave a pleasant smile as she shook off a few stray black hairs while stepping out of the black shadows behind the garbage bins. "She tasted disgusting. Got a whiff of her when I tickled her face—don't worry, I didn't *really* hurt her. It won't even leave a mark."

"What were you *thinking*?"

"*Hello* to you, too," she retorted. Zin glanced down at her nails, seemingly annoyed they hadn't yet retracted. "Ugh, stupid lady. I have blood under my fingernails."

"Zin, what *were* you thinking? I had control over the situation. What are you even doing here?"

"You had *what* exactly under control? The lady looked like she was going to eat you. She was a nut, Lily. You're lucky I was here."

"I don't mean to sound ungrateful," I said through gritted teeth. "So, I'll say thank you, first."

Zin finally caught the tremor of anger in my voice. "Whoa, girl. I was here independent of you. I caught your scent while I was prowling around as an alley cat and figured I should check the situation out. I saw what was happening, switched into a jaguar, and you know the rest."

"Yes, I do. But I was ready to handle the situation, Zin." I raised a hand and showed her the glimmer of the spell that lingered in my palm. "I could have taken her on my own."

"Sor-ry," Zin said, still sounding too casual for my liking. "Next time some psycho woman is trying to recruit you to be her *dolly*, I'll make sure to pull my punches and watch."

"That's not what I mean. Thank you. I appreciate your help, but...I'm confused. What are you doing on the mainland in the first place? Did Ranger X put you up to this? Were you *spying* on me?"

Zin's eyes blinked wider in surprise. "What are you talking about? Or course not. Why would I spy on you? I was working on my...er, my mission."

"Yeah, this secret mission I can't know anything about. I thought you were looking after Poppy, but it doesn't make a whole lot of sense why you'd leave her unprotected on The Isle and turn up here, in the exact alley that I'm in, at *this* exact moment."

"I told you I was following a scent!"

"Whose scent is around here except for mine and Binky's and the rest of the psycho posse?"

"Binky?"

I just shook my head. "I don't blame you for tailing me, Zin. I'm sure you were just following orders, but at least tell me the truth."

"I wasn't following you," she reiterated. "Come on, Lily. You have to believe me."

"I need to head home," I said on a sigh. "I've been off the island for almost two days, and it's time I return. I'm going to hop on the bus and take the ferry. Are you coming with me?"

"No, I have business here to attend to," Zin said sullenly. "I'm not watching over you, Lily. I'm sorry I stepped in and interfered."

"Yeah, me too," I said, then realized how childish I sounded. "Look, I really am sorry. I just...I wish Ranger X wouldn't do these things. I can take care of myself."

"He loves you," Zin said, frowning. "He's just watching over you because he doesn't want you to get hurt."

"By sticking my cousin on my every move?"

Zin realized her error as she shook her head. "I don't mean *me*. I already told you that Ranger X had nothing to do with this—I wasn't tailing you."

"Yeah, sure."

"Fine. You know what? I don't have to convince you. I'm sorry I ruined your moment of glory. Have a good night, Lily."

It wasn't a pleasant way to end the conversation, so I forced out another apology before Zin spun away from me and morphed back into an alley cat. I debated calling after her again, but she'd already disappeared.

I had no time to linger, either—*especially* not in these parts. I needed to get back to The Isle, and the last bus left in thirty minutes. From there, it'd pop me onto a paranormal ferry that would get me home just in time to collapse into bed and start all over tomorrow.

Tomorrow, I'd apologize to Zin again, once I'd had time to think, to calm down, to face X—and to find out why he'd stuck Zin on me in an assignment that showed he doubted my training.

I set off in a huff toward the bus, not stupid enough to ignore the wave of relief and gratefulness that followed once I was situated in the uncomfortable seat. No matter what I'd told Zin in my moment of anger, I *was* lucky she had arrived when she did. Though I knew I could've taken the woman out... that still left Binky and four others. Even a witch had her limits.

With a sigh, I tipped my head against the window and left a quick Comm memo for Zin. I wondered briefly if she had reverted to her jaguar form by now to track whoever—whatever—her target might be.

"I really am sorry, Zin," I muttered into my Comm. "I'm on my way back to The Isle. Stop by the bungalow when you get in, no matter what time. I want to give you a hug and say thanks in person. I...er, I love you."

I quickly disconnected once an older gentleman with an eye patch sat down next to me. He proceeded to flip open a spell book that hummed in an annoying buzz. Letting my eyes close, I fell asleep and didn't fully wake—shuffling in a zombie state from the bus to the ferry—until I returned to the bungalow and found someone waiting for me.

Chapter 16

"YOU!" I JABBED A FINGER at Ranger X as I burst through the door. "Why didn't you tell me?"

His face had been creased in a warm smile. He looked happy.

I stopped mid-stride, my mouth parting in surprise as I took in a completely transformed storeroom. Instead of the friendly clutter of bright colored potions and vials, curtains had been hung over the shelves in a deep burgundy, shielding the mess from view. And that was just the start.

Along one wall, the fireplace glittered warmly and two candlesticks as long as my arm dripped slow wax down their sides. Along the ceiling ran strings of fairy lights, twinkling in a cheerful glow. In the center of it all sat a beautifully adorned table containing a delightful-looking dinner: steak, all varieties of side dishes, and two goblets of red wine.

Ranger X already had one of the goblets in hand, and his smile perked brighter at my surprised glare. "Of course I couldn't *tell* you about this! That'd defeat the purpose of the surprise."

"Surprise...?"

"Happy anniversary," Ranger X said, standing, crossing the room to nip my neck with a soft kiss. "We started dating a year ago."

"A year..." I gasped. Already, more than a year had passed since I'd discovered my true roots, since I'd begun the transition into my role as Mixologist, since I'd met the love of my life. "Wow, that...I'm so sorry, I hadn't realized."

"You have a lot on your mind." Ranger X pressed a gentle kiss against my forehead. "And my assistant cares about these things. Yours doesn't."

"Where is Gus, speaking of the devil?"

"I sent him home. I figured it'd be late when you got back, and I didn't want to give up a second of our alone time."

"But..." I struggled for an argument. I'd burned through the door ready for a fight, ready to confront X about setting my cousin up to follow me, only to find a gorgeous meal with an even more delectable-looking man who was all mine. "Well, wow. Thank you."

"Sit down, have a glass of wine."

"I've been traveling, X—I really need to shower and—"

"Have a sip of wine, water, something—and then shower. It'll take me a few minutes to warm up our plates. I expected you, er, some time ago."

"I'm sorry." My shoulders slipped lower, and my heartbeat felt erratic in my chest. "I forgot about our anniversary, then I came home late...I'm oh-for-two, and I'm so sorry. Did you at least get my memo?"

"Yes—I knew you'd be late. It's no big deal. Shower, relax, we have all night together. I figured we could both use a little break. You were away from me for too long, and I missed you."

"Not enough to leave the tail behind," I muttered, then continued toward the stairs. "I'll be right down."

"What?" Ranger X stiffened. "What'd you say?"

"Oh, nothing. I'm going to shower."

"Not so fast." X grasped my wrist as I attempted to spiral away. "What did you say about a tail?"

"Forget about it. I understand why you did it."

"Did what?"

"I know you set Zin on me!" My voice raised in helplessness—I didn't want to bring this up now. If only I'd kept my mouth shut.

"And no, she didn't cave and tell me, so don't blame her. This is between me and you, okay?"

Ranger X's hand tightened further, his eyes darkened. "Why would I have set Zin on you?"

"Because I was away on the mainland, and apparently you believe I can't take care of myself."

"Do you believe for one second..." Ranger X pulled me distractingly close to him, "that I think that?"

My eyes flashed. I hadn't wanted to pick this fight, but it irked me even more that he was playing dumb. "I hadn't realized it until the alley."

"What happened in the alley?"

"Zin didn't report back on my movements, yet?" I bit back the sarcasm as the fire crackled and the table filled with celebratory drinks and eats loomed before us. "Look, I'm sorry. I shouldn't be talking about this now, but it stung a little."

Ranger X's eyes gleamed. Dark, glittering piles of onyx off which the fire danced with danger. "Zin told you all of this?"

"No." My eyes pooled with tears. I wasn't only ruining my night with X, I was ruining everything. I'd ruined Zin's night—or I was about to if X believed Zin had squealed to me. "She didn't say a thing, I swear. I guessed it."

"You guessed *wrong*."

"I wish you'd just let me figure things out by myself."

"I didn't stick a tail on you, nor did I instruct Zin anywhere near the mainland. If she's there, it's on her own time or as part of a mission."

"I just assumed... are you saying that this secret mission of hers has nothing to do with me?"

Ranger X squinted. "You're a grown woman, Lily. I love you. I want to protect you more than I want to breathe. But I didn't put Zin on your trail. I didn't think I *needed* to. I thought Ainsley and Frank would be enough."

"I looked into my mother's murderers," I said. "I know I should've told you, warned you, but I knew you'd tell me not to do it."

"And why would I have told you not to pursue it?"

"Because it was dangerous and stupid and didn't lead me to anything I didn't already know."

"And Zin was there...*why*?"

"I thought you'd sent her."

"I didn't."

"Then, I guess she wasn't lying. She said she was there on a confidential mission. I just assumed..."

"You assumed her last mission was my sticking her on you like glue."

"Basically." I shrugged, feeling stupid and self-centered. "I'm sorry, I don't know why I jumped to conclusions."

"I've considered assigning you a security detail before." Ranger X crossed his arms over his chest and surveyed me. "In fact, I did during the Trials because the circumstances were extreme. However, I told you about it. I don't go out of my way to hide things from you, Lily."

"Zin was being so evasive about it. Plus, she was there in the alley at the exact right time, so I just figured that was too much of a coincidence. It's weird, isn't it?"

"Very strange." He frowned. "What happened in the alley?"

I hesitated. "I'm not sure you'd actually care to know..."

He offered me a grim smile. "I think you've gone too far to backtrack, Miss Locke. Take a seat."

There wasn't exactly an alternative to his suggestion, so I sat heavily on the bench. Ranger X came around next to me, too stiff for light-hearted conversation. When his warmth leaned against me as he sat, I pressed into it, closed my eyes, and recounted the full story.

I included bits and pieces of the chase with the blond mystery man from the police station, the Forgotten Ferns from Ainsley's father, as well as his insights into the Master of Magic. I produced the books from the library onto a nearby chair with a heavy *oomph* as some sort of corroboration of my facts.

I finished the story with my visit to Miss Hubick and Sammy, along with Zin's valiant effort to save my life in the alley. "I owe her an apology," I concluded, feeling glum. "Poor Zin."

To my surprise, Ranger X threw his head back and laughed. He roared with laughter for so long that tears leaked from his eyes when he stopped.

"What's so funny?" I asked, frustrated at his response. "I was rude to her, and immature, and I'm sorry. To you, too."

Ranger X shook his head. "You have nothing to worry about. I'm sure Zin's on top of the world."

"But—"

"She's been itching for a mission. Almost hankering for a fight. After you got into it with those..." he searched for a word to describe Car, Binky and the rest of the gang, and failed. "Those *humans*," he spat, "how'd she seem?"

"Ecstatic," I admitted. "She didn't seriously hurt anyone, and she was very responsible," I added quickly. "But she seemed on a sort of high."

"Zin was just doing her job." Ranger X winked. "I only work with the best, and Zin will have been elated she had the chance to use her skills."

"If you only work with the best, then how'd you end up with me?" I asked. "I have been ruining everything lately."

Ranger X took my chin between his hands and raised my face until I met his gaze. "Why won't you believe you're perfect?"

"Because I'm not!" I pulled back from him and threw my arms to my sides. "Why aren't you lecturing me? Why aren't you mad at me?"

"I trust you. Do I wish you'd told me what you were up to? Yes. Would I have asked you not to do it? Probably." Ranger X let out a shuddering breath. "But I don't control you. You make your own choices, Lily. If I had it my way, you'd choose to marry me, but you haven't done that yet, either."

I froze, solid.

"I'm sorry," he said quickly. "I shouldn't have said that. I know you have reasons for wanting to wait, and I respect them."

"I'm going to shower," I said. "I think I've ruined enough for today."

"Lily..."

I left, climbed the stairs and went straight into the bathroom. I let my clothes fall from my body onto the floor as I cranked up the water to the hottest it could possibly go. Even the scorch of the heat wasn't pain enough to dull my senses as I stepped under the flow of boiling water.

I halfway suspected Ranger X to climb up after me, to wash away my tears with a few words, but he didn't come. I worried then, worried I'd pushed him too far. Worried he'd given up on me. Worried that I'd reached the limits of his seemingly infinite patience.

I savored the shower, then dressed in a satin nightshirt and tugged a robe on over it. I made my way gingerly downstairs, half expecting the room to be empty.

It wasn't.

Ranger X sat very still, staring deeply into the fire, a nearly untouched glass of wine still in hand. The image moved my heart. It shook me, rocked me, broke me.

I needed the man before me more than anything in the world, and the stresses of everything else had dulled that reminder until I could barely hear it.

I could never let that happen again.

I moved toward him, a few soft steps at first until the last few broke into a jog, thumping lightly across the floor. When he saw me coming, he set down his glass of wine and opened his arms. By the time I reached him, my arms clasped around his neck and he looked into my eyes with surprise. He reacted with the strength of a lion and the ease of a gazelle as he swung me into his lap.

I straddled him in my nightgown, my robe parting open to reveal the still-warm skin of my chest from the shower. While I probably looked ragged and worn, he looked absolutely dashing. Wearing a suit of the finest material—not his work suit, I noticed, but a special one just for tonight—he positively gleamed with perfection. With beauty and loyalty and all of the incredible qualities I could ever hope for in a mate.

"I love you," I said, and it came out a sob. "I love you so much, Cannon."

He opened his arms wide as I sunk into them, and he tilted his head so I could nuzzle against his neck. The smell of him was mine, the taste of his skin as I pressed my lips against his cheek was mine. All mine.

He was mine.

"Sweet Lily." He raised a hand, pushed my hair back. His eyes, dark and dangerous and sharp, swirled hot with concern. "What's wrong?"

I sniffed, but my heart was pounding too hard, and my lungs were struggling to pull in air. My hands shook as I grasped his neck, twined my fingers through his hair, and held him steady.

"Lily?" He looked alarmed. "What's wrong? You're trembling, sweetheart. What's wrong?"

"N-nothing."

He pulled me closer to him so that every inch of me ran along every inch of him. His body was hard—his chest, his abs, his thighs. His touch was soft but ferocious, lighting my skin on fire.

"Talk to me," he murmured. "Dammit, I love you. Tell me what's wrong."

"It's just..." I hesitated, gulped.

He cinched me tighter, ran his fingers through my hair.

"If you're not sick of me yet," I said on a hiccup, then paused. "I'd really like to marry you."

Chapter 17

THE NEXT MORNING BROUGHT happy sunlight through the windows. I laid with my *fiancé*, a new and foreign term on my tongue, as we rested with carefree abandon. I watched Ranger X sleep for a few minutes, hoisting myself onto my elbow to watch him with a bright smile.

He'd never slept in so late—not since I'd known him. He'd also never slept so closely against me. Normally, we'd fall asleep cuddled together, foreheads touching, and then roll to our respective sides as slumber settled over us.

Last night, we'd slept curled together, intertwined as one. Waking to kiss, to caress, to hold one another. To simply look into the other's eyes and smile, to wonder how we'd gotten so lucky. To merely be awake—because to go to sleep meant that we'd be apart, and the thought was unbearable.

I scooted back down, my arm over X's bare chest as he began the gentle process of easing into consciousness. A yawn, a groan, an arm thrown across my chest. I laughed softly, pushing the arm back where it belonged; it was simply too heavy. Like having a tree trunk land across my torso.

"Good morning," I told him, dotting a necklace of kisses below his chin. "How'd you sleep?"

"Sleep?" He crooked an eyebrow, his voice raspy. "Did we sleep at all?"

Another giggle. "Sorry," I said, clasping a hand over my mouth. "I don't know why I keep laughing. Something's wrong with me."

"I *know*," he said with a mock gasp. "It's almost as if you're *happy*."

"Happy?" I feigned uncertainty. "I don't know, maybe, I suppose. I guess."

He grinned. "If you're not happy yet, I can think of a few ways to improve your mood."

I laughed, squirming underneath him as he gained energy and pulled me to him. He nuzzled against my neck with touches that sent shivers throughout my body. When he began rubbing my shoulders, I sighed. "Okay, yeah. You can do that. That feels nice."

He flipped me over as if I were nothing but an omelet that needed turning and began the tedious work of rubbing out the tension in my shoulders. There weren't many spots he'd missed after last night, but...

Ranger X cursed, breaking the mood.

"What's wrong?" I tensed as his fingers stopped moving. "Did I say something?"

Moments later, I heard it. The opening of the bungalow door downstairs.

"I locked it," X said. "It must be Gus."

"I thought you told him to stay away until noon."

"I did. Does Gus listen to me?"

I shook my head. "He doesn't listen to anyone, if that makes you feel better."

X barked a laugh. "I hate to admit it, but I should be going, anyway. I have to report to HQ before noon."

I crawled into a sitting position on the bed, pouting as the thin strap of my nightgown slipped down my shoulder. "How can the world go on normally when we have so much to celebrate? Can't we take a break from all the *business* to just enjoy this moment together?!"

"Life's unfair, isn't it?"

Disappointingly, X slipped a black t-shirt over his thick bare chest, letting it settle over his waist and looking like an underwear model as he stepped into a pair of dark jeans.

"It is *so* unfair," I said, still pouting. "We didn't even get to talk much since I got back from the mainland."

Ranger X's glance was loaded. "I don't know about that. I said all that I needed to, and you, well—" he gave me a dark grin—"had a few words of your own."

"Cannon!" I blushed. "How *dare* you!"

I leapt for him, but he nimbly caught my arm and twined it around his back, placing it firmly behind him. I inched it down until I could squeeze his butt. Then, I squeezed it again.

He gave mine a pat back before pulling me into a more serious embrace. He lingered, sensual, as his kiss danced over my lips. "Aren't husbands supposed to tease their wives just a little?" His breath, fresh somehow, and minty, smelled delicious. "I'm just practicing, sweetheart."

I couldn't think of anything smart to say, so I poked my head forward and devoured his mouth in a kiss. Which turned out to be better than any witty retort because it ended up in a return groan from him, and then a topple of limbs and bodies as we collapsed back into bed.

"I hope you're decent!" Hettie yelled from downstairs. "I broke in because nobody answered my knock. Lily, you there?"

Ranger X and I froze, still entwined. "Your grandmother breaks into your house?"

"Not regularly," I said with an apology. "She must need something."

"Well, I need something too." His eyes hungered as he held me pinned to the mattress. "Can I see you again tonight?"

I flew to a sitting position. "Hold on a second."

"Lily, what's wrong? Why do you look terrified?"

"X, I didn't stop to think last night! Where are we going to live? I have the bungalow, you have your hut. Are we going to have kids? What about a wedding? Do *you people* invite families? Would your family come? Are witches allowed to elope? What does a paranormal wedding look like? *I don't know anything*!"

Ranger X hesitated. "You people? You do know you're one of us, right?"

"I just mean...I know what human weddings look like. What about paranormal weddings?"

Ranger X backed away, the mood apparently broken now that we'd reached logistics talk. "My job was to ask for your hand in marriage. I believe it's your mo—er, grandmother's job to help plan the rest."

The word hung there like an icicle. *Mother*. Eventually, I shook it off and forced a smile. "Just wait until Poppy and Mimsey and Hettie hear. They'll be overjoyed."

Ranger X winced.

"About that," I said. "What do you think about waiting a few days to tell people? I don't want to steal Zin's thunder as she's announced Ranger, and with all this business about the Master of Magic..."

"Let's wait until the weekend," X said. "Zin will be a Ranger by then. Everything else will be sorted. And if it's not sorted, it can be put on hold."

I sealed our agreement with a kiss. "Thanks for understanding."

He returned it, then glanced longingly at the window as if he'd prefer to climb down the wall rather than face my grandmother.

"Hettie's not so bad," I said, bunching a robe around me as I tottered toward my closet. I stepped inside, grabbed some clothes, and eased the door shut again before I changed. "Come on, she must need something."

"*There's* my granddaughter!" Hettie opened her arms as I appeared on the bottom stair a few minutes later. "The happy couple, I should say. The *very* happy couple, judging by the look on X's face."

Hettie's gaze swept over the half empty glasses of wine on the table, the overturned blanket near the fire that looked too unkempt to be innocent. She landed on our faces, studied them for a minute, then decided to stay silent with further commentary.

"Well," I said to X, awkwardly clearing my throat. "I'll see you tonight then. Oh, by the way, did you learn anything about the Soul Suck from the press conference?"

"You two didn't have enough time to talk about that yesterday?" Hettie asked, straining for innocence with her raised eyebrows. "Y'all must've been busy."

I turned red. Ranger X turned pale.

"We did find something peculiar," he said. "Oddly enough, the spell had traces of a foreign substance on it. Completely foreign."

"What do you mean *foreign*?" I asked. "And how does a spell have traces of things on it?"

"All spells leave some sort of a tiny trace. Usually, they're pretty standard, and we don't put a lot of time into analyzing them. This time, not so much. We found elements of a regular Soul Suck, but there are signs it wasn't conjured by a witch or wizard." Ranger X paused. "We're no longer looking for *who* launched the spell, but *what*."

"Who else can perform magic?" I asked. "Outside of witches and wizards."

"All paranormal creatures have some level of magic in their veins—that's what makes them paranormal."

"Right, but—"

"But this was completely unfamiliar to the normal patterns—I'm sorry, I don't know more yet. I'm headed to look deeper into it now, and I'll let you ladies know if I find anything further."

"What's this?" Hettie ignored X, sliding a piece of paper on the table toward her. "Oh! The Sixth Borough. Who's going to the Sixth Borough? I really need some Gerbil Geraniums, and they have the *best* bargain shopping in their marketplace." Hettie raised a hand and whispered to me. "They're supposed to bring good luck to any who plant them. That, and Tiger likes to eat them. They're flowers that taste like rodents. Weird, huh?"

"Very weird," I said. "What's the Sixth Borough?"

"The address." Hettie held it up. "Surely you've heard of it—it's the largest hidden magical city in the world! Next to The Isle, of course. But the Sixth Borough is denser, more highly populated. New Yorkers, you know how they are, my little formerly human grand-daughter."

"There are five boroughs," I said slowly. "Manhattan, the Bronx, Long Island, Brooklyn, and Staten Island."

"And *Wicked*," Hettie said. "That's what they call it. Used to be dark and dingy once upon a time, but now it's the place to be. Very hipster."

"You know where it is? And how to get there?"

"Boy howdy, do I! I know all the secret ways in and out. I once had a lover back there. Well, not so much as a lover, but when I was a wee little thing I went to Witch Camp, and I had *the* biggest crush on my counselor. Things didn't work out. I was eleven and he was forty-seven."

I wrinkled my nose. "Good thing it didn't work out."

"Anyway, I'm ready to make the trip if you are. Who are we visiting?"

X looked at me curiously. "Who *are* you visiting?"

I hesitated, realizing I'd forgotten this part of the retelling during my story the previous evening. "Have you heard of the Keeper?" I asked the question to both Hettie and X, but it was Hettie who nodded first. "Well, Frank received this address from the former Keeper. He said it was intended for me."

Ranger X considered this. "If you got it from Frank, I think you should go."

"Thank you, your highness," I said dryly, "for your *permission*."

"Take Hettie with you." X pulled me close, kissed my forehead, and turned to leave. "I love you."

I echoed the sentiment before turning back to Hettie. Her face was screwed up into an odd grimace, but she waited until X had gone and I'd locked the door before she spoke. Then she exploded.

"Congratulations!" Hettie burst, clapping her hands, dancing a little jig that showed off each and every sequin on her pants. "When can I have Mimsey start planning your wedding? Will you have a maid of honor? How will you choose between your cousins?"

I gaped at her. "How'd you know?"

"Grandmotherly instinct," she said. "Come on, dear, we can talk about it on the way to Wicked. In fact, it's the perfect day to get Wicked—I hear they have gorgeous bouquets. Maybe we can do a wee bit of shopping on the way back?"

"I have to get a potion started first," I said. "There's a new concept I've been gathering supplies to create, and it takes twenty-four hours to brew, I believe."

"What are you working on?"

"I don't have the name for it yet, and I'm not sharing what it'll do—just in case it doesn't work. Or it backfires. Or if it works too well, and I have to get rid of it," I said, thinking of Long Isle. I paused, flipping the book Gus had given me open to cross check it against a few herbology books I'd gotten from the library. "I have to get it started now because I'll need it sooner rather than later."

"What can I do to help?"

"See those ferns?" I gestured to the baggie of Forgotten Ferns from Frank. "Any chance you feel like grinding them to bits?"

"Oh, honey, you just wait to see my grinding skills." Hettie pushed back the curtain hanging in front of the shelves and found the mortar and pestle to mash it in. "I have grinding skills up the wazoo."

Hettie did, in fact, have quite fantastic grinding skills, and with my grandmother's help, and eventually Gus's upon his arrival, we were done with the preparations before the hour mark.

"This is just the base," I explained to Gus's questioning stare. "I need to let this brew overnight. Tomorrow will be the tricky part."

"I see you've got some treats for me." Gus changed the subject, looking greedily over my shoulder at the stack of textbooks on the table. The only thing more exciting to Gus than a new potion was a new *book* about potions. "May I?"

"Have a blast." I pushed the stack toward him. "While you're busy with these, my grandmother and I are headed to Wicked. How do we get there, Hettie?"

She reached out a hand. "Hold on tight, missy."

"What?"

"I said hold on tight."

"Where are we going?"

"Wicked."

"Are we going to fly?"

She shrugged. "I'm not sure exactly what you'd call it. Sympathy, maybe."

"What do you mean *sympathy*?"

"There's an easier route for us old folks to travel between The Isle and Wicked. The senior express." Hettie peered at me. "Never heard of it? The Senior Slide?"

I shook my head.

"Then you're in for a real treat."

I wouldn't call whatever Hettie had in store a *treat*, but she seemed to think it would work, which was what mattered to me.

After locking Gus into the bungalow with his books and sticking a *Closed* sign on the door of Magic & Mixology for the morning, I followed Hettie to a tiny little garden not far from the Lower Bridge. In the middle of it was a gleaming silver bench. I must have walked past it hundreds of times, but I'd never noticed it before.

"This is the easy access route for those scaredy cats who won't go near The Forest," Hettie explained. "Now, hold my hand."

"What?"

"Hold my hand."

"Hettie, what are you going to—"

"Grandchild of mine, I said hold my hand!" Hettie extended her arm and fingers toward me and waited a beat for me to grab her hand back. When I did, she squeezed tight and cackled. "Now, here we go!"

She plunked us down on the bench. My rear end barely touched metal before the world as I knew it was gone, and Hettie and I were floating. It felt like we'd entered a light, fluffy dream where clouds were made of cotton candy and everything around us was white and bright and clean. I looked over, surprised to see Hettie next to me, still holding my hand. Our bodies looked airy, almost ethereal. As if we didn't quite exist any longer.

"Hettie, did you go and get us killed?" I asked, glancing around. "Where are we?"

She laughed again. "No, but I see how you might think that. Maybe they really are getting us seniors ready for the pearly gates."

"How do we get..."

"Ah, *here* it is."

Hettie pulled me close to her as we drifted along. I was surprised to find her strength at an all-time high; she had the strength of a much younger woman, though I wondered if it had something to do with the halfway transparent way our bodies hovered over the milky white clouds beneath our feet.

"Sixth Borough for two," Hettie said as we reached a tiny, glistening pole in the middle of an otherwise untouched expanse of snowy white. "There we are—tickets are popping right up. Stay close, dear, you're definitely going to want to hold on tight for this part. Also, you shouldn't eat right beforehand."

"Isn't it a little late for the warning?"

It wasn't only too late for Hettie's food warning, but it was too late for me to finish my thought. As I watched, a fast-moving sidewalk appeared just to the right of the pole. It looked like a flat escalator on superfast speed, and it proceeded directly into a swirling mass of clouds and smoke, a little hole in the atmosphere that looked ready to suck us through.

And *suck us up* it did. Hettie had no sooner stepped onto the sidewalk and dragged me with her than my stomach lurched, swirled, and was gone. It was incredibly fortunate I hadn't had a moment to eat breakfast because in the next seconds, I lost anything I had left in there. Including half my lungs and most of my stomach lining.

We twisted, twirled, and turned at the speed of light. Zipping forward, never slowing. Others passed by, blurs as we leapt across the nation, presumably, but nobody looked at us. It was like we'd entered into an invisible wind tunnel that was trying to murder us.

"What in the *world* was that?" I gasped as the ride came to a stop, and I tumbled to the ground. I was on my knees, dry-heaving as Hettie stepped gently from the air next to me. "I swear you're going to kill me one of these days."

"If us old folks can do it, you should be able to, too. Then again." Hettie scratched her head. "It's not really made for people your age. How do you feel?"

"Horrible! What was that?"

"Isn't it neat? I just got my Senior Spellpass the other day. Helps us older folks who are weak and whatever—" Hettie paused to flex her muscles—"get places quicker. What if I had family living in the

Sixth Borough? How else am I supposed to travel for special occasions?"

I rolled my eyes, making my way to shaky feet. My legs wobbled like jelly. I wasn't ready to let this conversation go, until I turned and found something all the more distracting.

A pair of huge, intimidating wrought iron gates rose from the ground before me. The world around us was murky and dark, the air heavy with fog and dampness. We were on a narrow little path that led straight to the gates, a cobblestone thing that should have led to a quaint little cottage or a sweet gingerbread house in the woods.

Instead, there was only a set of gates larger than most giants. They were thick, sturdy, and sealed by magic so strong there was no unlocking them with a hex—I could tell from the crackle of protection sizzling on the black stakes.

"Where are we?"

"We came around the back entrance," Hettie said. "I know it's not much to look at, but just imagine a human arriving here. They'd turn their little tushies around and skedaddle back to the mainland."

"I'm ready to skedaddle. Why did we need to take the back entrance?"

Hettie raised the slip of paper she'd tucked into her pocket with the address on it, then stepped forward, unafraid of the intimidating gates as she rested a hand on the outside spoke. "It's closer to your friend."

"What, did you apply for a Senior Spellpass for that, too?" I asked sardonically. "No waiting in line for your entrance?"

"Yeppers."

I'd meant it sarcastically, but Hettie'd gotten us here after all, so I sat back and let her work her magic. As her fingers touched the gate, bolts of all shapes and sizes began to twist, unlock, and morph before our eyes. It took several minutes for everything to finish clanking and sliding into place, and when it did, a voice sounded from nowhere.

"What is your business?" The bodiless voice seemed directed at Hettie. It rolled low and deep, adding weight to the already intimidating landscape.

"I'm here with my granddaughter," Hettie said with a chirp. "Looking for Gerbil Geraniums. My cat, Tiger, has a real thing for them. My last visit was seven months and three days back." Hettie fluttered her eyelashes. "I had a date."

The voice didn't respond. However, he or she, or it, or whatever it was had apparently decided Hettie spoke the truth. Before our eyes, the path ahead lightened at once. Instead of a fog-filled road that led into an abyss of darkness and isolation, the sun peeked through the clouds and exposed an entirely new world before us.

Hettie gave me a moment to appreciate the sights and sounds. The road beneath our feet was paved with lightly shimmering gold stones, worn over the years into nothing more than a cobblestone path. Where the sidewalks ended, hundreds if not thousands of tiny stores lined each curb of the narrow path, many of them stacked haphazardly on top of one another, disappearing miles above us into the sky.

Not only did the busy road extend as far as the eye could see, but it extended upward, as well. Vendors hung from window sills and perched on clotheslines selling their wares. A whole new layer of traffic existed above us as witches and wizards on broomsticks haggled with store owners. The sheer volume of traffic reminded me of the photos I'd seen of Los Angeles or Tokyo or New York City.

"Excellent," Hettie said, dragging me through the gates. "Welcome to the Sixth Borough, my dear."

Chapter 18

I DIDN'T THINK MUCH could surprise me anymore.

After the shock of my life had hit just over a year ago with the discovery that I was a witch, I'd gone on to learn that I had a blood-intolerant vampire for a cousin, a Shiftling cousin, and a home on a magical island. I thought I'd seen it all.

I thought wrong.

The Sixth Borough was New York for magical folks. Crammed into a small, hidden city, an entire way of life existed here. Rich and fascinating, loud and dirty, bright and hopeful. Paranormal children breezed past our heads in dangerous games of tag. They hid behind chimneys, flying miles in the air as they ferreted one another out of impossible hiding spots.

Men and women wore clothes in all sorts of new fashions. Some wore robes of bright pink silks while others had feathers dangling from their ears to their shoulders. Others dressed in sharper velour suits, but most of it—all of it—was vibrant. This was a whole new world to me.

"Come dear, don't linger. You can spend as much time here as you'd like later. *Later*," Hettie chided as I stopped to listen to a vendor shouting broomstick prices at me. "Come on, now—if you give a second's pause, these vendors will be on you like vultures. Ignore, dearie. Look straight ahead or they'll strip you right solid of anything you have to barter."

I managed to mostly avoid eye contact as we traveled, but I couldn't do anything about the way my jaw hung open in amazement and wonder. Hettie didn't seem to mind that part; she kept glancing over to watch me enjoy the show.

"Magnificent, isn't it?" she said with a bit of pride. "Glad I got to show my granddaughter something new."

"Something new," I echoed dumbly. "Hettie, this place! It's terrifying. And wonderful, and busy, and fast, and...there's so much of it."

Hettie cackled. "Just when you think you're beginning to learn everything, you turn around, and...*voila*. A whole new world opens before your eyes. Ah, here we are."

"*Where* exactly are we?"

Hettie blinked, then laughed. "Your little friend's place."

When I stared blankly at her, she held up the slip of paper. That was enough to wipe the dazed grin off my face. "Oh! I see. How do we, uh, get inside?"

Hettie raised an eyebrow. "Um, knock?"

I surveyed the door before me. It made no sense to me whatsoever, and I stared quizzically at it hoping Hettie would help a sister out. She didn't. "Where do I *start*?"

"Well, what does the address say?"

I peered closer at the paper. I'd realized it to be a unique sort of address, but I hadn't spent much time studying it after Hettie told me she could get us here without directions.

"Uh, Senex Domus #364A, Wicked Way."

"Yes, this is the Retired Residences building. Now knock on #364." Hettie gestured around. "I forgot my glasses. Which door is that?"

Therein lay the problem. I studied the huge door, two times my size, and swallowed. Built into the door itself were hundreds of smaller doors the size of my palm.

"I won't fit through *any* of these little doors," I said, locating #364, which thankfully was near the bottom. "Even Glinda's forest fairies couldn't squeeze through there. What, ah—race—is the Keeper? He must be some sort of fairy."

Hettie cackled. "Just knock already."

I did, expecting something wild to happen. Maybe another bodiless voice or a mirage, or if nothing else, a crackle of magic. When none of that happened, I looked to Hettie.

She was focused on the palm-sized door where I'd knocked amongst a sea of other palm-sized doors. Suddenly, there was a *pop*, and the door seemed to hop right off its frame and bloom to a full-sized door like a flower opening before our eyes. It opened with the familiar *squeak* of rusty hinges, and Hettie smiled grimly at me. "Looks like someone was expecting you."

I didn't have time to wonder how a man I'd never met could expect a woman who didn't know what she was doing, but I didn't doubt Hettie. I'd had my quota of surprises today, and from here on out, I just planned to follow along.

So I followed my grandmother through the door, straight to a spiral staircase with steep steps that started moving on their own as we climbed them. They carried us upward toward the rooftops. "Where are we going?"

"The three hundred and sixty fourth floor," Hettie said simply. "What else would the address mean?"

I zipped my lips and waited until the staircase came to a stop outside a plain door. Black iron bars sat over the window, a show of defense in an otherwise friendly, residential-looking building. Before I could raise a hand to knock, it swung open.

"Do we go inside?" I asked Hettie. I cautiously peered through the door and found the room empty. "I don't see anyone."

"Of course," Hettie said. "These old folks' homes have the remote door openers so their inhabitants don't gotta get up when visitors come knockin'."

I wasn't certain she was correct, but Hettie knew the ropes better than I did, so I followed her diligently into a clean little apartment that had a ritzy, very human-esque atmosphere to it—as if it's owner had lived in the Roaring 20's.

A velvet chaise lounge sat in one corner while a mahogany desk stood as a solid centerpiece to the dining room. Over it hung a quaint chandelier that glittered with hints of sunlight that cast dancing little sparkles across the room.

It was only when I turned to face the living room that I saw him. An older gentleman who looked something like a butler. He wore a suit like a second skin, fitting into it so comfortably I could tell he'd spent much time dressed *just so*. His hair had grayed, but his eyes remained a bright green, and I could feel the very second his sharp gaze landed on me.

"Lily Locke," he said finally. "Welcome."

"Thank you for having me," I said. "And my grandmother."

"The pleasure is all mine." He cast a second, longer look at Hettie. "Please, take a seat, ladies."

Hettie obligingly took a seat in a plush armchair, and I followed her, finding a place in the armchair's matching cousin. The Keeper waited until we were both seated before he opened his arms, shifted his tie, and waited for us to begin.

"Thank you again for having us," I said. "I'd tell you why I'm here, but I imagine you're already quite clear on the subject. I'm looking for the Master of Magic."

"You got my address from Frank Shaw?"

I nodded.

"I've been waiting for this day for *years*. I wondered who it would be to finally require my help." His fingers stroked at his chin thoughtfully. "You're wondering how I knew to give him my address—*this* address, an address that wasn't mine to give so many years ago. Let's suffice to say that as a Keeper, there are certain...powers that are unexplainable. Just as the Master of Magic's work is pure art, entirely free from normal logic. The Keeper has talents similar in style."

Hettie's eyes widened. "What sort of powers are we talking? I'm into weird powers." She fluttered her eyelashes.

The Keeper nobly brushed off her advances. "As Keepers, we are individually no more important to this world than trees—we are not meant to be noticed. We're merely staples of the magic system as trees are staples of the environment. We Keepers live only to serve and protect. It is our duty, our pleasure, our joy, and our responsibility. We have a relationship to the Master much like the one I see between Gus and yourself."

I frowned at the intrusion into my personal life but pushed past it. "That must mean you know where I can find the Master?"

"You can't *find* him," he said simply. "I can't do anything for you on that front."

"Then why'd you give Frank this address for me?"

He took a breath and expelled it slowly. "I don't exactly know."

This threw me for a loop. "Excuse me?"

"I can't help you find the Master. That's simply impossible. I'm a retired Keeper, which means I've abdicated my duties to another. The next in line. I have no clue where the Master of Magic is located any longer."

"That seems harsh," I said, imagining if Gus left my side and feeling a pang of loss at the thought of losing him. "Weren't you friends?"

"This business is no more personal than the way trees exhale oxygen and we breathe it in. The Keeper is a cog in the wheel, a necessity. Sometimes we're granted beautiful magic, and it's like autumn then—a short burst of magic, similar to when the leaves change color and shine. They sparkle with glamor and glitz for a short while before they retire back into the useful lives they lead."

His words painted beautiful pictures, but my impatience at the task ahead wasn't muted. "I don't know why I'm here if you can't help me."

"Perhaps you can explain to me *why* you're here, and we'll go from there."

I was hesitant to start and looked at Hettie, not sure if I could trust him. I didn't even know his name—it felt crass to ask for one, and he hadn't offered. Hettie merely nodded, gave me the go ahead, and so I began.

I gave him the cliff notes version of my story. I included my suspicions about The Faction, though I left Liam's name out of it. I explained about the rest of my searches—from the magical library to The Isle—and the mentions of ancient gods. I included the theory of the demigod assassin for good measure, watching to see if his eyes lighted with surprise at the extent of my knowledge.

His eyes did light at the end of my explanation. He sat back, again running a finger over his non-existent beard, deep in thought. "Let me ask you this, Lily." His face held a deep severity to it, as if the following question contained life or death information. "Has anything *odd* been happening in your life lately?"

"Odd?" I snorted, surprised by his question. "Mr. Keeper, my life has been odd since the day I arrived on The Isle."

"Yes, yes, but anything particularly peculiar? Maybe not exactly in your own personal life, but in the events around you. Surrounding you. Little things maybe, out of the ordinary happenings..."

The first thought in my head was of the shadow I'd picked up on the mainland—the man who'd followed me through the police station for no apparent reason. Then I remembered the whole mess of the Forgotten Ferns on the island, along with the rest of the petty crimes. On top of that, Zin's uber private mission weighed heavy on my mind, as did the alley gang who'd cornered me after my meeting with Sammy.

"Yes," I said, striving for casual. "I guess you could say that things have been *off*."

"Ah. Then, there's nothing more that I can do. The Keeper is already in your life. He'll make the determination if you're worthy to be seen by the Master."

"The assassin," I said, ignoring the sting of his rejection. "You seemed surprised I knew about it."

"Surprised, no," the Keeper said. "I'm surprised you told me about it."

"Why aren't you more worried about The Faction finding the Master of Magic?" I hesitated. "Do you not trust my sources?"

"I trust your sources just as much as you do. I'm not worried because I also trust *my* sources—the Keeper will never give away the location to someone who isn't worthy."

"Right. But apparently there are ways around that little rule."

His eyes narrowed. "What are you insinuating?"

"I think my source is onto something. He said The Faction is getting ready to move—that doesn't make sense if they don't have a plan. How can they move forward if they don't know where to go?"

"Maybe it's a lie."

"I don't think so. I think The Faction realized the same thing I did. That there's a way to the Master around the Keeper. Find a demigod and have him do the dirty work. I'm sure for the right price, it could be arranged."

"I suppose you'd know better than most, seeing as your relationship with The Faction leader is quite..." The Keeper paused, lowered his voice. "*Familial.*"

I leapt to my feet. "How dare you! He's no more a father to me than you are."

"Lily." Hettie reached a soothing hand to my arm. "Sit. We're all on the same side here."

"I do agree with your grandmother," the Keeper said, leaning forward, his ears perked to listen. "I am intrigued. There is something about genes, don't you think, that connect us even when we sever all ties?" He didn't wait long enough for me to argue. "If you figured out an alternate route, it seems The Faction may have, as well."

"It wouldn't take much for The Faction to locate a demigod."

"Surely it would. They're carefully guarded and protected."

"You must have been out of the game for a while," I snapped, "because the Ghost, their leader, has resources beyond our wildest dreams. I think we need to consider the possibility has come to fruition."

"No." The Keeper shook his head firmly. "The only reason the assassin got through to the Master at all was because I failed my duties as Keeper. I wasn't there when he needed me."

A stony silence filled the room after his admission. It was hard for him to share—that much was obvious. As the truth left his lips, so did his shroud of control. In its place sat a curled, worn old man, quiet and still before us.

"I'm sorry," I managed. "I didn't know."

"The past is the past." He dismissed it with a wave of his shaking hand. "There was a man who tried to accompany the assassin on his mission. The wizard was left behind outside the walls of the city. It was impossible for him to follow through because he had no ancient blood, and he hadn't been granted access by the Keeper."

"What if—"

"What do you want me to do, Lily?" The Keeper was no longer able to hold back a shudder. "I have no clue where the Master of Magic is, and I cannot grant you access."

"What if the Keeper is the key?" I pressed. "Is there some way to speed the process along? If he already knows where I am, what's the harm in helping things along?"

"There is one thing..."

"Yes?"

"I believe we can catch his attention. There is a spell that will make you irresistible to the Keeper."

"Oh, well, I'm not sure about that."

The Keeper managed a small smile. "Let me mark you. Once you're marked, it'll be impossible for the Keeper to stay away. He'll be curious as to the magic that's touched you."

"What sort of magic?"

The Keeper raised his hands. "His own Keeper magic. I might no longer be the Keeper, but not all spells vanish with retirement. I have a few left behind."

I exhaled. "It won't hurt? Or affect me in any way?"

"You won't even know it's touched you. But all spells leave traces, and Keeper magic is no different. It's entirely unique, entirely separate from witch or wizard magic."

"What will I have to do after you complete the spell?"

"Live your life," he said with a dry smile. "I give you twenty-four hours before he's in your grasp. After that, it's up to you not to ruin your chances."

"Give me the chance," I said, "and I won't blow it."

"Close your eyes."

I did as he told me, feeling Hettie's hand clasp mine as the swish of fabric signaled the Keeper's slow, steady pace across the room. When his footsteps neared me, he raised a hand, sending a slight breeze across my face, and rested his thumb on my forehead.

I squeezed my eyes shut tighter still.

The Keeper began to murmur words, an incantation if I had to guess, one in a foreign, ancient language. The melodic sounds flowed from his tongue, drifting into one another with startling ease.

It lasted for so long I began to twitch with nerves. When the Keeper finally stepped back, murmuring for me to open my eyes, a sudden sense of peace fell over my shoulders. A contentedness.

"I feel...*fine*," I said to Hettie's searching eyes. "If anything, I'm calmer than before."

The Keeper smiled. "That's a very good sign. The spell took, then. I believe that was my duty to you. I, too, am content, and my work here is done."

That felt like a dismissal, a surprisingly quick one, but I realized that he was right. "Come on." I grasped Hettie's hand and pulled her to her feet. "We have work to do on the island and no time to waste."

"But, my Gerbil Geraniums," Hettie pouted. "Tiger will be so angry with me if I don't pick some up."

"He's a cat."

"He's got an attitude."

The Keeper stood, walked to his windowsill, and returned with a bright blue box of flowers in a rainbow of colors. "Here, take mine. I've tended them for years, and I believe they are also ready to take their leave from me."

Hettie grinned like a banshee, clutching them to her chest. "Mr. Keeper, thank you! How can I repay you?"

His eyes leveled first on me, then on Hettie. "Guide our young Lily, here. She'll need help."

Hettie's arm snaked around me. "She'll be safe with me."

"Yes," the Keeper said after a long pause. "I do think so."

"Where's the nearest Senior Slide?" Hettie asked. "I can tell our girl is getting antsy to get home."

"Miss Hettie, you are standing in the senior center. There's a Senior Slide on the bottom level. Safe travels to you both."

"What'd you make of him?" I asked once Hettie and I were safely out of earshot and on our way to locating the Senior Spellpass portal. "What strange magic."

"Strange magic is right," Hettie said. "But I think he's right. I think the road ahead of you will be a long and difficult one, and you'll need help. I'm here for you, Lily."

"I know, Hettie. You always have been..."

Before I could finish, Hettie gave me a nod, a yank, and we were off, hurtling toward The Isle without a backward glance. We arrived safely, one could say, though I felt as if I'd been battered against a wall of rocks by a raging ocean.

"Oh, my poor geraniums," Hettie said, patting them down. "They're a little windblown."

"Yeah," I said, pulling myself to my feet. We'd arrived back in the small garden with the silver bench. I caught a glimpse of my reflection in a small pond beside me and squeaked in surprise. My hair stood up on all ends as if it'd become frightened of my head. "Me too."

We set off for home from our location near the Lower Bridge. Hettie accompanied me as far as the turnoff to the bungalow where we stopped to say our goodbyes.

"I have to get these flowers home for Tiger," she said. "Will you be okay on your own for a bit?"

"Yes, Hettie—thank you for everything." I forced a crooked smile, still feeling off-kilter from the awful transportation system. "Thank you for showing me Wicked."

"Thank you for getting engaged," she said with a sly wink. "Congratulations, honey. I won't say anything yet, I promise—but I have to tell you that I cannot wait to go dress shopping! Please tell me you'll let me come with you."

"So long as we don't take the Senior Slide," I said with a grimace. "That is non-negotiable."

She laughed, agreed, and then we parted ways—her heading further north to The Twist while I veered along the beachfront path. I took my time on the walk, inhaling the fresh, sea-salt air as I attempted to regain control of my stomach.

"How was the trip?" Gus asked nonchalantly, as I stepped into the storeroom not ten minutes later. "Any news?"

I grimly set my jaw. "Not much. Now, we wait."

"Great," Gus said, too distracted to pry further. "I'm glad you have time to kill because there's something you need to see."

Chapter 19

"IT'S IN HERE SOMEWHERE," Gus muttered. "Ah, *here* we are."

I took a seat at the storeroom table next to Gus and tried to wait patiently as he ran his fingers over the stack of books before him. Eventually, he popped one off the stack I'd brought back from the library. The particular manuscript he'd selected was dusty and old, and at first, I didn't recognize it.

Then I looked closer, and it dawned on me. Instinctively, I clutched at my necklace, remembering the pain that had drawn me toward this very manuscript.

"I see you recognize this one," Gus said, watching me carefully. "I'm not as oblivious as you may believe, Lily. I know that necklace of yours glows more than ever these days, and I know it's been driving Trinket as mad as a werewolf under a full moon. What happened in the library?"

"Something in my necklace wanted me to have this book," I whispered, rubbing a hand over my chest at the ghost ache there. "It hurt—physical pain—until I selected *Ceres* from the shelf and brought it with me. I have no idea why."

"I think I might have an idea." Gus flipped open the cover to reveal a title page. "Take a look."

I leaned over, glancing at the exquisitely illegible script. The second I laid eyes on the familiar title, *Ceres*, a strange thing happened. The heart around my neck began to glow again, soft and sure, a gentle hum this time, as if content.

"Why does it do that?" I murmured absently, scanning through the first few pages of the book. They were littered with symbols and drawings. The text was smeared, and the captions were in a foreign language. "What is it trying to tell me?"

The answer came swift and sure. One second I was turning the pages and flicking my gaze over an ancient language, and then the next, I was staring at a drawing that was the mirror image of my necklace on the parchment beneath my fingertips.

"How can this be?" I looked up at Gus. "This book is decades old, probably centuries old. Much older than myself, much older than my mother or her mother or her mother's mother."

Gus kept silent, watching from over my shoulder.

"It's not possible," I whispered, leaning forward until the charm around my neck dropped onto the page. It matched, inch for inch. "What does this mean?"

The locket now glowed light pink, a color I'd never seen it generate before. The metal warmed against me—a pleasant warmth, one vibrating with energy. With urgency and anticipation. Even when Mimsey and Trinket had first presented me the second half of the necklace and both pieces had fused together, it had not reacted with such force.

Settling in, ignoring the world around me, I focused on reading the passage before me.

Ceres

Roman goddess of agriculture, grain crops, fertility, and motherly relationships.

Below was the caption for the drawing:

Amulet of Ceres

Sealed with a kiss from the goddess's lips, this piece of fine jewelry, priceless in its worth and abilities, is known as the Mother's Protector. With only one true amulet ever in existence, it is thought to be passed from

one generation to the next, finding its way into the hands of its true
owner when one bloodline stops and the next begins.
The amulet contains incredible healing powers along with the ability to
protect its wearer to an insurmountable degree. When Ceres's ancestors
wear this charm, they will be near invincible. However, it is prudent to
remember this necklace will not allow its user to escape death. True
death, true evil, will never be stopped by a charm. But when used for
good, for light, the amulet will guide the seeker to help during the deep-
est of despairs.

My fingers found the charm. I played with it lightly, gingerly. "Gus, is this... is this the true amulet? It can't be. That's impossible."

"I wouldn't say it's impossible." Gus raised bushy eyebrows. "There are enough ancestors of Ceres by this time that it's impossible to trace all of her bloodlines."

"But that would mean—"

"You may very well be a distant descendant of hers," he said, running a hand over his brow. "No wonder your powers are extraordinary. A Mixologist with ancient blood in her veins? Of course. I should have guessed."

"No, *no*—this can't be true."

"You're fighting a losing battle, Lily. Face the facts. I know you don't want to be any more different than you already are, but some things just *are*. They're neither good or bad; it's just the way of life."

Gus's words had a slight sting to them, a sharpness. I frowned. "Look—I didn't *ask* for any of this. It's not that I don't appreciate everything I've been given," I said coolly. "But that doesn't make me wrong for feeling like I haven't earned my gifts."

"Did Poppy earn her fangs? Did Zin earn her Shiftling status? Did Hettie earn that horrid sense of style, or was she born with it?" Gus let me consider this for an extended moment. "Actually, forget about the last one. Bad example. My point is you don't begrudge Poppy or Zin for what they are. Nobody begrudges you for being born a Caucasian female with brown, blond—whatever the hell color hair you have—so my point is to accept what you have and work with it."

I marked the conversation finished with a flick of my fingers as I returned my attention to the necklace. "This *must* be an amulet," I said, twining the chain around my fingers. "It has to be—there's no other explanation."

"It's certainly an amulet. The question is whether it belongs to Ceres."

"Gus, listen. I have a crazy theory—bear with me." I paced around the room, my breath coming in shallow gasps. "The Master of Magic is protected by ancient gods, right?"

"So the legends say."

"And the retired Keeper has confirmed it." I tapped a finger against my lip as I thought. "I suspected my necklace was acting up because of my mother. But what if that's not the reason the amulet has come to life at all?"

"You think that's a coincidence." Gus's eyes lit up. "Instead, the glow could have everything to do with your search for the Master of Magic."

"Exactly. Liam told us about the Master of Magic *just* after I first took Long Isle Iced Tea. The timing was so close that it was easy for me to think it had to do with the search for my mother. This whole time, maybe all the amulet was doing—if it truly is Ceres's amulet–is guiding me to protect the Master of Magic."

"I think you're onto something."

I frowned. "But if that's the case, why would it lead me *to* the Master of Magic? Theoretically, isn't that more dangerous than staying out of the situation entirely?"

"It might be, unless The Faction is preparing to destroy the Master of Magic," Gus warned. "Then, we're all in danger. And I'm sorry, but no amulet of the gods is going to save you if the Master is murdered."

I looked up, my gaze somber. "The amulet wouldn't be acting up unless The Faction is close. It must be a sign that Liam was right—they're getting ready to make their move somehow. Demigod or otherwise."

"I hate to bring this up." Gus peered through uncertain eyes. "But it needs to be said, I'm afraid."

"You're thinking about Lucian."

"You're blood related to the man, Lily—he's your father. If you have ancient blood, it's very possible you inherited it from your father's side. As far as I know, your mother wasn't a descendant. I don't know anything about Lucian's past."

"But I got the necklace from my mother."

"Right, but didn't you listen to the passage?" Gus peered intently at me. "It didn't say anything about being passed down to only the descendants of Ceres—it explained it's passed through one generation to the next until it reaches its rightful owner."

"You think my mother was just the messenger. The vehicle to get the necklace to me."

Gus cocked his head. "That would make sense if you're a daughter of Ceres through your father's bloodline. He wouldn't have given you the amulet—but you are clearly the rightful owner of it. It found you through your mother."

"You're implying..." I inhaled sharply, stopped. "You think my father is a demigod."

"It's not impossible, and if that's true, he *himself* can locate the Master of Magic. It could be the reason The Faction recruited him in the first place."

I raised my hands, pressed my fingers to my forehead as I sank back into the seat. "This is insane. I can't believe any of it."

"There's an awful logic to this whole thing." Gus thumped across the room and rested his hands on my shoulders. "If Lucian is the son of Ceres and a mortal man, then it would explain why you have the necklace. It'd help to explain why your powers are so strong—if, in fact, this is all true, you're two branches down the genealogy tree from Ceres herself. No wonder you are attuned to Empath magic."

I couldn't breathe. It was hard to say how long I sat there in a daze, but a sudden, sharp clap of thunder brought my attention back to the storeroom. I glanced through my haze to find Gus standing at the door, peering far over the horizon to where lightning leapt from the heavens and inky black storm clouds swarmed below.

"Lily," Gus said with a sigh that terrified me to the last atom of my being. "I'm afraid you're correct."

I gulped back a burst of fear. "About what?"

Gus pointed a finger up. It trembled. "I believe your father is close to finding the Master of Magic."

Panic clutched at my chest as darkness settled over the island. Eventually, beefy raindrops spattered onto the ground, thick as tears. We stood there until footsteps and a head of gleaming black hair tore our gazes from the skies.

"The time has come," Ranger X said, glancing behind him as if checking for a tail before he stepped inside the storeroom. He issued a somber glance in my direction. "What happened with the Keeper?"

"Come inside and lock the door," I told both men. "I have work to do, and I'll fill you in as I get started."

"What's so urgent?" Ranger X asked, peering over my shoulder. "Is it the potion you started this morning? The one with no name?"

I nodded, hesitated. "It has a name now."

Both Gus and Ranger X stopped short and waited expectantly. I clasped my hands nervously before my waist as I studied the ingredients simmering on the cauldron.

"Well?" Gus prompted. "What is it?"

With a grim smile, and a finger pointed to the story of Ceres, I whispered the name that'd come to me in a flash of understanding. "Amuletto Kiss."

Chapter 20

AFTERNOON BLURRED INTO evening, which blurred into night. At first there was chatter in the storeroom as I caught up Ranger X and Gus on the details from my trip to Wicked. After I completed the story, the two men lapsed into a quiet concentration and spent most of their time flipping through books, looking for any hint that might be of help in creating the Amuletto Kiss potion.

"I think it'll be done earlier than expected," I told the men sometime around midnight. "I'm going to stay up until it finishes. Why don't you two get some rest?"

Ranger X, bleary-eyed, looked like he hadn't slept in days. "We're here to help."

Gus, completely unruffled, nodded his agreement. "The storm outside's not going anywhere, so neither am I. Plus, I forgot my umbrella."

We all ignored the stack of umbrellas that lived permanently in the corner, almost never used thanks to the balmy nature of the island.

"Suit yourselves," I said. "This next bit is the tricky part."

"Maybe it'll help to explain what you're doing," X ventured cautiously. "I know it would help me stay awake if I could try to understand."

Gus didn't comment, instead waiting for my answer. Since I'd arrived on the island, he'd never once presumed to tell me *how* to work, he merely made suggestions and followed orders. When it suited him.

"Sure, I can do that." My voice sounded hoarse from lack of use over the last few hours.

I'd been concentrating so deeply and for so long that it felt like spiderwebs had taken over my brain. My fingers ached, my eyesight blurred, and I hadn't had a meal since the afternoon, but somehow, I'd never felt better. I was in my element.

I couldn't deny the thrill of the chase—the hours spent tinkering on the *exact* right proportions of hazel-seed to baby's breath, the slight flutter of satisfaction as the appropriate amounts eased into place, and the ensuing nerves as I waited to see if my work would be successful.

I took the two men step by step through my work, proceeding at a slow, steady pace while I explained. "The Amuletto Kiss will work similarly to the ancient potions Gus found theorized in the manuscript."

"Why didn't they work?" Ranger X asked. "The old ones, I mean."

"Because they're wrong," I said crossly. "But I think I've spotted the problem."

Gus stifled a grin of pride as satisfaction beamed from his face. "Lily Locke, proving the ancients wrong."

"You were right about something," I told Gus. "The reason they got the potions wrong was because the previous Mixologists were men."

That wiped the smiles clean off their faces.

"See, men tend to focus on *the thing*," I continued. "The problem."

"What are we supposed to focus on," X asked cautiously, "if not the problem?"

"Sometimes, the problem is *not* the problem," I said sounding snappish. "Sometimes, it's about the feelings. The emotions. The thoughts—not the *thing*."

Gus looked to Ranger X. Both appeared utterly mystified.

"Go on," Gus said. "Enlighten us poor creatures."

"See this here?" I held up a scrap of fabric, then smiled proudly. "I nabbed this off Sammy, the alleged killer of my mother. I sliced it from his shirt before he disappeared."

Gus's expression turned curious, while Ranger X leaned forward, perturbed.

"Previous Mixologists have focused on this." I wagged the cloth in front of their faces. "The thing. The piece of fabric. *That's* where they went wrong."

"If you don't need the fabric," X asked, "why did you take it?"

"It contributes to the potion, but it's not everything. More important than a piece of fabric are the emotions of Sammy. We need to know what Sammy was *feeling*, what he was thinking—the intangibles."

"You were talking about your mother," Gus said, "I'm assuming, so his thoughts and feelings would be focused on her."

"Exactly," I said. "Amuletto Kiss—if it functions as I anticipate—will allow me to relive the last few minutes inside of Sammy's head before I took this snippet of fabric. Not the factual thoughts, but *everything*. I'll be able to feel as he feels. I'll hear his thoughts, but I'll also sense what he's sensing. Is he panicking because I'm suspicious? Is he desperate? Sad? Lonely? After this, I should know if Sammy is guilty or not."

Gus looked down at the scattered array of ingredients I'd swept into neat little piles. He sucked in a breath. "It's comprehensive. It's not *mind reading* because you're stepping into another's body for a few minutes in time and taking over completely. The nightshade—"

Gus stopped abruptly, fingering one of the leftover ingredients. "Lily, this is genius."

"Thank you," I said with a smile. "I thought so. See here?" I pointed to a rare blend of chamomile Gus had tucked in the back of the storeroom. "This calms the user's body and enters them into a trance. The Forgotten Ferns—that's a key ingredient. It allows the user to entirely, completely forget themselves—forget their own wants and needs and desires, opening up their minds to inhabit another's."

"That's also part of the failed potions." Gus's eyes keenly studied the old texts. "They didn't clear the mind—didn't think it'd be necessary."

"But a woman knows that's not how humans work," I said with a tight smile. "Our heads, our hearts are so full of our own problems, loves, desires, wants, needs—we absolutely cannot experience another's wishes, thoughts, fears while we hold onto our own."

Gus's eyes sparkled. "I've never seen a thing like this."

"We've got to keep moving along," I prompted. "Here, I've added bits of powdered snail now that the potion is boiling. Any thoughts as to why I need them?"

"Because snails can shed their shells and move to another home. They can inhabit another's forgotten shell with ease," Gus said, his voice stilted in wonder. "Then you have the herb mix that'll stabilize everything, of course, and the...what's the yellow rose for?"

I smiled. "Color."

Gus looked up, shocked. "Color?"

"Why not make it pretty?" I asked. "I like pretty things."

Gus snorted. "You're kidding me."

"Now is not the time for criticism," I said lightly. "Of course, I added the standard reversals to the potion that will pull the user back to reality. I added guarana extract for an accelerator—more energy," I explained to X. "Because we only have a few minutes, and I want to hear and feel and experience as much as possible."

Gus stepped back and ran a hand through his thin, graying hair. He opened his mouth once or twice to try a response, but eventually, he settled for a pair of raised eyebrows. If I didn't know him better, I'd say he was shell-shocked.

"Well..." Ranger X struggled a few paces behind, far less familiar with the herbs and ingredients and their respective properties, though he fought valiantly to keep pace. "Why'd you name it Amuletto Kiss?"

"It's a member of the Kissing Curse family." I smiled and clamped a hand around my necklace. I exposed the heart charm for both to see. "And, with any luck, I'll be able to use this potion with the amulet. It's a gift from my mother, so..."

"Lily," Gus warned harshly. "I advise you not to use this potion with a relic so old. It's not only dangerous for you physically, but the mental distress could ruin you. That's if everything goes perfectly."

"It would be worth the closure," I said, ending the conversation before this turned into a whole different argument. "Now, if you don't mind, I have a few more steps to go before I close up shop."

Ranger X peered down at me. "When are you planning to test the potion?"

I tucked the necklace back into my shirt and smiled. "First thing in the morning."

Chapter 21

THE NIGHT BLEW BY US in a flurry. I forced Gus to go home after I'd set the final ingredients in the pot. He had stubbornly yanked an umbrella out of the corner stand, growled at the thunder, and went on his merry little way.

Ranger X had passed out hours before on a couch near the roaring fire. He continued to snooze peacefully, oblivious to the quiet work I pursued even as my eyes struggled to close mid-thought.

As the potion bubbled a thick golden yellow color, I finally eased to a seat beside the fire, pulling a blanket over my legs as the storm grew oily and black outside.

My legs creaked with exhaustion; I'd never stood for so long a period at once. But during the past twelve—fourteen, *or was it sixteen?*—hours, I'd been up and down, mixing and dicing, stirring and surveying, and I'd not realized how little I'd eaten or how much I'd waited hunched over the cauldron that now bubbled happily on a small burner in the middle of the table.

I pulled my eyes from the potion's complex swirls of color for a moment, letting my gaze wander toward the couch where Ranger X had simply tilted sideways a few hours before and fallen deeply into sleep.

He looked peaceful, the sharp contours of his face softer, more childlike. Innocent almost, as he breathed in and exhaled, a pleasantly carefree sound. Only a slight crease of his forehead along with the now-and-again flutter of his eyelashes gave away any sign of concern, and I hoped those would ease as the night continued.

I stood, hauling a blanket with me, and moved over to the couch where he rested. I'd covered him hours before with a large blanket, a long one that reached from his chin down to his feet. As I sat, I rested a hand on his forehead and noted his temperature was quite warm from the fire roasting several feet away.

My hand toyed through his hair, pushing a few strands from his face. The locks had fallen into his eyes and he blinked, twitching when they brushed against his lashes. As soon as my hand touched his skin, he relaxed.

I took pleasure in that small fact, the knowledge that even in the deepest of dreams, X seemed to know me. To ease nearer me despite the darkness in his subconscious mind. I'd have stayed perfectly still all night like that, but the distinctive pop of a bubble from the cauldron drew me back to work.

Bring to a boil, the last instructions said, *and nothing more.*

As I neared the center of the room after re-tucking in X, I glimpsed bits of sunlight fighting against the dredges of storm battering the bungalow. How quickly morning had come.

Time flies, they said, *when you're having fun.* If only my *fun* wasn't intended to lead me to my mother's killer, I might believe it.

I believed Sammy hadn't done it, but with this final test I would know for certain. After that, I had no clue what I'd do. Pursue the real murderer, I supposed, but when? How? Who and why? All questions I had little or no way of answering.

With quick hands, I ladled the finished version of Amuletto Kiss into several smaller vials that I tucked safely into my travel belt. *Just in case.*

Then I capped the remainder of it into a larger beaker and stashed that on the shelves of the storeroom that had reverted from its anniversary date night decorations to its typical happy chaos.

Though anxious to test out the potion, I forced myself to leave the tops on all vials and refrain. Now that the difficult part of the Mixing routine was over, the tiredness launched its attack, crippling me in waves. I was physically and mentally exhausted, completely drained.

Dragging my feet up the stairs, I decided on a shower and pajamas, and then I'd wake Ranger X. He'd have to leave for work about the time I crawled into bed, so the least I could do for his support was send him off with a kiss.

The shower came and went first. I stumbled out of the water and took a moment to bask in the trapped steam as it wrapped around my body. The makeshift sauna warmed me straight through, even as growling thunderclaps rocked through the walls.

I threw a towel around my body and limped toward the bedroom after a quick brush of my teeth. After grabbing clothes from the closet, I returned to the bathroom to change and, once there, shimmied into sleeping shorts and a tank top. I'd gotten a little paranoid about changing in my room ever since that whole *Surprise!* incident with Liam.

I returned a final time to my room to toss my dirtied clothes in the hamper when a sudden thought struck through my sleepy haze. I hadn't even considered the note I'd found in my nightstand lately. Despite all I'd learned over the past few days, none of it helped me to understand who had crept into my room to leave a message behind, or why.

I tossed my clothes in the laundry bin, then padded over to pull the drawer open. I hadn't checked on the note in some time, and for all I knew, my surprise guest had been back with an update.

As I bent to remove the paper, I heard it. The noise wasn't so much a creak, nor was it a breath—it wasn't anything I could put my finger on. It was the mere feeling that I wasn't alone. Someone else was in my room.

Nonchalantly, I climbed into bed, feigning a loud yawn as I pulled the covers to my chin and forced my breathing to slow. I carefully arranged the covers so they'd be easy to throw back. The last thing I needed was to trip over my sheets and hex myself senseless when I launched my attack.

With a subtle glance, I confirmed the closet door remained shut, just as I'd left it. The rest of the room looked empty as I scanned it a second and third time, which left precious few places for someone to hide—unless somehow the guest had skills to become invisible.

Just when I'd begun to doubt myself and chalk up my nerves to paranoia, it happened again. The slightest whisper of movement, intangible save for the confidence that burned through me.

Whoever had broken into my room was close, too close.

Another slight creak, and this time—it came from underneath my bed.

Closing my eyes, I inhaled and exhaled, struggling to feign sleep even as I raised my hands and mustered the most potent Stunner Spell I could master. I waited until it had grown as powerful as possible, and then I let loose.

Bellowing the incantation, I slashed my fingers toward the underbelly of the bed as I leapt from the mattress. I hoped X heard the incantation, but when the spell flashed and banged and there was no sign of footsteps, I realized the storm outside had drowned out any noise I'd made.

Ducking gingerly to peer under the bed, I lifted the edge of the sheet with caution, prepared to leap away at the first sign of movement. Luckily, I didn't have to do any such thing.

To my surprise, the spell had worked fantastically. Sure enough, there lay an intruder motionless under my bed. From this angle, I couldn't recognize him. I'd have to haul him out and to get a better look.

I debated running down to retrieve X first, but I couldn't risk the man somehow waking from the spell and escaping. He'd come here for a reason, and I needed to know what. I needed to know he'd worked *alone*.

With a heavy sigh, I grabbed one suspiciously large foot and yanked.

Together, we sailed away from the bed. I scrambled wildly to land on my feet, while the man remained rigid in his frozen state and thunked unceremoniously against my dresser. I winced as a picture teetered on top and then crash-landed onto the man's stomach.

The slightest *oomph* escaped his mouth, though his lips couldn't move with the effort.

"Sorry," I said, scrambling to my feet and snatching the frame. I tossed it onto the bed in my haste to not break eye contact. "Actually, why am I apologizing to you? *Who* are you and why were you creeping under my bed?"

The man's face was frozen, along with the rest of him, so I took a moment to study his appearance. He was short in stature, but a bit round in the middle, and he had one eyeglass—a monocle—that had fallen from his eye at my spell. It now dangled from the side of his face, and in another life, he could have been the Monopoly man. Except for the hat. He had no hat, only the firm salt-and-peppered hair color of someone who'd passed middle age a while back.

"I don't know if I should unfreeze you," I said. "Can you blink?"

The man attempted to do so; I could see the struggle in his glassy eyes, but he failed.

"I'm going to get Ranger X," I said. "Sorry in advance, since he won't like the fact that you made yourself comfortable in my private space."

I was halfway to the door when he spoke. The word was a pale representation of English, a guttural sigh, but distinct. "*No.*"

I spun on a heel. "No, what? Don't get him? No offense, but I'm pretty sure I shouldn't be listening to you. You're in *my* house."

"Wh—" gasp—"*Wait.*"

Still proud of how potent my spell had been, I decided to give him the benefit of the doubt. The spell would wear off slowly, unfreezing his face first so he could talk. The rest of the body would follow minutes later.

"Fine," I said. "But the second I see you wiggling so much as a little finger, I'm siccing the Head Ranger on you. If you don't know him, well, you should. He's nobody you want to mess with."

"Your fiancé," the man said, warming to the use of his voice. "*Congratulations*, by the way. I'll send a gift."

I narrowed my eyes at him. "Who are you, and how do you know that? Nobody knows we're engaged."

"I," he said, with a smile slow as molasses, "am the Master of Mischief."

"That means nothing to me."

"Surely it does." A disappointed gleam settled in his eye. "I had to test you, Lily Locke. I'm sorry for the hassle."

"Test me for what?"

He sighed, struggling for air.

"Wait," I said. "I know a better way to do this."

The travel belt had come with me upstairs since I'd worn it earlier, and I'd removed it only with yesterday's clothes. Moving to the mysterious man's side, I reached down and muttered a Sharpening Spell to slice off the smallest corner of his suit coat.

"Wha..." His voice faltered in and out.

"It's something new I'm trying out," I offered. "You won't have to explain aloud if I can see your memories. It's a new potion."

It seemed like the man tried to nod, remembered he couldn't, and settled for a sigh.

Uncapping the vial of shimmering golden liquid, I brought it to my lips, trembling with anticipation. This was it—the moment of truth. *Do or die*, as they said. Before I could back out, I arranged myself in a sitting position on the floor, closed my eyes, and swallowed the Amuletto Kiss.

The mixture tasted light and pleasant, floral almost, and sweet. It went down easy and sent a nice little shiver over my spine. I forced myself to relax as I felt the Mix moving through my veins, seeping into my legs, my back, and eventually, my spine and brain.

Then, it happened quick as the snap of a finger.

My thoughts, my feelings and concerns, my wants and needs—suddenly they were no more. Instead I floated freely, suspended in a vat of air somehow, waiting, waiting for something to happen. For what I couldn't quite say. I could hardly *think*.

Then at once, another shudder rocked my spine and a new set of thoughts, of feelings and concerns, wants and needs, descended over me. Even in my altered state, I could sense the potion had worked. Then, with a quiet bubbling sound, even that feeling faded to nothing, and I was *him*. Completely and utterly *him*.

My mind—*his* mind—flashed through a roll of memories too quick to decipher. There was a face looking down at me, old and wizened, with concern in his eyes.

Then there were more images—people, beautiful people everywhere. Women and men, and a sign. The sign was wooden with blurred text—*Olympia*—and then that vanished, too.

Next, I saw my hands pouring bubbles across a bridge, feeling Long Isle Iced Tea glide down my throat as I watched my body morph into Ranger X. I saw a field of Forgotten Ferns one minute, and then the next, they were gone. I saw tomatoes—so many tomatoes. I said a spell, and they were gone. I saw a note resting gently in the drawer beside the bed.

That was it.

The Amuletto Kiss left me with a whirl, and suddenly I was back. I was Lily, my memories slamming back into a shaky body. The familiar exhaustion and fear and frustration I'd felt before taking the potion hit with startling clarity. Along with those feelings came the end of a loneliness, and in place of the loneliness curled the warm embrace of all consuming love. With a start, I realized I'd learned nearly as much about myself as I had the man lying on the ground.

He watched me, his eyes having gained some responsiveness in the time I'd been swallowed by the potion, and he looked downright shocked. "That was incredible. What do you call it?"

"Where is Olympia?"

If he could've moved, he would've flinched. Instead, his face pinched incredulously. "What did you do? You can't have read my mind. That's impossible—you're not a registered mind reader."

"No matter." I stood. "So, Master of Mischief—"

I stopped abruptly. I sized him up. My brain clicked faster, faster still, until I understood. I smiled down at him as it registered. "*You're the Keeper.*"

He swallowed, sucked in a deeper breath that sounded painful. "I want to know how you did that."

"You serve the Master of Magic," I said. "Was that him I saw in your memories? The old man? It seemed..." I hesitated, remembering... "You feel love for him. A platonic, selfless sort of love."

"You did it. You read my thoughts, my memories." He looked utterly mystified. "You're even more peculiar than they told me."

"Shut up and talk to me—I still don't know if I trust you," I said. "You have been ruining my life, barging into my room, wreaking havoc on the island. Why?"

"I am the Keeper, and I do *not* have your best interests at heart. I serve the Master of Magic alone. I've merely been sent to you because he is in grave danger, and it's my belief you can help us."

"Why me?"

"You're the only Mixologist in existence. And, judging by how quickly you picked up on Olympia, you might have some descendent blood in those veins. Again, I'm sorry for testing you, but it's my duty to be thorough. It's only I who can expose the Master's existence, and I'd never forgive myself if I let the wrong person through to him."

"Explain. I saw that it was you pulling all those stupid pranks on The Isle. How is stealing tomatoes testing me?"

"Ah, you see, it was a test on so many levels. I had to strain you: your loyalties, your relationships, the goodness of your heart. I left you the note, you see, to *use what you have*. It was I, too, who took Peter's letter from your drawer and had it printed." He hesitated, looking toward me with an almost affectionate gleam in his eye. "In case you're curious, you have passed."

"What did I use that I already had? How was *that* a hint?"

"You used your loyalty, your love, your compassion, your intelligence and wit, and your determination." He offered a confident smile. "Look at yourself. You've created a Mix more complex and potent than anything I've ever witnessed. Your loyalty never once wavered, even in the face of great distress. Instead of pulling apart from your loved ones, you are closer than ever." He paused, then winked. "Again, congratulations on the engagement. A moment that could have torn you and your lover apart survived the darker days and flourished. I applaud you."

I fought back the boiling of my blood for all the unnecessary stress he'd caused. But even as I bit back a retort, I wondered if his hijinks hadn't been a blessing in disguise. It was true. The stress had broken me, worn me, pushed me further than I'd ever gone before.

The darkest times, however, brought out the brightest flame. And in the moment of bright flame, I'd created Amuletto Kiss. I'd found the courage to fall deeper into love and promise myself to my soulmate. I'd gone on my own journey and succeeded.

"I'm truly sorry," he said. "I'm also sorry for the Soul Suck—the mystery traces on the spell? That's Keeper magic. It's unique, probably as the former Keeper explained to you upon your visit. The Forgotten Ferns, that too."

"You ruined people's livelihoods," I told him. "It's not fair the others have to suffer because of me."

"Oh, they won't—not *really*. I will have everything returned before I leave—refunded, replanted, or otherwise."

"Fine," I said shortly. "What about the guy after Poppy? Or my tail on the mainland?"

He frowned. "I'm sorry, I don't know anything about either of those."

"Now's not the time to lie."

"I have no need to lie."

He sounded so convincing, I was tempted to believe him. "But if not you..." I trailed off, not wanting to give him any insights to more of my personal life. "Forget it. That's all you're responsible for?"

He thought back. "Yes."

"And?"

He raised his eyebrows. "And?"

"What's next?"

"Lily," he said, moving to a sitting position. He noted my defensive shift with a wave of his hand. "Please, come here."

"No."

"You already *know* where you need to go," he said patiently. "Now, let me show you the way to the Master. I won't hurt you—he's too precious to me. You're being sent to help him."

Against my better judgement, I eased forward and kneeled next to him.

"Close your eyes," he instructed, and I closed them.

The lightest touch came next, a feathery fingerprint against the center of my forehead. It gently warmed, and then faded to nothing.

"I didn't feel anything." I opened my eyes. "What did you do?"

"Think hard of the Master of Magic," he said. "Focus on his face, the city of *Olympia*."

I did as he asked, concentrating on the images that had flickered through my mind during the Amuletto Kiss journey. Suddenly, I understood. I knew the way to Olympia, to the Master of Magic. I could see it just as clearly as if he'd laid a map in the palm of my hand.

"Where...?" I squinted, trying to place it in a country or a state, but I couldn't. I just knew the turns to take, the roads to follow, the path toward my future.

"Go," he said gently. "You and one other will be guided there. My work here is now done."

"Someone's coming with me?"

"You'll have a friend," he said with a smile. "One other will join you on the journey, and a third will follow behind."

"Okay," I said, sensing that was all he'd say. "I have one more question."

"What's that, Mixologist?"

"Lily," I corrected. "Did you come here today because of the Keeper's spell? Whatever he did to me back in his home?"

"I'll admit, I was surprised to catch a whiff of an old friend. How is Jonah, by the way? He taught me everything I know."

"He's...content," I said, and I meant it. "I think he'd waited a long time to help me."

We shared an almost friendly smile. Then the Keeper's smile turned into a frown, a forlorn look in his eyes as the windows rattled and the storm shook the very bones of the house.

"Good luck, my friend," he said softly. "Though it won't be luck you'll be needing."

"What will it be?"

The answer never came.

As I watched, the Master of Mischief shimmered, then disappeared before my eyes. I didn't move for quite some time, the shock and awe settling around me as I waited.

"Lily?" Ranger X eased into the room some time later, looking first to the bed, then widening his eyes, his voice escalating as he saw the emptiness. "Lily?!"

I started, then pulled myself to my feet.

"Lily, what are you doing sitting on the floor? Did something happen? Are you okay?"

I managed to shake my head, though I couldn't seem to utter a response. Instead I looked into his eyes and saw confusion. "What's wrong?"

"I just got four Comms in the last few minutes," X said, cautious. "The Forgotten Ferns are all back, and the crop has been replanted and duplicated. The market is now overflowing with beautifully ripe tomatoes—ten times more than whatever was stolen. Other things, too. Little things. I can't even comprehend why someone would go through the trouble."

I bit back my comments, and not by choice. The pull to tell Ranger X about the Master of Mischief was strong, so strong it burned at my throat. Yet somehow, the words wouldn't form. I couldn't speak of the subject around him.

I understood somehow that Ranger X was not the one who would travel with me on the journey. Somewhere in the deep recesses of my brain, I knew this to be true, which meant the spell binding Olympia in secrecy wouldn't allow me to say the name in front of Ranger X. Only one person in the world had those permissions, and he'd just left.

But if not X, then who would be my companion?

Almost in answer to my curiosity, the front door to the bungalow opened. The noise startled Ranger X and I into action. I threw on

some jeans and a shirt before heading downstairs and following X into the storeroom.

"Lily," Zin said, shifting her weight uneasily at the sight of Ranger
X. "I need to talk to you. Any chance I could have a minute?"

"I have to get going." Ranger X pulled me into an embrace, kissed
my forehead and held me tight. "Get some rest, okay?"

I nodded, still mute. "I love you." Then I kissed him on the mouth
and lingered, wondering if he'd be able to follow me into the unknown whenever I was called to leave.

X left without a backward glance, and Zin's sharp eyes took in the
bedraggled sight of me.

"I need you to do something for me," she said, her voice sharp and
straight to business as her black hair swung in a line under her chin.
"You're going somewhere," she said, eyeing my clothes, the bookbag
I'd grabbed from upstairs, and my travel belt. "Where are you going?"

I hesitated, feeling the burn in my throat, knowing I couldn't
speak it aloud. Apparently, Zin wouldn't be the one traveling with
me, either.

"It doesn't matter," she said, a rush of relief sounding in her voice.
"It's better if you don't tell me, actually."

"What is this about?"

"Take Poppy with you."

Aha, I thought. *My fellow traveler.* The mention of Poppy's name
brought a soothing cool to my throat, and I had no doubt I'd be able
to say the name Olympia to her.

"Fine," I said. "What's wrong?"

"My mission is nearing its end," Zin said, a ferociousness on her
face. "There's a vampire hunter loose on the island, and he's after our
cousin. I need her safely gone—anywhere, so long as it's away from
here—until I can end this once and for all."

We looked at one another, the brief spat from yesterday's alley incident completely obliterated by our new bond to protect the family.

"Of course," I said. "How soon can you get her here?"

"Hello," Poppy said, poking her head through the door. "Zin said to meet here before breakfast. What's up?"

"I'm going on a trip," I said pleasantly, "and I'd like some company."

"Where to?" Poppy asked. "I'm always available for sidekick duties."

I smiled, took Poppy's arm in mine. "Come on, I think it's better if I show you where we're going."

Chapter 22

"I DO *not* understand how humans use these things." Poppy pumped at the gas pedal, slammed on the brake, then cranked up the heater and fiddled with the radio all in rapid succession. "Stupid death traps."

"I can drive if you want." I peeled one eye open from the passenger's seat of our borrowed corporate car, courtesy of Ainsley's string pulling at MAGIC, Inc. Apparently, paranormals didn't feel the need to keep well-maintained vehicles on hand, judging by the state of this one.

"No, look at you—you're exhausted. The bags under your eyes are horrendous. I'll drive."

"Thanks, Poppy. Do you need me to give you directions?"

Poppy hesitated, the thoughts in her head seeming to confuse her. "Actually, I know exactly where to go. Don't ask me how, but as soon as you said the name Olympia, the path just opened right up. Know what I mean?"

I nodded, just as the car roared to life.

"Ah," Poppy said, settling in and cranking up the stereo. "Much better. Rest now, darling. Relax and enjoy the ride."

It was a difficult ride to enjoy.

Driving wasn't Poppy's forte. We wove in herky-jerky patterns across the state, whizzing far too quickly down the highway and taking the side streets at a snail's pace. Don't get me started on the stoplights.

I eventually drifted off sometime after we crossed state lines. When I woke later, Poppy was muttering about a wrong turn, and I watched as we re-entered the state of Minnesota across an unfamiliar bridge. That's when I closed my eyes and opted to go with the flow, slipping back into nightmarish dreams to pass the time.

I woke what felt like hours later, mumbling after the remnants of a dream in which something—someone—had been chasing me. There'd been the dark of night, the pulse pounding thrill of the hunt, and a hooded figure.

Then I'd woken, sucking in deep, even breaths as I glanced across the console at Poppy, relieved to find her humming innocently along to the music while applying pink lip gloss.

"Where are we?" I asked, easing my seat upright from its reclined position. "How long was I out?"

"I have no clue where we are," Poppy said. "And to your second question, I think you slept a good six or seven hours."

"Wow. Sorry about that!"

"Oh, no problem. I've only been driving about four hours because I stopped quite a bit."

"Why'd you stop?"

Poppy thumbed toward the backseat, a sheepish glint in her eye. "I told you I've never been to the mainland."

I mentally smacked my forehead as I looked over my shoulder. There on the backseat sat every cheap token a human might buy at a rest stop. Postcards, candy, pre-wrapped cookies, random keychains. There was even what looked like a hot dog wrapper and a lottery ticket.

I groaned. "I totally forgot about that, Poppy! I'm sorry! We should have made this more of a special event. Instead, I was dead to the world for your first experiences here."

"Oh, it's alright! I had a great time. I wasn't sure how to get all the right money, so I had to ask for help. But anyway, now that you're awake, how about you explain *why* we're here in the first place?" Poppy's voice was light, but the glint in her eyes was hard. "You haven't exactly told me why we're here or where we're going."

I sighed. "I'm sorry."

"Stop apologizing and let me in on the secret," she said. "It can't be *that* serious, or else you would've invited Ranger X or Zin instead of me. I'm just a little confused as to what we're doing."

"No, I wouldn't have taken them. I couldn't have even if I wanted to because it's supposed to be *you*." I looked over at her, gauging her response. "I'm glad it's you, Poppy. This might be one of the most important things I'll have to do in my life."

"I-I don't understand."

"You and I are meant to be here," I said, and it was as simple as that. I reached for her hand and squeezed it. "And more importantly, I want you here with me."

"So, Zin didn't slough me off on you as a babysitting gig?"

I didn't respond for a long moment. When I did, I started at the beginning. The very beginning, figuring if nothing else, I owed her the truth. "Have you heard of the Master of Magic?"

Poppy's hands gripped the steering wheel tighter and tighter as we drove, her lips growing thinner and thinner as I launched into my story and piled one piece of information onto her plate after the next.

By the time I reached the portion where Zin had asked me to get Poppy off the island and away from the vampire hunter, I could see the light fading fast from Poppy's eyes.

"I knew it," she said, shaking her head. "I'm here because I'm a burden."

"No!" I crossed my arms. "I couldn't even *mention* the name Olympia to X or Zin or anyone else. I physically was bound from speaking it aloud. *Why*? I don't know, and I'm sorry. I wish I did."

Poppy settled back in her seat with a harrumph of agreement. Just in time, because at the next turn, her fingers loosened and she clapped her hand against the wheel in excitement. "Lily, we're here! Do you see it?"

I nodded, nerves skittering through my stomach at the sight of the sign. It was the very same sign with blurred text I'd witnessed through the eyes of the Keeper during my Amuletto Kiss journey into his memories. The word was scrawled on an old wooden thing, un-ceremoniously poked in the ground, the background cracked and the lettering painted in what looked like ancient script: *OLYMPIA*.

Poppy took the turn onto the marked road. As I glanced around, struggling to get a pin on our location, I adjusted my travel belt tighter against me. I'd taken a few vials of Amuletto Kiss, along with Aloe Ale, a few protective spells, and my usual array of traveling sup-plies. Since I couldn't be sure exactly why I was needed here, I'd tried to be prepared. I'd included a Long Isle Iced Tea for good measure, though I didn't intend to use it if possible.

"You know, I don't even know which state we're in," Poppy said. "I assume we haven't crossed state lines again after I made that wrong turn back in Wisconsin, but I can't be sure."

"I think that's probably the beauty of a hidden city," I agreed. "Hard to say exactly where it's located."

Poppy's gaze focused hard on the road ahead. "It gets really steep up ahead. I hope this stupid car doesn't roll backward on me."

The road grew more and more winding, curling, dangerous. We'd been driving through sparse forests for the past hour on a little two-lane highway, and we hadn't passed another car during the entire time I'd been awake.

"Is that a tunnel ahead?" I squinted to look. "It's so dark it's hard to tell."

The road to Olympia felt different than before, as if we'd crossed some invisible threshold a few miles back. We were still surrounded by tall, lean trees that cast sweeping branches over the road, and the dimness of forest lighting surrounded us with the same haze, but it was as if the air had shifted.

As we neared the looming darkness ahead, I realized we faced a sort of natural, living and breathing tunnel. Here, the trees knitted together tightly to form a near-solid tube of blackness. Poppy didn't bother to slow down as the car lurched into the tunnel, throwing us into a dark abyss. I reached over and demonstrated how to turn the brights on, causing the tunnel to flood with light. Poppy breathed a sigh of relief.

Then the bulbs went out, extinguished, and we were thrust back into complete darkness.

"Poppy!" I screeched. "Watch *out*!"

"I can't see!"

"Put on the brakes!"

"I can't seem to *stop*!"

We both broke into shrill screams, and I closed my eyes, picturing the deadly smash of our car into a tree as we hurtled forward. We shot through the black hole with a twist and a lurch, as if it were a portal into another world entirely.

When I finally sensed our journey was coming to an end, I forced my eyes open just in time to watch the car burst from the tunnel and skid to an abrupt stop on the other side. For a long moment, all was silent save for our racing hearts and our ragged breaths.

Then we began to see the world around us.

I noticed the light first. It was brighter here, as if more than just sunlight provided the rays. It appeared the very lands before us glowed, sparkled like the pages from a picture book. The reds of the berries on trees were brighter here, the greens deeper, the skies so pale blue they ached with clarity.

"*Wow*," Poppy gasped. "What *is* this place? It's stunning."

I shook my head, also staring at the expanse below us—a colony that felt freshly sculpted and placed here on earth, every atom of its

existence filled with a purity and rawness, an uncontaminated fresh-
ness ripe with wonder.

"Olympia," Poppy said, turning to look at me. "If the Master of
Magic didn't pick here to settle down, he's got problems. It's gorgeous."

Poppy and I sat still in the car for another few moments, struggling to absorb it all—to appreciate the beauty and bask in the new-
ness. We were perched on a hill high above the town, and from here,
it looked like a little Alpine colony tucked among mountains in Swe-
den or Switzerland or the like.

"Shall we head down?" I asked, tentative. "This is where my instructions end."

"What do you *think* we should do next?"

I shrugged. "I suppose we begin the hunt for the Master of Magic."

"Doesn't look like the peace has been disturbed here," Poppy said.
"It looks perfectly calm, unlike the rest of the world. I've never seen
The Isle so dark and stormy before."

"If we found our way here," I said, a grim set to my voice. "We
have to imagine that others may be right behind us. *Not* friendly
faces."

"Well then," Poppy said, shifting the car into gear with a clunk.
"Let's meet the gods."

Chapter 23

THE CAR PUTTERED DOWN the hill, a horrible knocking and banging sound coming from somewhere in the engine.

"Nothing like announcing to the world we're here," I grumbled as we backfired with enough intensity that several faces poked out the windows of nearby houses.

"Stupid MAGIC, Inc. and their budget cuts," Poppy said. "I really would've liked something prettier. This thing is a turd on wheels."

Houses had begun to pop up along the hillside as we swirled down a gentler road than the one we'd taken on the other side of the tunnel. That road had been a death trap; this one was a pleasant picnic.

"Oh, I'm famished," Poppy said. "And you must be, too. Can we stop?"

I looked up at a crooked sign marked with bright blue and red letters. "*Bean in Love*?" I muttered. "Is it a shrink or a coffee shop?"

"Both?" Poppy shrugged. "Come on, it's adorable. Let's take a look inside. We can ask around for some information."

Before I could disagree, Poppy pulled into the small dirt lot and parked. There were no other cars around, but through the window, I could see heads bobbing in line, others bowed over tables as people sank deep into their conversations or chattered lightly over plates of food.

Poppy pulled the front door open and waited until I passed through first. I landed in an explosion of *love*. Pale pink stools were the focal point, pushed up against a diner-like counter. Baby blue tables were scattered around the seating area while little paper hearts and window clings clung to every surface.

"I don't know," I said. "What is this place?"

"I love it," Poppy beamed. "So much love."

At the sound of our voices, every head in the room swiveled to face us. The chattering drew to a stop as all locals surveyed the newcomers. In an odd twist of reality, it was impossible not to notice the slight glow around each of their faces, some brighter than others. The smallest of halos, the palest of lights. As if these people weren't quite real.

The scrutiny continued, and I tried to ignore one particularly hostile gaze. I debated turning around and leaving when a slender hand landed on my shoulder and squeezed.

"Well, *hello*! We heard you might be coming." A bright, red-lipped smile turned warmly on us. "What can I get you ladies?"

The woman belonging to both the smile and the slender hand continued to grin at us as we blubbered around, trying to answer her basic question. The woman herself was beautiful: Her skin was the color of mocha, her hair black as night save for the neon pink tips, and her nails were dainty works of art doctored with hearts.

"Are y'all feeling okay?" she pressed at our dumbfounded gazes. "We have a special going on today with the Love Blend, but I understand if you're looking to start with something simpler."

The woman moved behind the counter and rested her palms against it. Her hands, I noted, were the only thing slender about her. The rest of the woman was round and soft, and just like her smile, friendly and warm.

"We've got a Hot Shot," she continued, "but that'll knock you right off your feet. Maybe just a little Love Brewin'?"

"Oh, um, coffee?" I asked. "What about regular? No love needed."

"Everyone needs love!" The barista gave a booming laugh. "But I think I have just what you want. And for little miss vamp?"

"How'd you know I'm a vampire?" Poppy frowned. "Is it that obvious?"

"Honey, you're not from around here. In the land of the gods, nobody has secrets. You learn it's useless to hide them soon enough."

"That's not true." The customer who'd spoken was a man sitting alone at a nearby table. "Everyone has secrets. Also, you didn't introduce yourself. That's Lucy—she's one of Aphrodite's, so just ignore her. I'm Derby. One of Hermes's."

"Hermes?" Poppy asked, stunned. "Like..."

The man stood, his physique the lean, taut build of a marathon runner. Not particularly handsome, nor particularly beautiful, but sturdy and efficient. He made a gesture as if he were running. "Hermes. You know. *Hermes.*"

"I'm not sure these ladies know, Derby. Now sit your skinny ass down and leave them alone." Lucy chuckled behind the counter. "I'm guessing the Keeper didn't give you all that much information about these parts when he sent you, huh, sugar?"

I shook my head. "No, we didn't have a whole lot to go on."

She sighed. "Sometimes I think Gerry takes his job too seriously."

"Gerry?" Poppy asked. "Who's Gerry?"

"Master of Mischief, the Keeper, the guy who made sure you knew how to get here. Don't get me wrong—" she held up a hand, defensive. "Gerry is the best man for the job. But his chest puffed up just a bit when they named him Keeper after Jonah retired."

"Gerry." I tried the name on for size. It fit like an old glove with my image of the little Monopoly man who'd hidden under my bed. "Is he here? Maybe he could help us out. We're a little lost."

"He'll be working now. Come, sit first and have a bite to eat. Y'all look shell-shocked."

Poppy bobbed her head. "I'll take a..." She blushed. "Did you say you have Love Brewin'?"

Lucy winked. "That's perfect for you, darlin', and for you, Miss Lily, I'm thinking a regular brew with a shot of celebration."

As Poppy and I eased onto the Easter-pink stools, conversation resumed around us. I leaned forward, elbows on the counter as I faced Lucy. "Any chance you could give us a little more information about this place?"

Derby moved from his seat, inching closer to our conversation. "Olympia is a city, a town, rather, created for the descendants of the ancient gods. In order to acquire residency here, one must prove the purity of their bloodline. They also must prove their intentions are pure, otherwise..." He made the *off with your head* gesture.

"How much lineage do you need to belong to the club?" Poppy asked. "Is there some sort of test?"

He shifted. "It's not really an exact science."

"Poor old Derby here is one parent away from being human," Lucy said with a wink. "On the other hand, both my parents were direct descendants from the Twelve, so I'm a shoe in."

"The Twelve?" Poppy asked. "Like, the Pantheon?"

"Exactly like that," Lucy said, pouring a coffee for me and sliding it over. "I'm a healthy mix—strongest bloodline is Aphrodite from my pop's side, but on my ma's side I've got the Hestia bloodline."

Poppy and I stared blankly at her. Finally, Poppy spoke. "What does that *mean*?"

"My Aphrodite genes are strongest, hence the specialty in love," she said, gesturing around her. "But Hestia—"

"Goddess of hearth, family, home—" I filled in. "I've read about her, too."

"Yeah, she's got a whole list of things she's famous for," Lucy interrupted. "I've got that too. It's a nice mix to run the coffee shop."

Our conversation quickly became the centerpiece of the shop as other patrons chimed in, adding their stories and heritage to the mix. I took a sip of my coffee, an absolutely delectable cup, while Poppy hesitantly took a sip of her Love Brewin'. And smiled.

"This is delicious," she said to Lucy. "What's in it?"

"Oh, nothing." Lucy leaned forward and squinted at Poppy. Then she turned her gaze to me. "*Huh*. Interesting."

"What?" I swiveled around to face her. "What's wrong?"

"Nothing," she said with a quirky smile, averting her eyes down to a carton of milk between her fingers. "Just excited for you."

"Why?" I looked at Poppy, then back to Lucy.

"Your love will be here sooner than you think."

I blinked. "Me? I have a love already—are you talking about Ranger X?"

"Oh, honey, I'm not talking about you," Lucy said dryly. "You're practically a married woman—Aphrodite's work with you is done, my friend. I'm talking about *her*."

"Me?" Poppy sucked in a breath and nearly inhaled her coffee. "Oh, no. No, I don't think so. No prospects on the horizon for me. I'll die an old maid, I'm certain of it. Nobody wants to marry a vamp." She blushed as she finished but stood by her word as she glanced my way. "What? It's true."

"It's not true!" I blurted. "Not at all. Poppy, I never knew you felt like that."

"Don't waste your breath reassuring her," Lucy said. "Love's on its way to find her, and there ain't nothing she can do to stop it."

"Yeah," Poppy breathed, half-dreamily, half-depressed. "We'll see about that."

"Come on," Lucy said, patting the counter as if she could tell we were spiraling away from her happy conversation. "Let me show you something."

"Where?" I asked. "We have, ah—some business to take care of, and—"

"Don't y'all want to see what it is we do here?" Lucy raised her eyebrows, knowing the question was irresistible. "Who we are?"

"Yes," Poppy said quickly. Then gave me a sheepish look. "I do, at least."

"Great. Follow me," Lucy said. "And Poppy, let me top off that Love Brewin' in a To-Go cup."

LUCY WALKED US DOWN the street at a pace so quick it was hard to see much of anything. Beyond the supernatural feel, the rest of Olympia seemed to be a traditional looking small town.

On the main drag sat an inn, a few restaurants, and a marketplace with small shops hawking their wares. Through it all, people shouted greetings to one another and stopped for chats in the middle of sidewalks.

We walked past all of it until Lucy came to a stop in from of a somber looking building at the end of the hubbub. The structure itself was huge—easily the largest in the entire Olympia zone that we'd seen so far. It rose above the city with a drab sort of grandness that came from decades old cement walls and promises of cold, empty chambers within.

"Come along inside," Lucy said in the reverent tones mostly reserved for churches. "You'll be wanting to see this."

We followed Lucy down an unadorned cement hallway. Shadows bounced off the walls and a soft dampness permeated my very clothes as we made our way through. The far end of the hall opened into a cavernous chamber with rounded ceilings that reached higher than most trees.

"What is all of *this*?" I understood Lucy's quiet tones as I surveyed the space around us and the statues that filled it. "Who are these people?"

"The Greats," Lucy said, gesturing to the twelve largest statues—stone carvings that towered over us, ten times our size at least. "These sitting on thrones are the original Olympians. The rest..." She drew a sweeping hand across hundreds more statues, all standing in neat rows as if prepared for battle. "The rest of the gods stand at attention."

I stepped closer to one, ran my hand along its leg, and felt the cool stone beneath my fingers. I bent to study the nameplate at the bottom and saw the label Dionysus etched deeply into the metal. A cluster of stone grapes, each one the size of my palm, dripped from his hands and towered over my head.

"Those of us who live in Olympia are all direct descendants," Lucy explained. "And it's our main duty to carry out the work of our ancestors." While I processed this, she began to stroll through the rows, gesturing for us to follow. "Gerry will probably be annoyed I showed you this before he did. He takes pride in this place. He set it up a few centuries back."

"How old *are* you?" Poppy gawked. "Er—are all of you centuries old?"

"I'm two hundred twenty-nine," she said with a grin, "but I say I'm not a day over forty-four."

"Sorry, but what does this have to do with the Master?" I asked. "Are these statues...to protect him?"

"Speak of the devil," Lucy said, coming to a stop. "Look where we are."

I looked up, and Poppy followed suit. Before us stood more statues, but these were smaller. Just barely larger than us, less formidable, more...*refined*. Modern.

"Welcome to the Hall of Masters." Lucy pointed to the one nearest us. "The most recent Master of Magic passed on—oh, I don't know. Seven hundred years ago? Give or take."

I blinked. "That's some lifespan."

"Yes, and it's a grueling one. Anyway, have a look around. There's not a ton to do in town when it comes to killing time, so I figured you might as well see the history of this place while you're waiting for the Master."

Poppy and I proceeded to wander through the statues. Poppy favored the statues of the twelve, while I studied the Masters—analyzing, wondering, thinking what they could possibly need from *me*.

All of the statues were men, most of them old and wizened. There was one near the back that looked no older than a child, but before I could ask more about it, Lucy gave a low whistle and called us back to her side.

"I have to get back to the cafe now," she said. "So, I'd like to set you up with a room at the inn."

"Oh, that'd be great," I said, then stopped, feeling my cheeks turn red. "One problem—do we need money?"

Lucy just laughed. "No, we'll take care of you, baby. Come on now, let's go."

"Wait," a voice spoke from the darkness, from the back of the Hall of Masters. "Let me take Lily."

I froze, listening. The voice was familiar, and the second time it sounded, the man it belonged to stepped into the light. Short and small and frowning. *Gerry*.

"C'mon, Gerry, stop doing that," Lucy said, annoyed. "You're startling the guests."

Gerry ignored Lucy and turned to me, his eyebrows furrowed and his voice reverent. "Lily, the Master is ready to see you."

Chapter 24

POPPY AND LUCY HEADED in one direction to get settled at the inn and find something to eat for dinner. I promised Poppy I'd find her when my meeting finished. So, while they headed back toward town, I turned to follow a quick-moving Keeper who didn't have a lick of patience for my more-human-style speed.

We came to what seemed to be a dead end behind the Hall of Masters. Or it was until Gerry rested his hand against an unmarked patch of cement wall, and a door sprung open to reveal a rickety old staircase curling upward.

I sighed as we began the climb. It was a steep spiral staircase, and the top of it was nowhere in sight.

"Keep up," Gerry said. "The Master is waiting."

I groaned, picking up the pace. I'd never gotten that bite to eat at Lucy's, and I keenly felt the gnaw of hunger. At least Poppy had let me sleep on the ride here, or else I'd be a walking zombie. Unfortunately, my improved attention allowed me to focus more directly on the sounds coming from my stomach.

"So," I said, gasping as I tried to make conversation. "What is he like?"

"He's..." Gerry hesitated, searching for the right words. He shook his head as we climbed. "There's nothing I can say that'll do him justice. You'll just need to find out for yourself."

"I'll find out if we ever reach him," I retorted. "Are we almost there?"

We hadn't actually left the Hall of Masters; we'd merely gone above it. Up, and up, and up, until my legs threatened to give out. I understood they needed to protect the man, but jeepers. An enemy's legs would fall off before they got to his front door.

Gerry merely frowned at my complaint. "Here we are," he said. "Brush your hair. It's horrendous and makes you look like a witch."

"I *am* a witch, Gerry."

"Don't call me Gerry."

I ran my fingers through my hair, tugging it into place. Gerry positively twittered with anxiety, wringing his hands and stomping back and forth before the door.

"Fine, it's fine," he muttered when I asked if I looked decent. "Be careful not to offend him. Don't say a word. Don't...*oh*, I meant to ask you. Who did you try and bring with you?"

"With me? You must mean Poppy, my cousin. She drove."

"No, the one who followed you and got left behind at the tunnel."

My blood went icy cold. "What are you talking about? I didn't—*couldn't*—tell anyone where we were going. It was just us."

"I know, that's the Gag Spell—prevents you from spilling information you shouldn't. But that can't be right."

"It *is* right," I repeated. "Are you positive there was someone behind us?"

"I thought it was one of your little friends."

"No. You did say another person will join us—a third. Could it be that person?"

"No, your third guest is not due until tomorrow. That's when her access begins." Gerry put a finger to his lips. "This is curious. I don't like it."

"Well, where are they now? Should we find this person?"

"They're outside; they were bounced."

"Bounced?"

"The boundaries succeeded in keeping them out, though they got further than I would've liked. Only the tunnel stopped them. You *should have* been more careful. Obviously, someone followed you."

"Nobody followed us here! We were careful."

Gerry shook his head like I was an idiot. "Seriously, you witches." He composed himself, straightened the little bowtie—the only adornment on his custom-sized suit—and cleared his throat. "No matter, I'll take care of it. Are you ready?"

"As I'll ever be."

Gerry swung the door at the stop of the staircase open. The result was wildly anticlimactic. Seeing as we'd been climbing for what felt like hours, I imagined we'd have a spectacular view of...*something*.

Instead, there was only a tiny room with a rickety little desk sitting right in the middle of it. One arched, stained-glass window cast a dim, dusty glow over the room. Fractures of colored light played against the bare surfaces, glinted off the few framed artifacts and documents against the walls. Dented floorboards ran below my feet, and a few half-dead plants starved of sunlight sat on abandoned shelves.

Peculiar arrangements of books sat haphazardly forgotten in every direction, some stacks towering up to my waist. The very air in the cramped space felt heavy with specs of dust that glinted royal blue and jungle green and murky red. Last, but not least, was the man sitting behind the desk.

The man who I presumed to be the Master of Magic was old, his eyes a clear, pale gray, the color of stone. His hair was white, unstyled—left to wisp in any which way it wanted, a bit eccentric.

He held only a pen in hand. A roll of parchment sat on the table before him. While he'd spared a look up at our entrance, he turned almost at once back to the desk before him and resumed scribbling.

I attempted to peek at the figures he wrote, but it was pointless. Not only were the marks on the page in no language I'd ever seen before, but they seemed to quiver and move before my eyes, making me nauseous.

Gerry caught me staring and hissed through his teeth for me to step back. I hadn't realized I'd stepped forward, ever so slightly, to peer over the desk. I tried to keep my eyes averted, but the draw toward his work was too much, and I disobeyed. I glanced down again, watching as more and more figures appeared, trembled, and then set still as the ink dried.

We stood there for quite some time, watching and waiting and listening. I couldn't be sure which I was supposed to be doing, so I tried to do them all. Every time I breathed too loudly or shifted my weight too quickly, I earned a look of scathing dismay from Gerry.

I was bottling up the courage to speak when finally, the silence broke.

"That's all for today," the man behind the desk said. "Good evening."

If Gerry was surprised by this development, he didn't show it. I, meanwhile, couldn't battle back the surge of frustration that leapt forth from a place of gritty darkness I'd let fester.

"*Sorry?*" I said, trying to understand. I'd set my life on hold, driven for hours across the state, left my fiancé without any explanation, and dragged my cousin from safety—all to protect a man who wouldn't so much as look at me? "Excuse me, but we came a long way today. Maybe I can introduce myself at least."

"He said that's *enough.*" Gerry's hand squeezed my wrist, and he tugged. "Lily, it's time to go."

I ignored the quiver of nerves in his voice and pulled my hand free from Gerry's. "I have to talk to him—I need information. Time's ticking, and I'm not here to sit around; I'm here to help."

"Lily." This time, Gerry made it clear he'd given me a direct command. "Come with me."

I hesitated, glancing at the Master of Magic to no avail. He continued to scratch drawings onto the page as if I wasn't in the room. "But..." I hesitated. "I don't understand. We're here to help."

The crack of magic sent a jolt through my spine, and the next thing I knew, Gerry and I stood on the first floor of the building just inside the Hall of Masters. Gerry closed the door to the staircase and sealed it with a touch of his hand. Without further ado, he stomped off.

"Where are you going?" I called after him. The sun had dropped while we'd been inside, and the wink of stars came out above our heads. "What happened in there?"

"An embarrassment," he said, whirling around. "Everything I asked you not to do, you did. And your hair is still horrendous, you *witch*."

"Where are you going? Where should I go?"

"I don't care." Gerry turned to face me. "The inn's around the corner, and your room will be ready. I'll let you know tomorrow if the Master requests your presence further, or if you're done here."

"You can't kick me out!" I raised my hands in frustration. "I'm trying to understand, trying to help. The Master of Magic is in trouble—can't you feel it? Couldn't you see those storm clouds on The Isle?"

Gerry shifted uneasily. "Let me show you something."

When Gerry rested his hand against the wall again and the staircase appeared, I groaned. "I'm sorry, I am not climbing up there again. I'm dead on my feet."

Gerry gave a resigned grimace, then reached for my hand, squeezed, and the crack of magic sent us spiraling away once more. This time, we returned to the same floor as the Master of Magic. The door of his office stood partially ajar, but it appeared he would be ignoring us again.

"This way," Gerry whispered, turning to the staircase. There was one more level to climb. At my intense expression of dismay, he scowled. "We can't Evaporate to this level."

I hauled myself up the staircase, following closely on Gerry's heels. He took soft, reverent steps, as if whatever waited behind the small, crooked doorway was a near-religious experience.

The paneling on the door itself was made from old driftwood-style material. A small crack above one of the wood's imperfections gave us a preview into the room. It appeared to be black, completely dark, until a bright, blinding flash of light clapped from the inside and bled outward. I watched, curious, as colors morphed and mutated from a pure white light into splinters of vibrant greens and blues and reds.

Gerry caught me gaping, and for the first time, looked pleased. "Maybe you'll have a greater appreciation for our Master of Magic after you see *this*."

On the last note, he pushed the door open and stepped through. I hauled my body up the remaining two stairs before the entrance and stopped once I'd joined Gerry inside. It was difficult to feel awe over the waves of confusion at the sights before me.

We stood on an observation deck of sorts. A glass cube with walls that ran only as high as my waist, and no ceiling. As I stepped onto it, Gerry rested his hand on the side of the glass and closed his eyes. The second he did, we jolted forward and began to move along with the platform.

Terror didn't come close to describing the sensation of standing on an utterly clear glass platform with an open top and an angry little man beside me. I had nightmarish visions of the floor cracking, or a fall over the ledge. I couldn't see where I'd land because beneath us was only a black abyss.

It took all the bravery I had in my body to look down. It wasn't that I had a fear of heights so much as a fear of falling into the unknown. It was a *long* way down, judging by the number of stairs we'd climbed—and I had no idea what might be at the bottom.

Then, the darkness broke.

The blackness cracked beneath my feet, little fissures in the seams of the atmosphere that allowed in brilliant streams of light.

Magic.

Delicate, exquisite rays of it. The finest threads of it, so slim they were barely visible. Quivering, trembling heartstrings. Like a musical instrument—a harp, a violin, a piano. These miniscule beams of light and magic moved to a silent dance, crisscrossing below us like a complex laser display—strangely beautiful, wildly mesmerizing.

As I watched, my heart rate slowed to a steady thump. A pulse to match that of the whispers of light below, the web that twisted and turned downward as far as the eye could see and beyond.

"This is where he works," Gerry said softly, serene as he gazed downward. "This is the core lifeblood of our universe. The heart of magic, if you will. It's *his*."

"What does the Master of Magic *do*?"

"These are the threads that stitch the universal magic consciousness together. He guides, maintains, balances."

"He controls all magic?"

Gerry looked at me sharply. "He never controls anything. It's not in his nature to control, but to guide and shape and balance. The balance, Lily. Good and evil, light and dark, laughter and sadness, hope and fear. Magic brings many things to our world, and it all hangs in a precarious balance."

I swallowed. "I don't understand."

"Nobody does, not fully." Gerry crossed his hands before his body, watching the flickering display once more. "Just because he does not *control*, does not take away from his power."

"Is he a wizard?"

Gerry frowned. "No."

"What is he?"

"The Master of Magic. There is nothing like it." Gerry pressed his hand to the glass siding once more and set us off, traveling back toward the stairwell. "That is exactly all he is. No more, and no less."

When the glass platform returned to the side of the abyss, Gerry disembarked and then stood waiting as I remained behind. I felt drawn to the edge, thirsted for more of this. The light, the magic, the intensity of it all.

"It's beautiful," I whispered, feeling the unwelcome sting of tears in my eyes. "I don't understand it, but it's..."

"Beautiful and horrible and wonderful," he agreed. Then, with a new crispness to his voice, he waved a hand toward the depths of the cavern. "One tug of the wrong thread, Lily, and your heart would stop. Now come, we're done here for the day."

I let Gerry pull me from the platform and back down the staircase until we reached the Master's office. Then with a flick of his hand and a grasp of my wrist, we Evaporated into a warm and cozy little space, a small room furnished with red squashy couches and warm, autumn colors popping against a pale wall. A fire roared just behind me, and I stepped forward in surprise, feeling the heat on my back.

"Welcome to the only inn in Olympia," Gerry said, much like an elevator attendant. And then he vanished.

"There you are." A smiling woman stood behind the desk, her hair in tight ringlets. "I'm Diana, one of Ceres's."

"Ceres?" I'd barely finished processing my visit with Gerry before I felt blindsided again. "*Ceres?*"

"I know, we mostly have the Greeks around here, but there are a few Romans scattered in the mix, too." She grinned, her face glowing far brighter than the auras around Lucy, Derby, or any of the other locals I'd seen. "I checked your cousin into the room upstairs. Would you like to join her? I'll have your bags sent up...er, you don't have bags. I can have dinner prepared if you'd like?"

"Oh, that would be wonderful." I rested a hand apologetically on my stomach. "I haven't had a thing to eat all day."

Her face brightened more around her full pink cheeks. "Of course! I've just prepared some dinner for myself as a matter of fact—loads of it, and it's not like I need to eat all of it." She fondly patted a healthy-sized stomach. "Will you join me? I was just about to take my break."

I glanced at the darkness outside, figured Poppy was probably sleeping already, or near it. Either way, I needed to eat, and I was desperate to learn more from Diana about her ancestors.

As the name Ceres flitted through my head, I felt the amulet weighing heavy around my neck. The closer I stepped to Diana, the warmer it grew, the brighter it glowed. A faded yellow sheen, quite similar to the halo around Diana's face. I took its happy hum and pleasant glow as a sign that my feet—and stomach—had pulled me in the right direction.

Diana invited me to sit at a small table in the living area, so I did, enjoying the fire crackling merrily behind us as she poured a deep, soulful burgundy wine into our glasses. A light tinkle of piano music flitted in the background.

The food itself was incredible. I ate until I should have been embarrassed, but I couldn't bring myself to stop. Meats and cheese and olives, salads and pastas, bits and bobbles of side dishes and sweets. Dessert was coffee and a slice of cake, and it was only then that I realized I'd been so busy eating I'd barely touched my glass of wine.

Diana sat back looking satisfied and smiled. "So, what brings you here? I know you're traveling with your cousin, and you've got Gerry's undies in a real bunch, so you must be important."

I laughed. "I would not say I'm important, just that I'm needed here. Or so they tell me. I'm actually not quite sure *why* yet."

Diana topped off her wine glass and sipped slowly. As she did, I weighed the pros and cons of taking a risk: The amulet was heavier than ever around my neck, but I'd kept it tucked under my sweater and safely hidden. I wondered if Diana would recognize it if I revealed it to her.

There was only one way to find out.

Reaching for the chain around my neck, I pulled out the amulet and rested it against my chest. I said no more, letting the glowing heart shine for itself as I watched Diana for her reaction.

Her eyes changed first. They widened and hinted at alarm as she focused on the heart around my neck. Then her hands gripped the table and her body froze still as death. "You have the amulet."

When her gaze made its way to mine, I hesitated, then nodded. "I'm beginning to think so. It was given to me by my mother."

"Of course it was," she whispered. "Where did she get it?"

"I don't know. She's dead."

"I'm so sorry."

"My aunts reunited both halves of the amulet on the day they told me I was a witch." I clasped a hand around it, amused for a brief moment thinking back over those early days, my shock and awe and fright at the declaration. Now, my witchiness was the least of my problems. "They told me it was to protect me. They told me a tale of its origin."

Diana nodded, her hand extended. At the last second, she hesitated. "May I?"

"Yes, of course."

"A long time ago, it belonged to *my* mother." Diana's fingers lightly gripped the heart charm. She smiled when her fingers connected with the metal. "I saw you staring at my Heritage when I mentioned Ceres's name—I wondered why, and now I know."

"Your heritage?"

"Ah, right. The glow you see around my face, around our faces. It's called *Heritage*. The closer one is related to the Twelve, the more attached they become to Olympia. The more attached, the stronger the glow." She twirled a hand around her face. "As you can see, I've got a strong Heritage."

"This necklace—it's not as simple a story as my aunts thought?"

"It *is* a protective charm as they suggested, originally from Hecate, but this one is a more particular variety than they'd ever bargained for." Diana let her fingers caress the charm one last time, then withdrew them to her side of the table. "You are wearing a *very* special heirloom. There is only one true amulet like this in existence."

"What does it mean?" I gestured downward at the changing shade of light. The necklace glowed a fierce orange now, vibrant and solid. I could hardly see the shape of the heart for the thickness of the glow. "What's happening to it?"

"It's found its way home. I'm a familiar face, Lily." Diana smiled at the necklace as if it were a beloved child. "It's part of the prophecy."

"Prophecy?" This wasn't the first time I'd heard the word thrown around. I hadn't thought much of it since Liam's proclamation, but I'd far from forgotten it. "Do you know the prophecy?"

"I know *of* the prophecy, though I hadn't realized it would be fulfilled so soon." She hesitated. "Then again, it makes sense. The Master's been hard at work these last few years. Uncharacteristically so."

"What do you mean?"

"His time is nearing an end, I believe. We can all see it. I am thinking this prophecy must have something to do with the relationship between you both."

A tremble rocked my spine, skittered across my skin. "You mean this Master is retiring?"

"Honey." Diana's expression filled with pity. "This isn't a job one can retire from. You see, there can only be one Master of Magic at a time. While one lives in power, the other...passes on. It's not a sad thing, honey, you poor thing. You're shaking."

"I came here to protect him. I'm—I'm the one who's supposed to stop that from happening. Are you saying I'm destined to fail?" I shook my head. "I don't believe it. I'm not giving up that easily."

"I'm not saying that at all. You both are connected in a pivotal way—as I said, there's some relationship between the pair of you. If your job is to save him now, save him you will." Diana retreated, her gaze softening. "Do you know what Ceres was known for during her time?"

I racked my brain attempting to picture the book from which I'd found the amulet story. "Grains or harvest...something to do with agriculture?"

"Yes, but in this case, more importantly, she was the goddess of motherly relationships."

"Okay," I hesitated. "And why does that matter?"

"The amulet you wear around your neck is the strongest protective charm for women that's ever been created. It was forged by gnomes, enchanted by elves, and sealed by the gods. The three creatures had never worked together before and have never since. It's a member of the Order of the Heart family of spells—an old witching tradition in which a mother passes down half of the heart to her daughter. However, this one is a very special version."

"What is its purpose? How is it different?"

"Its purpose is to protect its wearer. It is rumored to have, shall we say, a mind of its own. When it no longer belongs to you, it'll find its way to the next woman, and on, and on, until it's needed once more."

"Why do I have it?"

"This one is different because..." Diana hesitated, pushing her glass of wine away to make room for an elbow rested on the table. "It's specific to one owner. The amulet belongs to the Mother of Magic. All other owners are merely conduits to its true match."

"Sorry?"

"Every Master of Magic is born a human, a wizard, something. They don't become the Master until the time is right."

"He inherits his powers."

"Yes—and the challenge is that we never know when, where, how, or who, will bear the next Master. Therefore, the gods cannot protect the Master of Magic until he is found and named as such."

I frowned as I listened.

"The necklace was created to seek out the Mother of Magic and protect her, so she can safely raise her son until the time comes for him to live with us in Olympia. Once he inherits his powers, the Keeper will protect him."

I waited for a long moment, the silence stretching into discomfort. Then, I couldn't help it. I threw my head back and laughed. When Diana looked confused, I waved a hand and shook my head, slowly returning to a quiet grin.

"I'm sorry, but that can't be right. I must be one of the conduits you mentioned—one of the women who passes it onto the *true* owner. It can't be mine."

"You're just afraid." Diana patted my hand. "The prophecies are never wrong. If it's you who owns the necklace, and I think that it is, your son will be the next Master of Magic."

"Where is this *prophecy*?"

"The Master of Magic knows all prophecies, but I don't need the prophecy to know that this necklace belongs to you. You see, Lily, the amulet only glows so brightly when the time is nearing. I'd give you a few years maximum until your life changes. The Master of Magic must feel it, too. He's been working on something, a project—something big. I can only imagine it's his final one."

"You're telling me that I'll have a son who will be the next Master of Magic within the next several years? No," I said, shaking my head. "Absolutely not. I just got engaged *yesterday*." My hand circled around the amulet as I stood. "I can't—I'm sorry. I think you should take the amulet from me to hold for safekeeping."

"The amulet is yours to keep." Diana stood, too, matching my gaze. "Either you'll fulfill the prophecy..."

"Or I'll die trying, and it'll move on to the next woman in line."

Diana's silence was enough.

"I'm going to head upstairs. I need to get some rest and *think*."

"I can see you're not convinced," Diana said. "So, let me put it this way. The question isn't whether or not the amulet is yours... but for how *long* will it belong to you?"

I backed away from the table. Diana looked sympathetic, though amusement played at her lips.

"Fine, fine. That's enough conversation for tonight. Get some rest, Miss Locke."

I might have thanked Diana for dinner, but I couldn't be sure. I wound through the hallways of the inn and looked for door number nine as Diana had said, my head spinning with the day's events. I had come to a new town filled with the descendants of ancient gods, met the Master of Magic, and learned the truth about my amulet and its purpose in protecting a child I didn't yet have. I needed to lie down.

I spotted door number nine with relief. Finally, someone who could laugh at this with me. Who could help me process and forget, even for a minute, the weight of the world that pressed on my shoulders.

"Hey, Poppy, sorry I took so long!" I pressed my hand to the door and it unlocked at my touch. As it swung open, I called out again. "You will *not* believe what happened—"

The words died on my lips as I stepped into the room.

A scream followed—probably mine. I couldn't be sure.

Another bloodcurdling scream, and then, "*Poppy!*"

Chapter 25

THE SOUND STARTED FROM my lips, and then bled to hers.

Poppy lay on the bed as if she'd been sleeping. The covers were pulled up to her chest and the ruffle of pink pajamas peeked out at the top. Her head rested on the pillow, her eyes open, dead with fear.

The issue wasn't Poppy.

It was the figure standing over the bed—a tall man, broad and sturdy looking—blond-haired, dark-eyed with a look of utter concentration on his face. In his right hand, he gripped a stake.

At the sound of my scream, the intruder's eyes flicked up at me.

"Poppy, *move*!" I took advantage of the lag in time as we all digested the surprise and flung the door shut behind me before I pounced across the room. As I moved, I built a lightning fast Stunner Spell and hurtled it toward the intruder.

I missed my target wildly, but the ball of light caused Poppy's attacker to dodge its trajectory, stumbling backward and releasing his stake. As he scrambled for it, I moved further into the room and built another Stunner Spell. I held the pulsing ball of light in hand.

This time, I wouldn't miss.

I inched closer to Poppy, hoping to wedge myself between her and the attacker. Poppy had managed to roll off the bed and into a crouch on the floor. I crept toward her as I kept my eyes focused on the blond hair near the other side of the bed.

"Who are you?" I growled. "What are you doing here?"

He said nothing, though his face hardened as he stood, the stake in his hand. His knees bent as he got into position, and we faced one another, moving toward the end of the bed and away from Poppy.

"I don't want to hurt you." His voice was low, soft. Silky in its confidence. "Move aside and let me at the vamp."

I stiffened as realization hit me. The blond hair, the shiny blue eyes—shiny, shiny, *shiny*. This was the man from the police station. The person who'd tailed me on the mainland. The vampire hunter must have been tracking me to get to Poppy, and then I'd gone and led her right into harm's way.

"How'd you get into Olympia?" The thought came to me at once, and I blurted it out. "You're not a demigod, are you?"

"No." The man's eyes flashed. They were an odd shade of blue—an almost royal blue in their clarity. His hair was dirty blond and slightly curled, and his physique was...well, it was solid enough to kill a vampire, I knew that for a fact.

"Poppy's not a traditional vampire." I raised my hand, letting the Stunner Spell hold a warning as it glowed. "She doesn't drink blood, and certainly she'd never harm a *fly*, let alone a human or a fellow paranormal."

His eyebrows creased. "That's *impossible*."

"She's blood intolerant," I snapped. "It gives her...issues."

"Lily!" Poppy hissed. "Those issues are private."

"Not when I'm trying to save your life," I hummed back under my breath. To him, I spoke louder. "How did you get here?"

"I walked in."

I squinted, trying to decipher between obliviousness and deceit. After a long pause, I realized he wasn't lying—he truly didn't understand how he'd gotten into Olympia. An issue I'd address later, after Poppy was safe.

The hunter turned toward Poppy, and it was enough of a move for me to cry out my incantation and hurtle the Stunner Spell at him.

It clipped the man's shoulder, just enough to numb a bit of his arm. Unfortunately, it wasn't the arm with the stake.

He lunged toward Poppy, soaring over the bed and landing next to Poppy's crouch. With one strike, he had Poppy on the ground under him, holding the stake poised for the kill.

"*No!*" I couldn't say where the cry came from—inside me somewhere. A guttural, painful crevasse that sent fury and adrenaline rocketing through my body. "Stop!"

Even as I lunged at him, I knew it was too late.

The stake descended toward her heart.

I watched in slow motion as the vampire hunter looked directly into Poppy's eyes as he drove the stake downward, a hungry look on his face, as if he wanted to watch the life seep from her eyes.

He hesitated only for the briefest of seconds before completing the deed—one breath from Poppy's demise. That split second was enough.

A crash broke through the window across the room, the glass shattering to millions of sparkling pieces at our feet. A sailing blur knocked the tussling pair over, sending Poppy sprawling to the side where she fell with a sharp cry onto the shards littering the floor.

The snarl identified the jaguar as she tackled the vampire hunter, Zin's teeth gnashing mercilessly at the hunter's throat—not quite touching him, but close enough that her teeth glinted in the reflection of his eyes.

"Zin, stop," I said, breathing heavy. "Don't kill him—*yet*. We have to find out who sent him. Stay there, and I'll get Diana. Poppy, are you okay?"

A familiar crack of magic sounded as the Master of Mischief appeared in the corner of the room. Gerry stood looking quite ruffled in his pajamas: a two-piece outfit designed from cotton material, but still decorated to look like a suit. His eyeglass hung from around his neck.

"What's the disturbance?" Gerry looked around the room, dis-pleased. He examined the furniture first, then the shattered window, and then finally the man trapped beneath the snapping jungle cat. "I thought Diana didn't allow pets."

"She's not a *pet!*" I pointed to Zin. "She's a Ranger and my cousin, and her Uniqueness is that she's a Shiftling—she can shift into any-thing. Her name is Zin, and she just saved Poppy's life from this vam-pire hunter."

"She's not supposed to be in the district yet." Gerry frowned, fear spreading across his face as realization struck. "There's been a *breach*! But how?"

I toed the vamp hunter's shoulder. "I don't know how he got in, but he claims to have walked in."

Gerry's face paled further. "Something evil is upon us."

Our gazes locked.

"*They're* here," I said finally, and at the sound of my voice the world shook. It trembled and roared, as if the very ground beneath our feet was breaking apart. Thunder clouded the sky, winds whipped into a tizzy beyond the window.

"No," Gerry whispered. "Is there any chance you have more of that potion you used on me?"

"Amuletto Kiss? Why do you care?" I watched his quizzical gaze, followed his line of sight as he glanced down and saw the travel belt affixed to my jeans. The golden hue of Amuletto Kiss burned bright. "Oh. You want me to read the hunter's thoughts to find out how he got in—and who else might be here."

"Yes."

The earth shivered beneath us, and I figured I didn't have much of a choice. I had several more vials of the Mix and the suspect direct-ly beneath me. There wasn't time to waste in debate. I knelt beside the hunter and spoke in a frosty whisper. "If you want to live, if you want me to forget your name when I tell my fiancé what happened—"

"*Fiancé?*" Poppy shrieked. She had carefully pulled herself up from the floor of broken glass after Gerry's arrival and stood next to me. "You got *engaged* and didn't tell me?"

I gritted my lips. "Sorry, but—"

She burst into tears. "Congratulations, Lily. I knew it. I knew you loved him, and he loved you, and..." She stopped at my stern look. "Right, right. *Hold it together, Poppy*, you can do it," she coached herself.

"If you want to live," I continued to the hunter, "you better hope you were telling the truth about how you got in here." I prodded the hunter's shoulder as I snapped a piece of his shirt off with a quick Slicing Spell. "Otherwise, I'm going to let the cat take a bite out of you."

His eyes widened in shock, and he nodded in understanding.

Then I sat back, uncorked the vial, and took a sip.

The sensation was more familiar this time as the spell slipped over me; it had become easier to switch into and out of my own thoughts and put on someone else's—like a good winter coat or a pair of well-worn jeans. As I let my thoughts, worries, and exhaustion fade away, I prepared myself to enter a whole new mind.

I closed my eyes and waited. The visions began, the feelings, the sentiments along with it. As it did, Lily faded away, and I became the hunter—utterly and entirely *him*.

Images of Poppy appeared. I was tracking her. My earliest memories of Poppy were attached to an emotion resembling anger, frustration. She was standing in my way of a job well done. I had only one task remaining: kill the vampire.

My memories fast-tracked a few weeks, and I watched Poppy again and again as she went about her daily routine. Poppy sung and danced as she picked ripe strawberries in the garden. She packed a huge floppy hat and went to the beach, plopping onto a towel as she read a book for hours and hours on end. I felt myself stiffen as I watched her. The feelings of anger and frustration were replaced by ones of curiosity and fondness.

I continued to hunt her as she read a novel by the fire at night, knowing my time was drawing to a close. *She needed to be ended*, I thought, but the very notion was accompanied by horror as I watched her sleeping peacefully through the window.

Finally, my thoughts ripped forward to earlier this afternoon. I had followed Poppy here—tracking the car at a great distance. I'd arrived successfully in Olympia—or at least to the sign outside the tunnel. Then the car had driven straight through the tightly knit trees, and I'd tried to follow but couldn't.

Then a man appeared down the road in front of the tunnel. He drew a circle in the air and muttered words from a foreign language. The circle burned licks of green fire, and without hesitation, the man stepped through. I had no time to think; I simply acted. I leapt through the hole and found myself *here*.

Then my heart raced as I caught sight of Poppy and Lucy hugging goodnight outside the inn, and I knew the time had come. A horrendous, gut-wrenching sadness followed, a forlorn hatred, and then...

I opened my eyes, shuddering back into the mind and body of Lily Locke.

"Holy smokes," I said, startled as I looked to the hunter—understanding settling onto my shoulders with complete clarity. "You *love* her."

"Who?" Poppy asked mindlessly. "Who loves who?"

"He," I said, pointing to the man on the floor, "has fallen in love with you."

Poppy gave me one look, then laughed. "Well that's the craziest thought I've ever heard. He just tried to *kill* me." She turned to me, waited for the punchline, but at the severity in my face, she shook her head. "You're serious."

I gave a hesitant nod, but when the hunter merely closed his eyes in response, I followed it up with a more decisive one. "He hated to do his job. He's bound to kill you, but...he doesn't want to do it."

"Holy smokes, Lucy was *right*," Poppy said, then keeled over in a dead faint.

"How'd *he* get in here?" Gerry demanded. "Did you see? Lily, what are you babbling about?"

"Yes, I saw. He followed another man inside, but I couldn't see who because it was dark and he wore a cloak. This man drew a hole before the tunnel in the road—burning green flames—and stepped through."

Gerry's face, already pale, died a little more.

"Do you know what this means?" I pressed. "Gerry, talk."

"Come," he whispered. "It's already too late."

To punctuate his statement, the earth trembled, rattled, and then went still.

Chapter 26

THE KNOCK ON THE DOOR startled everyone.

"Hello, guests—I just wanted to check on y'all. Do you hear the thunder out there?" Diana called through the door. "Not sure what that storm's all about, but if you need anything, just holler."

I strode across the room, twisted the doorknob and pulled, revealing Diana. "Actually, we could use some help."

Diana's jaw dropped wider and wider as the door creaked open and she peeped over my shoulder. "Oh, ah, I see you have visitors. *Gerry*? What are you doing here?"

She caught sight of him over my shoulder, but my body was blocking the rest of her view. As I stood back, Diana took in the sight of a jaguar's gnashing teeth with a surprisingly calm demeanor. It didn't seem to startle her, nor did the strange man on the floor. Only Poppy's tear streaked face as she moaned and regained consciousness drew a concerned look from the innkeeper.

"What is it you needed me to do?" Diana's voice was riddled with curiosity, but the woman was cool as a cucumber under pressure. "I see we have a, *ah*, domestic sort of dispute here."

"This vamp hunter tried to kill Poppy," I said in a quick explanation. "My other cousin is a Ranger—she's the jaguar. This storm?" I held my hands out and gestured to the sounds, wincing as a particularly loud clap of thunder rocked the inn's foundations. "There are intruders in Olympia, and the Master of Magic's life is in danger."

Her eyes flicked briefly around the scene once more, then she nodded, accepting everything. "What can I do?"

"Any chance you can take care of him for us?" I kicked a leg in the direction of the vamp hunter. "Gerry and I will need to look for the Master. He's in danger, I'm sure of it."

"Of course." Diana clapped her hands and rubbed them together. "I have some magical handcuffs somewhere behind my desk. People leave the strangest things in hotel rooms. I'll be right back. I'll transport him to our holding area after that; he won't get out of there."

Poppy giggled, almost hysterically. "Handcuffs. Who leaves handcuffs behind?"

I turned to Gerry as Diana left. "Let's go—we can't waste any more time here."

Gerry nodded, still pale in his faux-suit pajamas. "How? Where? I don't understand."

"Focus, Gerry. I need you to get me something of the Master's—an item that belongs to him, something he's touched or used recently. Can you do that?"

There was a crack as Gerry disappeared without a word.

"What can I do?" Poppy whispered. "Don't you dare tell me nothing, Lily Locke. I'm sick of being protected. I'm here to help."

"You can..." I shrugged. "I'm sorry, I don't know. I don't know where he is or what we need to do. I didn't even see the intruder's face. All I know is that whatever that man wants—it's not you. It's me. I need to help, and I won't have you getting hurt on my account."

"You're not going in alone." Poppy's jaw was set, and Zin whined in agreement. "So, whatever your plan is, add two more to it. Probably three, since that Gerry fellow seems to adore the Master."

I was spared agreeing with her by the return of Diana. With assistance from Zin's paws, the two turned the vamp hunter over and slapped the cuffs onto his wrists. For good measure, I added a powerful Stunner Spell that'd last at least an hour, maybe more.

"You said you can transport him?" I asked her. "You have a prison or somewhere he'll be safe to keep?"

She nodded. "With that Stunner Spell, this guy ain't going anywhere for a while. I'll call Brucey and let him know we've got a pickup. He's got muscles."

Brucey seemed to have a lot more than muscles, based on Diana's *dreamy* sigh. She left once again to find Brucey just as a resounding crack signified the Keeper's return.

"Here," Gerry said, breathless. "It's the belt from his robe."

"Did he wear it today?"

"It was strewn on the floor of his home—the living room. So, yes," he clarified. "I can't be *positive*, but I believe this is what he was wearing when he was taken. He's nowhere to be found. I checked everywhere—that's why it took so long."

Gerry had only been gone a few minutes, but I didn't mention it. Instead I took the cloth and settled onto a chair in the corner of the room. "Be back," I said, raising the bottle of golden liquid to my lips. I drank.

My memories, my fears, my tensions disappeared more rapidly than ever before. I sat, patiently waiting until it wasn't me alone in my thoughts any longer. I was him; I was inside the Master's mind. Eventually even that realization slipped away as I *became* him and Lily was gone.

I stood at home in my robe, shuffling through the house—waiting. Runes and drawings and spells filtered through my brain; figures and fact swimming in colorful patterns as ideas flicked through me at the speed of light. My guest would be here soon.

Finally, a knocking sound drew my attention. I wasn't surprised, though a sense of exhaustion filtered through my old body. I dropped my robe to the floor, knowing it would be needed later in some way. It was essential I leave something behind for *her.*

My hand reached for the door, pulled it open, and I met—face to face—with her father. *Lily's* father. He'd come for me—and for her. He'd discovered the contents of the prophecy, and this evening, a piece of it was coming to fruition.

Underneath, I'd dressed in black, solemn robes for the occasion.

"I see you're ready." Lucian's voice spoke softly. "Good of you not to argue with me. Now, it's time we join your ancestors."

Wordlessly, I watched as Lucian raised his hands and murmured the curse he'd concocted for the sole purpose of paralyzing me. There was no use fighting fate, so I closed my eyes and accepted the spell. It connected with my heart, my mind, and my soul. My body collapsed, sunk into the blanket of darkness.

And then it was done.

My eyes—*Lily's* eyes—flew open. "It's him," I mumbled, disoriented. "It's him, my father. Lucian has the Master—"

"Where?"

"I-I don't know." I closed my eyes, thinking back for any clues. "The Master wanted me to see this—he left his robe behind on purpose *knowing* I'd be in his memories. He let himself be taken. I don't know why, but he did. He knew he couldn't stop it, so he went willingly."

"Why didn't he prevent it?" Gerry bounced with agitation on his toes. "I don't understand. He can control the universe, he could've—he could've prepared if he'd seen this coming. It's my job to protect him, yet he told me nothing about this!"

"This needs to happen," I said, slowly. "For one reason or another—fate, a prophecy. I don't know why; he didn't show me *why*. I think we need to trust him."

"He's in duress! How can we trust him?"

"He's not in duress," I said, slowly. "He felt no panic. He didn't feel much of anything except calmness. He knew," I said again. "He might even have left a clue, I just need to *find* it."

"What happened while you were in the potion?" Poppy asked. "If you tell us, maybe we'll be able to help."

"There were a lot of equations floating around. For a time, I understood them. I had his mind—now, they're gibberish. It wouldn't be the runes." I shook my head, remembering the dropping of the robe, the preparedness of his clothes underneath. He hadn't been ready for bed despite the robe, so that must be a clue. I squeezed my eyes shut. "Lucian said something about us—er, he and the Master—going to see my—*his*—ancestors."

Poppy frowned at my slip in point of view. It was too easy to get carried away, to feel like I'd been there, to feel as if I'd *been* him, existed in his shoes. *I hadn't*, I reminded myself. It hadn't been me there, it had been him, and I needed to remember that.

"That's *it*!" I raised a hand. "Is there some sort of private room in the Hall of Masters?"

Gerry looked confused. "Are you talking about the ancestors bit? I thought that was just a death threat."

"I'm *positive*." With astounding clarity, I knew this was what the Master of Magic had wanted me to hear. "Yes! That's our clue. Lucian said it's time for *us* to go meet your ancestors. If he'd wanted to threaten the Master, he would have said it's time for *you* meet your ancestors, or something of the sort. He distinctly said *us*. I think they're waiting for us—for me—in the Hall of Masters."

Gerry hesitated, then nodded. "There is something, a small..." his face paled. "You don't think they are waiting for *you*?"

"What?" Poppy pressed. "Where are they?"

"There's a small dungeon underneath the Hall. It used to be where the Masters would keep those who'd..." He swallowed. "Whose crimes against the world were unforgivable. A prison underneath the weight of all the Masters of Magic. Not one has ever escaped such a prison."

"Then that's where they'll be," I said grimly. "And that's where I'm headed. Poppy, Zin—help with this one." I nodded at the hunter. "Gerry, can you—"

"Nope," Poppy said. "We're in this together."

I exhaled a breath. "It's only me he wants. It'll do you no good to come along."

"Well, it just so happens that the three of us are a package deal," Poppy said with a grin. "Ain't that right, Zin?"

A snarl from the jaguar signified her agreement.

"Fine," I said, as Diana returned with a huge man by her side. "But I can't promise what we'll find. And I can't guarantee your safety."

"This is Brucey," Diana said with a pat on the shoulder of a massive man. "He's in charge of prisoner transport. He also runs the bakery."

We all stood in stunned silence, watching as a man who appeared to be part giant ducked into the room.

"This him?" Brucey grunted, tapping the hunter with his toe. "Lucky little fellow."

When I nodded, Zin backed away and began to slip back into human form as Brucey bent over and slung the hunter over his shoulder like I might carry a sack of potatoes. Except much less gently. The vampire hunter's head swung wildly as Brucey stood, his figure still immobile due to the Stunner Spell.

On his way out the door, Brucey stopped to give Diana a huge kiss on the lips. Her cheeks bloomed red. "Well, *thanks*," she said, and then cleared her throat with a tinge of embarrassment. "What else can I do to help?"

"Go with Brucey," I instructed her. "Continue on as normal. We can't risk anyone else's lives with this."

"All lives are already at risk," Gerry said, a whine to his words. "The Master is in danger."

"Lucian wants me," I said firmly. "Nobody else."

Diana nodded. "I'll...I'll wait for further instructions, and I'll alert the protectors."

"They've been alerted already," Gerry said. "They're gathering forces, but it'll take a few minutes. I don't think we have the time."

I shook my head, agreeing with him. Then I glanced to Zin, the golden glint still in her eyes, her hair shaggy and mussed as it returned to its short, severe bob. I turned my attention to Poppy, who watched me with glittering eyes. Gerry had a sense of determination about him as well, despite his nervously wringing hands.

"Let's go," I said simply. "No time to wait."

We found ourselves outside the Hall of Masters minutes later. Gerry bounced with agitation before us, one foot on the staircase leading inside. I held up a hand to still him.

"We stick together," I growled in warning. "*All* of us. But if something happens in there, you all leave me behind, understand? Get Ranger X, send the protectors inside, but don't *wait* there if things go belly up. Understand?"

I had to prompt the group a few times before they agreed. When I finally had their word, I nodded for Gerry to go ahead and let us in. The Keeper raised a hand and pressed it against the door to let us into the Hall.

"The chamber is toward the back," he said as the door slid open. "I'll show you. To unlock it, we'll need to—"

Gerry took one step over the threshold. Midway through, his eyes grew wide in surprise, his figure froze, and then his body crumbled and fell backward. I shouted for Zin to stay away, but it was too late. She barged ahead as I knelt to help Gerry, and she took a step through the doorway.

"Poppy, get *back*!" I yelled as she leaped forward to catch Zin. "The doorway's hexed!"

Poppy awkwardly clutched Zin's body to her chest and hauled her away from the cursed entrance. At the same time, I dragged Gerry further away and gave him a quick examination as we moved.

Both Gerry and Zin had fallen from the hex, and their symptoms were the same: glassy eyed, frozen figures, and a lack of speech. They were plenty alive, but immobilized.

"Poppy, you can't go through there," I said. "I think it's—it's a way for him to separate me from the pack. From my friends."

"You can't go through there, either," she said with a frown. "What if it happens to you?"

"Can you see anything?" I nodded toward the doorway. A blue haze shimmered there. I hadn't had the time to notice before two of our four had fallen.

Poppy shook her head. "Um, do you mean the doorway?"

"I can see the hex. It's blue, shimmering—I think it's meant for me, a sort of invitation. Please go get Diana. Have her bring Brucey and send for medical attention to care for Zin and Gerry. And get Ranger X here! Ask Diana, whatever you need to do—alert him and grant him access to Olympia."

Poppy nodded, then hesitated. "I don't want to leave you behind."

"Poppy, I need you—*they* need you."

"I don't need protection, Lily," she snapped. "I want to help."

"This is *not* me protecting you. This is me needing you. Don't you understand?" My hands reached out and shook her. "I need help—please, help me. Get X, get assistance, help Zin and Gerry. That's where you're needed."

She exhaled, nodded. "Fine, but..." Stepping forward, she pulled me into a hug. "Be careful, Lily. I love you."

"I love you too, Poppy."

We parted, surveyed each other for a second more, and then I turned to face the hexed entrance. Closing my eyes, I set my shoulders and stepped through.

I'd find him, and I'd end this.

Once and for all.

Chapter 27

THE HEX OVER THE DOORWAY bubbled shut behind me, as if the air had turned to rubber and snapped closed around my body. It had most certainly been customized as a portal just for me.

Charming, I thought wryly.

I moved briskly past the rows of statues. The Hall was dark this time of night, and the pale moonlight that had shown through earlier had vanished. I sent a quick Light Licker enchantment to kiss the torches hung on the wall, and once they'd lit, a faint flicker of flame guided me toward the center of the room.

The chamber wasn't hidden now that I knew to look for it. In between all the statues was a circle sketched into the floor, an oval of stone with words etched in the center:

If you must go,
To the depths below—
We must all agree,
It's your destiny.

I turned the words over and over in my head. It wasn't a spell in itself, it was more of a warning. A riddle. Just before Gerry had crumbled from the hexed doorway, he'd been about to tell me how to access the chambers. *To unlock it, we'll need to...*

"Come on, Gerry," I mumbled. "What were you trying to say?"

He hadn't gotten far enough in his explanation. *What needed doing?*

"*We must all agree*," I continued. "*It's your destiny*. Who is *we*?"

I racked my brain, looking around to the statues for help.

"Talk to me," I mumbled. "Help me out! Who has to agree..."

I looked up, surprised to find the answer settling before me.

"Of course! The magic of the Master lives on through the generations," I said, repeating Lucy's earlier words. "You all *are* the we. I guess that means I'll have to somehow get you all to agree that I need to go into the chambers."

I cleared my throat, unsure how to address a room full of stone statues. Since there seemed to be no better way than simply starting, I began to speak in earnest.

"Uh, Masters," I said, feeling like a fool. "I'm sorry to trouble you, but I think your brother is in danger. I need to go into the chambers below." I glanced at the words inscribed in stone. "I need your permissions. Please, I only want to help him."

My words were met by silence. Loneliness. The cavernous echo of a room without a living soul, without the beats of hearts or the whispers of breaths.

A room still, emptied of hope.

Until the lights went out. All of the torches extinguished at once, and the front door to the Hall slid closed with the crunch of stone against stone. Darkness was thrust upon me, my heart pumping furiously against my chest, the silence a wild cry in my ears.

Then—the lights began.

A glow of the purest white, tiny pinpricks of it all around the room. It surrounded me. Dull at first, then brighter, stronger. I realized as the brightness grew that each beam came from within the statues.

One by one the Masters' statues lit, glowing outward through the dark empty sockets where their eyes should have been. Flames had erupted inside of them and burned a blinding white, lighting the room on fire. Almost as if they'd come alive.

The whole room shone with it. I rotated in a full circle, watching as every last set of eyes flickered to life. The room filled suddenly and, though nothing besides the light changed, *everything* changed. There were no breaths, no heartbeats, but the buzz of life existed.

At that moment, the stones began to churn beneath my feet and the outline of the circle began to sink. With a start, I realized I'd gained permission to enter. I spiraled down with the platform as it descended, crouching to save my balance as the circle lowered far beneath ground level.

My eyes remained glued open, but I couldn't see much as darkness resumed underneath the Hall. The platform lowered to the floor of the dungeon, coming to a slow halt while I waited perfectly still. Then the stone crunched against the ground, shuddered, and stopped.

Torches flickered on the walls, a sign someone had been here recently. I couldn't see beyond the limited glow of the firelight. I straightened at the swish of fabric, then the shuffle of footsteps. *I wasn't alone.*

My heart pounded. I turned slowly in the direction of the sound. I prepared myself to meet my father again, the dark figure from the Master's memories, but my throat went dry and a familiar sense of dread crept over me.

When I faced the man, I gasped.

It wasn't him. *It wasn't my father.*

"What are *you* doing here—alone?" I gaped at the Master of Magic himself. "Quickly—we need to get you out of here. I saw...wait, I *saw* your memories. He—my father—took you away. How did you escape?"

"I'm not who you expected, am I?" The Master allowed himself the smallest of smiles under his cloak. "I'm sorry for the deception, but I needed to talk to you alone."

"Why didn't you just *ask*?" I struggled to get my bearings. I'd been wrong—wrong about everything. This wasn't about The Faction or my father. It was a ploy, a scheme, and I'd fallen for it wholeheartedly. "Yesterday when I saw you, you just stared at me—I was there in your office, and you could have talked to me then, but you refused."

"It had to happen this way."

"Why? Gerry is worried sick about you. The world…" I raised an arm to signify the faint booms of thunder and storms in the background outside of the near-silent dungeon. "What's going on?"

"I'm doing this for the good of all of us," The Master said. "Come here, come closer."

"What do you want with me?"

"The prophecy," he said. "I need you to tell me what's in the prophecy."

"That makes no sense." I stepped backward as he stepped forward. "You're the only one who *knows* its contents. I can't help you—I don't know what it says."

"You will tell me. You will find out." the Master spoke in a low slither. "This prophecy is *essential*. I have my suspicions as to its contents, but I need them confirmed. You're the key to it. But how? Why? What is it about *you*, Miss Locke, that's so special?"

"I don't know!" I wished I knew how to make the stone platform ascend, to return back to the Hall above so I could call for help. I fought the urge to run because there was simply no place to go. "I have no clue how I'm involved, or why. I wish I did know. I thought you'd be able to tell me."

"M-miss Locke," he said, but his voice drew to a choking halt.

The Master of Magic lurched forward. He held his stomach as if he were sick, but strange things began to happen around him. I couldn't bring myself to help, nor could I run. I could only watch, horrified, as his body morphed before me.

The robe on his back lengthened and his body grew taller, broader, stronger. Younger. *Impossible.* Then the figure stretched to new heights and threw back the hood of his robe. Finally, the new man standing in the chambers met my gaze.

"Hello, Lily," he said. "It's been too long since I've seen you."

"Lucian," I breathed. "But..."

"*How* did I do that?" he asked, amused. "It's thanks to you, actually. I'm sure you'll understand." Lucian brushed aside his robe to show me a travel belt not unlike mine, except his contained vials of a bright pink concoction.

"Long Isle Iced Tea," I said, aghast. "The woman—the one buying for the party. She was supplying you."

"It is a party," he said with a wry smile. "I would call it a reunion, as a matter of fact. Father and daughter."

"Never."

"Oh, Lily," he said, sighing heavily. "Don't play these games. You knew it was me you'd face tonight all along, and yet you still came. You didn't have to come here tonight."

"Oh, but I did." I forced myself to stand tall as Lucian stepped onto the platform with me. We circled the round stone, watching one another. "You took the Master to get me here. Why?"

"Isn't it obvious yet? The prophecy. I need it."

"I don't know what you're talking about." I banished every word about it to the recesses of my mind. Liam's mention of it, his belief that it was the very thing Lucian was after. It dawned on me that Liam had been right.

"You do." Lucian read the recognition in my gaze. "You know of it at the very least."

"I know of it," I admitted. "Nothing more than rumors."

"What do you suspect it says?"

He didn't know. He lacked the information Diana had given me about my mother's amulet—*her* mother's amulet. Diana suspected the prophecy spoke the name of the next Mother of Magic. She had guessed the name was mine, but only the prophecy could tell us that for certain.

I hid this information in the recesses of my mind and focused on my own curiosities. "I have no clue what it says, but it seems to concern me," I said wryly. "I'd like to know what my fate is, so if you *happen* to uncover more details, let me know."

"Lies."

"Sure, fine." I shrugged. "Lies."

This seemed to confuse him. "You *don't* know?"

"Why do you think I came here tonight?"

He frowned. "Because of me."

"Don't flatter yourself, *father*," I said, spitting the last word. "Despite your ego, surely you can see that I'm not happy to be related to you. I came here hoping to meet the Master and find out the contents of that prophecy. It'd be nice to know if I'm expected to live or die."

"What does it matter? You can't alter a prophecy."

"No, but I might try." I stepped toward him, my fear somehow at bay despite my defenselessness. "If I'm going to die anyway, I might as well find the one who's supposed to kill me and take care of him first."

I couldn't have disarmed him better with a curse. Lucian froze, uncertain, and stepped backward. He reached the edge of the stone pedestal and stumbled as he retreated to the ground behind.

I towered over my father, standing a good foot above him with the added height of the platform. He hadn't expected me to fight back, and when he glanced up at me, his gaze was uncertain.

"You can't change a prophecy," he repeated. "It's impossible."

"Has anyone tried?" I smiled grimly. "Don't forget, I'm the Mixologist."

"I *need* it," he said, anger darkening his gaze like storm clouds. "And I happen to have the one person who can enlighten us on the matter."

My heart skipped a beat as Lucian raised his hand and muttered a curse. Ropes sprung from his palm, affixing themselves to something in the distance. Or rather, someone.

He continued to mutter under his breath, drawing the ropes toward him. The figure on the other end dragged along as well, his robes filthy and his body battered with dust and grime.

"*Stop!*" The second I saw the body, I leaped toward the prisoner, cutting through Lucian's ropes with my own Slicing Spell.

Kneeling beside the old man whom I recognized as the true Master of Magic even through the filth, I pulled his head into my lap and brushed his hair from his face. I murmured soothing words to him as I pulled Aloe Ale from my travel belt and began to dab some on the more severe cuts and bruises. Despite my touch, the Master remained unconscious.

"Wake," Lucian instructed, and the man's eyes opened.

The Master's eyes met mine with startling clarity. I flinched in surprise. Recovering quickly, I eased him into a sitting position and then stood by his side. He stretched his muscles and flexed his fingers while I took a step back.

"Ahh, Lucian." The Master finally spoke, groaning as he stood. "So, the time has come, I'm afraid."

My father's eyes flashed at the name. "You don't know me."

The Master opened his arms wide. "But of course I do. How do you think you entered Olympia? Not by your own cleverness, certainly."

Lucian's gaze faltered. "But my portal—"

"I allowed you in. That is the sole reason you're here." To me, the Master gave a small smile and shake of his head. "Gerry will not be pleased with me."

Lucian bit his lip, then threw that idea away. "Impossible. I used the Rune of the Relics spell for entry."

"As you wish." The Master of Magic nodded easily, which visibly angered Lucian.

My father pulled up the sleeve of his black robe and exposed a bruised injection site. "I had to infuse myself with demigod blood to make it work."

"Why?" The Master's question was innocent. "Why infuse yourself when you had the bloodlines to begin with?"

"I did not. I am not a descendent."

The Master of Magic blinked once, twice. "But of course you are. As is Lily. You both belong to Ceres. Distantly, yes, but it's there."

"Then why couldn't I walk through the gates of Olympia?"

"Because we didn't want you here," the Master said simply. "That's what happens when you want to kill me."

"I don't want to kill you. But I will if that's what it comes to—I need to know what's in that prophecy."

"You will have to kill me," the Master said, and I started toward him, but he waved me off. "It's alright, Lily. I'm ready to die. I've been preparing for this moment."

Lucian's face scrunched as he fought back anger. The Master might be prepared, but Lucian wasn't. He'd clearly assumed the Master would fight for his life, would forfeit the contents of the prophecy instead of choosing willingly to leave this earth and join the statues above us in the Hall of Masters.

"My time draws to an end; we are all feeling it," the Master said. "Maybe you're the one meant to land the final blow. I don't know—I don't want to know."

"You'll fight back," Lucian said. "Just *watch*."

"No!" I yelled, seeing what was happening, but my reaction was too late.

With a snarl, Lucian sent a horrible curse screeching toward the old man.

The magic hit the Master straight in the chest, a festering ball of purple light and black smoke. It was meant to choke, to steal the victim's oxygen, and it worked. The Master fell to his knees, gasping for breath, his eyes wide.

"You idiot!" I shouted to Lucian. "If you kill him, neither of us will know the answers! Our world will fall apart!"

Closing my eyes, I summoned the most powerful curse-breaking hex I could muster without a potion to assist. I put my hands over the Master, muttering the chant until the electricity shorted out and the smoke evaporated to nothing.

Lucian appeared shaken. Both by my outburst and the Master's willingness to die for his secrets. The Master of Magic, all powerful, could have prevented the curse if he'd wanted; he could have fought back, could have overpowered Lucian. Instead, he'd let himself crumble.

A dangerous gleam returned to Lucian's eyes as a new idea settled over the old one. He turned to me, my stomach twisting under the horrible smile.

"*You* may die, old man, but not Lily." Lucian shook his head. "You won't let her die. She's the key, isn't she?"

Then with a whirl of purple light, he hit me with the same curse as he'd sent on the Master. I had no time to respond, to conjure another counter curse before my breath was gone and my eyes swelled with the lack of oxygen. I couldn't mutter a word, an incantation, or a goodbye. My body collapsed under me, giving out as I sank to the ground in a paralyzed slump.

After what felt like minutes, the flash of a green light streaked before my gaze and the pressure on my chest vanished. My breath returned in unceremonious heaves, and I treasured each round of oxygen as if it might be my last.

As I righted myself, I studied the picture before me. The Master of Magic's chest rose and fell in heavy pulses from the aftershocks of his complex counter curse. Meanwhile, Lucian watched us with a pleased, twisted smile. He'd found the Master's weak spot, and we all knew it.

"If you kill her," the Master breathed. "You'll be committing suicide. Mass murder. She needs to live, or we will all die. Kill me, kill anyone—but Lily *must* live."

"Why do I not believe you?" Lucian stepped forward, a ball of brilliant violet fire in his hands. "You are weak, old man. Your attacking powers are stripped, I made sure of that when I brought you down here. All you can do is fight *back*."

"Your attacking powers are stripped?" I looked to the Master of Magic. "But...how?"

Lucian laughed. "I'll show you my tricks someday, dear daughter—if the Master chooses to let you live. It's up to him, really."

The dim glow from the Master's eyes told me this was true. "The prophecy will do you no good, Lucian."

"It contains Lily's name, doesn't it?" Lucian pressed. "As her rightful father, I should hear it."

I couldn't help a derisive snort. "You might want the prophecy, but not because of familial ties—if you're going to lie, Lucian, do it well."

"This is how it'll go." The purple fire in Lucian's hands grew larger as he spoke directly to the old man. "I'll hit you first. Lily will have to choose to attack me or save you—it *can't* go both ways. She'll choose to save you because that's what she does. While she is helping *you*, I'll kill her."

I'd known my father was the enemy. I knew he led The Faction, led the group that challenged everything I believed in. Yet he'd never directly threatened to kill me before, and the words stung. I hated that they hurt, that they surprised me after all I knew about him already.

"You'd murder your own daughter?" I looked to him, my heart breaking at the familiarity I saw in them. "For *what*?"

The Master of Magic glanced my way, hesitated. There was no doubt in my mind about the truth of Lucian's words, and the Master must have felt the same. And so, the Master forfeited. He raised his hands, the fight seeping out of his posture. Lucian smiled grimly.

"Good," Lucian said. "I'm glad we can all agree."

"The prophecy is a simple one," the Master began with a heavy sigh. "It predicts the arrival of the next Master of Magic. I've been Master for centuries. Hundreds of years. My time is winding to a close."

"Who is it?" Lucian demanded hungrily. "Who will it be?"

"Why does it matter?" I snarled. "You don't control them anyway."

"That's exactly what he wants to do." The Master of Magic turned to look at me. "All Masters are born mere mortal babes. They grow into children, they love their families—as most children do. Should the future Master be born into a family that—" he turned to look at Lucian—"has less than ideal ethical beliefs, the world will be in grave danger. Masters are not immune to poor choices or unfortunate upbringings: *that* is why the amulet exists. To protect these children against such fates."

"But—" I gasped. "This amulet *can't* belong to me. It mustn't. I'm not—I don't have children."

"You might not now, but someday." The Master's eyes warmed. "I'm afraid, Lily, that Diana was correct."

My heart pounded, my hand fisted against the amulet. "But—"

"You are the Mother of Magic. You will give birth to the next Master of Magic, and he will replace me when he comes of age."

"I'm not—*no*," I said, sitting, gasping. "No, that's impossible."

Lucian's eyes glimmered with satisfaction. "This is... *better* than I thought."

"No," I rasped. "It makes no difference whether or not it's true; should I ever have a child, he'll never meet you."

"You might reconsider after you see this." Lucian extended his hands and formed a swirling cloud between his outstretched fingers. "I believe *congratulations* are in order?"

I moved closer to him as an image appeared above his palm, so clear it was almost like a window into another location. The figure was being tortured, disgustingly so, and with horror, I realized I recognized the man: the build of him, the dark hair, those tortured eyes, the screams of pain. He was *mine*.

"Let him go!" I shouted at Lucian, my eyes glued to the image before me. I moved closer, closer, the alarm bells in my head clanging at full force. "Where is X? What have you done with him?"

"He's being tended to," Lucian said with a slow smile. "If you'd like to save his life, let's talk."

"What more can you possibly want from me?" My voice was flat, my eyes dead as I studied their reflection in his. "You have taken everything I have."

"Not yet, I haven't." Lucian drew from his pocket a piece of parchment. It was blank, but as he looked at it and muttered an enchantment, words appeared there. "Review and sign."

"What is this?"

He pushed it toward me. I surveyed the finely inked cursive. The words were simple. The meaning was not.

"Sign," he encouraged, tapping a finger to the parchment and pulling a pen from his robes. "Or your husband-to-be dies."

My mouth was dry, the fight leaked from my muscles at the impossible choice. "No." I studied the page, pushed it back. "This is an impossible task. Give me something else, anything else."

"You heard him," Lucian stated. "You know the prophecy, and now you will choose between your future spouse and your future child."

"How can I sign away custody of my child if he doesn't even *exist*?"

The words on Lucian's parchment gleamed a blood red shade on the back of brown parchment: ***I, Lily Locke, hereby agree to grant full custody of my firstborn son to Lucian Blackmore, creator of this binding agreement.***

The words continued on for a few more paragraphs, but none of them mattered. The shield around my heart hardened as I looked up at the man who was supposed to be my family, my protector, my father. And found a monster.

"I know what's going through your head," he said, cool and composed. "You're thinking that if you sign this now, you might be able to find a way to break the contract. That you won't have to follow through on the terms and conditions."

I set my jaw and remained silent. That was *exactly* what I'd been thinking. I loved Ranger X more than life itself. But there was another way to solve the problem besides finding a way out of the contract, the simplest solution of all—a loophole: Ranger X and I could marry, but never have children.

With a new wave of hope, I reached for the pen. That was just the way things would have to be. At least I would still have my partner, my soulmate. Without X, my life would be empty anyway.

As I held the pen and prepared to sign, my necklace gave an encouraging hum, a slight glow and warmth that gave me hope I was making the most of an impossible choice. Or maybe, it was telling me that after all this, there would be a way out of the contract. Either way, I had to make a choice.

"Now you're thinking that instead of breaking the contract, you'll avoid this situation entirely and never have children," Lucian said smoothly, eerily narrating my thoughts. "Who knows? Maybe that's possible. Maybe you'll find a way to break the contract and change *fate*."

"Of course I will," I snapped through my teeth. "But I want it in writing—on this contract—that the minute I sign, Ranger X will be set free and left unharmed."

Lucian considered my request, then nodded as more words appeared on the page. I studied the binding agreement, satisfied with the addition. Then I lowered my pen to the page.

"You and I both know, Lily, that a magical contract cannot be broken," Lucian warned. "And prophecies must be fulfilled."

I bowed my head, bit down on my lip so hard the skin broke. I tasted blood, metal, as I began to scrawl my name. *What choice did I have?* If I didn't sign, Ranger X would be dead. We'd never have children anyway, and I would be left with scraps of nothing.

If I signed, I would at least have X. We could have *us*.

Together, we could get through anything.

I signed, swallowing the taste of blood.

As the electrical current of magic sizzled up my arm, the very one that bound me to the inhumane contract I'd been forced to sign, Lucian smirked. I glanced upward as my chest felt split in two, and watched as that smirk turned into a smile, a smooth, cold smile with all the smugness in the world because of one fact.

He was right, and we both knew it.

Contracts couldn't be broken; fate couldn't be changed.

The anger within my very spirit bubbled and boiled. It slithered into every crevice of my chest, my heart, my soul. A blackness invaded my every thought, a darkness blotting out the world around me.

Around my neck, the amulet glowed and burned. Its magic seeped through my skin, the burn no longer stinging against me but feeding off the wrath there.

Together, the heart emblazoned on the charm outside my body joined the pumping heart within, and they pulsed together, golden fingers of magic swirling around my body, dazzling and stunning, ripping and tearing at the air around me.

Gradually, the smile slipped from Lucian's face. I could only imagine the blaze in my eyes, the lightning from my fingers. Diana's words, repeated from the goddess Ceres herself, buzzed through my brain as I sensed the amulet's unrest: *the ancient Roman goddess had been angered.*

The magic seethed into a blooming black cloud and radiated from every part of me. Lucian stumbled, took a step backward, clutching the contract to his chest. I stepped toward him. It was just him and I—no one else existed. I laser focused on him, feeling the anger building to a level that might shatter this house of gods from its very roots.

"Lily, *stop*," Lucian pleaded. "Don't, I'll—"

"It's too late," I said, and as I spoke I lurched forward. The voice wasn't my own, but that of a powerful woman, an echo, a robotic intonation both deeper and stronger and more courageous than my own. "You have angered *us*."

Lucian looked over my head, startled, but there was nobody else. The Master of Magic watched from the wings. This was my moment, and he was letting me have it.

"By the power of Ceres," the voice said, radiating from my lips, though I had no control over the words, "you will be destroyed."

My hands rose of their own accord. My body seemed to stretch and grow as an unknown power coursed through me. Someone more powerful than any wizard was acting through me, possessing me. The ancient goddess, Ceres herself, had come to protect the wearer of the amulet. She'd come to protect *me*.

True fear blossomed on Lucian's face. "No—*Lily*!"

His shout went unanswered. The unembodied entity crashed through my limbs as my mouth shouted a spell in an ancient, foreign language. As the words rolled naturally from my tongue, a burst of magic shot from my palms straight to Lucian.

He clattered to the ground, unconscious, but I couldn't stop the magic. Power in spades filtered through my veins, out my fingers, radiated from every inch of me. Another day, the presence of this much power would have killed me. It would have broken me from the inside, destroyed every figment of my being. This evening, however, I had the rage of the past mothers of magic, of Ceres herself, of all owners of the amulet before me protecting me.

A rumbling began in the distance. It grew and grew until I felt the very crumbling in the depths of my stomach and the tips of my toes. I felt the collapsing sensation in the base of my spine and the beat of my heart.

The cement walls, thick and sturdy, began to crack around us. The dungeon started to crumble in on itself, the ceiling caving even as I stood still, the magic licking my fingers as it turned the world on its very axis.

A bolt of understanding hit me, and as the roof over us began to crumble, I launched myself across the room and threw my body over his. The Master of Magic allowed himself to be covered by me as hunks of cement thundered down around us.

It took minutes for the dust and debris to settle. Maybe hours. Maybe longer. I cowered in exhaustion over the Master of Magic as we breathed heavily amid the ruins.

When it was finally safe, I moved next to him and glanced upward to find starlight blinking above us. The damage I had inflicted with the help of Ceres was astronomical. More than half the Hall of Masters had fallen, the statues broken and battered and destroyed. I had barely been touched and not a scratch marred my body. The Master of Magic remained unscathed as well, save for the prior injuries inflicted by Lucian.

The Master studied me carefully as he eased into a sitting position. "Ceres has been at work here tonight."

"I know. I felt her. It was—I didn't have any control over what I was doing or saying." I shuddered. "She is so powerful, and she was so angry. I could feel things as if the emotions were my own. The spells she cast—I don't know what language they were in, but I knew the words, knew the extent of damage they would inflict. Yet I couldn't stop."

"That's the power of the amulet," he said, with a reverent nod toward the completely intact chain around my neck. "The mothers of magic—much like the Masters of Magic—are all connected via long, ancient bloodlines. An act of terror against you is an act of defiance against the entire line of Ceres's children. They rose to protect you in your time of need. Much like the Masters in the hall above have protected me."

"But I'm not—I can't be who you think I am," I said. "I don't have children."

"It's not my place to wonder at fate. All that's certain is the prophecy will be fulfilled." As he lapsed into silence, I scanned the wreckage surrounding us. My father was most certainly dead. I couldn't pull myself to look closer, but I didn't need to; the stones had fallen on him in a way that made it impossible for him to survive the collapse.

He was, after all, a mere mortal wizard.

While I might also be a mortal witch, I understood the gods had been on my side tonight.

Emotions flickered in the back of my mind. Ceres's thoughts, her powers, had vacated my body, and I now felt weak and frail in comparison. My hand crept to the amulet around my neck. I held onto it as the sobs began.

Sobs because of the complete and utter relief that we'd survived. Sobs because of the horrible knowledge that I'd killed my only living parent. Even greater sobs as I realized that the world was a better place due to his death.

Ranger X found me amongst the rubble sometime later that evening, and try as he might, he couldn't pry the amulet from my hand.

"Lily, sweetheart, I'm here. I'm here, you're safe." He cradled me, cocooned me in his warmth. His heart beat strong, fast, and I knew that behind those soothing words, he hid a rage almost as strong as mine.

"You're safe," I gasped, feeling his face, his lips, his chest. I couldn't get enough of his strong heartbeat against my cheek. "He had you, he tortured you."

Ranger X shook his head. "What are you talking about?"

"My father, he showed me..." I gulped back a wave of hurt. "He showed me an image of you being tortured, and he said that if I didn't cooperate with him, he'd kill you."

"I'm here, I'm safe, I'm fine. Lily, you're hurt, exhausted. Let me take you home. He never *had* me."

"It was a trick? What about the others? Zin, Poppy, Gerry?"

Ranger X didn't respond. When I resumed my sobs, he pulled me close. "It doesn't matter now. You're safe, they're safe—he's gone. Poppy got help, and Gerry and Zin are fine. You can see them as soon as we get you back to The Isle."

"I killed him," I whispered. "He's dead."

"I know, honey, I know." Ranger X pressed a kiss to my forehead. "You didn't have a choice. It was *always* going to be him or you. There was never another way."

"There was," I rasped. "But he didn't want it that way."

"I know." He stroked my hair, and in his own way, I knew that he understood. "I love you."

"I love you." I blinked, my throat raw, my eyes exhausted and my body a wet rag—completely spent. "Take me home," I told him, unable to stop the relief, the soaring in my heart as I realized he was safe, he was mine, and my contract with Lucian was null and void. "Take me away from here and marry me."

"You are mine," he said. "Forever."

Chapter 28

THE DAYS AFTER OUR return to The Isle flipped past, as if I'd thumbed through the pages of the calendar. The world continued on, surprisingly mundane despite the historic events marked by our time in Olympia.

The leader of The Faction was dead. The storm clouds had parted, and the Master of Magic had been safely returned to his tower. Life continued on at its regular, monotonous pace.

Life continued for all of us.

It continued for Samuel Palmer, too, the man wrongly accused of my mother's murder. On my first day back to The Isle, I'd arranged for Ranger X to set up Sammy with an apartment and enough money to get started. Ranger X had agreed easily and funded the venture with cash kept at Ranger HQ for specialized human missions. He utilized a few connections on the mainland and pulled strings to get Sammy situated in a decent job. Sammy was working to get on his feet and to face Miss Hubick with his chin held high.

The first weekend we were back was one of celebration. Though our hearts were still heavy, a cautious gleam of hope crept through the cracks as Zin became the first official female Ranger in the history of The Isle. With the vampire hunter locked away in prison, she'd completed her last task with flying colors, and this called for a celebration.

She was inducted on Friday, and the day after, Trinket held a small, vibrant party at her house to celebrate her daughter's accomplishments. We gathered there, toasting Zin's victories, eating luxurious foods, sipping warm and hearty wines.

Sometime during the party, Trinket showed up at my elbow, twitching with nerves. "Can I speak to you for a moment?"

"Sure, of course. What's wrong?" I asked as she led the way upstairs. A fire crackled near us as a cool wind blew across the open windows. "Why aren't you enjoying the festivities? Zin—"

"I'm terribly proud of Zin," she said with a frown. "Do you think she knows it?"

"Of course."

Not only had Trinket offered to host the party, but she'd been genuinely proud all evening. She'd boasted to her friends, eyes glittering brightly, about the many accomplishments of her stubborn eldest daughter.

"I've done things I'm not proud of," she said, her fingers playing with the edges of her long, flowing sleeves. "But the night when I confronted you at your bungalow might have been me at my worst. I'm terribly sorry for the mess with the Long Isle potion, Lily. I owe you a thousand apologies, and I want you to know I won't ever put you in that situation again."

"Trinket—"

"You're my niece. She was my sister. I loved her dearly, but...I love you, too. You are alive while she's not, and she won't come back—no matter what. It's time I come to terms with it."

"Listen." I placed my hand on her restless fingers, waiting until she stilled. "I have been needing to tell you something. I did some investigating and found information on her supposed killers. I met one of them, Trinket. His name is Samuel Palmer. He's completely human, and he served twenty-four years for the murder of my mother."

Trinket digested this, then gave a nod.

I met her gaze head on. "He didn't do it."

Her eyes whipped up to mine. "How do you know?"

"I don't know for a fact, but I will soon. I met with him in person, and I just don't think he killed her—for so many reasons." I hesitated, fingered the vial of Amuletto Kiss I'd tucked into my belt for this very reason. "I have a scrap of his clothing. I'll be able to read his thoughts, Trinket. We'll know for certain."

Trinket watched with hungry eyes as I pulled the scrap from Sammy's jacket out and placed it next to the vial. I let her take a minute to examine them both.

"If I take this potion," I told her. "The chances are good I will know for sure whether Sammy is guilty or innocent."

Trinket's fingers wobbled as she touched the fabric, her mouth parting with a gasp as she held it, knowing what this would mean for us. Closure, or confirmation. Either Samuel Palmer had committed the murder, or as Trinket had always believed, there was more to the story.

With a firm set to her jaw, she looked up abruptly. She raised the cloth, focused on it, studying the piece of fabric as if it were the last link to my mother. Tears sparkled at the corners of her eyes as she rubbed her forefinger and thumb over the material for an extended minute.

Then, with a quick twitch of her wrist, she tossed it directly into the fireplace. The flames gobbled it up in seconds.

"Trinket!" I gasped, mystified. "What are you doing? That's the only way I'll be able to know for certain. I needed something from Sammy to perform the spell."

Trinket gave me a tight, sad smile. "I know."

We stood in silence watching Sammy's coat fibers burn.

When they were nothing but useless ashes dusted beneath the logs, Trinket turned to me and rested a bony hand on my shoulder. "I think we should let her go," she whispered, and then pulled me into a hug. "Forgive me, Lily."

I held her tightly, our nails digging into one another's backs.

After releasing me from the embrace, Trinket grasped my elbow and steered me back downstairs. We ran headfirst into Poppy. She led a limbo extravaganza with an unwilling, but reluctantly grinning, Zin. Behind Zin stood Mimsey and Glinda, elbowing one another for the next spot in line.

A smile crept across my face, and as I looked to Zin, I took solace in her subtle happiness, her subtle pride, too. I shared a look with her over the striped limbo pole, and I could see the reassurance in her gaze that everything would be okay.

"There she is! We have one more announcement to make," Poppy said as she caught a glimpse of me. "Go ahead, Lily."

I blinked at her. "What?"

"It's okay." Zin stepped closer to me, lowering her voice. "This isn't just *my* party, it's for you, too. Congratulations, Lily."

Startled, I found Ranger X moving across the room to stand next to me, looking just as surprised. "Um, we—" I hesitated as he slid an arm around my back. "We didn't want to spoil Zin's night..."

"Oh, *stop!*" Zin shouted above my babbles and raised her glass. "Lily and Ranger X are getting married!"

We were swarmed by big hugs and sloppy kisses. Grinning faces asked how and when the proposal had happened—*and had we set a date yet*? Others gave us hearty pats on the back, while Hettie devolved into an impromptu planning session with Mimsey right there at the appetizer table.

The evening ballooned into a double celebration, and it wasn't until the wee hours of the morning that Ranger X and I finally found ourselves free to talk privately once more. After excusing ourselves from the party, we walked arm in arm across The Isle as the brisk morning breeze cooled our flushed cheeks.

We arrived at the bungalow happy, contented, and tired. Exhausted, really. I hadn't fully recovered from the events in Olympia yet, and though the party had been a raging success, I was ready for sleep. Working with the gods apparently sapped my energy supply.

"What's this?" I picked up a package from the porch as I climbed the stairs. It was a simple parcel, unmarked in brown packaging. "Any clue?"

Ranger X shook his head.

I unwrapped it as we slid inside and locked the door behind us. I pulled back the paper as I eased onto the bench at the storeroom table and balked when I saw the contents.

To Lily and Ranger X, the card began.

Congratulations. May this be the start of a wonderful life together.

—Liam

"What do you make of it?" Ranger X sat across from me, not looking at the parcel, but into my eyes. "Are you okay?"

"I'm fine." My fingers shook as I removed the card and slid it to the side. "An engagement gift? It's a little surprising, I'll admit."

Ranger X reached across the table and rested a hand on mine, relaxing it before I could unearth the rest of the package. "You don't have to open this now."

"What do you think?"

"About what?"

"Everything." My hands shook as I withdrew them from his grasp. "Everything, Cannon. We're engaged. I killed my father. The leader of The Faction is dead. We've barely dealt with *any* of it. We've been so caught up in celebrating Zin and getting back into normal life that I don't know what to make of the rest of it."

Ranger X drew me across the room and sat in a chair before the fireplace. He pulled me onto his lap and, one flick of his fingers later, and flames erupted to eagerly toast the bricks before us.

"Talk to me," he said. "You're shaking; you're worried. I know you, Lily. You didn't sleep last night. Whatever you're thinking, you'll feel better getting it off your chest."

He was right. Ever since we'd stepped foot outside Olympia, it'd felt like a large dragon had come and parked himself on my chest. Every breath was a chore, every blink a nightmare.

"I..." I inhaled, holding my breath to prevent the sobs from escaping. "I'm glad," I said finally. "I am so relieved he's gone, and I feel horrible about saying so."

The sobs broke free. They soared through me like a waterfall, tumultuous and unrelenting, draining what little energy I had left in my body.

I collapsed forward into Ranger X's arms. He knew it before I did and had prepared, cupping the back of my head with his warm hand, holding me strong against his shoulder. He let me cry.

When I finished, I sniffed and pulled back. "Are you sure you still want to marry me? How awful of a person am I to be *glad* my father is dead?"

Ranger X's eyes shone like black diamonds. "Oh, Lily."

Then he kissed my eyelids first, brushing away the tears. He kissed down my cheeks to my lips, from my lips to my throat, from my throat back to my mouth. He ended with a tender, lingering sigh.

"I adore you, Lily. My love for you will never waver. If you want to get married now, today, I'll do it. Tomorrow, I'll do it. Three years from now, I'll be waiting for you at the altar."

I found a smile. It felt weak and lopsided, but it was better than tears. Ranger X latched onto that, pulled me closer, and then shifted as if he'd remembered something.

"Here," he said, pulling a small card from his pocket. "I forgot. Gerry asked me to give this to you—he gave it to me as we were leaving Olympia."

"He *hates* being called Gerry," I said with a giggle, removing the neat little card from X's grasp. "He's a good guy."

"I'm not sure I can agree; he knowingly walked you right into that mess. He doesn't care about a soul except the Master of Magic."

"It's okay—everything worked out."

"Mostly." He pushed my hair back, shook his head in dismay. "Mostly."

"How sweet," I said, flipping the card up so Ranger X could read along with me. "An invitation to return to Olympia's finest inn for our honeymoon."

Ranger X closed his eyes. "The thought is nice, but I have no desire to return."

"Me neither," I agreed. "Poor Gerry."

The second present now felt like a bomb waiting on the table, demanding our attention. I slid from Ranger X's lap and pulled the parcel close to me.

"It's a folder," I said, sliding a stiff manila envelope out. "It's light, and—"

"I don't know if it's a good idea." Ranger X snatched at the folder. "Do we trust Liam? We haven't heard from him since he sent you on a suicide mission."

"It wasn't a suicide mission—I made it out alive. Also, he was right about the prophecy. I think we need to listen to him, even if we don't trust him."

"Yes, but where was he to *help* with everything?"

I didn't have an answer. I didn't even have a guess. Liam had simply vanished.

"I think we should open it." I spoke quietly, my hand extended. "It might be important."

Ranger X grudgingly handed the folder back. His wary eyes watched my every move as I slipped a sheath of papers from inside. All the pages were clipped together to form a file of sorts. The cover was stamped with a huge red **X**.

The few words printed underneath nearly stopped my heart.

TARGET TERMINATED.

It was an internal memo of sorts, marked with a unique symbol on the front I'd never yet seen. Before I could ask, X pointed to the marking. "That's the symbol for The Faction."

"This is an internal memo from Faction headquarters?" I repeated the information, stunned. "But who has access to this? Liam," I said, answering my own question. "But why?"

I flipped the cover open, my eyes staring into X's as I did so—I couldn't bring myself to look downward. I needed to study the file for its contents, but something held me back.

"You don't have to do this now," Ranger X said. "You're still not recovered from this week. Take some time, Lily."

"No," I whispered. "I need to do this."

With that, I tilted my eyes downward to find a picture staring back at me. The face of a familiar woman—a face I'd worn myself just days before. *My mother.*

The heading across the top boasted her name and date, a date just after my birth. The rest of the information stole my breath.

Target: DELILAH LOCKE

Alias: *Millie Banks*

Role: *Assassin of The Isle.*

Status: *Terminated.*

Epilogue

TWO DAYS CAME AND WENT in a blur.

The news of my mother's alleged profession had come as a shock. I hadn't known what to make of it. White nor black. Good nor evil. I had no thoughts on it whatsoever.

In fact, my mind was an empty hole as I reopened Magic & Mixology in hopes to move on with my life. It didn't work, not entirely. I served my customers with robotic motions, but I didn't truly process any of it.

Now that the storm had passed and some of the tensions had eased, business was back to its steady flow. Gerry had kindly published a counter-article to Peter's terror mongering one, and the islanders were more than happy to believe that life was settling back into its happy little norm.

Except for me. My life felt like it'd been flipped upside down. Ranger X dealt with the news better than me. Then again, he wasn't coming to terms with his mother's true identity—and then attempting to marry that to the stories he'd been told of her kindness and laughter and good-heartedness. Hettie and Trinket and Mimsey had seemed to adore my mother, so the image of her as an assassin was a difficult one to digest.

If Liam's file were true, my mother hadn't only been killed, she'd been murdered, terminated, assassinated. Before, I'd felt a need for revenge when I thought of her killers—a sense of fairness in knowing that her murderer should be punished as part of a rightful system of justice.

Now, whenever I dreamt of finding her killers and bringing them to justice, an uneasy churn moved through my gut. *Had my mother been a killer?* Had her death been warranted? Even if I wanted to dive deeper, it seemed impossible to uncover information from over twenty-seven years ago when nobody alive seemed to know the real identity of Delilah Locke.

The Comm came through after lunch. Ranger X asked to see me at HQ—he'd been keeping a careful watch on me every few hours, checking in, making sure every one of my movements was recorded. Normally, I would be annoyed, but under the circumstances, I found it sweet.

"Do you mind watching the shop?" I asked Gus after replying to X's Comm. "I have a meeting at HQ. I'll be back in an hour."

He grunted his agreement, then returned to the detailed process of adding a new entry into *The Magic of Mixology*. The pages for Amuletto Kiss were only halfway filled out, and already, it was the size of a tome.

I made it to the HQ entrance quickly, and Elle had an entry point waiting for me between the trees. As soon as she signed me in at the front desk, Ranger X approached and put his arms around my waist.

"Hi there," I said, leaning up to kiss his cheek. "What's up?"

"Sit, please."

My stomach continued to sink long after I'd sat on one of the couches in the lobby. "What's wrong?"

"I heard from Olympia."

I frowned. We'd left my father's body there, asking them to dispose of it respectfully. "Is there a problem?"

"A slight one." Ranger X ran a hand over his chin, his fingers scratching against the five o'clock shadow that'd grown overnight.

"Ah, when we left, you were under the impression your father was dead."

"You weren't? I saw him get..." I breathed. "All those stones—how could he *not* have been crushed?"

"His body had been protected by two pillars. He was severely injured and in a deep coma when we left. He was not expected to live more than a few hours."

"And?" My panic built. "He *has* to be dead, X. He has to be—I saw him die!"

"You didn't, Lily. You thought you did. However, he's still alive. His injuries are severe, but his heart is still beating."

"He *has* to die!" I said in a low growl. I reached for X's shoulders, shook him. "It's not *safe* for us while he's alive. You have to understand, he *must* die."

Ranger X's eyes hardened. "You're not a killer, Lily. If he lives, he *lives*. We'll put him away forever. He'll never get to you. Do you understand me? I won't let him. If it comes down to it, I will end him myself, but I can't—we can't—murder him in cold blood."

I gulped, my eyes wild. "No, you don't—you don't understand. He made me sign a contract that's binding so long as he's alive."

X's eyebrows furrowed. "When did you sign a contract?"

"In the dungeon. I didn't tell you because, well, as soon as I signed it I guess I got so angry, there was this prophecy, and..."

"Let's grab a conference room," Ranger X said. "And start from the beginning."

We sat in a quiet space. X brought me a glass of water, but it sat untouched on the desk as I poured every detail of my time in Olympia out to him—even the details I hadn't had time to process. It all returned and spilled from my lips in a discombobulated stream of consciousness.

When I finished the story, I tacked on the last part. "I had to choose between you and...and our potential son." It felt horrifyingly strange to speak about a child who didn't yet exist. However, the rest of the world seemed so confident in his arrival that this child was beginning to feel real to me. "There was no choice. You're here, you're alive, you're...I love you, Cannon. I didn't have an option. I thought he was prepared to *kill* you. The images..." I flinched.

"None of this is your fault—of course you didn't have a choice." He didn't step forward to comfort me because he *couldn't*. His entire body trembled with rage, and a golden glow appeared around his clenched hands. "We will find a way to break the contract."

"Or else?"

"I already told you." He stepped forward. "I will terminate him myself."

"But Cannon, you already said you can't do that. It would be murder."

"Lily." His eyes were soft. "I won't let anything happen to you or our family. I promise you. Can you promise me something?"

I hesitated, then nodded.

"Your father is alive," he said, resigned. "As far as I'm concerned, that news changes nothing. He'll be transported to The Isle and locked in our prisons. He will *not* escape."

"But—"

"I'm not finished." Ranger X held up a finger. "Should we have children, they'll be ours, and ours alone. That's my promise to you."

I nodded, comforted by his determination. "What do you need from me?"

Ranger X waited until I looked him in the eyes. Then he knelt and pulled a small box from his pocket. "I didn't properly propose to you before," he said with a soft smile. "In fact, you might have proposed to me."

I gave a giddy, nervous laugh as my hands clasped over my mouth, and I suddenly lost the ability to properly breathe.

Ranger X opened the box to reveal the most stunning stone in the universe. Mounted on a pristine, thin silver band, the stone sparkled like moonlight, glittered with the sheen of a thousand stars. It was like nothing I'd ever seen before—completely unique, exceedingly magnificent. *Perfect.*

"My love for you is brighter than all of the stars in the universe and greater than the distance to the farthest moon. It's stronger than the deepest of magics and more consuming than the air we breathe." X reached for my hand and pulled it to him, slipping the ring gently onto my finger where it belonged. "I love you more than life itself, and I can't imagine continuing on without you by my side. Marry me, Lily."

THE END

Author's Note
(and super-exciting announcement!)

THANK YOU FOR READING! I hope you enjoyed the roller-coaster that Lily, Ranger X, and the gang rode as they struggled to save the Master of Magic. The adventures on The Isle will be continued in book six, however, I also have a brand-new spin-off series that will be releasing this summer. I will have THREE BOOKS coming out back to back, and they all take place in the magical Sixth Borough of New York—yes, the very same place that Lily and Hettie visited in *Amuletto Kiss*.

I am so excited to introduce you to this new cast of characters! You will meet Dani DeMarco—pizza connoisseur and superstar detective—and her impossibly gorgeous and mysterious and (sometimes) boyfriend Matthew King. To check it out, head over to ***THE HEX FILES: Wicked Never Sleeps*** on Amazon now! Click HERE[1] to read a synopsis.

To be notified of new releases, please sign up for my newsletter at www.ginalamanna.com.

Thank you for reading!

Love,

Gina

---

1.   http://bit.ly/TheHexFiles

Now for a thank you...

To all my readers, especially those of you who have stuck with me from the beginning.

By now, I'm sure you all know how important reviews are for Indie authors, so if you have a moment and enjoyed the story, please consider leaving an honest review on Amazon or Goodreads. I know you are all very busy people and writing a review takes time out of your day—but just know that I appreciate every single one I receive. Reviews help make promotions possible, help with visibility on large retailers and most importantly, help other potential readers decide if they would like to try the book.

I wouldn't be here without all of you, so once again—*thank you.*

List of Gina's Books!²

Gina LaManna is the USA TODAY bestselling author of the Magic & Mixology series, the Lacey Luzzi Mafia Mysteries, The Little Things romantic suspense series, and the Misty Newman books.

List of Gina LaManna's other books:

The Hex Files:

Wicked Never Sleeps

Wicked Long Nights

Lola Pink Mystery Series:

Shades of Pink

Shades of Stars

Shades of Sunshine

Magic & Mixology Mysteries:

Hex on the Beach

Witchy Sour

Jinx & Tonic

Long Isle Iced Tea

Amuletto Kiss

MAGIC, Inc. Mysteries:

The Undercover Witch

Spellbooks & Spies (short story)

Reading Order for Lacey Luzzi:

Lacey Luzzi: Scooped

Lacey Luzzi: Sprinkled

Lacey Luzzi: Sparkled

Lacey Luzzi: Salted

---

2. http://www.amazon.com/Gina-LaManna/e/B00RPQD-

NPG/?tag=ginlamaut-20

Lacey Luzzi: Sauced
Lacey Luzzi: S'mored
Lacey Luzzi: Spooked
Lacey Luzzi: Seasoned
Lacey Luzzi: Spiced
Lacey Luzzi: Suckered
Lacey Luzzi: Sprouted
The Little Things Mystery Series:
One Little Wish
Two Little Lies
Misty Newman:
Teased to Death
Short Story in Killer Beach Reads
Chick Lit:
Girl Tripping
Gina also writes books for kids under the Pen Name Libby LaManna:
Mini Pie the Spy!